Six Strings and a Dream

Songwriters Series Book One

Ali Spooner

Sasha Thibodaux Series
Sugarland
Bayou Justice
Line of Sight

Strong Southern Women Series
Diamond Dreams
Gator Girlz
True North
Footprints

Cast Iron Farm Series
The Mountain Whispers
The Star Child
Soul on Fire

Co-authored with Annette Mori
Heart Strings Attached – TWC3
Free to Love
Trouble in Paradise – TWC4

Co-Authored with
K.L. Gallagher
Hat Trick

Six Strings and a Dream

Dream

Songwriters Series Book One

Ali Spooner

2022

Six Strings and a Dream
Songwriters series book One
© 2022 by Ali Spooner

Affinity E-Book Press NZ LTD.
Canterbury, New Zealand

1st Edition

ISBN: 978-1-99-004984-2 (paperback)
ISBN978-1-99-004981-1 (EPUB)
ISBN: 978-1-99-004982-8 (PDF)
ISBN: 978-1-99-004983-5 (KINDLE)

Editor: Angela Koenig
Proof Editor: Alexis Smith
Cover Design: Irish Dragon Designs
Production Design: Affinity Publication Services

ACKNOWLEDGMENTS

I would like to thank my fans for following my stories, providing great feedback, and encouragement. Writing wouldn't be so much fun without you. Thanks to Affinity, Irish Dragon for the cover art, and the team of editors, readers, and publishers who continue to help me grow as a writer.

DEDICATION

I dedicate this book to the friends and family that have supported me moving forward in life without Rhonda. Many of you, I've never met in person. I appreciate that on those hard days there is always someone I can count on to lend a hand or a shoulder to cry on. Your strength and compassion have been a tremendous help. Thank you, more than you will ever know.

TABLE OF CONTENTS

CHAPTER ONE

Hank Tyler closed the hood on the beat-up pick-up truck his daughter had saved for two years to buy.

"You are good to go, Cedra," he said, wiping his hands on an oily rag. She wasn't the prettiest truck, but she was well made. He felt the tears welling in his eyes as he looked at the young woman before him.

"Thanks, Daddy," he heard her call out as she climbed in behind the wheel.

"She's not much to look at, but she's reliable and should get you to Nashville," he said with a grin.

Cedra returned his smile. "That's all I can ask; the rest is up to me."

"I will pray for you every night. Call me as often as you can," he said with tears blurring his eyes. "Follow your heart and your dream." He patted the side of the truck.

"I will, Daddy," she promised.

1

†

Cedra saw the emotion building in her father's face and knew she had to go before she changed her mind.

"I love you," she said as she cranked the truck.

"I love you, too."

Cedra put the truck in gear and pressed the gas pedal as she slowly pulled down the drive. She looked in her rearview mirror and watched her father wave as she drove away. When she reached the hard road, she turned right. Looking back at the only home she had ever known, Cedra honked her horn and waved a final goodbye to her father with tears flowing down her cheeks.

†

"Good luck Cedra," Hank said to himself. He watched as his only child drove away in pursuit of her dreams, and turned to make his way slowly back into the empty house. He sat down in his favorite chair and looked at the photograph of his beloved wife, Melinda, who had passed away a year ago. She had suffered a debilitating stroke just after Cedra had graduated from high school, and the two of them had provided her care until she suffered another massive stroke and died.

"Watch over our baby girl," he whispered to the face smiling back at him from the frame.

For almost a year now, he and his daughter had continued aimlessly until one night a month ago, he sat her down for a talk.

"I know you have big dreams of going to Nashville and breaking into country music," he told her. "Now that your mother has gone, I think it is time that you pursue those dreams."

Cedra had immediately replied, "But Daddy, who will be here to take care of you and the house?"

"I'm fifty years old, and I think I can take care of myself and keep the house from falling around me. I appreciate your sticking around to help with your mom, but now it's time you move on."

Cedra once more had started to protest, and Hank cut her off. "I'm not kicking you out, but you were born to follow your dreams, and I fully expect to hear you on the radio someday."

Hank had breathed a sigh of relief when she smiled and nodded her agreement and then walked back to the kitchen to finish preparing their dinner. Hank could imagine Cedra going to bed that night with a million thoughts running through her head.

"You're going to do just fine, Baby Girl," Hank had whispered and turned off his bedside lamp.

CHAPTER TWO

Cedra followed the county road until she reached Interstate 65 and entered the ramp to head north to Nashville. Her heart was hammering in her chest as she merged into the heavy traffic flow to start a drive that should take her seven hours if she had no complications. She cranked up her radio and settled in behind a semi hauling new John Deere tractors.

The sun had been up for hours and was beating down on the Interstate as she counted down the green mile markers. She was relieved to see a blue sign indicating a rest stop ahead and pulled over for a break two hours after leaving home. Cedra used the facilities and stretched her legs before climbing back into the cab of her truck. She hoped to make it to Montgomery before she would have to gas up and reached for a bottle of water in the small cooler her father had packed. When she opened the top, a plastic bag dropped out, and she bent to pick it up. Cedra found an envelope tucked inside, and curiously opened it to see a note from her father, along with five twenty-dollar bills: *It's not much, but I wanted you to have a little extra to fall back on if you need it. Good luck, and always remember how much I love you.*

Cedra tucked the bills in her pocket with tears threatening to fall. It would not take much effort to pull a U-turn and head back home, but she knew her father would be disappointed if she did. In a way, she was pursuing a dream he had when he was a young man before he met and married her mom. He had been part of a small band, and when Melinda had told him she was pregnant, he quit the band to become a "responsible provider" for his wife and child. Holding back the tears, she put her truck in drive and continued her journey.

She stopped just out Montgomery to gas up, pleased with the truck's performance, and drove on to Birmingham. Cedra had never been farther north, so she had studied the *Rand McNally Atlas* her dad had given her for weeks to memorize the route. She passed the Vulcan statue with a smile and entered the virgin territory.

The miles were quickly fading with the sunlight as she passed the NASA rockets of Huntsville and approached the state line. She could feel the truck's engine strain as the landscape began to increase from rolling hills to small mountains and decided on one last rest stop in Alabama. She pulled off an exit and topped off her gas tank before entering the small store to pay for her gas and buy a snack. She chuckled to herself as she selected an RC Cola and moon pie; such a country girl selection.

Cedra ate her snack and a sandwich her father had packed and walked back inside to use the restroom before she started on the last portion of her journey.

The scenery was beautiful. Everything seemed such a deep shade of green as she drove through mountain cutouts and deep valleys and, as the sun was setting, Cedra caught her first glimpse of Nashville as she crested a large hill. She pulled over and looked at the lights that were beginning to twinkle in the growing darkness.

An hour later, darkness entirely upon her, Cedra pulled into a driveway in Mt. Juliet at the boarding house owned by Ma Bentley. Cedra had talked to the woman several times over the past few weeks and already had a growing affection for her. She looked forward to being her new boarder, and the price was certainly in her favor.

She took out her most enormous bag, carried it to the front door, and rang the bell. She fidgeted as she waited for someone to answer the door.

Cedra was surprised when a young man opened the door. "You must be Cedra," he said with a warm smile. "I'm Keith," he added as he reached through the door to take the bag. "Ma says to come on in and join us for dinner, and we can get you settled in afterward."

"Thanks," Cedra managed to say as he quickly lifted the colossal bag, placed it in the foyer, and then led her to the dining room.

Ma Bentley and another young man were sitting around a small table enjoying a meal. She looked up at the sound of their approach.

"Welcome home," Ma said. "Come have a seat and some dinner, then the boys can take your bags upstairs." She pointed to an empty seat next to her.

"That smells fantastic," Cedra said as she looked at a platter full of fried chicken, a bowl of mashed potatoes, and corn on the cob.

"I'm Wayne," the other young man said as he handed her the platter of chicken.

"Nice to meet you all," Cedra said.

"Wayne and Keith are my other renters," Ma explained. "They are good boys but will leave you hungry if you are late for meals. Juliet will be your neighbor, but she won't be back until late tonight after a gig."

Cedra chuckled at her comment. "I will make sure I'm on time then." She speared a chicken breast and placed it on her plate.

"There's iced tea in the pitcher or cold water at the tap if you prefer."

"Iced tea is fine," Cedra said as she poured a glass.

"So, you're from Alabama?" Wayne asked.

"Yes, from Monroeville down by Mobile."

"I'm from North Carolina, and the red neck here is from Kentucky," he said, punching Keith in the shoulder.

"I reckon you're here just like us, chasing the dream," Keith said between bites.

"Will you two calm down and let the poor girl enjoy her dinner?"

"Sorry, Ma," Keith said.

"It's okay, Ma. Yes, I hope to one day record some of my songs," she answered.

"You write and sing?" Wayne asked.

"Write mostly. I haven't had too many opportunities to perform live."

"We can help you with that," Wayne said with a smile. "Keith and I both play at the Iron Horse for tips, and I'm sure we can get you included in the rotation."

"That would be awesome."

"Have you lined up work yet?" Ma asked.

Cedra nodded her head then swallowed. "I have an appointment at the Redbird Café the day after tomorrow, in the morning at ten to discuss a serving position."

Ma smiled brightly. "That's great news and a fantastic spot. A lot of the music industry big wheels have lunch there regularly. In my opinion, the Redbird is much more popular than the Bluebird. They've stuck with the traditional café fare, and writers and performers to showcase new talent. The Bluebird doesn't have much in food options and is more into the entertainment aspect of the business."

"What do you boys do?"

"I work at the Ryman as a lighting tech," Keith said. "That reminds me that I need to get a move on or I'm going to be late. Another great meal, Ma," he said and carried his dishes to the kitchen sink.

"Have a good night and be safe," she said.

"Sorry I have to duck out on your first night, but welcome to Ma's," Keith said.

"Duty calls," Cedra said as she reached for a home-baked roll.

Keith disappeared, and moments later, they heard the front door close behind him. Cedra looked at Ma. "So, is Dierks Bentley one of your boys?"

Ma chuckled heartily. "Lord, no. I would gladly claim that adorable young man, but no, my Harold and I never had children."

"I'm sorry to hear that."

"It was probably for the best. Harold died young when he was only forty-five, from a heart attack. I would have been left to raise kids on my own."

"I'm sure you would have been just fine," Cedra said. "Did you ever dabble in the music business?"

"Seems like a thousand years ago, but yes, I sang some backup for Patsy and Loretta on occasion. I just never had the gumption to try to make it on my own," Ma said with a dreamy sigh. "So, I opened my house up as a boarding house, and I live that dream through the young people who come through here."

Cedra considered her response for a moment. "I bet you have seen many folks who have come here to chase their dreams."

"Hundreds," Ma said.

"Any of them ever make it?"

"Several of them have made it as singers and songwriters. Some have sold a few songs, but most run out of money and ambition after a few months and head home," she said bluntly.

"I hope I won't be in the latter group."

"It is a hard business to break into and takes a lot of determination and grit. Wayne can tell you. It took him almost a year to get a gig as backup vocals."

"Congratulations," Cedra said.

Wayne grinned at her. "I got fifty dollars and a copy of the CD for my first gig."

"That's fifty dollars you didn't have before," Cedra said.

"True, and it's opened the door to some studio time and other gigs. Otherwise, I'm a full-time bartender and bouncer at Wild Bill's Honky Tonk."

"I bet that's an exciting job."

"Especially on the weekends, the crowds can get a little rowdy."

"When you two finish eating, I will clean up here, and Wayne can help you carry your bags upstairs so you can settle in," Ma suggested.

"I can manage if you have other things you need to do," Cedra said.

"Nonsense, it won't take as long if two of us are toting bags," Wayne said.

"Thanks, I appreciate the help then."

Cedra and Wayne left the dining room and walked out to her truck.

"Cool ride."

"She's not much to look at, but she gets me where I need to go."

Wayne ran his hand down the heavy fenders. "They don't make 'em like this anymore."

Cedra had two more bags. Wayne picked up the larger of the two, leaving a small one and her guitar case. Cedra closed the door behind them and followed him into the house. He picked up the large bag they had left in the foyer earlier and started up the stairs. He led her into a small but comfortable room and set the bags next to the bed.

"If you need anything, just give me a holler. I am right across the hall from you. Oh, the bathroom is through there," he said, pointing to a door across the room. "You and Juliet share."

"Thanks for all your help, Wayne."

"My pleasure, ma'am," he said, and pulled the door behind him.

†

Cedra saw a note on the small desk and a key to the front door resting beside it. The message was from Ma, explaining the few house rules she had and the meal schedules. Cedra slipped the key on her key chain and then lifted the first bags onto the bed.

She opened the bag and smiled. Her father had purchased a cell phone for her, and he had wrapped it up in a note. *Call me when you can*, it read, and she opened it to find it fully charged and her home number programmed in to speed dial.

She pushed a button and listened for the phone to ring. Two rings later, her father answered.

"Hello."

"Hi, Daddy, thank you for the phone," she said.

"I thought that would be the best way I could ensure you would call me," he said, and she could imagine his grin across the phone. "Did you make the trip okay?"

"Yes, it wasn't a bad drive at all, and I am about to get settled into my new room."

"That's great, Baby Girl. I hope everything is to your liking."

"It's not big, but it meets my needs, and Ma and her other boarders seem nice."

"I'm glad you feel comfortable, and will have a day to get settled and see some of Nashville tomorrow."

Cedra smiled. "I've got my maps, and I will drive around some to get familiar with routes to and from work," she said.

Her father was silent for a minute.

"Daddy, are you okay?"

"Yes, I'm sorry, the house is just so quiet with you gone."

The sadness in his voice tugged at her heart. "I can be home tomorrow, Daddy."

"No way, Baby Girl. I am a big boy, and I will adjust. You need to stay up there and realize all your dreams. Earlier, I was thinking of getting a puppy or a kitten to occupy some time and give me a companion."

"Aw, that would be an excellent idea, Daddy."

"Maybe I will take a ride to the shelter tomorrow and see who needs adopting," he said.

"I will call tomorrow night then, to see how many animals you bring home," she teased.

"You call me whenever you want. You don't need a reason."

"Okay, Daddy, I just don't want to run up a huge bill."

"You let me worry about that. Besides, I'm only buying groceries for one now, so I have some money left over."

Cedra chuckled at her father. "I will call several times a week then."

"Thanks, honey. Finish getting settled in and try to get some rest. I will look forward to your call tomorrow night."

"Okay, I love you, Daddy."

"I love you too, Baby Girl."

Cedra ended the call and then tackled the first of her bags.

An hour later, she had all her clothes hung in the closet or tucked away in the dresser, and had placed her hygiene supplies in the small bathroom. She stored her empty suitcases under the bed and looked around her new home. She smiled to herself then placed her journal and notepads on the small desk before pulling out her guitar. She stroked the smooth wood and checked her strings. The

Gibson guitar had initially been her grandfather's. Her father passed it down to her after his father's death at his request. She sat back on her bed and began to play.

CHAPTER THREE

Juliet Tucker slipped quietly through the house, trying desperately not to wake the others as she climbed the stairs. She was hungry and knew there would be leftovers from supper in the fridge, but she was too tired to eat. All Juliet wanted was to lie down on her bed and sleep for days. When she topped the stairs, she could see a sliver of light escaping beneath the door next to hers. The new girl had arrived she thought as she approached her room and heard the soft music of a guitar. Juliet checked her watch; it was nearly two in the morning. She hoped her suitemate wasn't an insomniac who would keep her awake all hours of the night. She turned the knob to open her door and didn't bother with the light as she headed straight for the bathroom.

The sound of the music was louder in the bathroom since it joined the two bedrooms. Juliet could hear a low voice singing lyrics with the music from the guitar, and it was an enjoyable sound. She found herself leaning against the bathroom door listening to the haunting melody. Juliet used the restroom, and when she flushed the toilet before slipping into her bedroom, the music stopped suddenly.

†

Cedra had finished unpacking and arranging her room and had attempted to go to bed around ten, but her mind and body disagreed. Despite the long drive that had left her body exhausted, her mind was running a mile a minute. She squeezed her eyes shut in an attempt to lure sleep, but lyrics to a song kept dancing through her mind. Finally, just after midnight, she had given up, turned the small desk lamp on, and opened her notepad to write the words that were haunting her sleep. The first stanza flowed into the next, and Cedra was amazed when she read what she had just written.

She picked up her guitar, intending to match some music to the lyrics and was softly strumming the well-worn strings when she heard a car pull up in the yard. That must be the other renter coming home from her gig, she thought as she tried in vain to remember the woman's name. She listened as footsteps crept up the stairs, and she heard a faint click when the woman closed the door behind her.

Cedra smiled when she heard the toilet flush and looked at her clock to see that it was two. Cedra finished the music to the last stanza and rested her guitar beside the desk.

She reset her alarm from six to seven and turned off her lamp to return to her bed, desperately in search of sleep. In the darkness of the room, she heard herself still humming the tune she had just played, then as the music faded, she slipped into a deep, restful sleep.

†

Juliet also heard the soft humming, and a smile came to her face. It was a wonder she could still hear anything after spending two hours with amps throbbing, energizing the room as she performed her gig. Juliet preferred the soft sounds of a love story or ballad, but the paying crowd wanted upbeat rockabilly to dance to with their dates. Juliet complied for now but yearned for the day when she would dictate what style of music she would perform. She closed her eyes and fell asleep as her mind kept hearing the enchanting melody the woman next door had been playing.

CHAPTER FOUR

The following day Cedra found Ma sitting on the front porch sipping coffee. "Good morning, Cedra. I hope you slept well."

"Good morning, Ma. Yes, I did once my body relaxed enough for sleep."

"Well, yesterday was a long day for you, I'm sure, and a lot of changes for your body. I'm sure you will adjust quickly to your new home," she added with a smile. "Would you like some breakfast?"

"I will just make some toast and join you in a cup of coffee if that is okay."

Ma stood and stretched. "That sounds good. Let me show you where everything is," Ma said as she shuffled her feet into her well-worn house shoes.

Five minutes later, they had returned to the front porch and were comfortably sitting in cane-bottomed rocking chairs. The morning fog lifted, and Cedra noticed the Honda Accord sitting beside her truck.

"Did you hear Juliet come in last night?"

"Ah, so that's her name. I couldn't remember," Cedra said. "Yes, she came home around two."

"Mercy, don't tell me you were still up at that time."

Cedra chuckled at looked at Ma. "Yes, I was. My mind wouldn't let me sleep until I wrote down some lyrics."

"Ah, the price of creative genius," Ma said. "There's no rest for the wicked when a song needs to be born."

Cedra nodded her head. "That's very true and nothing else to be done until you sit down and write them out of your head."

"Has this always been a pattern with you, that you are up all night writing?"

"I guess I got in the habit when I would sit up nights caring for my mother, when she was ill," she said with a note of sadness.

Ma could hear the heartbreak in Cedra's words and knew that the illness had not turned out well. "I'm sorry to hear that she was ill."

"Thanks, Ma. She was my best friend and is now my guardian angel," Cedra said with tears welling in her eyes.

†

Juliet had walked to the front door and stood listening to their conversation, and she felt this was a good time to interrupt them. She pushed through the screen door stifling a yawn and carrying a cup of coffee. "Mind if I join you two?"

"Not at all, but I'm surprised you are up this early," Ma said.

"Me too, but the irresistible smell of coffee woke me."

"I hope it wasn't me making too much noise," Cedra said, smiling up at her.

"No, not at all. You were quiet as a church mouse."

Ma laughed. "Now, there's an expression I haven't heard in a while. Cedra, this is Juliet, your neighbor, by the way."

"Very nice to meet you," Cedra said. "I heard you come in last night. I hope I didn't disturb your sleep. I tried to be quiet, but you know how that goes."

"Cedra had a song that needed writing last night," Ma said.

"I heard part of it, and it sounded terrific," Juliet said.

Cedra blushed at her compliment. "Thank you."

"Maybe later today, you can sing the whole thing for us," Juliet suggested. "Sometimes, the boys and I have jam sessions out on the porch. It helps to get feedback when you have writer's block, or you need an opinion on a tune."

Cedra felt a smile grow on her face. "I would like that."

"Cedra's going to spend the day in town getting to know the place," Ma said.

"Would you like some company?" Juliet asked.

"That would be great. I've studied the maps, but I would never turn down a guided tour."

"I've been here almost six months, so I think I know my way around pretty well."

"Where are you from?" Cedra asked.

"Blue Ridge, Georgia," Juliet answered. "And you?"

"I'm from Monroeville, Alabama," Cedra said.

"Ah, the home of Harper Lee. Her novel has always been one of my favorites."

"Yes, she's a quaint old broad," Cedra said with a sigh. "So much talent but never another story."

Ma surprised them both by saying, "Sometimes when you start with perfection, there is little desire to repeat and take a chance at failure."

"I guess that's true, but she has so many stories that she has shared with us over the years that would have been such tremendous reading," Cedra said.

"Maybe that was her lot in life then, to pass down her stories to others in hopes that one day they will write them."

Cedra smiled at the older woman. "I hadn't considered that, Ma."

"Don't forget I'm supposed to be older and wiser," Ma said with a chuckle. "What would you like for breakfast?" she asked, turning to Juliet.

"I could enjoy some of your French toast," Juliet answered. She turned to Cedra. "Will you join me?"

"I've already had a piece of toast, but that does sound good."

Juliet smiled at her and then said to Ma, "Ma's French toast is to die for."

"How can I resist that then," Cedra agreed.

"I can see already that I'm going to have to keep an eye on the two of you."

Juliet placed a hand on her chest in mock rejection. "Ma, whatever do you mean?"

Ma chuckled. "You alone are too smooth but combine the two of you and look out world. That is all I'm going to say."

Juliet roared with laughter. "See, Cedra, you are doomed to be my partner in crime already."

Ma shook her head and lifted her heavy carcass from the rocker. "Let's go get you two some breakfast so you can hit the road," she said with a grin.

†

Cedra followed Ma's instruction to heat the syrup in the microwave while Juliet placed two plates and utensils on the table, then poured two glasses of orange juice.

Ma cooked up several slices of French toast and served it on their plates. "Get started on these, and I will have more ready in a jiff."

Juliet was right. Ma's French toast was delicious. The smell of the homemade butter and thick maple syrup made Cedra's mouth water, and when she took the first bite, a low moan escaped her lips.

Juliet hiked an eyebrow and smiled at her. "Told you so."

"Yeah, you did. It looks like I'm going to have to start exercising if I'm going to be eating like this every day."

"Nonsense, you need to put a few pounds on that skinny little frame of yours anyhow," Ma teased.

"She's just giving us her starving artist look, Ma."

"There will be no starving around here," Ma said in mock disgust. "Not as long as I can still drag this old carcass into the kitchen to cook."

Cedra smiled at Ma and took another bite of the wonderfully sweet breakfast treat.

Juliet and Cedra finished eating and placed their dishes in the dishwasher. They were about to start up the stairs when Ma called out.

"Do you think you girls can stop by the Farmers Market for me?"

"Sure, Ma, what would you like?"

"I thought some fresh green beans would go well with tonight's pot roast. Here's a ten, so get as many as you can," Ma said, offering Juliet the cash.

"Keep it, Ma, I can afford the beans. Do you have any plans for dessert?"

"Not yet. What did you have in mind?"

"I thought we could pick up some strawberries to go with that angel food cake you have tucked away in the pantry."

"Oh, that does sound good," Ma admitted.

"Consider it done then," Juliet said.

Cedra followed Juliet upstairs. "You can have the first crack at the bathroom."

"Okay, I won't be long," Juliet replied with a grin.

Ten minutes later, they were bounding down the stairs. "Do you learn better by driving or riding?" Juliet asked.

"Driving usually, but if you wouldn't mind driving, I can pay better attention to landmarks," Cedra said. "I will gladly pay for the gas."

"Not a problem, and my tank's full," Juliet said. "See you later this afternoon, Ma."

"You two be careful and have fun," Ma hollered to them from the kitchen.

†

"Cool truck," Juliet said as they walked to her car.

"Yep, that's my baby," Cedra said. "It took me two years to save up to buy her."

"Money well spent then. This one is a hand-me-down from my father," she said as they climbed inside the Honda.

Juliet carefully backed out of the drive, and they began the short ride into Nashville. "So," she said, looking at Cedra. "Tell me all about you."

"Not much to tell. I am just a country girl from Alabama. I'm almost twenty-one, and like you, came to Nashville to see if I can make it in the country music business."

"Most folks come straight here after high school," Juliet said. "They are just dying to break free of the small town and make it big in Nashville."

"I took a slight detour," Cedra said. "My mom had a stroke right after my high school graduation, and I stayed at home for two years to help my father with her care. She died almost a year ago."

Juliet could have kicked herself for being insensitive. "I'm sorry for your loss."

Cedra looked away from Juliet and stared out the window. "She was my best friend, and I still miss her terribly," she said as tears welled up in her eyes.

"She hasn't left; you just can't see her, is all."

"I do believe that. Sometimes I feel Mom watching over me, and I can smell the fragrance of her perfume. If ever there is such a thing as a guardian angel, my mom would surely be mine."

Juliet reached over and squeezed Cedra's shoulder in a motion of caring. "We could all use one of those. Is she who you were singing about last night?"

Cedra whipped her head around at Juliet. "I didn't think I was that loud."

"You weren't. I had to strain to hear the lyrics, but what I heard was beautiful."

Cedra smiled. "There was no way I was going to sleep until I got up and wrote them down. Does that ever happen to you?"

"Heavens no, I struggle to write anything decent," Juliet said. "I've got a strong voice and can play almost any type of instrument, but I can't write a respectable lyric to save my soul."

Cedra chuckled at Juliet's complete honesty. "Writing is the easy part for me. It comes very naturally. I can play the guitar and piano, and my voice is so-so."

"I think you have a better voice than you let on," Juliet remarked. "I bet you just need to practice to let the words flow through your voice like they do your pen."

"Those are sage words from someone so young," Cedra said.

"Hey, I'm only a year behind you. I will be twenty on March thirteenth."

"We will have to have a birthday party together then. My birthday is the fifteenth."

"No kidding?"

"Nope, kind of strange, don't you think?"

"Strange but cool that we are so close together. Did you get tons of comments in High School about being born on the Ides of March?"

"Probably about as many as you did about being born on a Friday the thirteenth."

"Damn, you are quick," Juliet teased. She dropped her hand from Cedra's shoulder as Nashville came into view. "What would you like to see first?"

"I have an appointment tomorrow at the Redbird Café," Cedra said.

"That's an easy spot to find. It's right down here on the left," Juliet said and pointed the building out as they drove past.

"That is a lucky break," Cedra said. "I don't think I can get lost trying to find that."

"I would be worried about you if you could," Juliet said and shot her a wink.

†

Cedra felt very comfortable with Juliet and was relieved to have made her first new friend. She listened to Juliet as she pointed out many of the notable spots in the downtown area.

"Keith can hook you up with a tour of the Ryman," she said as they drove by. "There is so much more to Nashville than the Grand Ole Opry and the Ryman, but they are two of the most historic sites. Printer's Alley is an exciting part of town as well. Not one I would recommend you venture to alone at night. It can get pretty rough down in that area."

"I've heard that the nightlife is pretty interesting down there," Cedra said.

"That's one way of putting it. A lot of trouble to get into with drugs and other less than pure activities," she added with a grin.

"Not your choice of a local hangout then, I take it," Cedra asked?

"Me? I'm as pure as the driven snow."

"Uh-huh, and what bridge are you going to try to sell me next?"

Juliet's laughter filled the car. She pointed out Wild Bill's, the Iron Horse, and some other local fare as she continued her tour. "I have a gig at the Wild Bill's three nights a week for the next two weeks," she said.

"Then what?" Cedra asked.

"It's back to the pickle jar at the Iron Horse unless something else comes along."

"Keith and Wayne mentioned that last night."

"It is where a lot of up-and-coming artists pay their rent, and the crowd appreciates the struggles. Generally, tips are pretty good." She looked over at Cedra. "Now and then, one of the big names drops in to listen and remember the humble roots they were grown from."

"Do they expect to hear you perform cover songs, or can you do some original stuff?"

"I have found a mixture of both works the best. Grab their attention with a few covers, then mix in something original."

Cedra soaked up all the information Juliet offered, and made a mental note to sharpen up some cover tunes. She would spend a few nights checking out the various clubs to get a feel for the environment, and when she felt she had a handle on the atmosphere, she would take up Wayne and Keith's offer to get her into the rotation at the Iron Horse.

Juliet drove to the local Farmers Market, and they spent time wandering through the aisles of fresh fruits and produce. They had more than the strawberries and green beans they had come after when they left. There were fresh peaches and apples that neither of them could resist. Cedra's stomach growled when they got back to the car.

Juliet looked over at her and asked, "May I buy you lunch?"

"Sure, where did you have in mind?"

"If you are interested, I thought we could sneak you into the Redbird so you can catch a glimpse of it before tomorrow."

"I would like that."

Juliet checked her watch. "I think we have missed the major lunch crowd, so maybe we can get a table and still have plenty of time to get these beans back to Ma."

It was nearly two in the afternoon when they pulled into the lot behind the Redbird and found a parking spot.

"That's a good start," Juliet said as she whipped into the space. "You know this may be the perfect spot for you."

"How's that?" Cedra asked.

"The Redbird has Open Mic nights and Sunday Writers' Shows. It caters more to songwriters instead of performers." She cocked her head to the side as they walked around to the front of the building. "Are you a member of the NSAI?"

"Apparently not since I don't know what it stands for."

"The Nashville Songwriters Association International," Juliet said. "We need to get you signed up quick. You have to be a member to be eligible to perform here."

Juliet swung the door open and held it for Cedra. Cedra stepped inside the building that turned out to be much larger than she had expected and stood in awe. Juliet chuckled and guided her to an empty back table where they took a seat.

"Are you meeting with Lisa Marie tomorrow?" she asked.

"Yes, I believe that was the name."

"That's her behind the register," Juliet said.

"Good afternoon, ladies," a server said when she approached the table. "Hey, Juliet, I didn't recognize you."

"Hey, Suzy, I'd like you to meet Cedra. Hopefully, after tomorrow she will be working with you."

Suzy gave Cedra a close once over and then smiled. "I hope you know what you are getting yourself into," she warned with a wink to Juliet.

"I've done some serving before, so maybe I won't be too bad."

Suzy let out a quick laugh but let the topic drop. "What can I get you to drink?"

"Sweet tea, please," Cedra said.

"Go ahead and make it two."

"Anything for you, Juliet," Suzy said and sashayed back to the counter. She stopped to say something to Lisa Marie, and Cedra saw her potential employer look up to catch a glimpse of her.

"This place is awesome," Cedra said, taking in the small performer's stage placed in the center of the room.

"I will take that as a compliment," an unfamiliar voice said, and Cedra turned to see Lisa Marie standing there. She blushed furiously and managed a hello.

"Suzy told me that you are our new waitress, and I wanted to stop over to welcome you and harass Juliet for a second."

"Would you care to join us?" Juliet asked.

"Let me grab a tea, and I will be right back."

Juliet grimaced, "I should have asked you if you mind."

"No, not at all," Cedra answered.

She returned to the table. "I am Lisa Marie, and you must be Cedra," she said as she held out her hand. "Welcome to Nashville."

"Thanks, and you do have a marvelous place here."

"You need to change that to 'we' if you are going to be working here," she said with a smile. "I thought I would start you off slow with the breakfast crowd. Can you be here at five in the morning instead of ten?"

"You bet I can," Cedra said with a huge smile.

Lisa Marie turned to Juliet. "Don't let this one get you into too much trouble," she teased. "I caught a bit of your show last night. You sounded pretty good up there."

"Thanks," Juliet said. "Can I vouch for Cedra and get her in the NSAI?"

Lisa Marie turned back to Cedra. "Are you a songwriter?"

"Yes, ma'am, I am," she proudly said.

"Excellent. I will see what I can do about getting you an application for tomorrow then, and when you are ready, you can perform on one of our Open Mic nights since you are new to the area."

"That would be great. Thanks for the opportunity and the job," Cedra said.

"Don't thank me just yet. This place becomes complete chaos during the rush hours," she said with a chuckle. "What do you ladies want to eat, and I'll give Suzy your order?"

"Chicken fingers and fries for me, with honey mustard," Juliet said.

"Make it two, please."

"That should be easy enough for Suzy to remember," Lisa Marie said. "I will see you tomorrow, Cedra."

"I hope you are an early riser," Juliet said.

"I can handle it, I think," Cedra said. "I take it there is no uniform."

"Blue jeans are the norm here. It's a very casual atmosphere if you haven't noticed."

The door opened, and a tall, dark-haired woman walked in, followed closely by two men dressed in western-cut suits. "Well, I'll be damned," Juliet said, and Cedra followed her gaze, which led her to the woman.

"Someone you know?" she asked.

"Maybe in the future," Juliet said with a chuckle. "She is one of the hottest agents in Nashville at the moment. Her name is Carrie Brooks. She has a reputation of being a royal bitch, but she represents some of the best new artists in the business."

Cedra noticed the air of arrogance that emanated from the woman as she waited for one of the men to pull out a chair for her. She looked around the room to see if any other important people were present, then took her seat.

"She's a regular here, so maybe you can strike up a friendship with her," Juliet suggested.

"Only time will tell," Cedra said as she felt the woman's eyes glance past their table.

"She doesn't sing or play a lick, but she knows how to promote new talent," Juliet said.

Suzy arrived with their food and left them to eat in peace. Cedra noted that Lisa Marie stopped by the agent's table and took their orders after having a brief conversation, and then headed back to the kitchen.

She and Juliet finished their meals and picked up the tab to pay on their way out. Cedra followed Juliet across the room, and she felt Carrie Brooks's eyes on her as they walked across the room. When Cedra looked her way and saw her gazing at her, Carrie smiled as their eyes met and immediately turned away.

"That was some serious eye time," Juliet whispered as she handed a twenty to Suzy.

They exited the building, and Cedra asked, "What did you mean by that?"

Juliet chuckled at Cedra's innocence. "The woman watched you all the way across the room."

"And, what am I missing here?"

"Nothing, my friend, just an observation," Juliet said, and they walked back to the car.

"Thanks for lunch and the tour," Cedra said when they reached the car.

"My pleasure," Juliet answered.

When they returned home, Juliet quickly told Ma that Cedra would be starting work early the following day as they carried the bags into the kitchen.

"You will need to get a good night's rest tonight," Ma said. "I'm usually up by four, so I can make sure you are awake and have some coffee ready for you. You will get a meal at the café, but if you need something before you leave, I can have it ready."

"I can't imagine eating at that time of day," Cedra said. "Coffee and a wake-up will be great, though."

"I will snap these beans and get them cooking if the two of you will clean and slice the strawberries," Ma replied.

"I can handle this if you want to go get your clothes ready," Juliet said.

"Thanks. Ma do you have an iron and ironing board I can use?"

"In the laundry room behind the door, there's a fresh can of starch on the shelf."

"Oh man, you are going to show us all up by ironing your clothes?" Juliet groaned.

"It is important in making a good first impression," Cedra said.

"I rather prefer the I-slept-in-them look," Juliet said.

"Well, that's you. My mother would roll over in her grave if I left the house without looking my best."

"You could do well to listen to Cedra," Ma teased.

"Thanks, but that's just not my look."

"To each their own then," Cedra said with a wink and left the room.

†

"It appears you two are hitting it off well," Ma said when Cedra disappeared.

Juliet kept slicing strawberries. "Yeah, she's nice."

"I think you both could use a good friend."

"You are right about that, Ma. I love you and the boys, but it is nice having another female around who is close to my age."

Ma chuckled to herself and kept snapping the beans. She had seen the way Juliet looked at Cedra with raw hunger in her eyes and could sense more than a friendship brewing on the horizon. She only hoped that Cedra, who appeared so innocent, could handle the wild child that Juliet unleashed from time to time. Ma felt they seemed to be so opposite in many ways, yet Ma could sense a magnetism that brought the two of them together. *Fate knows what it is doing*, Ma thought as she hummed a tune while she worked.

†

Keith and Wayne returned home just in time for dinner. They both had the night off and had gone in search of some studio time earlier in the day.

"We both managed to cut a demo," Keith told Ma as he settled into his seat.

"Oh really?"

"They don't sound half bad either," Wayne chimed in.

"Let's have a listen after dinner then."

Both boys were grinning from ear to ear.

"Afterwards, if your heads aren't too swollen, I thought we might have a brief jam session on the porch. Cedra has to be up with the chickens to start work in the morning, but I thought we might play for an hour or so."

"Sounds good to me," Keith said.

"Me too," Wayne agreed, and they all looked at Cedra.

"Of course, I'm in," she grinned.

The group finished in record time, and the girls cleared the dishes while Ma prepared the strawberry shortcakes. The boys sat at the table, their mouths watering as they watched Ma serve up the desserts.

"Those look heavenly," Keith said.

"You have Cedra and Juliet to thank for the strawberries."

"Thanks, girls," he said as he passed a dish to Wayne.

"You are welcome," Juliet said as she dried her hands on a dishtowel and walked back to the table.

They settled in for dessert, and the boys finished off the remaining strawberries and cake as hungry boys tend to do.

"Do you feel like listening to us tonight, Ma?" Juliet asked.

"Y'all go get set up. I'm going to make myself a cup of coffee, and I will be out."

†

All four of them rushed upstairs to grab their instruments. Cedra opened her case, took out her guitar, and then picked up her songbook. She noticed it was getting full, and she would have to buy a new one soon, but that was a good thing.

Wayne and Keith had pulled the rocking chairs close together in a circle. Wayne surprised her by having a banjo to accompany their three guitars.

"Hey, let's listen to your demos before we get started," Juliet said as she brought out a small CD player.

"You first," Keith said to Wayne.

Wayne took his CD from the case and placed it in the player. Juliet pressed play, and the soft notes of a guitar started to play. The tune was a tender love song he had written, and Cedra was very impressed. It had a beautiful sound and was pleasing to her ears. Keith removed Wayne's demo and inserted his CD when the song had finished. It was a much different sound, more of a rockabilly tune, and Cedra immediately picked up Wayne's voice in the backup vocals.

"That would sound even better with some female voices mixed in," Juliet said.

"You feel like giving it a try?"

"Play it through for us once and let us hear it live," Juliet said.

They picked up their instruments and began to play as Ma sat down in one of the rockers. Cedra and Juliet picked up the rhythm and played along with the boys halfway through the song. The lyrics were simple, and when they began playing it for a second time, all four sang along together. Ma rocked in her chair as she sipped her coffee and smiled at the beautiful music they were making. Cedra had to admit they did sound good together.

"What do you think, Ma?" Keith asked.

"I think the four of you sound fantastic together. You blend with a fantastic southern voice."

Keith glowed with pride from Ma's praise. Ma's words caught her attention, and Cedra had a thought begin to grow in the back of her mind.

"Okay, Cedra, your turn," Keith said.

Caught off guard, Cedra struggled to decide what to play for them as she flipped through her notepad.

"Are all of those songs?" Wayne asked.

"Yeah, they are."

"Holy cow, someone's been busy," he said with a smile. "You gonna let us have a look at that?"

"Maybe," Cedra said. "But then again, you might not like any of them."

"I find that hard to believe," Keith said. "I think you are a diamond in the rough, Baby Girl."

Cedra smiled at the name he called her, and it reminded her of her father. She would give him a call before she went to bed to check in with him and share the good news of starting work.

"Play the song you were working on last night," Juliet said.

"It's still pretty rough," Cedra said.

"Let us be the judge of that," Juliet said.

Cedra nodded her head and turned to the back of her notepad. She picked up her guitar and began to play. Her eyes were down on the tablet reading the lyrics, so she did not see the reaction the song was making on her new friends until the song ended, and she looked up to see their shocked faces.

"Was it that bad?"

Wayne was the first to chime in. "I want to see that notepad. Cedra, that was so beautiful."

"It sounded even better than last night," Juliet said with a smile.

"I loved the song, but I would recommend just a bit of a change on the music," Keith said.

"Show me," Cedra said.

Keith picked up his guitar and played the first part of the song exactly as she had, but when he reached the chorus, he used a very different key, which blended in much better.

"Oh, I like that," Cedra said and jotted the notes down on her pad.

"One more time then," Ma said.

Cedra smiled and repeated the song, this time with the changes Keith suggested, and it did sound much better.

"I think that's the tune you should lead out with on Open Mic night," Juliet said.

"You've got a slot already for Open Mic at the Redbird?" Wayne asked.

"No, not yet," Cedra answered and chuckled at the shocked look on his face.

"I was gonna say, damn, you work fast, girl," he grinned.

"Give me a couple of weeks at least."

"That is a beautiful song," Ma said. "Where did the inspiration for those lyrics come from?"

Cedra smiled at Ma. "I was lying in bed last night, thinking of my mother and all of the changes that are occurring in my life, and they just started to flow."

"I am so jealous," Juliet said. "It would take me a week to write a song, and you did it in a couple of hours."

"It just happens like that sometimes."

"Would you mind if we do look through your book at some of the others you have written?" Juliet asked.

"No, not at all, just drop it off when you come upstairs."

They could all hear the clock chiming on the wall in the foyer. "I can't believe it has gotten this late. If you all will excuse me, I need to give my dad a call and then get some sleep."

"Thanks for playing with us," Keith said.

"I enjoyed it," Cedra said as she picked up her guitar and made her way upstairs. As she slowly climbed, she heard Juliet's voice drifting across the soft breeze as she broke into Garth's "Shameless." She could not help but smile at her choice of songs. That had always been one of her favorite songs, and Juliet's voice was beautiful as she lowered her voice to sing the lyrics.

†

Cedra put her guitar away and reached for the cell phone to call her dad.

"Hey, Baby Girl," he said when he answered. His voice sounded a bit winded, surprising Cedra.

"Are you okay, Daddy?" she asked, worried.

"Yes, Lord, I have just been playing with these danged kittens. They are so funny," he said.

"They? How many did you come home with?"

"Just two," he answered. "They had a brother and a sister, both solid blacks, and I couldn't stand to separate them."

Cedra could hear the joy in her father's voice.

"I discovered that they like to chase shadows in the kitchen," Hank said. "So I have been making shadows on the walls and watching them trying to catch them. I swear I haven't laughed this hard since your mother was alive."

"That sounds like a lot of fun. What have you named them?"

Her dad let out an evil-sounding chuckle.

"Elvis and Elvira," he said and broke out laughing.

"Good Lord, how can you tell them apart?"

"Elvira has a tiny bit of white on her throat, and Elvis is a lot longer than she is."

"You will have to take some pictures and send me some."

"I will. How did your day go?"

"It was awesome. Juliet, one of the other boarders, gave me a guided tour, and we stopped off at the Redbird for a late lunch. The manager asked me if I want to start earlier tomorrow, so I have to be there at five."

"Five in the morning?" he asked.

"Yes, Daddy."

"I hope you are ready to get into bed then. Five o'clock comes way too fast."

"I'm going to take a quick shower, then I'm off to bed," she promised.

"Okay, Baby Girl, I am very proud of you. I love you."

"Thanks, Daddy. I love you too and will call in a couple of days."

"Goodnight, Cedra."

"Goodnight." Cedra ended the call and then picked out some pajamas and headed to the bathroom.

After a quick shower, she brushed her teeth and climbed beneath the crisp sheets. She closed her eyes and was asleep as fast as her head hit the pillow.

†

Juliet, Keith, and Wayne were bent over on the porch, looking at the notepad that Cedra had left with them.

"This is some good stuff," Juliet said, letting out a low whistle between her teeth.

"She's got a wide range of songs built up here," Keith said. "I totally like this one," he said, pointing to a song called "Backwoods Boogie." "I could get into some rockabilly with this."

"Ask her if you can use it," Juliet said. "I get the impression from her that she much prefers writing over performing. Some local exposure certainly couldn't hurt her."

"What do you think her chances are of getting an Open Mic invitation?" Wayne asked.

"From what I have seen in here, I'd say pretty damned good," Juliet answered. "We need to help her choose five or six songs and help her clean them up to get her ready."

"That may be the hardest part, choosing which ones," Keith said.

"Definitely the song she sang for us tonight," Juliet said.

"She's got some neat ballads in here that I think suit her well. Has anyone picked up on the artists Cedra has noted at the top of the page?"

"What?" Keith asked.

"Scribbled at the top is a list of artists that she would write the song for to suit their style," Wayne said.

"I didn't notice that," Juliet said as she flipped back through the pages. "I wonder if she hears their voices as she writes the lyrics?"

"That would be interesting to know," Ma chimed in. "I don't think I've seen the three of you this excited before."

"This is incredibly good. You can feel the passion that Cedra writes with and almost taste it," Juliet said.

Ma smiled at Juliet's comment and climbed to her feet. "I hate to leave such good company, but my old bones are aching, so I'm going to call it a night. Don't stay up too late," Ma said and entered the house.

"I think I will call it a night, too," Wayne said as he stood and opened the door for Ma.

"Goodnight then," Juliet said.

"I'll hang with you a bit," Keith said as he picked up his guitar and started playing a tune.

Juliet continued to read the lyrics as she listened to Keith play. The more she read, the deeper she fell into the heartache and longing Cedra conveyed in her words. When Keith finally called it a night, Juliet picked up her guitar and played several times through one of the songs. The words rolled off her tongue so smoothly it felt good, and she found her face aching from smiling so hard.

When she felt like she had the tune and lyrics down, she entered the house and locked up behind her before climbing the stairs. As quietly as she could, she crept into Cedra's room and left the notepad on her desk. A small nightlight softly lit the room, and her heart caught in her throat when she saw how peacefully Cedra was sleeping, her hair framing her face like an angel as she slept.

Juliet stretched out on her bed and couldn't stop thinking about Cedra. Juliet knew Cedra hadn't recognized the look of hunger that burned in Carrie's eyes as she watched the sensual sway of Cedra's body as they crossed the room. It was apparent to her that Cedra had never seen that look before.

"So innocent and sweet," Juliet whispered. "I have my work cut out for me to keep you from Carrie's clutches."

CHAPTER FIVE

Cedra rolled over to turn off her alarm just as a soft knock came from her door, and Ma poked her head inside.

†

"Cedra, are you awake?"

"Yes, Ma, just stretching before I get up to shower."

"Do you want some breakfast?"

"No, ma'am, just a big mug of coffee to go."

"I have some travel mugs that will keep it hot for you and will have a mug ready when you come down."

"Thanks, Ma," Cedra said and tossed her covers back.

Ma closed the door and descended the stairs, her old knees creaking with each step. She entered the kitchen, started the coffee pot, and then moved to the cupboard to retrieve a travel mug. Darkness still cloaked the house as she looked out the window. She knew Reggie, her old rooster, would be strutting around in the yard, and at the sign of first light, he would crow his morning greeting.

†

Cedra raced through the shower, dressed, and finished her preparations before going downstairs. She crept from her room and descended the stairs as quietly as she could to find Ma sitting at the kitchen table, sipping her first cup of coffee.

"Here's your mug," Ma said as Cedra entered. "Are you sure I can't fix you something to eat?"

"I'm way too nervous to think about putting food in my stomach," she admitted.

"Relax, Cedra, and you will do just fine," Ma promised.

"I hope so, Ma," Cedra said and started for the door. She stopped and turned back to Ma. "Is there anything you need from town today?"

"No, not that I can think of, but thanks for asking," Ma answered.

"I will see you this afternoon then," Cedra said and slipped through the front door. She walked across the yard to her truck and cringed when the door creaked loud when she opened it and climbed inside. Cedra closed the door as quietly as possible and fired up the motor.

†

Juliet lay in her bed and smiled at the sound of Cedra's motor. Damn, but it was too early to be up, she thought, as she listened to Cedra pull away, and then raised the covers back over her head to return to sleep. Tonight, would be a late night for her, so she would take advantage of the opportunity to sleep in for a bit.

†

Cedra backed out of her parking spot and turned on her headlights when she put the truck in gear. Her heart was beating like a hammer as she pulled onto the hard road for the short drive to Nashville. The darkness made everything look different, but the sky was beginning to lighten as she approached the city limits. She breathed a sigh of relief when she came to a familiar four-way stop and turned left to the Redbird. She pulled her truck into a back parking lot she assumed was for employees, and parked beside a canary yellow Ford F-150. Nice truck, she thought as she plucked her keys from the ignition and locked the door behind her. She was about to knock on the back door when Lisa Marie threw the door open.

"Good morning," she said. "I hope you don't mind being up with the chickens."

"No, not at all. I like the peacefulness of the early morning."

"Enjoy it while you can because we open the front door at 5:30, and all that peace will be gone. Come on, and let me introduce you to the rest of the morning crew."

Cedra followed Lisa Marie inside where she met Teddy, the short-order cook, and Vanessa, another early morning server. "Pleased to meet you," she said.

"I hope you can keep up," Vanessa said as she walked past Cedra and started wiping down tables.

"I will give it my best."

"Don't worry about Grumpy," Teddy said. "Her bark is much gentler after she gets a pot of coffee into her."

"Hilarious, Romeo," Vanessa sneered from the dining room.

"Now, children," Lisa Marie said. "You are not making an excellent first impression on Cedra here," she scolded.

"It's no problem. I get up on the wrong side of the bed too sometimes," Cedra said with a wink to Lisa Marie.

Lisa Marie roared with laughter. "Yes, you are going to fit right in. Get an order pad off the counter, and here is a small apron to store some supplies," she said as she handed it to Cedra. The back door chimed, and a sleepy-looking, dark-haired youth came strolling in.

"This zombie would be Tom," Vanessa said. "He buses the tables and washes dishes" she snarled.

"Hi Tom, I'm Cedra."

"Morning," he said as he made a beeline to the coffee pot.

"Okay, let's get these tables wiped and menus set up," Lisa Marie said.

Vanessa and Cedra went to work.

A few minutes later, a small crowd was forming at the door. Lisa Marie grabbed her keys and unlocked the front door. Four men walked past her to barstools at the front counter, and another group of four took a nearby table. "Cedra, take the counter, and Vanessa can have the table," she said.

"Yes, Ma'am," Cedra said and approached the men at the counter. "Can I get you fellows coffee to start?"

"Yes, please, and keep it coming," one of the men said over the top of his menu.

Cedra poured four cups of coffee and started taking orders, using the shorthand she had learned at a previous waitressing job. She took the first order, called it out to Teddy, then placed the ticket on an order line for him and returned for the following order.

†

Lisa Marie watched her and was pleased with the friendly banter she kept up with the customers as they teased her about her first day at the Redbird. Cedra took their gentle teasing in stride and received a generous reward with good tips as the morning began to fade. Cedra managed the counter, and when the dining room began to fill, both she and Lisa Marie assisted Vanessa.

After the morning's first rush, Lisa Marie told Cedra to take a fifteen-minute break. Cedra nodded and walked out the front door to sit on a small bench in the early morning sun. She took a small notepad from her apron and quickly jotted down several lines of lyrics that had been floating through her head all morning.

†

Lisa Marie looked up from the cash register to see Cedra sitting on the bench, her head bobbing with an imaginary tune as she wrote on the small pad. She smiled and shook her head at the energy of her newest server. Cedra had been a good choice, and even some of the most cantankerous of her early morning customers seemed pleased with her good-natured personality.

†

Cedra finished her break and returned inside to pour herself a cup of coffee. "Why don't you order some breakfast and come join me," Lisa Marie suggested.

"Yes, ma'am," Cedra answered and gave Teddy her order; then she took a fresh pot of coffee to freshen up the coffees of customers that were still eating.

Lisa Marie had watched her closely and was impressed by her willingness to work hard and stay busy. Even the hard-natured Vanessa seemed to soften a bit around Cedra.

"Order's up, Cedra," Teddy hollered from the serving window.

Cedra walked over to pick up her plate of food and then joined Lisa Marie at a table.

"You are doing very well this morning," Lisa Marie said. "Do you have any questions?"

Cedra picked up her coffee cup and asked, "Is it always busy this early in the morning?"

Lisa Marie chuckled. "We always have a good breakfast crowd, even more so when there is a big event in town. I can remember having a line backed around the corner of the building by six when the Music Festival's in town."

Cedra's eyes must have grown wide as Lisa Marie talked. "Don't worry; we always have extra staff on hand during those times."

"That's good," Cedra said and took a bite of toast.

"I noticed you were jotting some notes while you were on break," she said.

Cedra's face flushed a little. "I had some lyrics floating around that I wanted to capture before they disappeared."

Lisa Marie chuckled softly. "Does that songwriter brain ever shut off?" she teased.

"I sure hope not," Cedra said. "Writing has always been so easy for me. I would hate to hit a writer's block, so whenever a line comes to mind, I try to write it down."

"I have a feeling you are going to be successful here in Nashville," Lisa Marie said.

Cedra was shocked by the honesty of Lisa Marie's comment. "Why do you think that, if you don't mind me asking?"

"Well, first, you seem to have a good flow of lyrics going through your brain, and second you have a strong work ethic. Your determination will take you where you want to go." She sipped her coffee and looked at Cedra. "So many young people come to town expecting instant fame and fortune and fail because they don't know how to be persistent or don't want to put out the effort it takes to be successful."

"I have promised myself that I will stay at least a year, and if I don't feel I have what it takes, I will head home."

"Work hard, and you will know if you have what it takes to be successful. There's a world of opportunity here in Nashville, so stay true to your dream."

"I will," Cedra said with a smile. "Have your dreams come true?" she asked.

Lisa Marie smiled. "When I first came to town, I was able to do some backup work, but I soon realized that my best bet to be a part of the music business would be to feed the masses and help some struggling new artists as much as I can by showcasing their talents."

Cedra could not detect a single hint of regret in her words. "You have a great place here, and business seems to be good."

"It is, and I have had the pleasure of hearing some outstanding talent before they hit the big time."

"I look forward to being here for an Open Mic night."

"It will give you a good idea of some of the talented artists that are just waiting for that first big break. I have your application for the Songwriters Association, so take it home with you and get brushed up and ready."

"That may take a few weeks," Cedra answered.

"There's no hurry, but the sooner you get started, the better."

"Yes, ma'am," Cedra answered with a nod. Having finished her breakfast, Cedra stood to carry her plate to the kitchen. "I better get back to the counter," she said as several new customers were coming through the door.

"Thanks for having breakfast with me," Lisa Marie said.

"Thank you," Cedra said.

†

Around eleven, two other servers came in to prepare for the lunch crowd. Cedra was glad to see them, as the flow of customers had not let up since she had finished her breakfast. She was having a great first day but would be grateful when one o'clock arrived, and she could stop for the day.

Just before it was time for her to end her shift, the door opened, and the dark-haired woman she and Juliet had seen the previous day walked in. Cedra wracked her brain to remember the woman's name and was relieved when Lisa Marie said, "Hey Carrie."

Carrie Brooks took a seat in Cedra's section, so she took a deep breath and walked over to the table. "Good afternoon. What may I get you to drink?"

"Good afternoon," Carrie said, her dark eyes shining. "I would like some sweet tea."

"I will get that right out to you while you look at the menu," Cedra said and left the table.

†

"Thanks," Carrie said and appeared to peruse the menu. She had eaten at the café so often she had the menu memorized but continued the ruse.

Cedra returned moments later with the glass of tea. "Here you go. Have you made up your mind about what you would care to eat?"

"I would like the spinach salad, please, Cedra," Carrie said after glimpsing her nametag.

"I will get that order right up for you," Cedra said and walked back to the counter.

Carrie's eyes followed Cedra back to the counter.

†

Cedra called out her order, and when she turned around toward the dining room, she found Carrie watching her.

"That's your last customer of the day," Lisa Marie said loud enough for Carrie to hear. "You did a great job today, and you are well deserving of a relaxing afternoon."

"Thanks, Lisa Marie. It was a great day, and I can't tell you how much I appreciate the job."

"I think I got the better part of this deal," Lisa Marie said as she rang up a charge.

"Order's up," Teddy called and then handed Cedra a large salad loaded with steaming bacon dressing.

She carried the salad over to Carrie's table and placed it in front of her. "Other than more tea, is there anything else I can get you?"

"Some company if you don't mind. I heard Lisa Marie say I was your last customer, so I'm sure she won't mind if you join me for lunch."

"I'm not hungry, but I will grab a drink and join you if you wish."

"That would be nice."

Cedra walked back to the counter to refill Carrie's tea glass and pour a glass for herself. "She asked if I would join her at her table. Is that okay with you?"

Lisa Marie stepped close. "That would be an excellent friendship to strike up. Do you know who she is?"

"Juliet says she's a hotshot talent agent," Cedra whispered back.

Lisa Marie chuckled. "That sounds just like Juliet. Carrie Brooks represents some very high-powered talent. You would be fortunate for her to hear some of your songs, so by all means, do join her."

"Yes, ma'am," Cedra said with a grin.

Cedra returned to the table, placed the fresh glass of tea in front of her customer. She pulled out the chair across from her and sat.

"Thanks. My name is Carrie, by the way."

"You are welcome."

"Tell me about Cedra," Carrie said as she took a drink of tea.

"Well, there's not much to tell yet. I'm an aspiring songwriter from south Alabama, and this is my first day at the café."

"Welcome to Music City then," Carrie said. "What type of songs do you write?" she asked, genuinely interested.

"Mostly ballads and love songs, but I do have several that Juliet calls rockabilly," Cedra said, a warm smile playing across her face at the mention of Juliet.

"Juliet Tucker?" Carrie asked.

"Yes, we live together at Ma Bentley's boarding house."

"She's got a good voice and is a great musician, but Juliet's songwriting still needs to be developed."

"I hope I can help her with that," Cedra said.

Carrie cocked her head to the side in a curious gesture. "Most newcomers to town would never consider helping out a competitor in the dog-eat-dog world of music. That is very kind of you," she said.

"I am not all that invested in performing live," Cedra admitted. "My heart lies in my writing."

"A good writer is worth their weight in gold in this town," Carrie said. "There are hundreds of newcomers that can sing a decent tune, but it's rare to find a good young songwriter. Have you joined the Association yet?"

"Lisa Marie has an application for me and said she would be a reference for me. Juliet also said she would be a reference."

"So, you only need one more. Feel free to use me then," Carrie surprised her by offering.

"Thank you, Ms. Brooks," Cedra said.

Carrie laughed loudly. "No one calls me Ms. Brooks unless they want something, so just call me Carrie," she requested.

"Thanks," Cedra said. "Let me get you some more tea. May I offer you some dessert?"

"Do you have buttermilk pie on the menu today?"

"Yes, ma'am, we do."

"Will you at least join me in a slice?"

"Sure thing," Cedra said, and walked back to the counter to place two slices onto small plates.

Lisa Marie smiled at her and gave her a wink as Cedra carried the plates and the tea glass back to the table.

"Here you go, one guilt-free slice of buttermilk pie."

"You must be a magician as well as a songwriter if you can take the calories out of this pie," Carrie said with a grin.

"I won't tell if you won't," Cedra said, returning Carrie's smile.

"So, will you be working the morning shift here?"

"So far, I think Lisa Marie will keep me on the five-to-two shift."

"Good, I will see you almost every day then," Carrie said. "I usually eat lunch here if I don't stop in for breakfast."

"I look forward to seeing you again then," Cedra said. "Thanks for the pie," she added, standing to clear the table.

"Thanks for the company. It is rare I get a moment free from the office that one agent or another does not smother me. Good luck with your writing, and I hope to hear some of your work soon."

"Thanks. Lisa Marie said she will slide me into a slot at Open Mic night when I'm ready."

"Be sure to keep me posted then," Carrie said.

"Is there anything else I can get you?"

"Just the check, thanks."

Cedra pulled her ticket from the pad and placed it down on the table. "Have a good day," she said, and carried the dishes into the kitchen.

Carrie picked up the check and followed her back to the counter, where she handed Lisa Marie cash to pay her bill.

"I hope you enjoyed your meal."

"It was great as usual," Carrie said, taking the change Lisa Marie offered. "Give this to Cedra for me, please." She handed Lisa Marie a ten-dollar bill.

"Will do," Lisa Marie said. "See you tomorrow."

"Yes, you will," Carrie said and walked to the door.

Cedra returned to the counter. "I'm off unless you need something."

"Here's your tip from Carrie," she said with a grin. "Looks like you made a good impression."

"She seemed pretty nice and even offered for me to use her as my third reference for the Songwriters application."

"Really? That has to be a first. Let me get that for you before I forget," she said and walked into her small office. "Fill it out and bring it back in when you have it done with the application fee."

"I will, and thanks again for everything," Cedra said.

"Get some rest, and I will see you bright and early tomorrow."

"See ya," Cedra said and walked out into the bright sunshine.

CHAPTER SIX

Cedra drove home, enjoying the sunshine pelting through her window. It was warm, but the heat and humidity were still tolerable. When she pulled up to the boarding house, she saw Ma and Juliet sitting on the porch. Juliet was finishing off a sandwich while Ma shucked corn.

"Welcome home," Ma said when she walked up.

"Thanks, Ma. How are you all?"

"I think it's safe to say we are good," Ma answered. "How did your first day at the Redbird Café go?"

"Pretty well, I think. We were busy the whole shift, but I didn't spill anything on any customers, and Lisa Marie seems pleased with me."

"That does sound good."

"I see Lisa Marie got you an application for the Songwriters Association," Juliet said, pointing to the papers Cedra carried.

"Yes, she did, and you will never guess who volunteered to be my third reference."

"You have my curiosity, so who?" Juliet asked.

"Carrie Brooks."

"No way," Juliet said.

"Yes, way, she was my last customer today and asked me to join her for dessert. When we started talking, she volunteered to be my third reference for the application."

"Oh girl, you are a shoo-in now," Juliet said.

"That is very impressive," Ma chimed in. "I have never met the woman, but I know she controls a great deal of power on Music Row."

"I was excited," Cedra said as she settled into a rocker next to Juliet.

"Are you hungry?"

"No, Ma, I believe I am too tired to eat anything right now. I think a shower and nap are in order for this afternoon."

"That's not a bad idea. I will have supper ready at six."

"After supper, I will have an hour or so before I head off to my gig if you would like some help with that application," Juliet offered.

"That sounds good," Cedra said as she stood to enter the house.

"Have a great nap," Ma said, and Cedra entered the screen door.

"Thanks, Ma. I will see you two later this afternoon."

Cedra climbed the stairs, placed the application on the small desk in her room, and began emptying her pockets. She was surprised to find that she had accumulated ninety-five dollars in tips during her first day, and she used a pushpin to tack the ten-dollar tip from Carrie to her wall. It was by far her largest single tip. Cedra stripped the rest of her clothes off and headed for the shower.

The warm water flowing across her skin finished relaxing her entirely, and she barely set her alarm before her body collapsed on the bed.

†

"Do you think I should invite Cedra to listen to my first set tonight?" Juliet asked.

"I think she would probably enjoy that. Wait until you see how well she rested this afternoon, and if she seems refreshed, I would ask her," Ma suggested.

"She could be home by nine-thirty at the latest," Juliet said.

"I think she could handle that."

"Do you need some help with supper?"

"No, I have everything under control," Ma answered.

"I think I will work on some songs for my first set then. I will be in the parlor if you need anything."

"Okay, Juliet," Ma said as she disappeared into the house.

Ma finished shucking the corn, carried the fresh ears into the kitchen, and placed them in the refrigerator. Then she returned to the porch, carried the cornhusks over to her compost bin, and dropped them inside. She decided she would sit on the porch a while longer and soon found herself dozing in the warm sunshine.

†

Juliet put her final changes to her playlist for her night and hoped that Cedra would allow her to use one of her songs in her first set. They had talked about the song briefly the day before, but she would ask her permission to use the music later when Cedra awoke from her nap. She walked out onto the porch to find Ma dozing. Juliet walked over and softly placed a hand on her shoulder to rouse her from her slumber.

"Why don't you go take a nap, too," she suggested.

"I guess that wouldn't be a bad idea," Ma said as she pulled her body up from the rocker.

Juliet followed Ma up the stairs, then crept into her room, careful not to awaken Cedra, picked out an outfit for the night, and then lay down on her bed. She listened for any sounds coming from the room next door and drifted off to sleep as a calm wind blew through her window.

†

The house remained quiet for several hours as the three women slept deeply inside. Ma woke and she immediately set to work preparing supper, and Juliet joined her in the kitchen.

"What can I do to help?"

"You can make some fresh tea and then whip us up a fresh salad."

Juliet had brewed the tea and had it cooling in the refrigerator when she heard someone enter the kitchen. She looked up to find Cedra sleepily walking in.

"Hey there, sleepyhead, did you have a great nap?"

"Yes, I did, thanks. I feel very refreshed."

Juliet put the finishing touches on the salad and then placed it in a large bowl.

"You can put that in the fridge, too," Ma said.

"Is there anything I can do?" Cedra asked.

"You can rinse and slice the okra," Ma said.

"Do you want some of these tomatoes sliced, too?" Juliet asked.

"Yes, please."

Cedra walked to the sink, rinsed off the okra, and then sliced it on a cutting board as Juliet prepared the tomato slices. Ma battered pork chops for cooking.

When Cedra had finished, Ma pointed to a cabinet. "There's a Tupperware bowl in the cabinet. Please put the okra inside and cover it with some of the buttermilk in the fridge," she instructed. "Juliet, when you finish, can you get the bag of cornmeal from the pantry for me and then set the table?"

"Yes, ma'am," she said.

"You two are going to get me spoiled with all this help," Ma teased.

"There's no reason why we can't help when we are home," Juliet said.

"I do appreciate it," Ma said as she pulled down a large platter that she covered with paper towels to drain the cooked pork chops.

They heard a vehicle approaching, and moments later, Keith and Wayne came bounding into the house. Wayne had picked Keith up after an early shift at the Ryman, and the boys had stopped off at a bakery and brought home dessert.

"What's that you two are carrying?" Juliet said, eyeing the bakery box.

"We brought a caramel cake for dessert," Wayne said with a grin.

"You better go ahead and set the coffee pot then," Ma told Juliet.

"You two can go get cleaned up and ready for supper," she said to Wayne and Keith, knowing they would only congest the small kitchen workspace if she allowed them to stay.

"Yes'm," Wayne said, and then raced Keith upstairs.

Ma got the first batch of pork chops started, and Juliet took the opportunity to ask Cedra about using her song. "Cedra, would you mind if I used one of your songs tonight?"

Cedra looked at her, a bit surprised. She and Juliet had talked about several of her songs, but she had not dreamed that Juliet would perform one of them live.

"Oh, I was also wondering if you would like to come down and listen to my first set tonight. I start at eight, so you should be home at nine-thirty at the latest."

Cedra smiled at Juliet, lighting up the room. "Yes, and yes," she answered.

"Great," Juliet said. "Keith is going to join me on a few numbers so you can ride with him or follow us in your truck."

"I think I will follow you, so there's no chance of ending his night prematurely," she answered.

Ma was still fussing around the stove as the two girls chatted. "Cedra, will you pour some of that cornmeal into a plastic bag for me?" Ma asked.

"Sure, Ma," she answered and took a plastic zip lock bag from Juliet. "Thanks."

"Now, will you strain the buttermilk from the okra, and pour the okra in the bag, and give it a good shake?"

Cedra followed Ma's instructions and handed her the bag of okra. Ma began fishing out the sticky vegetable slices and dropped them into a pan of hot grease. "Juliet, will you cover another platter with paper towels for me, please?"

"Sure, Ma," she answered.

"Man, something sure smells good," Wayne said as he entered the kitchen.

"You can pour the drinks, and I will have supper done soon," she told him to keep him from standing over her shoulder.

"I haven't had okra fried like that since my mom passed away," Cedra said.

"I hope it is half as good as hers then," Ma said.

"I bet it will be. It looks like you cook it the same way. I've tried a few times, but it always comes out like mush."

"I've learned you need to have the oil at just the right temperature to make it light and crispy," Ma said as she took the last of the pork chops out to drain and handed Juliet the platter. "Just another few minutes on this okra, and we are good to go. Juliet, can you get the salad and sliced tomatoes and put them on the table?"

"Yes, Ma," she said, and got busy setting the goods on the table.

Cedra held the platter while Ma scooped out the fried okra and carried it to the table where the boys and Juliet were eagerly waiting. Cedra and Ma joined them around the table, and they held hands as Ma said a short blessing over the food.

Cedra scooped out two helpings of okra, then took a bite and moaned. "Tastes just like Mom's," she said.

"Eat your fill then," Ma said.

"I could eat this whole platter," she said as she passed the dish to Wayne.

She kept an eye on the platter of okra throughout the meal, and when it appeared everyone had finished, Cedra asked, "Does anyone mind me finishing off the okra?"

"Go for it," Juliet said, passing her the platter.

"This is just too good, Ma," Cedra said as she spooned out the remainder of the dish.

"I am so thrilled you approve," Ma teased. "We will have to serve it more often."

"That's alright by me," Keith added.

Ma and Juliet served coffee and slices of the caramel cake. When Cedra had finished, Juliet said, "Let's go upstairs, and I will help you knock out that application before I need to head out."

"I need to help Ma with the kitchen first," Cedra said.

"Nonsense, I have these two knuckleheads left to help me clean up. After all, you two helped with the cooking," she added.

"We can handle this," Wayne said, so Cedra followed Juliet upstairs.

"I filled in most of it already," Cedra said as Juliet sat on the end of her bed. "I just need help with a few things."

Juliet moved closer to read over Cedra's shoulder, and within minutes, they had finished the application. "Do you have the money for the application fee?" Juliet asked.

"I do now," Cedra said with a grin. The tips she had made today would be enough to cover the fifty-dollar application fee and still have a few bucks for gas.

Juliet noticed the ten-dollar bill pinned to the wall but refrained from asking questions. "I better run through the shower and get moving. I will have a small table reserved for you by the stage," Juliet said and left the room.

Cedra took a couple of outfits downstairs to the laundry room to iron while Juliet showered. They passed one another of the stairs.

"There you go, showing me up again," Juliet teased when she saw crisply starched jeans on the hangers.

"Someone around here has to keep up a good appearance," Cedra shot back at her.

"Ouch, that stings," Juliet said with a wink. "Keith, are you ready?" she hollered into the kitchen.

"I will be right there," he yelled back.

"I guess I will see you shortly," Cedra said, and climbed the stairs to change clothes.

"Drive careful," Juliet called to her.

"Always," Cedra answered.

She closed the door to her room and decided to call her father before dressing to update him. Her father was very excited to hear about her first day of work and gave her the rundown of what he, Elvis, and Elvira had been doing. Cedra was pleased to listen to the excitement and joy in her father's voice when speaking of the kittens. It had been a long time since his voice had sounded so good. When they ended the call, Cedra changed into her best jeans and newest shirt before bounding down the stairs.

"Hey, can I catch a ride with you?" Wayne asked.

"Sure, you can. I will see you later, Ma. Thanks for a great dinner."

"You are most welcome," Ma said. "Have fun, and I will see you bright and early."

Wayne rushed ahead of her and held the front door open for her. "Thanks," she said, and they walked out to the truck.

"This is one fine piece of metal," he said as he climbed into the passenger seat. "Maybe when you hit the big time, you will think about selling her to me."

Cedra laughed softly. "She may not be running by the time that happens."

"Oh, I'd bet this old gal has at least another five years in her, maybe ten if you stay on top of her maintenance."

"I sure hope you are right. I've never had a truck payment, and I sure can't afford one now."

"That will all change once performers start seeing your songs," he predicted.

Cedra shifted into gear, and the truck bounced along the driveway as she contemplated Wayne's words. When they pulled up in front of Wild Bill's, Wayne quickly pointed out a parking spot, and Cedra pulled the truck to a stop.

"It looks like a good crowd already," Cedra said.

"This place is usually crammed on just about any night of the week."

"I sure hope Juliet remembered to reserve us a table then," Cedra said, worried as they walked toward the entrance.

"I'm sure she did," Wayne said with a grin. "She is very excited that you agreed to come tonight."

"I am happy she invited me."

"Keith is going to be performing a few songs with her, too, from what he told me earlier."

Wayne held the heavy door open for her as they stepped into a large building. The crowd was busy dancing on the large dance floor to some recorded music. Juliet looked up to see them enter and pointed to a table to the left of the stage. She and Keith had nearly finished setting up their gear, and when Cedra sat at the table, she approached with a wide grin.

"Welcome to Wild Bill's," she said.

"Thanks. Are you all set?"

"Yes, we will be turning the lights down low in just a few minutes."

"Can I get you a drink?" Wayne asked.

"A cherry coke, please," Cedra answered.

"Lightweight," Juliet teased. "Thanks again for coming tonight and letting me use one of your songs."

"Don't thank me yet. The crowd may not like it at all."

"Oh ye of little faith," Juliet said as the light flickered to clear the dancers from the dance floor.

"Break a leg," Cedra said as Juliet turned toward the stage.

Wayne returned to the table carrying drinks just as Juliet and Keith opened the set with an old Garth Brooks tune. The crowd sang along with her as she belted out the song. The next song was a new one by Thompson Square. She and Keith carried off the duet brilliantly, and when they sang the chorus, "Are you gonna kiss me or not?" Juliet's eyes met Cedra's as she sang. When the song was over, the crowd roared in appreciation, and it took several minutes for Juliet to get them settled down again.

"That was a popular song with this crowd," Cedra said as she watched Juliet on stage.

"This next song is written by a songwriter brand new to Music City. I want you all to give a fine 'How to do' to Miss Cedra Tyler," Juliet said as her hand guided a spotlight to the table where Cedra sat in morbid shock. Her face was scarlet as she lifted a hand to acknowledge the crowd, and the soft sounds of guitars filled the air.

The room fell silent as Juliet began singing the lyrics, and time seemed to move in slow motion. Keith chimed in on the song's chorus, and Juliet's eyes sparkled with excitement as she sang the song. Cedra found herself mouthing the words to the music along with Juliet as she sang, and when the song came to an end, the crowd erupted with applause.

Cedra was pleased with the reaction of the crowd. She knew it was just as much for Juliet's performance as it was the song itself, but she felt a pulse of pride growing within.

"The crowd liked the song," Wayne said to a broadly smiling Cedra.

The excitement of the crowd's reaction buzzed through her body until the set ended and Keith and Juliet joined them at the table.

"You sounded fantastic," she said.

"I think the crowd genuinely liked your song," Juliet said.

"Or your performance of it at least," she answered. "Thanks for making it such a lovely tune."

"I hope you were pleased with the few changes we made to the music."

"It was an incredible performance," Cedra said. "I am very proud of how it sounded."

Keith walked up with two beers and handed one to Juliet. "We did alright together, huh?"

"We did more than just alright," Juliet assured him. She took a long pull from the cold beer and smiled at Cedra.

"I hope I can get another glimpse or two at that songbook of yours."

Cedra chuckled. "I already told you guys you can use anything in there you like."

"Would you mind if I borrow it tomorrow and go out to make three copies? I'm afraid Juliet will drool all over your original and ruin it," Keith said.

Cedra broke out in laughter. "Juliet knows where it is on my desk, just don't lose it."

"I will guard it with my life," he promised.

"I hate to be the party pooper, but four comes mighty early," Cedra said.

"I appreciate your coming out to listen," Juliet told her.

"I had a great time, and you both did well."

Juliet beamed at the praise. "I will walk you out to your truck, if that's okay."

"I will see you all later then," Cedra said and stood to walk from the bar.

She was amazed that several patrons spoke to her as she and Juliet wound their way toward the door, and told her they enjoyed the song she had written. Cedra felt lightheaded as she stepped outside into the cool air.

"This is much better," she said, taking in a deep breath.

"Yeah, it is. It can get a little overwhelming inside sometimes."

They walked to Cedra's truck, and she slipped in behind the wheel then rolled her window down. "I did have a good time."

"I'm glad you did, and maybe soon you will get a day off and can stay out a little longer."

"I hope so, too."

"Be careful, and I will try to be quiet and not wake you when I come in."

Cedra smiled. "I will be long gone by the time you come in."

†

"See you tomorrow then," Juliet said as Cedra started the truck. She watched her back away and then turned to walk back to the building. When Juliet reached for the door, it swung open rapidly, almost catching her off guard. She was surprised to find herself eye to eye with Carrie Brooks.

"Well, hello, there," she said.

"Great show," Carrie said, never missing a step.

"Thanks," Juliet said as Carrie walked quickly away.

She was somewhat surprised that Carrie was in the audience and she could not remember ever seeing her at Wild Bill's before. Maybe, just maybe, that could be a good sign, she thought as she walked through the door into the smoke-filled bar.

†

Cedra drove home thinking about how Juliet had looked into her eyes as she sang and about the warmth that had filled her body. It was a completely new sensation for her and one that left her confused. She made it home and climbed the stairs before collapsing onto her bed. It had been a great day, but she was exhausted and grateful for the soft pillow beneath her head as she remembered Juliet's soft voice singing, "Are you gonna kiss me or not?" Cedra slipped into sleep with a smile growing across her face and a gentle rumbling in her soul.

CHAPTER SEVEN

The next few days sailed past in a blur of activity. When the weekend arrived, and Lisa Marie informed Cedra she would have Saturday and Sunday off, her heart soared. Lyrics had flooded her mind, and she had not the time or energy after the long day's work to write them all down. She hoped to settle in and get some of the lyrics out of her head during the next two days.

The only downside to having the weekend off was that Juliet would be out of town playing a gig, too far away for Cedra to travel. They had spent little time together during the week, and Cedra felt an empty spot growing in her chest in her absence. She was amazed at how close they had grown in such a short time. Cedra did not have many close friends in high school but was surprised at how easy it was to talk with Juliet. In the few short weeks they had spent together,

Cedra felt Juliet knew more about her and her feelings than anyone else had in the world, even more so than her father, whom she had grown so close to after her mother's death. She could look deep into Juliet's eyes, and her heart burst open, and everything, every feeling she had bottled up, would just come pouring out. Juliet would smile softly and listen intently to her every word.

"What are you going to do this weekend?" Wayne asked to bring Cedra's attention back to the dinner table. She had not even realized her mind had drifted away from the conversation.

"I was hoping to relax and get some writing done," she answered.

"Keith and I were thinking about going to the Shoals tomorrow before work, if you'd care to join us," he said.

"What, and where is that?"

"There's a small river down near McMinnville, and the rocky shoals are a great place to hang out, relax, and soak in a bit of sun on a beautiful day," Keith said.

"It's also a make-out place for teenagers on Friday and Saturday nights," Wayne said with a grin.

"Yeah, but they will be long gone by the time we get there."

"Sounds like fun. What time did you plan on going?"

"We both have to work late tomorrow afternoon, so I thought we could leave here around eight."

"If Cedra helps me, we can fix a picnic basket for the three of you," Ma said.

"Why don't you make it four and join us?" Keith asked.

"No, thanks. I will settle these old bones in the sun on the front porch. You youngins go and enjoy the shoals."

"I wish Juliet were here to join us," Cedra said.

"She will be back by Tuesday, right Ma?" Keith asked.

"Yes, I believe that's what she said."

"Seems like such a long time yet," Cedra replied aloud, voicing the thought she was thinking.

"I do believe someone is missing her friend," Wayne teased.

"Yes, I am," Cedra said, using her fork to move the food around on her plate.

Ma smiled warmly at Cedra. "You've become good friends. It's fine that you miss her. Have you tried calling her since she left?"

"Just once last night, but it went straight to her voicemail."

"Did you leave a message?" Ma asked as she began clearing the table.

"I started to, but I didn't know what to say." Cedra felt the warmth creeping up her neck.

"Why don't you try again tonight, before it gets too close to the showtime?"

"I think I will, but after we finish here." Cedra stood and carried an armful of dishes to the sink.

"Nonsense, I've got this. Go make your call." Ma made a sweeping gesture with her hands.

Cedra nodded and turned quickly to climb the stairs. Wayne and Keith had rushed to get ready for work and were coming back down.

"See ya in the morning," Keith said as they danced around Cedra on the stairs.

"Have a great night and be careful," she said as they reached the bottom of the stairs.

†

Cedra walked into her room and picked up her phone to find Juliet had called. Cedra smiled and pushed the button to play the message. Loud music filled the background.

"Hey, I'm at sound checks right now, but I'll try calling back at seven before the show starts. Sorry I missed your call."

Cedra looked at the clock to find it was a quarter to seven. She took a seat at the small desk and opened her song pad. She looked through the lyrics she had scribbled on an order pad at work and smiled. She picked up her pen and wrote them on a blank page, and her mind whirled with lyrics that she frantically wrote down. She was lost in the words when the jarring of her phone brought her back to reality. Juliet's name flashed on the screen, and she hit the button to accept the call. The background was quiet as she spoke into the phone.

"Hey there."

"Hey there yourself. Sorry I missed your call last night. We were late arriving, so everything was rushed. We had a good show, though."

"That's great to hear. Are you all set for tonight?"

"Yeah, we've got a sold-out show. How are you?"

"I'm doing great. I've got the weekend off, so the boys are going to introduce me to the Shoals tomorrow."

"I am so jealous," Juliet groaned into the phone.

"Why? Because we're going?"

"Because I can't be there to go with y'all," Juliet replied. "It's gorgeous there and so peaceful."

"That's the price you pay for being an up and comer," Cedra teased.

"Cleveland, Ohio, is not Nashville, but hey, it's a gig," Juliet said.

"I'm very proud of you. I wish it weren't too far to drive to see your show."

"There will be other opportunities. I promise. The crowd loved the songs you allowed me to play. Several of the guys in the main act asked me who the writer was, so hopefully, we'll both get some perks from the performance."

"That sounds wonderful. I've got so many lyrics in my head right now it feels like it will explode. I should not have agreed to the trip tomorrow, and stay home and write."

"Nonsense. You need a break. You've been working so hard at the Redbird. Take your tablet. The Shoals are relaxing, and the beauty might inspire you to write once you see how peaceful it is there."

"I will pack it along in my bag then."

"Don't forget the sunscreen, unless you want a sunburn. It's beautiful, but there aren't many shady options at the shoals."

"Thanks for the reminder. I don't usually burn, but I don't want to risk it ruining my weekend." The sound of a microphone test in the background filled her ears. "It sounds like the show is about to start."

"Yes, in just a few minutes. I miss you, and I hope you have fun tomorrow."

"Have a great show, and call me when you can." Cedra paused. "I miss you, too. Goodnight, Juliet."

"Goodnight, Cedra."

Cedra placed the phone back on charge and returned to her lyrics. The excitement of talking with Juliet filled her mind with words that she couldn't write fast enough to put them all down. She was surprised when she heard Ma climbing the stairs and then the soft knock at her door.

She rushed to the door and opened it. "Ma, I completely lost track of time. I intended to come back to the kitchen to help you clean up."

"No, worries. I have cleaned up a kitchen for many years. I boiled some eggs and thought we could whip up egg salad for you and the boys to make sandwiches tomorrow. You can cut up some fresh fruit, and we'll pack a cooler for you all to take."

"That sounds fantastic. You sure you won't come along?"

"No, thank you. I may take advantage of the quiet and catch a nice nap while you youngins play. It'll just be you and me for dinner since both the boys are working, so what would you like for dinner?"

"How about a break from cooking? I'd love to treat you to dinner at the Redbird."

"I haven't been there in so long," Ma replied.

"I'll get us a table reserved about six then, if that's a yes. There should be an Open Mic Night, so maybe we can hear some great new music."

"That sounds great. I'll get my nap in and see if this old woman still cleans up good," Ma chuckled as she turned away. "Get you up at six or seven? It shouldn't take us long in the morning."

"Six if you're up. That way, we can have some coffee while the boys wake up."

"Don't stay up writing too late then," Ma said with a nod toward the tablet on her desk. "Did you talk to Juliet?"

"Yes, ma'am. She called at seven before the show started. Said things were going pretty well so far. They have a sold-out show tonight."

"That's excellent news. Juliet needs that one influential person to hear her sing to send her on her way. One day soon, I hope."

"I hope so, too, Ma. She works hard, and she's got a lot of talent."

"Just like somebody else, I know." Ma shot her a wink. "See ya bright and early."

"Goodnight, Ma." Cedra watched until Ma disappeared into her room before closing her door. She walked back to her desk and picked up her pen. "Just a few more lines," she promised herself.

CHAPTER EIGHT

The following morning, Cedra woke with a start. It was barely six, but she couldn't remember going to bed the night before. She rinsed off in the shower, dressed in her swimsuit, shorts, and a T-shirt before going downstairs to find Ma sitting at the kitchen table cutting up fruit.

"Hey, I thought that was my job?"

"I couldn't sleep another minute, so I came down and got to work. The egg salad is ready, and I've almost finished the fruit. You can still pack the cooler, but after we have a cup of coffee."

"Are you ready for a refill?"

Ma nodded. "I sure am."

Cedra took Ma's cup and pulled one down from the cabinet. She carried them to the table once she had them poured and sugarfied, as Ma called it. "Here, or do you want to go out on the porch?"

"Let's go see what the morning looks like." Ma cut the last strawberry and placed it in the container. She snapped on the lid and took the knife and cutting board to the sink. "I'll get those later," she said as she picked up her coffee and took a sip. "Is it my imagination, or does it always taste better when someone else makes it?"

Cedra smiled. "I think you may be right. We sure do get a lot of traffic at the café just for coffee."

The sun was shining as they stepped onto the porch. The morning dew was fading, and the songbirds sprang to life. "It looks like it will be a beautiful day," Ma said as she carefully sat in a rocker.

"Yes, it does, if this morning is any indicator." Cedra took a seat beside Ma. "I heard there's a chance for an afternoon shower, but I think we'll be on our way home by then."

Ma, let out a laugh, "You can't count on the weatherman to give you a perfect forecast. In Tennessee, the weather can change in fifteen minutes. Be sunny one minute, and thunderous clouds roll in the next. Especially this time of year."

"I'm looking forward to seeing the color change with the seasons. We have green for more of the year in south Alabama and then brown. I can't wait to see the palette of colors Mother Nature will paint in this area."

"It's predicted to be a nice autumn," Ma answered. She shrugged, "Who knows, though? Sometimes we get a late tropical storm that blows through, and it rips all the leaves off."

"I hadn't thought about tropical weather reaching this far inland," Cedra said with a frown.

"We get our share of snow and ice in the winter, too," Ma added. She shook her head. "It's always fun to see drivers trying to navigate the roads when they are icy."

"Careful, I might be one of them. I've seen a total of about four inches of snow in my lifetime," Cedra replied.

"It's just like driving in the rain. Slow down, don't be in a hurry, and don't hit your brakes or the gas pedal too hard."

Cedra broke out laughing. "I may be the driver everyone cusses at for driving twenty miles an hour."

"That's okay. You can get the last laugh when you pass those drivers in a ditch on down the road."

The screen door opened. "What's so danged funny this early in the morning?" Wayne asked.

"Cedra and I were talking about driving in snow and ice," Ma answered.

"You know, if we got you a tow strap, you could earn some extra bucks pulling these fancy cars out of a ditch when they get stuck," Wayne chimed into the conversation. "They race around you like you're on a NASCAR track and end up stuck in a ditch."

"Is Keith up yet?" Ma asked. "I thought I'd whip you up some French toast before you go."

"If not, he will be in a minute," Wayne said and walked back inside.

"I guess our quiet morning coffee has come to an end," Cedra smiled. She reached for Ma's hand. "Come on, and I'll set the table while you cook."

Ma used Cedra's help to get out of the chair. "You have a deal. Pour us another cup, too, if you would."

"Yes, ma'am," Cedra replied and held the door open.

After a delicious breakfast, Cedra went upstairs for her bag and returned to help Wayne pack the cooler.

"Did you all remember to take towels?" Ma asked.

Cedra and Wayne both nodded. "Yes, ma'am."

"I laid out a worn blanket y'all can use to stretch out on. Let me go get it for you." Ma left the room and returned with a large bundle. "This should work nicely."

Cedra took the blanket as Wayne hefted the cooler. "I reckon we'll take my truck," he said.

Keith rushed down the stairs and grabbed the other end of the cooler. "Let's roll," he said.

"We'll be back later, Ma. Give me a call if you need anything," Cedra hollered back to her.

"Y'all be safe and have fun," Ma said and waved before stepping back into the house.

"Good times, here we come," Wayne said as he slid in behind the wheel with Cedra sandwiched between him and Keith. "Sorry, there's not much of a backseat."

"No problem. I've got plenty of room. Just don't take the curves too fast." Cedra laughed.

"Yes, ma'am." He grinned and put the truck in gear.

Cedra marveled at the canopy of trees that covered the road as they drove deeper into the country. "I bet this will be a beautiful drive in a few more weeks."

"When the colors start to change?" Keith asked. "It's gorgeous."

Cedra took in the countryside as they began to cross rivers and creeks. "Is it my imagination, or is the elevation changing?"

"My ears pop every time we come this way. It's so gradual, you don't realize it until your body lets you know," Wayne said.

When he turned on his blinker and slowed the truck, Cedra asked. "Have we arrived?"

"Not quite yet, but this is our turnoff. It may be a bit bumpy on the next section, so hold on." Wayne grinned.

Bumpy was an understatement Cedra thought. She felt as if her teeth were jarring out of her mouth after every rut and bump in the trail. It couldn't even be called a road, but the view was well worth a few minutes of discomfort. When the truck pulled into a clearing, the shoals came into view. The sun glistened off the quickly moving water, and the grass was a deep green along the edges of a pristine stream. Wet rocks protruded from the water, and Cedra could guess that, for the most part, the water was shallow, with a few deeper pools. As Wayne pulled closer, he lifted his hand and pointed.

"Look," was all he needed to say.

Cedra gasped at the beauty of three small waterfalls that ran down a cliff, depositing fresh water into the stream. "Wow, this place is gorgeous."

"It doesn't get much prettier than this." Wayne pulled to a stop. "Keith and I'll grab the cooler and our bags if you'll spread out the blanket."

"Deal," Cedra replied and slid off the bench behind Keith. Even the air seemed fresher and chillier this close to the water. Cedra shook out the blanket on a small patch of grass, careful to find a spot without rocks.

The boys sat the cooler on one corner and their bags on the other three. Wayne walked back to the truck for his guitar case and propped it next to the cooler. He smiled at Cedra. "In case we get inspired."

"This would be a great place to set down some tracks," Keith replied. "It's normally very peaceful here."

"Well shit, that may have just ended," Wayne said as he heard another vehicle approach.

Cedra took out her notepad. "You didn't seriously expect to have all this beauty to ourselves, did you? It's too pretty of a day to be stuck inside."

"That it is. Come on, before you go all songwriter on us, join us in the water for a few minutes," Wayne said as he reached out his hand to her.

Wayne quickly lifted Cedra to her feet. "We have to warn you. At first, it's cold, but your body will adjust quickly."

"That's right. You just gotta suck it up and take a quick plunge in the pool," Keith added.

Cedra pulled her T-shirt over her head and shimmied out of her shorts. "I'm game," she replied.

Keith took off at a run, and Cedra followed behind him. A nano-second after her body hit the water, and she felt the shock of the cold, Cedra came up with a gasp. "Holy shit, that's cold. Is it always this cold?"

Keith pushed the wet hair out of his face and nodded. "Even in the heat of the summer, but it's a bit more refreshing then."

"It's deeper than I thought."

"Some people put in here and tube down about fifteen miles." Wayne nodded to the group that had pulled up behind them. "Looks like that's what they have in mind."

"I sure hope so," Keith groaned. "You see who that is, don't you?"

Wayne turned his head to look more closely at the group unloading the truck. "Viper?"

"Yeah, and her gang of misfits."

"Would you guys like to fill me in?" Cedra asked.

Keith nodded toward the group. "The blonde with the purple streaks in her hair, we call her Viper. I'm not even sure I remember her real name anymore. She and her two bonehead brothers and one of their girlfriends form a band called Crimson. Not all that talented, but you would think they owned Broadway the way they act."

"They do okay with cover tunes, but they have been on stage for two years and haven't cranked out a decent original song. Viper thinks her looks make the men in the audience forget about the words she sings."

"Ha! The women too," Keith reminded Wayne. "She sank her fangs into Juliet one night, and she's been chasing after her ever since."

Wayne chuckled. "That's why Juliet is more careful of who she drinks around now."

Cedra had a puzzled look on her face. Wayne and Keith shared a panicked look. "I think we'd better leave it at that," Wayne said.

"Too late. Viper has spotted us and is coming our way."

"Well, hello boys, and girl," Viper said as she looked at Cedra. "Where is that gorgeous leader of yours?"

"If you're referring to Juliet, she's on the road on a gig," Wayne said.

"Well, that's good news for her." She turned to look at Cedra. "Are you the fresh meat?"

"I'm Cedra. New to town, but I'm holding my own."

"She's an incredible songwriter, but you wouldn't know anything about writing lyrics," Keith said.

"Maybe we should get together sometime then," Viper purred to Cedra.

"Sorry, Juliet and the boys have first dibs on anything I write."

"You'll have to come to see her soon on Open Mic night," Wayne said.

"You've got a slot at the Redbird already?" Viper arched an eye.

"She's getting worked into a date," Keith said.

"That's impressive. I've been waiting months for Lisa Marie to get me a slot."

"Lisa Marie knows good talent when she sees it. Carrie Brooks is also one of her referrals," Keith added, further twisting the barb into Viper.

"Did you have to sleep with her to get that? She doesn't refer just anyone," Viper growled.

"Nope. I didn't have to do anything like that. She was present to hear Juliet singing one of my songs, and she liked what she heard."

"Good luck with that. That woman eats new artists for breakfast," Viper snarled.

"Actually, she prefers French toast with country ham and eggs over easy," Cedra tossed back at her. "She's pretty nice once you get to know her."

"Hey, Sis, daylight's wasting," one of Viper's brothers called to her.

"Have a nice float," Wayne said as he waved goodbye to her.

"See you around, newbie," Viper said and spun away from them.

Wayne held up his hand for a high five. Cedra slapped his palm. "What was that for?"

"For putting Viper in her place. That couldn't have been more fun to watch," Keith said and slapped her palm.

"I can handle a mean girl," Cedra smiled.

Wayne nodded. "Yes, ma'am, you certainly can. I think you heated the water. It's not nearly as cold now."

"I agree. I just hope one of you didn't pee yourselves laughing," Cedra teased.

"Damn, my secret's out," Keith said and broke into laughter.

"What did Juliet see in her?" Cedra asked.

Keith shook his head. "I don't think Juliet was seeing anything well that night. When she came home the next morning and told us what happened, we made her promise not to drink unless one of us was around. That could have turned out terrible. I mean more terrible than it did."

"Juliet was still new to town and was probably a bit lonely. Viper kept buying her shots, and Juliet drank way more than she should. A hard lesson learned," Wayne added.

"I don't think I've seen her drink more than one beer," Cedra replied.

"You probably won't either. It's dangerous and harmful for a career to drink too much when you first hit town. Once you hit the big time, there are all kinds of tour parties, but you've got to earn that first."

"In case you haven't noticed, Wayne, I'm not much of a drinker, period." Cedra paused. "I don't like anything that dulls my senses."

Keith smiled at her. "Smart girl. You don't want anything to blur those beautiful words of yours."

"What have you been working on this week?" Wayne asked.

"I have had all kinds of lines going through my brain. I managed to get one down last night and hope to take advantage of the weekend off to write more."

"Just don't forget to mix some fun in there," Wayne reminded her.

Cedra splashed water at him. "What do you think I'm doing with the two of you?"

"That's our girl. I can't wait to brag to Juliet how you handled the Viper," Keith said.

Cedra shrugged. "Nothing there to brag about. I didn't fall for any of her bait."

"You handled her perfectly. I never thought I'd see the day when Viper was speechless, but she had to think hard to try to trip you up."

"That comeback on breakfast was priceless. Did you see the look on Viper's face?" Wayne looked at Cedra with admiration.

"When you wait tables, you learn to interact with a variety of people, some pleasant, others not so much," Cedra replied.

"Maybe we should apply for a server position at the Redbird," Wayne suggested.

"Um, no. I love y'all, but you're way too clumsy when it comes to passing plates. The last thing you need is to dump a plate of food in the lap of some record executive or big-name artist." Cedra looked at the shocked faces and broke out laughing.

Keith placed his hand over his heart. "Oh, that hurt bad."

"Come on, bro, you know she's right," Wayne teased. "Let's eat, and you can share that new song with us."

Yeah, now we're talking," Keith said, instantly healed from his wounded heart.

†

Cedra stored the remainder of their lunch while Wayne took his guitar from the case and started strumming. "Do you mind if I play while you get ready?"

"Not at all," Cedra returned with a smile.

Wayne pulled out his copy of Cedra's songbook. "I've been working on something I'd like to play for you. I think this song would work well for your Open Mic event."

"I'm glad you're confident I will get a chance," Cedra said as she opened her book. "Which song?"

"I have no doubt you will. Page thirty, the song called 'Longing'."

Cedra smiled when she turned to the page. She had written the song at the beginning of her mother's illness. The lyrics had multiple meanings for her at the time. Cedra had prayed her mother's health would improve and that she would one day hear her daughter on the stage of the Grand Ole Opry, playing one of her songs. Cedra felt a pang of sorrow when she remembered singing the song for her mother. Her mother had shed a tear, which she promised Cedra had been of joy, but even then, Cedra felt that her mother would never see her perform. Cedra pushed her sadness away and began to sing as Wayne started playing.

Wayne and Keith smiled as she sang the tender words of longing. Keith's head nodded as she sang. "That was perfect," he praised.

"I like how you changed the music," Cedra told Wayne. "I think it blends so much nicer."

Wayne returned her smile. "There are so many good songs in here that I'm almost overwhelmed."

"I agree," Keith said. "I've been thinking about something for a few days, and I want to run my idea past you."

Wayne stopped playing, and he and Cedra looked at Keith. "What's on your mind, bro?"

"I've been thinking a lot about the four of us. We've got the instruments down pat, our vocal talent is strong, too, but we were missing a good songwriter. Now that Cedra has joined us, what do you think of us forming a band together?"

"None of us individually is making a huge impact," Wayne said. "I mean, Juliet has been the most successful playing a few gigs, but I think collectively as a group, we could all do better."

Keith looked at Cedra. "I know your heart is in writing versus performing, but I think as you grow more comfortable, your performing voice will amaze us all."

Wayne nodded. "I agree. You have a beautiful voice that blends well with the three of us. Your passion comes out in your writing and your voice."

Cedra looked from Keith to Wayne's eager faces. "I wouldn't have a problem with that. I play a decent guitar and keyboards."

"I could play drums as needed," Wayne said. "You, Juliet, and Keith can handle the strings."

"I even have a suggestion for a name," Keith blurted out excitedly. "We'd have to have Ma's approval, of course, but how about The Bentleys? That's where our music is grounded?"

"I love it," Cedra said and clapped her hands. "I bet Ma would like it as well."

"Should we ask her now or wait to run it by Juliet first?" Keith asked.

Cedra's phone rang, and she pulled it out of her bag. "Her ears must have been burning. It's Juliet. Let's ask her now." Cedra answered the call. "Good morning. You're on speaker. The boys and I have something to run past you. But, how are you?"

"Good morning, everyone. I'm good. The venue we're playing is having some issues. I'll be home tomorrow night instead of Tuesday so they can shut down for repairs."

"I'm sorry to hear that, but I'm glad you'll be coming home early," Cedra replied. "We're out at the Shoals, and Keith has just made a proposal we'd like for you to consider."

"That sounds serious. Hit me," Juliet replied.

Keith took a deep breath and let it out slowly. "I know you are starting to get some successful gigs, and the rest of us are playing here and there, but I think we are now complete. Since Cedra has arrived, we now have our missing link. Someone who writes the songs we haven't been able to produce on our own."

"Okay, I agree with you so far, and I think I know where you are heading, but go ahead," Juliet replied.

"I think we should form a band called The Bentleys," Keith blurted out.

Juliet burst out laughing over the phone, leaving the boys and Cedra with startled looks on their faces.

"Why is that so funny to you?" Cedra asked.

"I'm sorry," Juliet said. "I've been having the same thoughts running through my head for days, except for the name, but I love the idea. Collectively, I know we will be successful. I've been struggling with a name, but that will be perfect. Has anyone approached Ma about it yet?"

"No, it is coming to life right now," Keith said. "If you'll be home tomorrow night, why don't the four of us make a pitch to her?"

"That sounds like the perfect plan to me. It will allow Ma's dream to come true, too, to see her name in lights," Juliet said. "I think the idea will tickle her."

"I do, too," Cedra agreed.

"Hey, Cedra was about to sing her newest song for us, if you have time to listen," Wayne told Juliet.

"I've got all the time you need this morning. Go ahead, Cedra. Are y'all having fun at the Shoals?"

"A blast, and we'll have to tell you about Cedra meeting Viper, but that can wait until after the song. You want to use my guitar?" Wayne asked.

"Oh, the Viper. That sounds interesting, too. Go ahead when you're ready, Cedra."

Cedra took Wayne's guitar and started playing. She cleared her throat and began to sing the new lyrics for the group, watching the smiles grow on their faces. When she played the last chord, she handed the guitar back to Wayne.

"You need to sing that for Open Mic," Juliet said. "That was beautiful."

"Every song you write just keeps getting better," Keith added. "We will have to get serious about selecting songs and getting some demos cut."

"That may be the most challenging part, deciding on which ones to use. Let's do this," Juliet said. "We can all pitch in to pay for some studio time once we make our selections and have them planned out."

"I think if we work hard, we could cut three to four songs in a session," Wayne said. "We can circulate those and see what response we get."

"Once Cedra gets her Open Mic slot, that will also give us some extra exposure," Juliet added.

"Will I be allowed to use the band for Open Mic?" Cedra asked.

Juliet paused. "It can't hurt to ask, but I think you need to go solo to get your name out there. Once we get some demos cut, we can circulate them, and I bet we can get some playtime at The Wild Horse or other places."

"I'm sure Wayne and I can start working on that," Keith said.

"That sounds great, guys," Juliet replied. "Now tell me about Cedra and the Viper," she chuckled.

"She and her two brothers and I assume one of their girlfriends showed up a few minutes after we arrived. She was disappointed to find you weren't with us and tried her best to bait Cedra, but our girl shut her down quick," Wayne said. "It's the first time I've ever seen Viper at a loss for words. She spun on her heel and stormed off when Cedra stumped her."

"Great job, Cedra. Oh, I would have loved to see that. She's a snake in the grass, so you all watch your backs when she's around. I can't believe I fell for her tricks, but that's water under the bridge."

"I'm excited you will be home sooner than expected, but disappointed your gig got canceled." Cedra frowned. "I wish you could be here today. This place is gorgeous."

"Maybe we can go out again on your next days off if it isn't too cold," Juliet said. "What am I saying? That dang water is always cold."

Cedra laughed. "It's still such a beautiful spot. We could have a fire in the pit if the temperature continues to drop."

"Yes, there is that. Well, I won't keep you all from having fun. I'll be home sometime tomorrow."

"Be safe. We miss you," Cedra replied and ended the call. She turned back to the boys. "This is so exciting. What's next?"

"I think we pick out several songs that we want to consider for demos," Keith answered.

"Can you two handle that for a bit? I've got something bouncing around my brain that I need to write down."

"Go for it. Will we be a distraction? We can move to a different spot if you want us to," Wayne asked.

"Nope, you're good," Cedra replied and picked up her pen.

An hour later, the wind picked up, and dark clouds began to roll in. "I think we'd better pack up and head for home," Wayne suggested. "We need to get ready for work anyhow."

"That's perfect. I can get a nap in and get ready to take Ma out for dinner. I've got a table reserved for us at the Redbird tonight," Cedra informed them.

"That's great. Ma deserves a night out on the town. She works so hard to keep us well fed," Keith said.

"Yeah, she does. Let's roll before this rain hits," Wayne said as he placed his guitar back in the case. "I'll get the cooler if y'all will get the rest."

"Deal," Keith said, and reached out his hand to pull Cedra to her feet.

†

They barely made it to the paved road before the skies opened and the rain pelted down. The combination of the sound of the rain and the rhythmic motion of the windshield wipers lulled Cedra to sleep. Keith shot a grin to Wayne when Cedra rested her head and his shoulder for the ride home.

"I guess we wore her out," he whispered.

Wayne nodded. "She can have an early start to her nap."

Cedra slept until Wayne pulled into Ma's drive and hit a bump. She shot up in the seat and wiped her face. "I fell asleep, didn't I?"

"Yes, but that's no problem. You didn't even drool on me," Keith teased.

"I'm so sorry. The sound of the rain does that to me sometimes. It's so relaxing. I had a great time with you two today. Thanks for sharing the Shoals with me."

"Thanks for coming along with us. I wish we could have stayed longer, but Mother Nature had other plans today," Wayne said as he shifted into park. "We'll go again."

"I'd like that. When did the rain stop?" Cedra asked.

"Just a few minutes ago, but I think it's heading this way. Let's grab our stuff and get inside before it hits," Wayne suggested.

†

Ma heard the truck arrive and walked over to turn on the coffee pot. There was caramel cake that needed finishing, and they had returned home early so they should have enough time for a quick snack. Ma smiled when Keith rushed through the door carrying a load, followed by Cedra and Wayne with the cooler.

"You are home early. Did you bring the rain back with you? It's been thundering for a while," Ma stated.

"I'm afraid so, Ma," Keith answered. "There's a storm just minutes behind us."

"Drop your stuff and come have some coffee and cake with me before you go rushing off upstairs then. Maybe it will give the storm a chance to pass through."

"If not, we can all have a quick nap. Cedra's already got a head start on us," Keith teased.

"There's nothing quite like the sound of the rain on a tin roof," Ma said.

"Or a truck roof, apparently," Wayne smiled at Cedra.

"That's a compliment to the two of you that she feels comfortable and safe around you," Ma informed them.

"As she should. We're like family," Keith replied.

"The coffee is ready, and I'll slice the cake," Ma said with a note of anticipation in her voice. "We can't let this go to waste."

"Heavens no. I can't believe it lasted this long before getting devoured." Cedra pulled some paper plates from the pantry, handing them to Ma. She watched Ma cut three slices, passing each of them a plate, leaving only a tiny sliver for herself. "Why do you get the small piece?"

"Because I am saving room for the fried chicken plate at the Redbird," Ma grinned. "Dessert afterward, too, if they still have homemade pies."

"That's a guarantee," Cedra answered.

"This tastes wonderful," Wayne said. "I think I'll pass on the coffee and have a glass of milk. Anyone else?"

"Naw, I'm good," Keith answered, and Cedra shook her head.

"Did you enjoy visiting the Shoals?" Ma asked Cedra.

"I did. It is so beautiful there. Peaceful too. I got some writing done, and the boys are helping me select some songs for an Open Mic event."

"That's fantastic news. I will be in the audience for that," Ma smiled. "Do you have a date yet?"

"Not yet, but Lisa Marie is eager to get me on stage. I'll ask about it this week." Cedra took a bite of the cake. She wanted to ask Ma about the band name, but they had agreed to wait for Juliet to return. "Oh, Juliet is coming home tomorrow. The venue they were playing has some maintenance issues they had to close down for, so she'll be home early."

"In time for dinner?" Ma asked.

"I would think so," Cedra replied. "Are you thinking of something special?"

"Juliet loves homemade lasagna. If you help me with a salad and maybe a dessert, we could have a special homecoming meal."

"Leave the dessert and garlic bread to us," Wayne offered. "We can hit the Farmers Market for a pie or cake and some fresh bread in the morning."

Ma smiled. "I love it when a plan comes together. I'll check the pantry for supplies before we go to town tonight if we need to make a grocery stop. Is there anything special you want on next week's dinner menu?"

"How about a pot roast? We can pick up the vegetables while we're at the Farmers Market," Keith suggested.

"That does sound good. I'll buy the roast if you pick one," Cedra offered. "I never can pick a decent roast."

"Too many people go for meat that has no marbling or fat content, and that's where all the flavor lies." Ma grinned. "After we get done, you'll know what to look for."

"We can shop after we go to the Redbird, right?" Cedra asked.

"Yes, there will be plenty of options to choose from. If we don't find the roast we like, we can go back to town in the morning." Ma stretched. "Now, I'm going to take a nap. I'll be ready by 5:30. Is that good?"

"Perfect, Ma," Cedra answered.

"You boys have a good night at work."

"Will do, Ma. Have fun on your night on the town," Keith replied.

"Oh, I plan to." Ma left them with a wink and started upstairs.

Cedra cleared the utensils while Wayne tossed the paper plates. "Thanks for a fun day. Y'all be good tonight, and we'll see you tomorrow."

†

Cedra slept soundly and dreamed of being on stage with Juliet. Juliet left no doubt that the lyrics she was singing were for Cedra, and Cedra's heart raced. She was leaning into Juliet for a kiss when her alarm sounded, jolting her from dreamland. "Well damn," she said and walked into the bathroom to start the shower. Cedra picked up her phone and smiled to see a text from Juliet. *See you soon. Don't corrupt Ma tonight.* Cedra typed in a quick response. *Miss you. Be careful. See you soon* She waited for a reply as she gathered her clothes and then undressed to shower.

96

Ma was sitting at the table when Cedra bounded down the stairs. Ma looked up and smiled at her.

"Ma, you look fantastic," Cedra said as she stepped into the kitchen. Ma had taken the time to do her hair and makeup, and she looked years younger. "Do you have a walking stick?"

"No, I'm not that old yet, Cedra." Ma scowled.

"Not for you, for me to beat the men away from you tonight. Wow, you do look nice." Cedra sniffed. "You smell good too."

"This old gal can clean up pretty well. Besides, I can't accompany Nashville's hottest new songwriter looking like a country bumpkin," Ma teased.

"Are you sure you don't have some man meeting us that you dressed up for?"

"Nope, it's all for you. If I happen to catch someone's eye, then so be it," Ma chuckled.

"Now I wish I'd gone to get the truck cleaned up," Cedra smirked.

"Pfft, I've seen the inside of your truck. It's spotless."

"Are you ready to ride?"

"I'm ready to eat. I've been dreaming about that fried chicken all day."

"Let's go then." Cedra held out her elbow for Ma to hook into as they walked out the door. Cedra locked the door behind them and escorted Ma to her truck. "She ain't the prettiest, but she's reliable and paid for," Cedra said as Ma climbed inside.

"The prettiest things aren't always the best," Ma said.

Cedra grinned, walked around to the driver's side, and climbed inside.

The sun was setting as they drove toward Nashville, and the city started to glow as lights illuminated the skyline.

"No matter how many times I've seen it, this is one of my favorite views of Nashville—another day has gone, and a night is just beginning."

"It is beautiful," Cedra agreed. She had rolled down her window when they left, but the night air was rapidly cooling, so she cranked it up. "You can feel the fall approaching in the air."

"Yes, it changes fast when it starts here," Ma agreed.

†

Cedra pulled into a parking spot, and when they entered, Lisa Marie called out to them from the cash register. "I've got you two set for table three. I'll be over in a minute to get your orders."

Cedra scanned the room as they walked over to the table. "It looks like someone must have called off for the evening shift," she told Ma as they took their seats.

Lisa Marie walked over to their table. "What can I get you ladies tonight?"

"Did someone call out tonight? Do you need my help?" Cedra asked.

"Betty is running late. It's your off day, but thanks for the offer." Lisa Marie smiled back at Cedra.

"I'm here if you change your mind and need some help," Cedra offered.

"Okay, I accept, but just until your food arrives or Betty gets here," Lisa Marie said and blew a stray strand of hair from her face. "What can I get you?"

"Fried chicken, rice and gravy, green beans and corn for me. Tea to drink," Cedra said as she stood and walked to the door to greet the next guests. "I've got them."

"That's why I love that young lady," Lisa Marie told Ma. "Such a hard worker. I haven't seen you in ages, Ma. How have you been?"

"Great, thanks. I'll make it easy on you. Double the order Cedra gave you. She's going to insist on getting the check, but please make sure I get it."

"You got it. I'll try to send Cedra back as soon as possible, but I appreciate the help."

"No worries, we are staying for the music afterward. Do you think Cedra will get a spot soon?" Ma asked.

"As soon as it calms down in here, I'll join you if that's okay? I wanted to run a few dates by her."

"That will be perfect, Lisa Marie. Thanks."

"Let me get these started, and I'll bring out your drinks."

Cedra got the new guests seated and took their orders. She was more than happy to help Lisa Marie out in a bind. "I'll get these orders in and be right back with your drinks."

"I thought you were off today?" one of the customers said.

"I am. I'm just helping Lisa Marie out for a few minutes," Cedra replied.

"Thanks for helping. I'm starving." The customer grinned at Cedra.

"We'll have you all taken care of in just a few minutes." Cedra walked to the serving window to place the order.

Cedra delivered a fourth order when Betty came bursting through the back door in a whirlwind. "I am so sorry I'm late."

"No biggie. Cedra came in for supper and has been filling in until you arrived. Now she can enjoy her meal." Lisa Marie carried two platters filled with their orders to Ma.

"This looks so delicious," Ma said.

"I'll send Cedra over so it doesn't get cold. Enjoy."

Lisa Marie walked over to Cedra. "Thanks for your help. You were a lifesaver. Betty and I can take it from here. Supper is on the house also, so don't even think of arguing with me. Dessert included."

Cedra nodded. "Thanks. We will enjoy every bite."

"Go before it gets cold." Lisa Marie nodded her head.

Cedra dropped the order pad at the cash register and returned to their table. "Man, that smells good," she stated as she sat next to Ma.

"That was very nice of you to help out," Ma said.

"No big deal. Lisa Marie has been good to me. She also informed me our supper and dessert were on the house, so I can't argue with my boss."

"That makes everything taste a little better," Ma said. "As if it could get any better." She bit into the chicken and moaned.

As they were wrapping up their meals, Lisa Marie brought a pot of coffee and three mugs. "Mind if I join y'all?"

"Not at all. Have a seat." Cedra smiled up at her boss. "You look like you could use a break."

"I wanted to chat with you for a few minutes while you decide on dessert," Lisa Marie grinned. "I have a sixty-minute slot open in two weeks for Open Mic. Are you interested?"

"Hell, —I mean heck yes," Cedra replied. "I've been working on cleaning up some songs to get ready."

"I figure you could introduce yourself to the crowd and perform 3 to 4 songs during that time," Lisa Marie offered.

"Is it strictly a solo event, or could I get Juliet, Wayne, and Keith to perform a number with me?" Cedra asked.

"Normally a solo event, but hey, it's your sixty minutes to work the crowd. If you want them to accompany you, I'm game. Just make it the last number."

"I'm not even sure if they will want to play with me," Cedra replied.

Ma scoffed. "Who do you think you're kidding? They love jamming with you. I'm sure they will jump at the chance."

"I've got another piece of news for you," Lisa Marie teased. "Carrie Brooks asked to be notified when you perform. She wants to bring in all her big guns. That never happens."

Cedra's mouth dropped open. "Aw, now I'm going to be nervous," Cedra replied. "She told me she'd be there, but I just thought she was being nice."

Lisa Marie chuckled. "Carrie is always friendly when she wants something, and I think she senses talent in you."

"Just close your eyes and imagine being on the front porch before you start to play," Ma said. "The audience is going to love you. Never in my life have I had four more talented youngsters under my roof."

101

"That's saying a lot, Ma," Lisa Marie said. "You've had some good talent living with you over the years."

"Yes, I have, but these four are electric. Just wait until you hear the way they play together, and you'll know what I mean." Ma reached over to cover Cedra's hand and turned to Lisa Marie. "Can I reserve this table?"

"I will make it happen," Lisa Marie promised. "Carrie will be right beside you. She always asks for that table." She pointed at the table closer to the stage.

A young man walked out on stage to prepare for his show. "He's pretty good, too," Lisa Marie said. "Have you two decided on dessert?"

"Do you have coconut cream pie?" Ma asked.

"We sure do. I'll grab some and bring fresh coffee. Have you decided?"

"That coconut cake looks good, too. I think I'll have that," Cedra answered. "I don't think we can go wrong with either of them."

"I'll be right back," Lisa Marie said and picked up the rest of the dishes. She returned carrying a tray of cake and pie slices and a pot of coffee. She placed a portion of each in front of them. "In case you want a little of each."

"Little?" Cedra said. "That's half a pie."

"Oh hush, and just eat it," Lisa Marie teased. She looked at Cedra. "This is Stone Watson. He's a new songwriter to the area, too. You may want to meet him later."

Cedra looked at the young man on stage, and when he raised his head to see them watching him, he smiled. Finished tuning his guitar, Stone took a seat on a barstool and adjusted the microphone.

"Good evening, ladies and gentlemen. My name is Stone Watson. I arrived in Nashville a few months ago from

Ocala, Florida, where I grew up watching racehorses train and cattle grow. I want to thank Lisa Marie and the Songwriters Association for allowing me to perform for you tonight. I'll be sharing a few songs that I have written, and I hope you will enjoy hearing them." Stone began strumming his guitar, and Cedra relaxed back in her seat.

Cedra felt the softness of the guitar open the song and was surprised by the warmth in Stone's voice as he began to sing. Her body swayed with the music as her mind listened to the lyrics. He was good, and Cedra could feel the heartache, reaching out to the audience, pulling them into the song. When he finished the first song, Cedra joined the crowd in a round of applause.

"He is good," she whispered to Lisa Marie.

"I think the two of y'all would do well to collaborate on a few songs to see how well you create together." Lisa Marie smiled. "After you train him on how to handle the breakfast crowd."

"He's going to work here?" Cedra asked.

"Yes, at least a few days a week at the start. Stone's living in a camper on the back of his truck, but needs some extra income to pay lot rent and buy groceries."

"I'll be glad to show him the ropes," Cedra replied.

They watched the remainder of the performance, and when Stone finished and packed his guitar away, Lisa Marie waved him over to introduce him to Cedra and Ma.

"It's nice to meet you ladies," Stone said in a softly spoken voice.

"Would you care to join us?" Cedra asked.

"I'd love to if you wouldn't mind. Lisa Marie tells me you will be teaching me how to serve tables next week."

"Yes, she will. Have you eaten yet tonight?" Lisa Marie asked.

"Not yet," Stone answered with a blush.

"How about a cheeseburger with the works? Sound okay to you?" Lisa Marie asked and disappeared before Stone could answer.

Cedra saw the startled look on Stone's face. "Get used to it. When Lisa Marie makes her mind up on something, there's no arguing with her. She's good people," she added.

"She's been very kind to me," Stone replied. "She also tells me you are a songwriter," he said as he shifted in his seat.

"I'm trying my best to be. Lisa Marie just gave me a date for an Open Mic slot in two weeks. I hope I'm ready."

"Lisa Marie wouldn't have offered the spot to you if you weren't," Ma said. "She has a knack for knowing when the time is right for an artist."

"She speaks very highly of you," Stone replied. "She tells me every free moment you have at work that you're jotting down lyrics."

Cedra laughed. "Maybe she exaggerates just a bit, but the words are flowing well right now, and if I don't write them down, they are gone in an instant."

"I understand that. I've got notes on napkins, post-it-notes, and even the want ad section of the newspaper. Sarah, my wife, teases me all the time about writing on every scrap of paper."

"Is your wife up here with you?" Ma asked.

"No, she's back home in Florida with our little girl. Destiny is almost two now. They are living with my parents while I try to break the ice up here," Stone explained. "I've given myself a year to chase this dream before I go home to work on the ranch owned by my family. If I can't make enough to support myself and my family, I have to face the reality of being a husband and father."

"I think that's where a lot of us come from," Cedra replied. "I have set a limit of a year, but I don't have a spouse and family to support. I can't imagine how difficult that is for you."

"I miss them something terrible. I would feel successful if I could just write the perfect song and get it into the right hands. Then I wouldn't necessarily have to be right here in the heart of Music City to make a songwriting career."

"I hate to burst your bubble, but unless you are super lucky, you will need to be here, rubbing elbows and pitching songs to artists and agents. Not that it is impossible, but I wouldn't think it was very likely to work remotely. I could be wrong." Cedra shrugged.

Lisa Marie had returned. "I'd have to agree with Cedra on that point. Unless established and in high demand in Nashville, your chances of success become limited by proximity."

"I guess I've got a lot of working and thinking to do then," Stone said.

Cedra reached out to touch his arm. "Don't be discouraged. There are probably hundreds of us with the same goals. Whoever works the hardest and has a decent bit of luck will make it to the next level. You've got talent and passion in your writing. Don't give up on it too easily."

"Thanks," Stone replied with a blush.

The next artist came on stage and got set up to perform. She was a bit older than Cedra and Stone. Her songs were good, but she didn't have the passion or charisma

Stone had demonstrated to pull the crowd into the music. When she finished her set, Cedra looked at Ma, who was stifling a yawn. "You ready to go, or you up for one more?"

"I think I can hang for one more set," Ma said. "I'll need more coffee, though."

"I'll be right back," Cedra said, and returned with a fresh pot and a mug for Stone. "Do you want a mug?"

"Sure," he smiled. "You know you're going to have your hands full teaching me to wait on customers. I need to learn quickly to keep from starving or running out of gas," he chuckled.

Cedra shot a look at Lisa Marie. "I don't think Lisa Marie will allow you to go hungry, but I'll teach you the best I can. As long as you don't have five thumbs, I think you'll survive. A big part of being a good server is interaction with your customer. It's even more important because influential people in the industry often eat here. We can't have you dumping food into someone's lap that may be able to open doors for your future."

"Geesh, no pressure there," Stone replied and took a sip of coffee.

"Relax, and we'll have fun. You'll be fine," Cedra reassured him.

The next performer was another male, but Cedra was not impressed with his songs. She leaned over and whispered to Stone. "You are the cream of tonight's crop by far."

"Thanks. I need to hear that I do have some talent. I worry and try not to doubt my ability," Stone admitted.

"Do you have a songbook?" Cedra asked.

"Several." He laughed.

"Pick out your best and bring it with you next week, and we can start looking at them together. I'll show you mine if you show me yours," Cedra said with a wink.

Stone looked at her. "Seriously? Not, showing me yours, but you will take a look at my work?"

"I will. I would appreciate you reviewing mine as well. We may have thoughts from a different perspective that can help us both create stronger lyrics."

"You have a deal." Stone reached out to shake Cedra's hand. "Thank you."

"Don't thank me yet," Cedra teased.

"I'll be right back, and then I think it's time for you to take Ma home. She's about to fall asleep on us." Lisa Marie stood and walked to the counter.

Cedra nudged Ma. "Are you ready to roll? We still have to make a grocery store stop."

"Maybe a walk in the store will wake me up. I'm still so full from supper," Ma replied.

Lisa Marie returned with a box. She placed it on the table along with two twenty-dollar bills. "What's this?" Cedra asked.

"A cake for y'all to take home and your tips from helping out earlier."

"Free dinner was enough," Cedra replied.

Lisa Marie smiled. "The tips are from your customers. The cake is my way of saying thanks."

"Any time you get in a bind, just call me. I'm more than willing to help out," Cedra said. "Thank you for everything tonight." Cedra looked at Stone. "I'll see you at five a.m. Monday."

"I'll be here," Stone said and stood as they left the table.

Cedra guided Ma through the crowded venue and out the door. The night had cooled significantly, and the air felt good against her skin. "Are you sure you're up for the store tonight?"

"Yes, I'll get my second wind. That way we don't have to worry about it tomorrow. Lisa Marie fixed us up with the dessert, so we just have to keep the boys out of it until then." Ma grinned as she climbed into the truck and took the box from Cedra.

"Yes, she did indeed. Alright, pot roast, here we come."

†

Cedra tried to remember all the details Ma had schooled her on for selecting good beef. Her eyes roamed over the freshly stocked cooler section full of various cuts of meats. She spotted a large roast with marbling and a thin rind of fat. "How about this one, Ma?"

Cedra picked up the roast and held it out for Ma to see.

Ma looked closely at the selection. "I think that will work just fine. Good job, Cedra."

"I remembered what you said to look for." Cedra beamed back at her. "Will it be big enough?"

"It's a plenty good size and will be surrounded by fresh vegetables from the Farmers Market. With the bread and maybe a side salad, we will have a feast."

"Is there anything else we need?" Cedra asked.

"Better pick up some milk. You know how those boys love a cold glass of milk with their sweets."

"Better get two then," Cedra replied, and guided them to the dairy section. "Did you have everything you needed for the lasagna?"

"It wouldn't hurt to have a bit more cheese," Ma answered.

"Pick out what you need," Cedra told Ma. "Do the others go home for Thanksgiving, or will we have a feast at home?"

"I haven't discussed it with anyone yet. Are you planning to go home?" Ma asked.

"I probably need to work," Cedra answered. "Would it be okay if I invited my father up for Thanksgiving? There are plenty of hotel options."

"Nonsense, there is a spare room downstairs, but it's nothing to write home about. Big enough for your father to sleep in, and that's about all." Ma dropped a package of cheese in the cart. "Remind me to ask the others for their plans. It would be great to have a nice dinner together."

Cedra guided them toward the checkout line. They passed through an aisle of candy.

"Dang, this year is flying by. Halloween will be here soon. I'll have to stock up on candy for trick or treaters."

Cedra pulled the cart to a stop. "Do you want to get some now?"

Ma laughed. "It wouldn't make it until Halloween. I'm as bad as the boys when it comes to sweets."

"Okay, next weekend then. Surely it can last a week? Oh, hey, that's the night after my Open Mic."

"Yes, it is. We'll have to party all weekend," Ma chuckled.

Cedra loaded the bags into the back seat and smiled to find Ma dozing on the ride home. It wasn't late by young people's standards, but Ma was an early riser, and they were hours past her bedtime. When Cedra pulled into the yard and stopped the engine, Ma was startled awake. "Welcome back, sleeping beauty."

Ma wiped at her face. "Thank you for a fun night. I had a good time, and the food was fantastic. It was nice to have a break from cooking."

"We need to have a girls' night out more often," Cedra said. "Maybe try out a few other restaurants."

"We can do that. Just let me know, and we can arrange it around the boys' work. Pick a night when Juliet is available too."

†

"I'll put the groceries away if you want to head upstairs," Cedra told Ma, who had stopped to lock the door.

"I won't argue with you tonight. This old body is ready for the bed. I'll see you in the morning. Goodnight, Cedra."

"Rest well, Ma." Cedra stored the groceries and set the coffee pot for the morning. Grinning at the box on the table with the cake, Cedra walked to Ma's small foyer table and plucked a pen. *Hands off until Sunday dinner!* She returned the Sharpie and turned off the light before starting up the stairs with a tune playing in her head.

†

Cedra changed into shorts and a T-shirt, pulled out her chair, and flipped open her songbook. At the top of the page, she wrote, *The Perfect Song*. Cedra rarely knew the song's title until she had finished the lyrics, but she knew this title right away. She had been thinking about Stone's comment about writing the perfect country song since they left the café. On the top line of the page, she wrote, *Six Strings and a Dream.*

Underneath, she began jotting notes, not lyrics.

That's why we all come to this dog eat dog town, with six strings and a dream.

We leave our family and loved ones behind to follow our dreams with six strings and a dream.

Pouring our heart and soul into the lyrics to be danced on by a two-step or shuffle,

Long lonely nights, long days scraping enough to get by,

Barely fed, same clothes on my back day after day, but fighting on,

Praying it's enough to make the sacrifice worth the risk, holding on tight to six strings and a dream.

Yeah, six strings and a dream.

Hands trembling as the big night is near, cold sweat running down my spine,

Fingers poised above the strings, prayers sent up as the first chords break the silence,

Vibration from the strings charge my heart to racing,

Eyes close as the music dances in front of my eyes,

Yeah, with six strings and a dream.

My voice breathes out the heartache and longing from this life of chasing the dream,

Yeah, with six strings and a dream.

Heart smiling to hear the crowd singing along,

The journey has just begun, pushing forward, not burning up the two-lane back home, still chasing the dream,

Yeah, with six strings and a dream.

Cedra read over her notes several times and then turned off her lamp and stretched out on the bed. Rough lyrics, but she wanted to capture the gist of the song forming in the back of her brain. Something every artist could relate to as they started on their professional journey. Most hit Nashville alone or with a small group of friends in hopes of breaking into the big time, but for every dream realized, hundreds shattered. Maybe not for lack of talent, but a lack of drive or even luck to have that right person hear the passion in your words. Humming the melody in her head, Cedra smiled and whispered to the night, "Yeah, with six strings and a dream."

CHAPTER NINE

Juliet had packed and was on the road right after breakfast, eager to get home. The gig had been a good road experience and was more than enough to pay for gas and the hotel with a bit leftover. She felt the crowd had enjoyed her performances, and she regretted not having any demo cuts to sell after the show. Fans approached her after shows for photographs and autographs, but she would need to rethink the whole marketing process. She needed to leave something in their hands other than a scribbled signature. If indeed she was going to be in a band, they needed to do things much differently. They would need to arrange photoshoots for autographed prints and copies of singles to be made available before even the smallest gig they would play. Solo was a gamble for only herself, but a band would have others to consider. Juliet loved the idea of a band, but the devil of self-doubt climbed onto her shoulder as she drove home.

Juliet felt confidence reforming as she crossed over the Tennessee state line. *It won't be long now until I'm home.* She turned the dial to pick up a local Nashville station and sang along as the final miles slipped away in her rearview mirror.

†

Cedra was surprised when she awoke to find she had slept in beyond eight. She couldn't remember sleeping that late for years. She stretched and slowly sat up in the bed, her tangled hair falling into her eyes.

"Juliet comes home today," she spoke aloud. "I've got to get moving." Cedra made her bed and pulled out an outfit for the day before heading off to the shower. She was sure Ma had been up for hours, and hopefully, the boys were at least awake so they could go to the Farmers Market. Ma would probably insist on making them breakfast before sending them off to shop. Cedra dressed, and when she opened her door, the smell of bacon teased her down the stairs.

"Good morning, Ma," she said as she walked into the kitchen.

"Good morning, Cedra. I hope you slept as well as I did," Ma replied.

"Like a rock. Not even the sun beaming in the window woke me this morning."

"Did you hear any activity from the boys' rooms when you came down?"

"I might have heard a shower running, but the tempting aroma of bacon had me distracted."

"I thought a hearty breakfast would be nice. Will you go with the boys to the Farmers Market so I can be sure to get what I need?"

"Do you not need my help here?" Cedra asked.

"I've got the lasagna ready to bake. I just need the salad fixings and bread. I've written down a list of things I'll need for the roast, too," Ma said, pointing to a notepad on the counter. "If you see any other veggies or baked goods that strike your fancy, pick them up, and we can work them into this week's menu. There won't be many more opportunities for locally grown vegetables."

"That sounds good to me. If I can find some nice yellow squash, maybe I can make a squash casserole to go with the roast."

"That does sound good," Ma agreed.

"What can I do to help with breakfast?"

"Go upstairs and round up the boys, and I'll start scrambling some eggs. The grits are warming, so we'll just need toast and a table setting."

"That sounds easy enough. I'll be right back." Cedra started for the stairs where Keith was coming down. "How far behind you is Wayne?"

"He's still primping but should only be a minute or two," Keith answered.

"You two can set the table and pour our drinks while I help Ma finish breakfast," Cedra said and returned to the kitchen.

"Morning, Ma," Keith said. "You've got it smelling heavenly in here."

"Food will be ready in just a few minutes," Ma answered. "Add eggs, some bacon, and sausage if you can find some at the market. Country ham, too. If you can find a decent amount of corn, I'll make some homemade cream corn, biscuits, and fatback one night this week. Better add fatback. Sliced if you can get it. Otherwise, I'll slice it."

"You're making my mouth water, Ma," Cedra said as she removed the toast and added fresh slices. "I'll look for more okra, too. That would go well with creamed corn."

Ma filled a large bowl with scrambled eggs and carried it to the table. "You better take the toast you have and get to the table before the bacon starts disappearing," Ma told Cedra. "I'll finish up the toast and bring fresh coffee."

"Thanks, Ma," Cedra replied and took a seat. Keith was taking a serving of eggs, so Cedra grabbed the platter of bacon, placing several slices on Ma's plate before taking some for her own.

"That was a clever play," Ma said as she brought their coffee cups to the table.

"If nothing else, I'm a quick learner," Cedra replied and passed the bacon back to Keith.

"You have to be if you plan on surviving meals around here."

"How did your night on the town go?" Wayne asked.

"Fantastic, and Cedra got good news," Ma said.

Both boys turned to look at Cedra. "Well?" Keith said impatiently.

"My Open Mic night is in two weeks, the night before Halloween."

"That's great news," Wayne said. "Congratulations."

"Lisa Marie also said I can bring you guys and Juliet on for my last number if you're game."

"Oh, hell yes," Wayne replied. "We need to go ahead and make sure we can get off that night," he told Keith.

"That works for me," Keith said as he bit into a slice of bacon.

"There was also a songwriter that performed last night who has got some skills. He starts work with me at the café on Monday, so maybe we can help each other with songs. His name is Stone Watson."

"That's a great name for a country singer," Keith said. "Where's he from?"

"Ocala, Florida," Cedra answered. "He has a wife and a two-year-old daughter who are living with his parents right now. Stone is living in a camper on the back of his truck."

"That's roughing it," Wayne said. "How long has he been in town?"

"Just a couple of months."

"He interacts well with the audience, and his songs were pretty strong," Ma added.

"Well, if any of us can help his writing, it's you, Cedra," Wayne said. "He'd be a starving artist if he depended on Keith or me."

"You guys aren't bad at writing. You just need more practice," Cedra said.

"Not my cup of tea. I'm a performer all the way," Wayne said. "As long as I can have access to your songbook, I'm excellent." He winked at Cedra.

"That won't be a problem," Cedra assured him. "I do need your help cleaning up the songs we chose for my performance, though. I'm only allowed four songs."

Keith nodded. "We'll be more than happy to help. If it works that we can play together as a band for one song, I think we should pick a piece with some tempo to showcase your range of skills."

"Something like 'Backwoods Boogie'?" Cedra smiled.

"Exactly like that." Keith grinned. "I love that song. It's perfect for some rockabilly music."

"He's right though, it will showcase the range you have," Ma said as she sipped her coffee. "Carrie will be more interested in variety."

"Carrie, as in Brooks?" Wayne asked.

"Yeah, she told Lisa Marie to notify her when Cedra would be performing," Ma replied.

Wayne nearly choked on his food. "Damn, girl, that's impressive." He turned to Keith. "We better get cleaned up for this performance."

"I might spring for a new pair of Levi's." Keith grinned.

"I'll iron for you two if you give me what you plan to wear," Ma volunteered. "A haircut wouldn't hurt either," Ma teased.

"I am getting a bit shaggy." Keith chuckled.

"I'm sending Cedra with you two knuckleheads this morning, so I know I'll get everything on my list."

Wayne looked at Keith. "Should our feelings be hurt?"

"Naw, man. You know Ma's right. We'd forget half the stuff on her list," Keith replied.

"Do you know what time Juliet will be home?" Ma asked Cedra.

"Not for certain, but I'd guess early afternoon. Juliet's excited about coming home."

"You've got lots of good news to share with her," Ma replied.

"Yes, I do. Maybe we can work on the songs after dinner for a bit if y'all aren't too full of lasagna."

"I have to work for a few hours tonight, but that sounds good to me," Wayne replied.

Ma reached for the last slice of bacon. "I'll have dinner ready early so that y'all can get busy."

"That works for me," Wayne said, then he rinsed his dishes and placed them in the dishwasher. "I'm going to brush my teeth, and I'll be back to help with the kitchen. I'm driving?" he asked.

"I'm good with that," Cedra replied.

†

When they were ready to head out, Ma stopped Cedra and handed her a list and a hundred-dollar bill.

"I guess the list would help," Cedra said as she plucked the paper from Ma's hand. "We've got this, so no arguing."

Ma nodded and watched as they walked out the door. "Y'all be careful," she called out to them.

Cedra looked back at Ma. "We will, Ma."

Cedra and the boys sang along with the radio as Wayne drove to the Farmers Market. "Stay focused, boys," Cedra said as they parked and walked into the aisles filled with delicious aromas and tables filled with goods.

†

Juliet was almost home when she dialed Cedra's number. "I'm only about twenty minutes away," she said when Cedra answered.

119

"The boys and I are at the Farmers Market doing some shopping for Ma. Do you want to join us or head on home? We're only about halfway through the list."

"I'm coming up on that exit now. I'll see you in a few."

"Juliet's going to join us," Cedra replied. "Should I call Ma and let her know she's earlier than expected?"

"I'll give Ma a call, and you go meet Juliet. We'll continue down this aisle, so we should be easy to find. Better grab another cart. This one's getting full."

"Will do," Cedra said, and handed Keith the list. "Don't miss anything."

"Yes, boss," Keith answered.

Cedra felt her face beaming with a smile when she saw Juliet approaching the market. The gentle sway of her hips and her hair blowing in the soft breeze was hypnotic. Juliet smiled when she looked up to find Cedra watching her, and Cedra's heart skipped a beat.

"Hey, stranger," she said and pulled Juliet into a hug.

"Hey, yourself. Did you miss me?" Juliet teased.

"Yes, I'll admit I have. I'm glad you're home."

"Me too," Juliet said and linked arms with Cedra. "Let's go see what we can find."

"Oh wait, I've got to get another cart," Cedra said, and veered off the aisle. She returned a moment later with an empty cart. "We've got a healthy list."

"If it's Ma's cooking, it's all good. There's nothing like home cooked meals. I've missed her meals the last few days."

"Is that all you missed?" Cedra pouted.

"Of course not. I missed you all, too. What have you been up to since I've been gone?"

"Working mostly. Last night at the café, Ma and I had a wonderful time meeting a talented young songwriter who performed at the Open Mic."

Juliet stopped in the aisle. "Should I be jealous?"

"No. Stone is married and has a daughter back in Florida. He's got some good writing skills and will be working at the Redbird starting tomorrow."

"As good as you?" Juliet quirked an eyebrow.

"No, but a different style." Cedra smiled.

"You'll have to invite him out to jam with us then. If he's impressed you, he must be good."

"I also got my date," Cedra said. "The thirtieth of October."

"For Open Mic? Oh, my goodness, that's excellent news. Congratulations. I am so excited for you."

"Wait, there's more. I asked if you and the boys could accompany me for a number, and Lisa Marie agreed to the last song in my set."

"Oh, heck yeah."

"Wait. There's more."

"What could be better?"

"Carrie Brooks will also be there. She specifically told Lisa Marie to keep her posted on my date."

Juliet stopped in her tracks again. "You're kidding me?"

"Nope, I swear with my last breath, those were Lisa Marie's exact words. Please say you'll jam with us."

"Hell yes, I will. That could be a great launching point for the band," Juliet said. "The more I think about it, the more excited I get."

"Me, too," Cedra admitted. "The boys want to use 'Backwoods Boogie' to show the range of my songs."

"That will be perfect. We need to start jamming soon," Juliet said.

"Tonight, after dinner, until Wayne has to go to work. Then we can work on my other three selections." Cedra smiled. "This is all so exciting and nerve-wracking."

"Relax. The crowd will love you and hopefully will enjoy the band as well. It is exciting. I'm very happy for you." Juliet bumped shoulders with Cedra. "You must have caught Carrie Brooks's attention."

"The only song of mine she's ever heard was the one you sang when she was in the audience. So, maybe it's not just me she's interested in promoting. Only time will tell."

Juliet pointed to Wayne and Keith.

"Hey, you guys are supposed to be picking out corn, not eating cookies," Cedra teased.

"We had to wait for the empty cart for the corn. We did get most everything else except the meats," Wayne said as he offered them a cookie.

†

The boys loaded the goods in Wayne's truck when they finished shopping. "I'm going to ride home with Juliet," Cedra told them.

"Okay, we'll see you there." Keith grinned.

Juliet laughed. "It gets a bit cramped between those two, doesn't it?"

"Yeah, it does, but I love those two goofballs," Cedra replied as they walked to Juliet's car.

"I think that feeling is mutual," Juliet said as she opened the driver's door. "Man, it's good to be home."

Cedra fastened her seatbelt. "Did you not have a good time?"

"The performing part was great, but I felt like a third wheel around the band. The guys were nice enough. I guess I just felt out of my element."

"I can understand that. You won't have to worry about that when The Bentleys hit the road." Cedra smiled at Juliet.

"Do you honestly think we will be successful?" Juliet pulled into the traffic.

"Yes. I do. I think we have a better chance together than individually, and you have to admit we have chemistry. Ma even thinks we sound good together, and you know she doesn't sugarcoat anything when it comes to music."

"How do you think she's going to react when we ask her about using her name?" Juliet glanced over at Cedra.

"First, I think she's going to cry. Then I think she will be very honored that we want to use her name. Regardless, she'll be our number one fan."

Juliet chuckled. "You're right about that. How are we going to approach her?"

"We thought we would casually drop it on her at supper tonight," Cedra answered. "You've been with her the longest, so we thought we'd let you do the honors."

"Whose idea was that?"

"Wayne's actually, but Keith and I didn't object," Cedra replied.

"Fortunately, I'm up to the task, but not until dessert. I heard Keith talking about coconut cake from the Redbird."

"Yes, we brought it home with us last night. I'm sure it was hard for the boys not to dig into it last night when they got home, so I left a warning on the box."

"That was probably a smart move. Those two could have devoured the whole cake if left unsupervised." Juliet turned on the blinker to enter Ma's drive. She slowed as she followed Wayne's truck. "There's no place like home."

"Speaking of which, do you have plans to go home for Thanksgiving?" Cedra asked.

"I hadn't thought about it, to be honest. Why? What do you have planned?"

"I want to invite my dad up for a holiday, and I'd love for you to meet him."

Juliet parked the car and looked over at Cedra. "That settles that. I'm staying here for the holiday."

"Fantastic," Cedra replied and stepped out of the car. Ma was sitting in her rocker on the porch. "Look who we found at the market." She nodded toward Juliet.

"Best find of the day," Ma grinned and looked at Juliet. "Welcome home."

"Thanks, Ma. It's good to be home."

"Did you youngins buy out the market?" Ma called to the boys as they started unloading the truck.

"We tried our best, Ma," Keith said. "Cedra was a taskmaster and only allowed us to sneak off once for cookies."

Ma turned to Cedra. "Good job. I knew it was the right decision to send you along to monitor. Let's get these goodies stored. You can leave that corn out here, and I'll shuck it later while y'all are jamming."

"Yes, ma'am," Wayne said, and placed the large box of corn beside Ma's chair.

"Do you need help with your bags?" Cedra asked Juliet. "I think the boys can handle the groceries."

"Sure, you can grab my guitar, leave it on the porch, and come back for a bag. Thanks."

"No problem," Cedra said. She propped Juliet's guitar case on the wall beside Juliet's usual spot. She returned to the car and took a small bag from Juliet.

Ma and the boys were in the kitchen when Juliet stepped inside. "Is that lasagna I smell?"

"It sure is," Ma said. "It'll be ready by the time you make it back downstairs."

Juliet dropped her bag and rushed over to Ma. She picked her up in her arms and swung her around before setting her back on her feet. She kissed Ma's cheek. "I love you, Ma. Thanks for cooking my favorite."

"We all thought it would be nice to celebrate your homecoming," Ma replied.

"I couldn't ask for anything more perfect." Juliet looked at Cedra. "Let's get these bags upstairs so we can eat."

"Pour the drinks, boys, and I'll bring the lasagna," Ma said as Cedra and Juliet climbed the stairs.

†

The group ate a fantastic meal and chatted about the events that occurred since Juliet had been gone, and she gave them an update on her road trip. Cedra began clearing the dishes while Ma cut the cake. When she took her seat, she shot a grin to Wayne and Keith, then nodded to Juliet.

Juliet cleared her throat. "Ma, there's something we want to discuss with you."

Ma looked at Juliet, Cedra, and then the boys. "This must be serious. No one is pregnant or in trouble with the law, are they?"

"Heavens no, Ma. Nothing like that," Cedra replied.

125

"We have been tossing an idea around about forming a band. We think our chances for success will be much better than if we remain solo artists."

"That does sound like a good idea. I think that collectively, you all are very talented together. So, what do you want to discuss with me? You certainly don't need my permission." Ma chuckled.

Juliet smiled at Ma. "The name of the band. We want to call ourselves The Bentleys."

"What?" Ma asked, surprised.

"If it weren't for you, we might not have ever met and grown together as a family. We want your permission to use your name for our band," Cedra explained.

"Hell yes," Ma said with a whoop. "I love it."

"I reckon it's official then. Now can we have some cake?" Wayne asked.

Laughter broke out around the table. "I know you've been dying to eat that cake since we got home last night, bro," Keith said.

"I think I even dreamed about it," Wayne said as he accepted a slice from Ma. "Thanks, Ma. For the cake and allowing us to use your name."

"I am so honored," Ma said, with tears glistening in her eyes. She handed the cake to Cedra. "Your idea?"

"Joint effort. It does have a ring to it, and we all live here together. The more we talked about it, the more it seemed so right for us," Cedra replied.

"It will be great to see my name in lights when y'all hit the big time," Ma said.

"I love your confidence," Juliet said.

"The four of you together have no other choice but to be successful. None of you would settle for anything else. Am I wrong?" Ma asked. "I just have one thought."

"What's that, Ma?" Cedra asked.

"That you consider adding Stone to your group. He's an excellent musician, and I believe the two of you could write great songs together."

"I have got to meet this guy," Juliet said. "He doesn't live with us, though."

"That's easy enough to remedy," Ma said. "He sleeps in a camper on the back of his truck. He can park it in the side yard and come in for meals and showers. He would be officially a Bentley then."

"He could carpool with me," Cedra shrugged.

"Wait to decide until you meet him, but I think he would be a great addition," Ma said. "Will you invite him out to supper this week?" she asked Cedra.

"What night is everyone free?" Cedra asked.

"I'm good Tuesday or Thursday," Wayne said.

"Me too," Keith answered.

"Let's do Tuesday, and we can have the creamed corn for dinner," Ma suggested. "I can do the roast tomorrow night."

"Sounds good to me. Even if we don't all like Stone enough for the band, he could live out here," Keith said.

Ma grinned at Cedra. "Oh, I think you will all like him, but we'll wait and see."

†

Once everyone settled on the porch, Juliet looked at Cedra. "What selections have you chosen? I know "Backwoods Boogie", but what else?"

127

Cedra picked up her songbook. "The first one that I shared with y'all, which we've already cleaned up well, and the songs on pages twelve and twenty-five."

"I was going to suggest twenty-five," Keith said. "Play it for us, and let us listen."

Wayne and Juliet turned to the correct page and read the lyrics as Cedra picked up her guitar. Ma was shucking the corn, and her smile grew as she watched the four young artists.

When Cedra finished the song, Ma was the first to chime in. "It's missing something. Not the lyrics, but the music."

"Like what, Ma?" Wayne asked.

"Your banjo," Ma answered. "Go get it and play with Cedra."

"Is that okay with you?" Wayne asked Cedra.

"Absolutely," Cedra replied. "I think you're right, Ma. That would spice it up some."

"You could play it as your third song before the rest of the band joins you," Ma suggested.

Juliet clapped. "Brilliant as always, Ma. Great idea."

The group played for the next hour until Wayne stretched. "I hate to leave such fun company, but I need to head into work. I think you've pretty much got the music and selections down. I want to play through "Backwoods Boogie" several more times before we go live."

"I don't think that will pose any problems," Juliet replied. "I'd like to see if we can get some studio time scheduled soon. I've got a few favors I can collect on to get some free time. It may be odd hours."

"That's no problem. Let us know what you can get. I think we've all agreed to pitch in to pay for studio rental if we need it," Cedra answered.

Juliet smiled. "If things go well during your Open Mic, Carrie will make sure we get all the studio time we need."

"I hadn't considered that. Do you think Carrie will make an offer to us?" Keith asked.

"She appears to be interested," Juliet replied. "I've never heard of her going out of her way like this before."

"I don't want to be a Debbie Downer, but she could just be interested in Cedra," Keith said.

"There is no just Cedra. It's all or nothing," Cedra responded.

"That's a fine gesture, but you don't have the luxury of driving that decision with Carrie," Juliet warned.

"I have all I need right here. If Carrie is not interested, then it's her loss. I think we've all agreed that together we can be more successful, so we need to stick to our plan." Cedra looked at each of them. "Carrie Brooks is not the only agent out there."

Ma looked up from her seat. "Cedra's right on this one. Carrie would be a fool not to sign all of you in one package. Have faith."

"Hey," Juliet said. "I've got an hour at Wild Bill's the Thursday before your Open Mic. Why don't we use that as a practice run?"

"It could get some interest stirring, and we would be practicing live."

"I'll ask for that night off tonight when I go to work," Wayne said.

"It shouldn't be a problem for me," Keith added.

Cedra smiled. "I work days, so I'm good to go."

"If Stone works out, it shouldn't be a problem for him either," Juliet added.

Cedra was pleased that Juliet was considering Stone even though she hadn't met him. She was the only one who had a foundation for a solo career established, so she would be sacrificing the most by joining a band.

"I'll see y'all tomorrow," Wayne said as he left the porch. "Don't have too much fun without me."

"Have a good night and be safe," Ma told him. "Keith, will you carry these corn husks to the compost bin and help me take the corn inside."

"Sure thing, Ma. Do you plan to cut the corn tonight?"

"I thought I would," Ma answered.

"We can help you," Cedra offered.

"Too many cooks in the kitchen." Ma looked at Keith and winked. "Keith can help me while the two of you catch up."

"You got it, Ma," Keith answered and carried the corn inside.

"Well, I guess it's down to just you and me," Cedra said. "What do you honestly think of all these changes?"

Juliet looked into Cedra's eyes. "I think it's too good of an opportunity to pass on. I know we have the talent, so with a bit of luck, we can make this work for everyone."

Cedra nodded. "I think so, too, but I worry about you passing on a chance for a solo career."

"That's not as important as having you in my life," Juliet said.

"That wouldn't change. You'd still have first dibs on anything I write," Cedra replied innocently.

"That's not what I was referring to," Juliet smiled. "Would you mind taking a ride with me?"

"I'd love to," Cedra replied. "Let me put this stuff up, and I'll be ready."

†

Cedra's response left Juliet wondering if she had been misreading the chemistry between her and Cedra. She was much more interested in Cedra than her beautiful lyrics. Juliet had to know for sure if there was interest from Cedra for something more before she fully committed to the band. She couldn't imagine how difficult it would be to remain so close to the woman she loved if Cedra was not interested in a romantic relationship. Juliet stuck her head inside the door.

"Cedra and I are going for a ride. We'll be back later."

"Be safe," Ma replied.

Juliet started the car and waited for Cedra. Her hands were sweating as she gripped the wheel. Her heart raced when Juliet saw Cedra walking towards the car. She second-guessed if this was the right time to have this talk with Cedra.

"Better now than later," she voiced to herself to bolster her courage.

Cedra climbed in and fastened her seatbelt. "Where are we going?"

"There's someplace I want you to see," Juliet answered cryptically.

"Alrighty then," Cedra answered. "I like surprises."

Juliet secretly hoped that was true for all aspects of her life as she drove to a nearby bluff with a view of Nashville on the horizon. She had stumbled onto the spot one

131

day and watched a beautiful sunset. That was what she hoped to share with Cedra.

"This is a beautiful view of the city," Cedra said when Juliet placed the car in park and killed the ignition.

"Just wait a few more minutes, and you will witness the true beauty of this place," Juliet promised as she lowered the windows to breathe in the fresh air. "I ran across this place a few months ago, and the sunset was amazing. I thought you might appreciate seeing it for yourself."

Cedra nodded and turned toward Juliet. "Have I done something wrong? I feel like there is something you want to talk to me about."

Juliet looked into Cedra's eyes and saw tears pooling in them. Her heart ached to hear that Cedra thought she had done something wrong. She reached up and softly stroked Cedra's face. "No, you haven't done anything wrong. If anyone is at fault, it will be me. Do you believe in love at first sight?"

"Yes, of course. I'm enough of a dreamer to believe it happens," Cedra answered.

"I have a confession to make to you, and I don't know how you will react," Juliet said.

Cedra frowned. "You can tell me anything."

Juliet took a deep breath and let it out slowly, willing her racing heart to stay in her chest without shattering. "Ever since I heard you singing the night you first arrived, my feelings for you have grown. When I was on the road this trip, my heart ached to be away from you. I need to know how you feel about me because I'm not sure I can move forward without you in my life."

Cedra's frown softened on her face. "I'm not sure I follow, but I'm listening."

Juliet felt the tears in her eyes. She had never felt like this for anyone, and Cedra's innocence made it so difficult. She wiped at a tear that had escaped and smiled at Cedra. "What I am trying to say, and doing a poor job of communicating, is that I fell in love with you that night, and my feelings for you have grown with each passing day. I know this may be confusing for you and much different, but I have to put my heart in your hands before it bursts completely."

Cedra stared back at Juliet for several long seconds.

"I will understand if you think I'm crazy, but I have to get this off my chest," Juliet said as the tears continued.

Cedra reached between them and brushed away Juliet's tears. "I feel like such an idiot. I can write about all kinds of emotion and passion, but I hadn't realized what I felt until I saw it mirrored in your eyes. You stir something inside of me that I have never experienced before. If this is love, then I welcome the strangeness of it." Cedra leaned forward and brushed her lips against Juliet's.

When Juliet realized Cedra was about to kiss her, she closed her eyes and fought the overwhelming desire to allow the kiss to escalate too quickly. The tender kiss evolved into more when Cedra's tongue parted her lips, and they tasted one another for the first time. When the kiss ended, Juliet opened her eyes and found Cedra smiling.

"Wow."

"Wow, indeed," Cedra agreed. "I'll admit, I know very little about being in love, but I'm eager to follow your lead and allow you to guide us in a relationship."

"Oh, thank goodness," Juliet replied. "I thought my heart would burst right out of my chest if you didn't feel something towards me."

"For someone who can write so effortlessly, I find the words to describe how I feel about you out of reach. It's more than incredible that I'm complete whenever I'm near you, that the hole of something missing disappears. Does that sound crazy?"

"Not to me. I'll admit, I've lusted after others before, but the sex just satisfied a temporary need. Not to say I don't desire to be with you because the thought of making love with you drives me crazy, but how I feel when I'm with you is different."

The change in the atmosphere drew Cedra's eyes to the windshield. The sky appeared enflamed with brilliant red and gold hues as Cedra watched the sun disappear beneath the horizon.

Juliet's eyes followed Cedra's as they silently watched the sunset. "This spot was beautiful to me before and tonight, sharing the sunset with you, it's now even more spectacular."

"This is an incredible view," Cedra replied. "Thank you for sharing it with me." She reached over and stroked Juliet's face with both hands, looking deep into her eyes. "I promise to hold your heart gently next to mine and love you with all that I have."

"That's all I could ever dream for," Juliet said, and closed the distance between them for a fiery kiss.

When the kiss ended, Cedra chuckled. "My entire body is trembling. I want so much more of you, but I don't know what to do."

"I feel like I could explode right now, but I don't want our first time together to be in a car, either. Let's go home, and we can continue this in a comfortable bed," Juliet suggested.

"What about Ma and Keith? Will they hear and know what's going on?" Cedra felt the blood rush to her face.

"I promise to be quiet if you will," Juliet teased. "I think they know what has been growing between us all along. I know Ma has."

"I'm not sure I can keep that promise, but I'll try," Cedra replied. "You really think Ma knows?"

"Yeah, I think so. I've caught Ma watching us many times, and she has a way of giving us things to do together."

"You may be right. I need to shower when we get home. I've got my clothes ready for this week, so I don't have to worry about that." Cedra looked at Juliet. "Let's go home."

Juliet nodded and started the car. "I'll hang out with Ma for a bit and shower after you get done."

†

Cedra nodded and reached for Juliet's hand. Her small hand fit into Juliet's perfectly. She felt a rush of heat pass through her as the thought of Juliet's hands bringing her pleasure raced through her veins. Cedra was glad the night had fallen and would hide the flush on her face.

When they arrived home, Cedra held the door open for them, and they found Ma sitting at the kitchen table working a crossword.

"Keith rode into town for a while, so it's just us girls," Ma said with a grin. "I was thinking about another slice of cake before the boys come home and destroy it."

Cedra was having a hard time looking Ma in her eyes. She felt that her excitement and nerves would show, and she didn't want Ma to worry or question if she was feeling okay. Cedra didn't have a word to describe what she was feeling, so when Ma asked if they would join her, Cedra shook her head.

"I'm going to shower and call it an early night. I'll see you in the morning, Ma."

"Four will come early," Ma agreed. "Sleep well, and I'll have your coffee ready."

"Thanks, Ma," Cedra replied and started for the stairs.

"Are you drinking milk or coffee with your cake?" she heard Juliet ask. "I think I'll have a cold glass of milk."

"That sounds good to me," Ma replied.

Cedra rushed up the stairs and straightened her room. She grabbed a T-shirt and panties to head to the shower. Her body trembled as she thought of the kisses they had shared and the slickness between her legs she couldn't wash away. At least she would feel clean when she stepped out of the shower. She brushed her teeth and hair after dressing. Cedra sat at her desk, opened her songbook, and wrote while waiting for Juliet.

†

"Did your trip go well?" Ma asked as Juliet sat across from her.

"It was a decent gig, but I was glad to come home early," Juliet answered.

"That wasn't the trip I was referring to," Ma teased.

"We rode to the bluff to watch the sunset. It was beautiful," Juliet said.

"What else? I feel like something has changed between you and Cedra. Did you finally tell her how you feel about her?"

"You don't miss anything, do you?"

"Cedra hasn't failed to look me in the eyes since she arrived. So, what's going on?"

136

"Yes, I told her how I feel about her, and we shared a few kisses," Juliet grinned. "I think she's worried about how you and the boys will accept our relationship."

"I hope you will share with her that we've all been cheering the two of you on," Ma said. "It's been evident to us from the beginning. Tell her we don't judge people for who they love."

"I'll share that with her, but she needs to hear that from you," Juliet said.

"I'll make it a point to have a chat with her soon." Ma smiled at how quickly Juliet had devoured the cake. "Just don't keep her up too late. Four in the morning does come early," Ma teased.

Juliet smiled and stood to place her dishes in the washer. "Yes, Ma."

She walked back to Ma and leaned down to kiss her cheek. "Thanks for everything, Ma."

"I haven't done anything yet," Ma said. "Goodnight, Juliet."

"Goodnight, Ma."

†

Juliet rushed up the stairs and shed her clothes quickly before starting the shower. She found an oversized T-shirt to pull on after showering. Putting on anything else would just slow things down, and Juliet couldn't wait to be skin on skin with Cedra. She smiled as she looked at the door to Cedra's room to see a sliver of light coming under the door. Juliet showered quickly, then dressed and took a deep breath before reaching to open the door. She felt her fingers shaking and a smile on her face as she saw Cedra sitting at her desk. She crept over to the desk. Cedra was focused on

137

her writing and did not hear her approach. She leaned down and brushed the hair away from Cedra's neck, and planted a soft kiss.

"Is this a good time to disturb your writing?"

"It is now," Cedra replied and closed her songbook.

"I don't even get a peek at the new song?" Juliet pouted.

"It's not ready yet," Cedra replied. "I think I can make it up to you, though." Cedra stood and took Juliet in her arms and kissed her deeply.

"That's an excellent start," Juliet said. "I'll be right back."

Cedra stepped back and watched as Juliet left the room and returned with a lit candle. She reached over and turned off the lamp. "That's much better."

Juliet set the candle on the desk. "Now, where were we?"

Cedra opened her arms, and Juliet stepped into them. Cedra saw the flash of bare skin beneath the shirt Juliet wore and smiled as her hands snaked under the shirt. Her hands glided slowly up the curve of Juliet's hips. "So soft," Cedra whispered into Juliet's ear. Her hands continued up Juliet's body and felt her shiver. "I want to see you." Cedra was surprised by the low growl in her voice.

Juliet's eyebrow shot up. She placed Cedra's hands on the bottom of her shirt. She nodded, and Cedra lifted the shirt above her head and tossed it onto her chair. "Just as I thought. You are beautiful." Juliet's eyes followed her as Cedra's fingers explored her body with soft caresses. Her thumb touched a small scar on her right side, and Juliet shivered. Cedra's fingertips rose slowly to circle Juliet's breast, causing her breath to catch.

"Too fast?" Cedra asked.

"Not at all, but you have too many clothes on," Juliet smiled. "I want to feel your skin next to mine."

Juliet removed Cedra's shirt and led her to the bed. She wasn't ready to remove Cedra's panties yet as she stretched out on the bed and guided Cedra next to her. She placed her leg over Cedra's thigh and leaned over for a tender kiss. Her hand caressed Cedra's stomach as their tongues danced and the kiss deepened. The heat built between them as Juliet's hand explored Cedra's body. Her hand lowered to cup Cedra's mound, and she gently squeezed the moist area. Cedra released a soft moan.

"You like this?" Juliet asked as her fingertips traced her lower lips through the damp panties.

"Oh, hell yes," Cedra answered. "You've got me soaking wet."

"That's a perfect thing," Juliet answered as she continued to tease Cedra. Her lips kissed down Cedra's neck. "Trust me?"

"Implicitly," Cedra breathed.

"Good," Juliet's mouth moved down to cover Cedra's breast with gentle kisses, and then her tongue flicked across Cedra's fully erect nipple. Her right hand slipped beneath the fabric of Cedra's panties.

"I think we can get rid of these now," she whispered against Cedra's skin.

"Yes, please," Cedra replied as she lifted her hips to allow Juliet to remove her panties.

"That's much better," Juliet said and took Cedra's breast in her mouth as her fingertips traced Cedra's entrance, dipping lightly into the wetness. Juliet felt Cedra's body writhing under her touch and nipped at her nipple.

Cedra buried her hand in Juliet's hair, pulling her mouth firmly onto her breast. "More," she groaned.

Juliet sucked Cedra's breast into her mouth, trapping her nipple against the roof of her mouth as a finger slipped between her lips into the velvety wetness. She could feel Cedra's muscles clenching around her finger as she slowly withdrew and added a second finger, sliding them deeper into Cedra.

Cedra gasped and then relaxed.

"Too much?" Juliet asked.

"No, it feels too good. Please, don't stop," Cedra answered.

Juliet curled her fingers inside Cedra and felt her walls quiver with excitement as she began a slow rhythm, withdrawing and sliding deep. Cedra's hips began moving to match Juliet's movement, pushing her fingers deeper as her breathing became labored. Juliet raised her body to cover Cedra's mouth with a deep kiss as her thumb pressed into her clit with every stroke of her fingers. Juliet could feel Cedra's body shaking as her orgasm was close and kissed her deeply to muffle the moan that ripped through her. When Cedra's hips crashed back to the bed, Juliet's kiss became tender.

†

Cedra's body continued to quiver as she tried to steady her breathing. "Holy shit," she managed to say when Juliet smiled down at her. "That felt incredible."

Juliet slowly withdrew her fingers. "I'm not done with you yet."

Cedra's eyes grew wide as Juliet moved between her legs and her tongue began tracing the inside of her thigh. Juliet's fingertips opened her entrance like a blossoming

140

flower, and Cedra had never experienced a touch so sensual before. Her heart was thundering in her chest as Juliet's mouth hovered just above her entrance, and the tip of her tongue licked slowly. Cedra's experience had not prepared her for the pleasure of Juliet's touch, and the realization of Juliet's mouth enclosing her center sent her mind whirling. Juliet's fingers had been firm and demanding, but her tongue was soft as it caressed and teased her to the brink of a second climax. When her body reached the boiling point, Cedra covered her mouth with a hand as her body erupted, sending a gush of juices from her body. Juliet's tongue moved slower as Cedra's hips writhed beneath her, and she raised her head, leaving a tender kiss behind before she crawled to lay between Cedra's legs, their mounds pressed together as she kissed Cedra. She supported her weight on her hands, pressing their bodies together. Juliet's eyes were shining as she looked into Cedra's, and Cedra knew from that moment that Juliet had taken her heart. Not that she had doubted Juliet's intentions, but the love she saw in Juliet's eyes felt so right.

"That was rock my world amazing," she whispered. "Promise me it will always feel this good."

Juliet returned her smile. "I will do my best always to make you feel this well-loved."

"That's all I could ever ask," Cedra said as her hand stroked down Juliet's face.

Juliet rolled over onto her back and chuckled. "I can't believe it's already past midnight."

"I don't care what time it is. I want you to feel this good," Cedra replied.

"Not tonight, sweetie. Four will come way too quickly. I enjoyed every moment with you tonight, and I will be satisfied to sleep next to you. Tomorrow night, I promise we will continue."

Cedra pouted, but she knew Juliet was right. She would get little sleep as it was, but she was disappointed. She turned and blew out the candle before snuggling into Juliet.

Juliet leaned over and kissed her. "We have just begun." She wrapped her arm around Cedra and pulled her close.

Cedra rested her head on Juliet's shoulder and draped a leg across her body, her hand resting on Juliet's chest. "Thank you for loving me."

"I will always love you," Juliet replied. "Sweet sleep, my love."

Unfamiliar with sharing a bed, Cedra woke several times when Juliet moved or sighed in her sleep. Each time brought a smile to her face as she looked at the woman she had fallen in love with and snuggled in closer. When the alarm went off at four, she lunged for it to turn it off before Juliet woke.

"Is it four already?" Juliet murmured.

"Yes, time for me to get going, but go back to sleep," Cedra said. She kissed Juliet's lips and crawled from the bed. She walked to the bathroom and smiled at an unfamiliar soreness in her muscles. A pleasurable feeling reminded her of their lovemaking as she reached inside to turn on the water. As she ran the soapy washcloth over her body, Cedra was surprised to find how sensitive her skin remained, and her thoughts returned to Juliet. She wished she had the luxury of time to crawl into bed beside her and love the morning away. Cedra sighed. *One day,* she promised herself, *we will have all the time in the world.*

After dressing, Cedra picked up her songbook and kissed Juliet's forehead. Lyrics were dancing through her mind, and she couldn't wait to write them down before they disappeared.

Ma was sitting at the table sipping coffee when she entered the kitchen. "Good morning, Ma."

"Good morning to you. You seem excited this morning," Ma said as she watched Cedra sit and open her songbook.

"Something just popped into my head," Cedra confessed.

"Well, get to writing, girl, and I'll make your coffee," Ma said with a chuckle.

Cedra quickly wrote the thoughts dancing through her head and barely realized Ma had placed her coffee next to her and sat down across from her. She could smell the rich aroma of the coffee but couldn't tear her eyes away from the page.

"I hate to interrupt your writing spree, but if you don't get a move on, you're going to be late for work. That's not a good first impression to make on Stone. Don't forget to invite him out for supper."

Cedra snapped the book closed. "Thanks, Ma. The time has gotten away from me. I'll see you tonight."

"Yes, you will, but keep your eyes on the road. Those lyrics will still be there when you take a break."

"Yes, ma'am." Cedra grabbed her travel mug and headed out the door.

Ma watched her back out and shook her head. "I thought for sure she'd come dragging down the stairs this morning." She grinned and then laughed at her comment. "Oh, young love. Must be invigorating."

†

Cedra arrived with three minutes to spare, but instead of picking up her songbook, she resisted the urge and left it sitting on the seat of her truck. The new lyrics would have to wait on her first break. When she entered the café, Stone was sitting at a table with Lisa Marie, who looked up when she entered.

"Here comes your trainer. Pay attention to everything she does today, and you will be successful," Lisa Marie praised.

"Good morning," Cedra said. "Let me clock in, and I'll be right back."

"Come with me, and I'll give you the rundown on the cash register while we wait," Lisa Marie told Stone.

Cedra returned with an extra apron for Stone and a new order pad. "Is it okay if we take the counter this morning to start him off slow, and if he picks up quick, we can move him on to tables?" Cedra asked.

"I think that's a great idea. Stone can watch you for a few orders and help with coffee refills, and then he can start taking some orders under your supervision." Lisa Marie looked at Stone. "How does that sound to you?"

"I can handle that," Stone replied with a smile.

Cedra nodded to Stone. "Let's grab a cup of coffee, and we can review the menu until the doors open at five-thirty." Cedra viewed some shorthand notes to help Stone take efficient orders and some tips for interacting with the customers. Right on schedule, Lisa Marie unlocked the door, and the team sprang into action.

†

After the initial morning rush concluded, Cedra looked at Stone. "You did well. You didn't spill anything, and you were very attentive to your customers."

"Thanks. I have a good teacher," Stone replied.

"Are you hungry?" Cedra asked. "Now would be a good time to get a break."

"I could eat."

"Let's put in our orders and have a seat at the counter. The usual for me, please," Cedra told the cook. "I'll be right back."

Cedra walked out to her truck to retrieve her songbook. The lyrics from this morning were still running through her head. She took a seat at the counter and began scribbling her notes.

Stone brought mugs of fresh coffee and sat beside her. When Cedra looked up, he asked, "Always the writer, huh?"

"Yeah, you know how it feels when something's bouncing around your brain and won't give you peace until you write it down?"

"I know that feeling all too well. I've been guilty of writing words on my hands if I don't have anything else to write on," Stone replied.

Cedra nodded and pulled out her order pad and turned it over. "I scribble on everything."

"I'm sure I will join you in that soon."

"Order up," the cook called from the window.

"Sit tight, and I'll get our breakfast," Stone said.

Cedra looked back at the page and added a few words before closing the book. When Stone placed the food on the counter and sat next to her, Cedra looked up at him.

"Are you free for supper tomorrow night? Ma and I would like to invite you out to discuss a few things with you and let you meet the others living with us."

"Tomorrow night will be great. Just give me a time and directions, and I'll be there. I'd never give up on a chance for a home cooked meal."

"Ma is doing her creamed corn and fatback with homemade biscuits," Cedra informed him. "Oh, and fried okra too."

"That sounds delicious. Breakfast looks good, too, and the portions are bountiful. Does it cost us much?"

"Meals are on the house while we work. Lisa Marie wants us to stay well fed."

"I'm going to love working here." Stone picked up his fork and dug into the breakfast.

"We have to keep up our energy levels so we can provide good service." Cedra dropped some butter in her grits and seasoned her food. "Where did you park your truck?"

"There's a little campground about twenty minutes from here. It's cheap but still convenient to town."

"That's great," Cedra said, then took a bite of food.

Lisa Marie walked over and sat with them. "It looks like you're picking things up well," she said to Stone.

"He did good," Cedra said. "Even once we moved into the dining area."

"You ready to tackle a lunch crowd? It's a bit more varied from breakfast."

"Yes, ma'am. I believe I can handle it. I may not be as fast as Cedra, but I'm getting the process down."

Cedra smiled and nodded to Lisa Marie. "He can handle it."

"That's excellent news." Lisa Marie nodded toward Cedra's songbook. "Is the writing going well?"

Cedra beamed. "It's going fantastic. I've got the songs ready for my Open Mic, and we've been practicing, so I pray everything goes well."

"I shot Carrie an email this morning about your date, and she responded and sounded excited."

"Did you mention the last song?" Cedra asked.

"About the group of you performing together? Nope. I thought we would keep that a surprise."

"Juliet has a time block at Wild Bill's the Thursday night that week, so we are going to use that to practice," Cedra replied.

"That's not a bad idea to give you some live experience and exposure. Be sure to mention your Open Mic, so maybe the audience will come to hear more," Lisa Marie suggested.

"We will," Cedra replied. "I'm excited to see how this turns out."

"I don't think you'll be disappointed. You've got a great deal of drive and talent, and that's a great combination to have." Lisa Marie smiled as a customer walked through the door.

Cedra turned around and was about to get up from her seat when Lisa Marie said, "Sit tight, I've got this one."

"I think I'm going to like working here," Stone said. "Good people and atmosphere for work."

"Some extremely influential people come to eat here, so it's important to build rapport with all the customers. You never know who can open a door for you in Nashville, and first impressions are critical."

"I'll keep that in mind. Do you think we can get together soon to discuss some ideas I have for songs?" Stone asked.

"I think we could do that sometime this week after work. What's good for you?"

"How about Wednesday?"

Cedra thought for a second. "That should be doable."

As they were finishing their meals, the door opened again. "No rest for the wicked," Cedra teased. "You get them seated, and I'll drop these plates in the kitchen."

Cedra monitored Stone's first few lunch orders and then cut him loose on his own. The diner was filling quickly, and everyone stayed busy, including Lisa Marie, who operated the cash register while they concentrated on filling orders.

When the rush died down, Cedra poured a glass of tea. "That was quite a crowd today."

"It's been a great Monday so far," Lisa Marie replied as Carrie Brooks walked into the café. "I think you should take this one," she said with a wink to Cedra.

"I'm on it." Cedra followed Carrie to her favorite spot. "Welcome back. What can I get you to drink?"

"Let's start with some sweet tea. Will you be able to join me for a few minutes?" Carrie asked.

"Let me get your drink while you decide on what you want to eat. I think it's slow enough that I can take a short break."

"Excellent. Go ahead and place an order for a spinach salad then," Carrie answered.

"Very good. I'll be right back," Cedra said, and went to place the order. "You mind if I take a quick break?" she asked Lisa Marie.

"No problem. Take what time you need. I doubt we will get busy in the next few minutes," Lisa Marie replied.

"Thanks." Cedra picked up her drink and took Carrie's to the table. "Here you go. The salad will be up in a few minutes."

"Thank you. Is that Stone Watson at the counter?" Carrie asked.

"Yes, it is. Stone's just starting today and has done well," Cedra responded.

"The young man has some talent for songwriting," Carrie said. "The two of you would make a great team."

"We've talked about working on a few songs together. Our styles are close enough. We would do well collaborating."

"I agree. Lisa Marie emailed me this morning about your Open Mic date. Are you excited?"

"Very much so. I've got my songs picked out and a surprise planned."

"What kind of surprise?" Carrie asked.

"If I said, it wouldn't be a surprise, now would it?" Cedra replied.

"Just don't let it backfire on you," Carrie warned.

"I don't think it will, but thanks for the advice. Will you be here that night?"

Carrie smiled before taking a drink. "I wouldn't miss it for the world. Don't be surprised to find a few other agents in the audience. There seems to be a buzz of energy around you already. I hope I can beat my competition to the punch."

"Only time will tell. I will be as prepared as possible, and hopefully, the audience will enjoy my performance." Cedra was shaking on the inside, but she wanted to sound confident but not cocky. She watched Carrie's face for any signs of emotion, but Carrie remained as stoic as ever.

"I appreciate your confidence and have no doubt the audience will like what you have to offer. Can we go ahead and set up a meeting for the following Monday afternoon at three in my office?"

"I'll have to leave work a bit early, but that won't be a problem." Cedra felt her heart pounding against her chest.

"Order up," came the call from the kitchen.

"I'll be right back," Cedra said, and did her best not to knock her chair over, getting up from the table. She walked calmly to the kitchen and returned with Carrie's salad. "Is there anything else I can get you right now?"

"More tea in a few minutes. Will you join me for dessert? I'm hoping you have pecan pie today."

"We sure do. I'll refill your tea and get your dessert ready," Cedra replied.

"Thank you, Cedra," Carrie's voice purred.

Cedra was surprised by the tone in Carrie's voice and more surprised by the look of desire in Carrie's eyes. Maybe her recent experience with Juliet had her more sensitive to external cues, but Carrie's response seemed different than their previous encounters. She returned to the counter feeling a bit confused and overwhelmed.

Lisa Marie was separating the tips for the day when Cedra returned. She must have seen the puzzled look on Cedra's face. "Is everything okay?" she asked.

Cedra looked at her. "Yes, I need to talk to you after Carrie leaves, though, if that's okay?"

"Perfectly fine," Lisa Marie replied with a grin.

Cedra served up two portions of pie to take to the table with a pitcher of tea. She could feel Carrie's eyes on her as she worked and looked up to see her smile as she returned to the table.

"Here you go," she said as she placed the pie on the table.

Carrie had pushed the empty salad plate away and eyed the pie eagerly.

"Let me clear your plate, and I'll be right back," Cedra said and took the plate to the kitchen.

"Thanks for joining me while I eat," Carrie said. "I hate eating alone, but it's nice to get away from the suits sometimes."

"It's not a problem. You usually come in after the lunch rush, so it's not hard to break then," Cedra replied.

"It gets me fueled up for afternoon meetings," Carrie said. "I'm usually stuck in meetings from two until six."

"You sound like you stay extremely busy," Cedra replied.

"It takes long hours to sign and promote the best Nashville has to offer. I usually hit the clubs at night to see what talent is playing to determine if any of them catch my interest," Carrie went on to explain.

"Do you get any downtime or sleep?" Cedra asked.

"On occasion. Right now, there are so many new folks coming to Nashville; it's hard to take my foot off the gas pedal. I don't want to miss an opportunity to sign a diamond in the rough."

"I'm new to all of this. What does an agent do for a performer or a writer?" Cedra asked.

"A multitude of things from scheduling studio time for recordings to setting performance plans in place. I put writers in touch with other songwriters and bands looking for new material. Many artists think they are good songwriters when they genuinely aren't, and they need fresh material to record and market."

"No wonder you stay so busy."

"It takes significant commitment to stay on top of this market. There seems to be a flood of new talent coming in these days, some with great promise and others nothing more than cover band material. It takes a good eye for talent to pick the best of the crop, and I've got a good track record I intend to maintain."

"Do you promote one more than another? I mean, more bands or songwriters or a mixture?" Cedra asked.

"I'm always on the lookout for both, but a good writer is priceless in this town. It doesn't take a genius to play the guitar, but the songwriting is an entirely different skill set. Any good musician can add music to lyrics, but not every musician can write a great song."

"I can feel your passion for what you do. It's not unlike how writing feels to me," Cedra admitted.

"If the song that Juliet sang was a prime example of your writing, then yes, I can agree to that. I'm betting that it is."

The door opened, and a large group of men entered. Cedra tore off the ticket for Carrie. "It looks like you weren't the only one out for a late lunch. Thanks for the pie. If you need anything else, just catch me."

"Thank you, Cedra. It is always a pleasure to share your company."

†

Juliet had the luxury of sleeping in and took full advantage of the opportunity. She climbed out of Cedra's bed at ten and headed for the shower. After dressing, she made the bed and went downstairs.

Ma was on the front porch still sipping coffee when Juliet peeked her head out to find her.

"Good morning, sleepyhead. I'm glad you finally made it up. I was beginning to get worried."

"No need to worry, Ma," Juliet replied. "I was more tired than I thought, and it sure felt nice to sleep in." She leaned against the doorframe.

"Are you hungry? I can whip you up some breakfast," Ma offered.

"No, I think I'm good for now. I may rustle up some leftovers for lunch in a bit."

"Grab a cup of coffee and join me on the porch then. Here, you can bring me another cup, too," she said, reaching her cup out to Juliet.

Juliet smiled as she took the offering. "I'll be right back."

Ma kept rocking and began humming a tune.

Juliet poured two cups of coffee and added an extra spoon of sugar into her cup. She needed a quick energy boost. Even though she had slept for hours, she still felt tired. That wasn't like her at all. She could usually go for hours on minimal sleep. Did she overdose on rest? *Naw, I'm just feeling a lazy day.* She picked up the coffee and walked to the porch.

"Here you go, Ma."

"Thanks, sweetie. You must have needed the sleep."

Juliet ran her hand through her damp hair. "I think I may have gotten too much. I feel like I could go back to sleep even now."

"Are you coming down with something?" Ma asked.

"Lord, I hope not. I mean, I don't feel bad. I'm just tired."

"Maybe just adjusting from being on the road a few days?" Ma suggested. "Do you have anything to do today?"

Juliet smiled. "Nothing at all. Tomorrow, I'm playing some studio backups, but nothing today."

"Just relax then and enjoy a day off," Ma suggested. "How did last night go with Cedra?"

"It was wonderful," Juliet said. "I slept like a baby and barely remembered her leaving this morning."

"She had a beautiful glow about her, even at that time of day. She came downstairs and began scribbling away in that book of hers." Ma chuckled. "She didn't even break for a sip of coffee, and I had to shoo her out of here before she was late for work."

"She's working on a new song but won't even let me take a peek at it yet."

"Give her time to finish it. I'm sure it will be worth the wait."

Juliet took a sip of coffee. "I'm sure it will be, Ma. She's incredibly talented."

"I know you've got a blossoming solo career going. Are you going to be okay with the band idea?" Ma asked. "You have more to sacrifice than anyone so far."

"I'm not thrilled being on my own, and I feel at peace with Cedra and the boys. It's like my spirit comes alive when we play together."

"That's so good to hear. You all sound great together. I think the chemistry between you will only make success an easier road to travel."

"You won't rent out our rooms if we manage to go on the road, will you? As long as we keep ya paid up?"

"This is your home until you decide it's not," Ma said. "You will always be welcome under this roof no matter how rich and famous y'all become."

"That's good to know. I feel like this place has allowed my roots to spread and grow. It feels like home."

"I hope it will always feel that way for you. I've enjoyed having the bunch of y'all living here. I've had plenty of boarders, but never a group as we have now. I'd be proud to call you my kids, and when people ask, I'm going to claim every one of you."

Juliet broke out laughing. "I can't wait to see those faces. None of us look at all alike."

"Doesn't matter. I'm still claiming you." Ma chuckled. They fell silent for a few minutes, enjoying the peaceful day together.

"Is there anything you need me to do around here today?" Juliet asked.

"Funny you should ask. I was thinking about picking up some pecans out back and shelling them to make a pie this week. Are you up to helping an old woman out?"

"No, but I'll help you out. You're no old woman, Ma."

"I feel like it some days, especially as the seasons start to change. These old bones get stiffer than they used to," Ma replied. "Why don't you heat some lasagna up, and we can harvest some pecans after your meal has settled?"

"Will you join me for leftovers?"

"Don't mind if I do. I've got chicken ready to go in the oven for dinner tonight with a fresh tossed salad and some veggies as well."

"That sounds delicious, Ma. I'll go in and preheat the oven. Your lasagna is too good to heat in a microwave."

"Okay, I'll hold down the fort. Just holler when you're all set."

†

Cedra walked over to welcome the group and took their drink orders. Stone assisted her with the customers, and Carrie slipped out while Cedra was at the kitchen window placing orders. When the group of men finished eating and left, the evening shift came on, and Lisa Marie called Stone and Cedra to her office.

"You two had a significant shift. Here are your tips from the customers who cashed out while you were busy." She handed a pile of bills to each of them.

Stone's eyes grew wide. "This is all mine?"

"Yes, Stone, it is. You had a wonderful first day," Lisa Marie said.

"I can fill my truck up with gas and still have money left." He grinned.

"Don't spend it all in one place. We'll see you again in the morning," Lisa Marie said, permitting him to leave the office.

"Thanks. I'll see you tomorrow then. Thanks for showing me the ropes, Cedra."

"My pleasure. You did a great job. Have a good night. I'll bring you directions to Ma's tomorrow."

"Goodnight, ladies."

Cedra watched him leave and then turned to Lisa Marie, smiling broadly.

"Well, spill it."

"Carrie has already scheduled a meeting for me the Monday after the show for three, so I'll need to leave early to go home and change."

156

"That sounds very promising. Do you want to take the day off?"

"No. I think I'd just be a bundle of nerves if I didn't stay busy."

"I'll ask one of the evening shift crew to come in at twelve. That should give you plenty of time. I am so excited for you."

"Don't be just yet. I'm sure it's just an introductory meeting, but Carrie did say that other agents would also be in the audience and that there was a buzz going around about me. I don't know where that came from, but it surprised me."

"Don't sell yourself short or your talent. You've got eyes and ears all around you, and I'm sure Wayne and Keith have been doing a bit of bragging about you."

"I told her I had a surprise planned for the performance but didn't tell her what it was. She did warn me not to let it backfire on me, though. Do you think I'm making a mistake by bringing the others into my performance?"

Lisa Marie smiled warmly. "What does your heart tell you?"

"That it's the right thing to do. To show the variety of my songs and showcase the group's talent. We've decided to form a band called The Bentleys after Ma, and are considering asking Stone to join us."

Lisa Marie clapped her hands. "I think that's a wonderful plan, and he'd be a great addition."

"We've invited him out to supper tomorrow night to discuss it, and Ma said he can park his truck on the side property so he'd truly be a Bentley too."

"That is such exciting news. I'm happy to hear that, and I don't think it will be a mistake, especially since you know other agents are in the house. Carrie's the best, but she's not the only good agent in town. Make her work for you."

"What if she's not interested in a group?"

"If the group is what you want, you hold your ground. All or nothing, but that could eliminate a solo career for you. Are you ready for that?"

"Yes, I think I am. If things don't work out as planned, I can go my own way."

"But maybe not with the advantage you have right now. Give it some deep thought before you meet with Carrie. Dedication and friendship are important, but you have to look out for your career, too."

Cedra let Lisa Marie's words sink in for several long seconds. "I reckon I better to get to thinking then. Thank you for the advice. I know you've been around here much longer than me."

"Whatever you decide, leave it on good terms with Carrie. She's a powerful woman in the field right now, and you wouldn't want her as an enemy," Lisa Marie said.

"That, I understand completely." Cedra smiled and stood to leave. "I'll see you in the morning."

†

Cedra left and drove home with mixed feelings of excitement and apprehension. How much did she tell the others about her conversation with Carrie? She had always believed in being open and honest with people, so she decided this wouldn't be any different. Her heart skipped a beat when she pulled into the driveway and saw Juliet's car. She parked and took her songbook and travel mug inside.

The house was eerily quiet, which Cedra found strange. Ma was generally on the porch or in the kitchen when she got home from work. She placed her empty travel mug on the counter and laid her songbook on the table before climbing the stairs. There was no sign of Juliet in her room, and it was just as quiet. She looked out her window to confirm Juliet's car was in the drive, and it was right there beside her truck. She went back downstairs and walked toward the laundry room. That's when she heard the beautiful sound of laughter coming from the backyard. She peered out the back door and saw Juliet throwing a handful of colorful leaves at Ma. She stood there for several minutes, watching the two of them play in the leaves like children on a lovely early fall day. Cedra opened the back door and stepped out on the porch without either of them noticing.

"What on earth has gotten into y'all?" she asked as she walked towards them.

"Oh, hey, Cedra," Juliet said. "Ma and I were picking up pecans for a pie when all these wonderful leaves just got the better of us." Juliet was still breathing hard from laughing. She fell to the ground beside Ma.

"Welcome home," Ma said from her spot on the ground. "Did you have a good day at work?"

"Busier than a one-armed paper hanger, but it was a good day. I was worried when I came home and couldn't find you all, but it looks like you've been having fun."

"We did harvest some nuts," Ma said as she pointed to the nearly full bucket. "I'm not sure it will be enough, but our inner children took over, and these leaves were just too tempting."

"So, I see," Cedra said and plucked a colorful leaf from Ma's hair. "There's nothing wrong with having some fun. I think we should all play more." She took a seat on the ground next to Ma then flinched. She reached under her hip

159

and pulled out a large nut. "I think you missed one," she said and tossed it into the bucket.

"I think we missed a bunch, but there's still daylight left," Juliet said.

"That's true. It might make it easier to find the nuts if you raked the leaves into a pile," Cedra suggested. "Then you would have a big pile of leaves to play in," she grinned.

"Are you volunteering for the raking?" Ma asked.

Cedra nodded. "Just point me to a rake, and I'll rake while y'all pick up nuts."

"I'll run get it," Juliet said. She stopped next to Cedra and bent down to kiss her. "Welcome home."

"Thanks, sweetie," Cedra replied as Juliet took off.

"Y'all been at this long?" Cedra asked Ma.

"Only an hour or so. Juliet was dragging when she first woke up, but I think she's gotten her second wind. Why don't you rake for a bit and then take a nap? I know you probably didn't get much sleep last night."

"That is the best idea I've heard all day," Cedra replied.

"Once we get enough nuts, we can start shelling while you rest."

"You have a deal, Ma," Cedra replied and stood to offer a hand to pull Ma up.

†

Stone survived his second day at the café, and when he pulled into the yard at Ma's, they were all sitting on the porch practicing "Backwoods Boogie." They continued to play as he took a seat on the steps to listen. Stone admired how the four of them played together, and the harmonies were perfect. He had never met any of them other than

Cedra, and he was impressed by their sound together. When the last chord ended, Cedra looked over at him.

"You guys sound amazing. That's got an authentic rockabilly feel to it. One of yours?" he asked Cedra.

Cedra nodded. "The lyrics are mine, but the music is ours. Wayne and Keith put the sound together. I'm glad you liked it."

"Have you played it to anyone live yet?" Stone asked.

"Nope, but we plan to introduce it next week at Wild Bill's," Keith answered quickly. "Juliet's got an hour slot on Thursday that she's going to share with us."

"I will plan on being there to listen," Stone said.

Juliet nodded to Cedra.

"I have to confess to you, Stone, that's part of the reason we wanted you to come out for supper tonight. We are forming a band called The Bentleys, 'cause we all live and met here, and we wanted to see if you'd be interested in joining us."

Stone felt his mouth open and his jaw drop. "Are you serious?"

Cedra nodded. "We thought it would be good to add a second songwriter and musician to the group."

"But I don't live here with y'all," Stone stammered.

"Ma came up with the perfect solution for that," Wayne said. "She reckons you could park beside the house and come in for meals, showers, and such."

"Then you would be a Bentley, and you could carpool with me to work," Cedra added.

"Wow, you've got it all thought out, don't you?" Stone smiled.

"All we need is an answer from you," Juliet replied.

"You've never even heard me play a lick," Stone replied.

"Ma and Cedra have, and that's proof enough for me. Give it a go if you are up to it," Juliet said and handed him her guitar.

Stone took the instrument from Juliet and let his fingers caress the strings for a few seconds.

Then he began singing one of the songs Cedra recognized from his Open Mic performance and gave him a smile of encouragement. She looked at the faces of her friends and watched their smiles blossom as Stone's voice showed a range of skill. Again, listening to his voice left Cedra confident that he would be a welcome addition to the group.

When Stone finished the song, he handed Juliet back her guitar. "Do you think I'd blend in with you guys?"

Ma was standing in the doorway listening as Stone played. "I think it would be a win-win all the way around. You'd have two strong songwriters, some excellent musicians, and voices together. Solo, each of you could make it in time, but I believe a band is a way you should go. Just my two cents."

"Your two cents are always valuable, Ma," Juliet said. "Think about it if you need. We will continue with or without you."

"I always think you make the best decisions on a full stomach, so take a break and come eat. You can get back to jamming after," Ma instructed.

"You don't have to ask me twice," Keith said. "I'm Keith, by the way." He shook Stone's hand and headed for the kitchen.

"I'm Wayne, and this is Juliet," Wayne said as he held the door for them. "Welcome to Ma's."

Cedra directed Stone to a chair beside Keith. "What do you need help with, Ma?"

"You can grab the bowl of biscuits, and I'll bring the pitcher of tea," Ma answered as she wiped her hands on a dishtowel and tossed it on the counter.

"Ma, this looks delicious, and it's the first real home cooking I've had in months," Stone said.

Ma settled in a seat beside him. "Eat until your heart's content. Just go light on the fried okra. Cedra always likes finishing it off." Ma chuckled.

"I don't think anyone will go hungry tonight, Ma," Juliet said as she took a spoon of the creamed corn. "Is that pecan pie I smell cooling on the counter?"

"Yes, it is. I had enough nuts for two pies. One for Keith and one for the rest of us," Ma teased.

"Oh, heck yeah," Keith grinned at Ma. "Are there still nuts on the ground? If so, I'll harvest them as long as you keep making pies."

"This is all so wonderful," Stone said. "Do y'all always eat this good?"

Cedra nodded to him. "Pretty much. Ma feeds us well."

"I pay a hundred fifty a month to park at the campground. How much more would I need to park here?" Stone asked between mouthfuls.

"Just kick in for some groceries from time to time," Ma said. "If you want a special meal, you buy the fixins, and we cook it up."

"I can grill a mean steak and BBQ chicken if you've got a grill," Stone offered. "I'm not that great in the kitchen, though."

"We all pitch in for cleanup and if vegetables need shelling or peeling. I'm sure we can teach you that," Keith teased.

"That, I think I can handle," Stone replied with a smile.

After the meal, everyone pitched in to clean up while Stone and Ma chatted on the porch. Stone would plan to move at the end of the month. "Are you sure I won't be an inconvenience?" he asked.

"The more, the merrier. We will just need to coordinate shower schedules with the boys, but it will all work out. I'm so happy you are joining us," Ma said.

"I like the idea of working with a band. I've played some backup music, but that's about all since I've been here. I miss playing."

"What are your favorite instruments?" Ma asked.

"Drums, fiddle, and guitar," Stone replied. "I don't have room for my drum set in the truck, so it's the guitar for now."

"Drums are easy enough to rent. Most studios have them already set up for artists who don't own a set. Don't fret over that."

Juliet and Cedra were the first to join them. "Do you want to stay and jam with us for a while?" Juliet asked.

"I'd love to," Stone answered.

"Here, you can have my copies of the songs we will be playing at the Wild Horse. We will also perform the one you heard us playing with Cedra at her Open Mic," Juliet said as she handed him a clipboard.

164

"You can use my guitar," Cedra offered.

"No need. I'll be right back." Stone left the porch and jogged to his truck.

"He's planning on moving out on the first," Ma told them while he was out of range. "He seems very excited."

"He's got a nice voice," Juliet replied.

Wayne and Keith returned from the kitchen and took their seats. "Can we jam for a bit and then take a break for some pie?" Keith asked.

Ma chuckled. "I swear you've got the worst sweet tooth I've ever seen."

"I can't help it, Ma. Your baking is just too good." Keith grinned back at her.

"Do we want to take another run at 'Backwoods Boogie' before going down the list?" Juliet asked.

"That's fine by me," Wayne said.

"What if we add another instrument to it?" Stone asked. "I have a fiddle we could add to the mix."

"Hell yeah, go get it, man," Wayne responded.

Stone rushed back to his truck to retrieve the instrument. "A fiddle will add some depth to our music," Keith grinned. "I've always wanted to cover "The Devil Went Down to Georgia" but I can't play a fiddle."

"No need to now. We can take a run at it tonight if Stone knows it," Juliet replied.

"What country boy wouldn't know it?" Wayne teased. "Hey, Stone, can you play "The Devil Went Down to Georgia"?"

"Hell yeah, I think that's a requirement for playing a fiddle," Stone shot back.

"Great, we'll give it a shot after the next song," Juliet said.

Ma sat in her chair and listened to the beautiful sounds as she rocked in time with the music. When one song ended, she opened her eyes and looked around at them. "The harmony on that was exceptional," she praised. "I'll head in and brew a pot of coffee and start serving pie if y'all want to break after the next song." She looked at Keith and Wayne. "Milk for you two?"

"Yes, please, Ma," Keith answered.

"Coffee for us, Ma," Cedra replied.

"Me, too, please," Stone requested.

Ma headed to the kitchen. "Come in when you're ready."

"One more, and then it's pie time," Keith said. "Any preferences?"

"I think Cedra needs another run at that first ballad," Juliet said.

"All right, Cedra, it's on you."

Cedra picked up her guitar and started playing. Her eyes met Juliet's as she began to sing, and she saw a sparkle of excitement in her lover's eyes. Cedra felt a rush of warmth flow through her body and tore her eyes away to make contact with the rest of the group. When she finished, Wayne was the first to respond.

"That was killer eye contact. For a second, I thought you were singing the song to me. We all need to practice that more. I know I have a habit of closing my eyes," Wayne admitted.

"It's easy to get lost in the music," Juliet said, "but it's important to interact with the crowd during live performances."

After storing their instruments, the group walked into the kitchen. Ma was pouring coffee, and two glasses of milk sat on the counter. "Grab those," she instructed Keith. "Cedra can help me bring the coffee."

"Holy crap, I almost forgot something," Juliet said as she went to take a bite. "We can get some studio time on Wednesday night, but it's 9 pm to 11 pm. I know it's late, but will it work for everyone?"

"I work, but I'll see if I can get off early or go in later," Wayne replied.

"I'm good. I have an early shift that day," Keith answered.

"It will be a late night for us, but if we can get a nap in after our morning shifts, we should be good," Cedra said, and looked at Stone for confirmation.

"I'll probably be too excited to nap," Stone admitted.

"I know that feeling, but we need to try so we don't drag on Friday. That's usually a busy day for us at the café," Cedra informed him.

"If we play well, we should be able to cut a few tracks," Juliet said. "All we need to pay for is the cost to burn multiple copies. We'll also need to get some cover shots done."

"I'll check with the guys at the Ryman to see what they'd charge for a photo shoot," Keith said.

"This is all so exciting," Stone replied. "What can I do?"

"Get with Cedra and write us some great songs," Juliet said. "Once we get a photo we all agree on, I'll work on the CD insert. I can start drafting those now on my laptop."

"We are really doing this," Wayne said with a grin.

"Yes, we are," Juliet smiled back at him. "Let's try to get another practice session in later this week if we can."

"How about Saturday afternoon?" Keith asked. "Do you and Stone have to work this Saturday?"

Cedra shrugged. "I don't know. I'll have to check the schedule. If not, we can do Saturday morning."

"All right, just let us know, and we can be ready," Keith said. "It was great meeting you, Stone, and welcome to the band."

"Thanks. It's exciting, and I can't wait to be able to play more with you all," Stone replied. "I'll see you bright and early," he told Cedra as he packed up his instruments.

"Yeah, you will. Goodnight, Stone. I think it's time for me to get some sleep as well. Goodnight, y'all."

Juliet, Wayne, and Keith talked for a few more minutes, making plans for the week. "This is so exciting," Juliet said. "I'll get to work on our CD inserts tomorrow."

"I'll call my friend at the Ryman and see when we can get a photo shoot. Group and individual shots?" Keith asked.

"Yes, I think that would be great. Thanks," Juliet replied.

"What can I do?" Wayne asked.

"Spread the word about our performance next Wednesday to anyone you can. I'd really like a packed audience," Juliet said. "We are going to light the place up." She gave Wayne a high five.

"Amen, sister," Keith said.

"Goodnight, Ma," Juliet said as she passed by the kitchen.

"Goodnight, Juliet. I'll see you tomorrow." Ma smiled as Juliet nodded and headed for the staircase.

Juliet knocked lightly on the door leading to Cedra's room from the bathroom and stepped inside when Cedra called out, "Come in." Cedra was seated at her desk, her songbook open, as Juliet entered the room. Cedra turned to face her, and Juliet planted a soft kiss on her lips.

"You smell delicious," Juliet said. "French vanilla?"

"Yes, a new shampoo," Cedra replied. "Do you like it?"

"It smells lovely. I'm going to take a shower. Will it bother you if I stretch out on your bed to watch you write?"

"I don't know, but we can try it and see. I think I'm getting close on this one. Maybe I'll finish it up tomorrow. Stone and I are planning a writing session after work tomorrow afternoon."

"That's cool. Is Stone coming out here?" Juliet asked.

Cedra nodded. "That would probably be best. What are you planning to do tomorrow?"

"I'm going to town to do some clothes shopping in the morning, but it won't take all day."

"New clothes? That sounds like fun," Cedra replied. "Anything special?"

"I'd like something new for our night at Wild Bill's and then for your Open Mic night. Any suggestions?"

"You look sexy in anything you wear. Just make it something comfortable."

Juliet smiled and kissed her again. "You are so good for my ego. I'll be back shortly."

†

Cedra read over the lines she had written so far and made a few additions while waiting for Juliet to shower. She smiled when she heard Juliet singing the lyrics to one of her songs.

"Damn, Juliet even sounds good in the shower," Cedra said aloud. She flipped the page and looked at the notes she had jotted down earlier in the day. The words perfectly conveyed her emotions during her first time with Juliet. The tenderness and soft kisses and then the fiery passion that had burned so hotly between them. Cedra felt herself grow moist at the memory. She added another line about the sweet anticipation of being together again when she heard the shower turn off. She imagined the towel caressing Juliet's skin as it glided down her body and shivered.

"Girl, you have got it bad." Cedra laughed at her comment then turned to wait for Juliet to enter the room. She felt her breath catch in her chest as Juliet entered, wearing a black tank top and black boi short underwear. *Oh, dear woman, you are killing me.* She smiled as her eyes climbed upward to Juliet's face.

"Do you like what you see?*"* Juliet asked.

"Like, no, love, yes. You are beyond sexy in black, my love," Cedra answered. "You look good in bright colors, too, though. Hell, you look good in everything."

Juliet walked over and stretched out on the bed, tucking an arm under a pillow to prop her head. "Do you know what you will be wearing yet?"

Cedra laughed.

"What's so funny?"

"Do you know how hard it is to think about clothes when I see you so sexy laying there, and all I want to do is get you naked?"

"Focus," Juliet teased. "I'm serious. What will you be wearing?"

"Jeans and boots for sure. I haven't decided on tops yet."

"Would you mind me looking in your closet?" Juliet asked.

"Knock yourself out," Cedra replied and tore her eyes away from Juliet to return to the songbook.

†

Juliet walked over to Cedra's closet and started searching through her wardrobe. She noted the size jeans and shirts Cedra wore with the anticipation of buying her something new. She didn't want them to match, but she did want them to complement each other.

"What is your favorite color?" Juliet asked as she searched through the row of shirts. "I'd guess, blue or green." She chuckled.

"I probably would say blue, but I'm open to any suggestions," Cedra answered.

"You've got a couple of options here I can work with," Juliet said as she rifled through the hangers.

"That's good to know, that I'm not a complete wardrobe failure," Cedra said.

Juliet resumed her position on the bed and watched Cedra scribbling notes onto the pages. She smiled at the intense look of concentration she saw on Cedra's face as she scratched through a line and added another. "Has anyone told you how cute you are when you're writing?"

Cedra looked up from the desk. "What?"

"I asked if anyone has ever told you how cute you are when you're writing?" Juliet repeated. "You get this little wrinkle between your eyes when you're concentrating."

"Oh, stop it," Cedra said and felt a blush rising.

Juliet rolled onto her side. "You don't have a clue of how beautiful and talented you are, do you?"

171

"If you are trying to make me blush, you are succeeding," Cedra answered.

"I'm as serious as you will ever find me," Juliet said. "Cross my heart."

"I don't feel like I'm anything special," Cedra replied. "Just another country bumpkin trying to make it in the big city." She turned toward Juliet.

Juliet sat up quickly on the side of the bed. "Cedra, you are so much more than that. You have a heart of gold that you pour into the words you put on paper, and if you don't make it as a songwriter for some insane reason, you could do modeling." Juliet took her hand. "I'm not saying this just because I'm in love with you. Other's see and feel that way, too. Carrie Brooks nearly goes into heat when she sees you." Juliet laughed softly. "Ma made a mention of that. And all three of the guys can't help but smile when talking to you. Even Stone, a happily married man, lights up when you speak to him."

"I think you are exaggerating quite a bit," Cedra replied.

Juliet rapidly shook her head. "No, if anything, I'm underestimating how people react to you. You've got the 'It' factor, the charisma that people would die to have, and you don't see it in yourself. That's what makes you that much more special."

Cedra reached over and flipped the book closed, then climbed onto the bed next to Juliet.

"You still aren't finished with the new song yet?" Juliet asked.

"Songs. I have two that I'm working on, but neither of them is ready yet. Close, but not finished. I have this beautiful woman stretched out on my bed that is more important than any written word." Cedra leaned over and kissed Juliet.

"You are such a smooth talker," Juliet teased.

"I've been ready to be in your arms all day," Cedra replied. "I miss you during the day, but it's nice to know you will be here when I get home."

"I had fun with Ma today. It was great just to unwind and enjoy a slow-paced day for a change."

"I enjoyed watching the two of you together. The laughter was contagious, so I knew I had to join y'all. The pie was awesome also."

"I don't ever want Ma to think we take her for granted. She's more than just a landlord to us. A surrogate mom and friend as well," Juliet said.

Cedra snuggled in close. "She works hard to keep us all well-fed and on our toes. She makes me feel like she genuinely cares for each of us."

"I wonder if we can talk her into a night on the town when we play at Wild Bill's? She needs more fun time away from here. I know she's already planning to come for your Open Mic," Juliet informed Cedra.

"All we can do is ask. I think Ma would have fun, and she's our number one fan," Cedra whispered against Juliet's neck.

"When we get our group photos done, I want to make her a shirt to wear," Juliet told her. "Maybe get some T-shirts printed, too, for some free advertising."

Cedra's fingers traced the strong muscles of Juliet's right arm. "I sometimes think I am in the middle of a fabulous dream. Things are moving much faster than I imagined they would." She looked into Juliet's eyes and saw a sparkle of excitement in them. "I couldn't ask for better partners in this journey." Her hand slid beneath Juliet's shirt and caressed warm skin as she explored Juliet's body. "I didn't mention this to the boys tonight, but Carrie has an appointment for me for the Monday after my Open Mic." Cedra watched Juliet's eyes fly open.

Juliet lifted Cedra's face to look into her eyes. "That's fantastic news. It sounds like Carrie is very eager to sign you to a contract. Do you still think it wise to join the band? She may only be looking to add a songwriter."

"That won't be the deal. It's all of us or nothing," Cedra boldly stated.

"Oh, sweetie, you need to give that some serious thought. If Carrie only wants you as a writer, that's too good for you to pass up. She's the best in the industry right now."

"I have been thinking about it all day and discussed it with my dad. He advised me to follow my heart in making the decision and agrees that a band is a great idea."

"I can't wait to meet him. Did you invite him for Thanksgiving?"

"I did, and he's tickled to death to meet everyone. He's going to love this place and you." Cedra smiled. "Before you ask, yes, I told him about us. He said he sensed something different and exciting in my voice. He doesn't care who I love as long as they treat me well."

Juliet reached out to trace the line of Cedra's jaw. "That's good to know, and I promise I will always try my best to make you happy."

Cedra took Juliet's hand and brought it to her lips. She kissed her knuckles. "That's all I could ever ask. I know there will be good times and some difficult ones ahead for us, but if we work together, there's not much we can't overcome."

Juliet brushed the hair from Cedra's face. "I just don't want you to pass on something that can be good for you because you feel obligated to the rest of us."

"I am part of 'us,' and if she doesn't want that, then somebody else will. I don't think once she hears us perform, there will be any doubt she won't sign The Bentleys."

Juliet laughed softly. "I love your confidence."

"What's not to like about us? Two quality songwriters, good musicians, and one heck of a sexy lead vocalist. That sounds like a winning combination if I ever heard one."

"Just don't go looking to buy a tour bus yet," Juliet teased.

"Well, darn. I've got my eye on one of those cute VW popup van campers," Cedra replied. "Between that and Stone's truck camper, I reckon we could sleep five."

Juliet pulled away from her. "You're serious, aren't you?"

"Absolutely," Cedra replied with a straight face.

"I love them, but there's no way I'm sleeping in a camper with one or more stinky boys," Juliet said.

"They don't stink," Cedra replied in defense of Keith and Wayne.

"Okay, so you haven't done laundry with them yet or smelled those boots and shoes once they've taken them off. There's not much ventilation in a camper van, and we'd have no private time together."

"We could get one of those signs that say, 'If the trailer's rocking don't come a-knockin' you see in truck stops."

Juliet burst out laughing. "You need to stop this nonsense before I pee myself." She smiled at Cedra. "I can't believe my innocent little Bama girl would say something like that."

"Whoever told you I was innocent?" Cedra said with a raised eyebrow, but she couldn't keep a straight face and started laughing at the expression on Juliet's face.

Juliet moved quickly and rolled Cedra onto her back. "You're a little vixen, huh?" She pinned Cedra beneath her longer body and leaned down to nibble at Cedra's neck.

"You keep making me feel like this, and you can call me a vixen or anything else you want," Cedra replied, followed by a moan.

Their gentle teasing continued until Cedra let out a soft growl and rolled Juliet onto her back. She listened and felt the response of Juliet's body as she mimicked the lovemaking they had shared the night before. Cedra's heart raced each time Juliet's body reacted to her actions, and when she came for the first time with Cedra's fingers deep inside her, Cedra thought she would explode. She kissed her way up Juliet's body and whispered in her ear, "That felt almost as good for me as it did you."

"I can do ya one better," Juliet said, and they made love until they were both exhausted.

Juliet held Cedra in her arms, softly stroking down her side until Cedra drifted off to sleep. She watched her rest for a long time before rolling over to turn out the light. Her eyes fell onto Cedra's songbook, and for a second, Juliet considered opening it to get a peek at Cedra's new work but resisted the urge. When Cedra was ready, she felt sure she would be one of the first to hear the new songs. *I know they will be worth the wait.*

CHAPTER TEN

The rest of the week passed in a whirlwind of activity. Stone and Cedra wrote for a while together during the week, and Keith was able to schedule a photo shoot for Saturday morning, so they pushed the jam session back to Sunday.

The studio session went well, and they cut four tracks that they left with the engineer to tweak and burn into CDs for them. He wouldn't make any promises, but he hoped to have them ready in time for the Wild Bill performance.

When they left the studio that night, they were all feeling the high of the session, and it was hours before Juliet could convince Cedra to get some sleep. They all had a busy weekend planned and needed to get what rest they could.

Ma had accompanied Juliet to town to shop earlier in the week, and they came back with several bags of new clothing. Juliet bought new denim shirts for the guys, a long-sleeved black oxford for herself, and a bright blue one for Cedra. She also purchased a lightweight red sweater for Cedra to wear for her Open Mic event. Red was a power color, and Juliet was confident Cedra would look terrific wearing the gift. She bought a similar sweater for Ma in a bright orange, which she found was Ma's favorite color.

Cedra and Ma spent hours Friday night ironing outfits for each of them to wear the following day for the session. Even Juliet caved when Cedra asked her what jeans she planned on wearing.

"I swear you're going to ruin my image," Juliet complained, but handed her the newest pair she owned with a grin.

Ma placed towels around the boy's necks Saturday morning so that they wouldn't spill food and ruin her and Cedra's hard work. Even Stone complied with Ma's request.

"I can't wait to see these photographs. You all are a handsome group," Ma told them after breakfast before they piled into two trucks and headed to the Ryman.

†

Ma had a plan of her own, and after cleaning up the kitchen, she got in her car and headed to town. She had bought a gift she would give to the kids before Wednesday's performance. It wasn't much, but she wanted them to know how proud she was of them. She would cook an early meal Wednesday and give it to them then.

†

The photographer started with group shots and then took many photos of each individually. When he felt like he

178

had a variety to choose from, he called them all together around a large computer screen. He popped the memory card from his camera and slipped it inside his computer.

"Damn, we do look good together," Wayne said as they scrolled through the various group photos. "Hey, can you Photoshop me and make me a few inches taller?" Wayne joked.

"I'm good, but I can't work miracles," the photographer replied, and the group broke out in laughter.

"These look great, Chuck," Keith told his friend when they got to the individual shots. He looked at Juliet and Cedra. "Do we have what we need?"

"Yeah, we have plenty of great shots to work with," Juliet answered. "Thanks, Chuck."

"When you burn your first CD, be sure to send me a copy," Chuck said.

"You will have it soon, we hope," Cedra answered.

"I'm going to try to sneak into Wild Bill's to get some live shots of y'all performing, and I will be at your Open Mic night," he told Cedra. "I hear so many good things about you from Keith. Maybe one day soon you'll be performing here."

"One day we hope to," Juliet said. "We'll just have to take one step at a time."

Chuck popped out a memory stick and handed it to Juliet. "Let me know if you need any help with formats or anything else."

"Thanks, Chuck. We appreciate everything you're doing for us."

"Just get out there and break a leg, guys, so I can say I knew them when." Chuck grinned. "Good luck."

When they arrived home, Juliet asked, "Do we still have some time to jam for a bit before you guys go to work?"

"Yeah, but let's get out of these nice clothes so we can have them ready for next week," Keith said.

"Go change and bring them back down. I'll do the laundry and get the outfits pressed for next week," Ma told them. "You, too." She grinned at Stone, who laughed and ran out to his truck to change.

Ma made sandwiches while the band played on the front porch. When she carried out the plate filled with sandwiches and a bag of chips, she arrived just in time to hear Cedra make a request.

"I've been working on something new that I'd like to share with y'all. Initially, I wanted to use it for the Open Mic night, but I think it would be better with multiple voices."

"Holy crap, is this the one you've been hiding all week?" Juliet asked.

Cedra nodded. "One of them, yes."

"Do you want to take a food break or sing first?" Ma asked.

"It will wait a few more minutes. My stomach has been growling for an hour," Cedra replied.

"You and you," Ma pointed to Keith and Wayne, "come help me with tea."

"Right behind you, Ma," Wayne said and followed her into the kitchen.

"Are you going to share the other one, too?" Stone asked.

"I want to share that one with Juliet first," Cedra replied.

Stone looked at Juliet. "You're going to love it."

"So, you've already seen them?" Juliet protested.

"Not the first one," Stone replied and held his hands up in mock surrender. "She wouldn't even let me peek at that one."

Ma and the boys had returned with drinks. "That's because I got the idea for the song during our conversation the first night we met," Cedra told Stone. "It's been driving me crazy since."

"This is going to be interesting," Keith said and bit into a sandwich.

"I think you'll like it. I had each one of us in mind as I wrote it. That's why I think it needs all our voices." Cedra looked at her friends. "It's our song."

"Does it have a name?" Ma asked.

Cedra nodded. "Six Strings and a Dream."

"Forget the sandwiches. I need to hear this now," Juliet said. "Please?"

"Y'all keep eating, just make them save me some, Ma," Cedra said as she picked up her guitar and opened the songbook beside her. "I don't know if you remember telling Ma and me that you hoped to write the perfect song to help you get started in the business?" she asked Stone.

"That sounds like something I would have said," Stone replied.

"Well, it got me thinking about why we all come to Nashville. Not just us, but all the dreamers who hope to make it big. So, this is what I came up with."

Cedra began playing, and for each verse, she looked at the person she had written it for, and she felt the connection with them grow ever deeper as her words spilled into their hearts. When she finished, no one was eating. They were all just staring at her.

"I don't know if this is a good reaction from y'all or you think it's a piece of crap," she finally said.

Juliet swallowed the bite she had been holding in her mouth. "Do you not honestly know how good that is? Big names will be fighting over the right to sing this."

"You've hit it beautifully on the head," Wayne said. "You took a bit of each of us and blended it into the perfect country song. I don't know any artist that wouldn't connect their struggles with those lyrics."

"Will you sing it one more time, just like that?" Keith asked.

Cedra nodded and repeated the song.

Keith smiled. "I'm not sold that it needs our voices. You sing it so perfectly."

"I think you should lead off your Open Mic with that," Juliet said. "Then, if everything goes well and we can get more studio time, we can record it as a group."

Cedra nodded. "I'll make some copies of it for y'all after work. Now pass those sandwiches."

Ma handed her a glass of tea, and Cedra could see tears in her eyes. "That was so beautiful. I am so proud of you, all of you, for what you are doing. I couldn't be prouder if you were my own."

Juliet smiled as she passed the plate to Cedra. "We are yours, Ma. We're The Bentleys."

Ma wiped her eyes and continued smiling until the group broke up for the day. "Thursday night, I want you all back here by five for dinner before the show," she said, then walked back into the house.

"We'd better get a move on before we're late. That was a great session, guys," Keith said. "Beautiful song, Cedra."

"Thanks," Cedra replied.

"I'm going to mosey on, too, and try to get some writing in. I'll see you in the morning," Stone said.

"Yes, you will," Cedra answered.

"Bye, Stone," Juliet said with a smile.

After everyone had left them sitting on the porch, Juliet looked at Cedra. "That just leaves us. What do you want to do?"

"I want to go watch the sunset with you," Cedra answered. "Take your guitar up and meet me at my truck."

"Do you want me to take yours up?" Juliet asked as she picked up her instrument.

"No, it's going with us. I have one more song to sing for you tonight."

"I'll be right back then." Juliet rushed inside the house while Cedra took her case and songbook to the truck.

When Juliet returned and climbed inside the truck, she looked at Cedra. "Do you remember how to get there?"

"I think so." Cedra grinned and put the truck in gear. When they arrived at the bluff, Cedra backed into position. "Drop the tailgate for me if you will, please."

Juliet raced to the back of the truck and dropped the tailgate as requested. She held Cedra's guitar while she took a seat and then sat beside her as the sun was quickly fading. Cedra picked up her songbook, opened it to the last page, and handed it to Juliet.

"You don't need it?" Juliet asked.

"Nope. I've got it right here," Cedra replied and tapped her chest above her heart. "This song is how I felt when I found love for the first time with you."

Juliet swallowed hard as she watched Cedra begin to play. The words rolled off her tongue like the sweetest love song Juliet had ever heard, and she felt the tears rolling down her cheeks as Cedra sang directly to her from her heart. Juliet placed the songbook beside her. Tears blurred her vision too much to read along anyhow, and she smiled as Cedra finished the song.

"That couldn't explain our love any more perfectly," she finally said when Cedra looked to her for approval. "Thank you for playing it for me first. I would have been blubbering like a baby in front of the others."

"Do you think we can sing this together?" Cedra asked.

"Eventually, yes, but I'm not sure I can do it right now. I'd like to maybe take a run at it in the studio first before we try it live."

Cedra nodded and put her guitar back in the case. "I can live with that."

"I need to be able to contain my emotions before singing it in front of a crowd," Juliet explained. "It will always be our song, but it's too good not to share. Just not yet, anyhow."

"I can understand that," Cedra replied as she scooted closer to Juliet. "A beautiful sunset to finish off a great day," she said, and sighed before leaning into Juliet.

Juliet wrapped an arm around her. "With a beautiful love to share it with."

They sat in silence as the sun disappeared beyond the horizon, and then Cedra turned her head up for a kiss. Juliet lowered her face to Cedra's and stopped just inches from her lips. "I do love you."

"I know you do," Cedra replied and pulled Juliet down to meet her lips.

Once the darkness surrounded them, they started for home. Ma would have supper ready, and they didn't want to make her wait. Juliet held Cedra's hand as she drove them home. "I think I'd like to work on the CD covers a bit more tonight, now that we have photographs. Do you think you and Ma could help me with some selections so I can make some drafts for all of us to review?"

"I'd like that, and I bet Ma would, too," Cedra replied.

"I hope Ma didn't go out of her way to cook since it's just the three of us tonight," Juliet said.

"Why don't you call and see what she has planned. We could always pick something up to bring home," Cedra suggested. "Maybe some BBQ or pizza."

Juliet pulled out her phone and had a short conversation with Ma. "She's planning on breakfast, but she would eat some brisket if we brought it home."

"That makes it easy. Will you call us in an order? I'd like brisket, too, with fries and beans," Cedra replied. "A large portion of brisket. I'm hungry."

Juliet smiled and called in their order and added three ears of corn. She ended the call and slid her hand into Cedra's. "It will be ready by the time we get there."

"Thank you for ordering. This meal is on me," Cedra replied.

"I won't argue with you, especially since I didn't bring my wallet," Juliet chuckled. "I was in such a hurry to get back to you, I didn't think to grab it."

"Keep the truck running, I'll grab dinner, and we can be on our way," Juliet said as she took the cash Cedra pulled from her wallet. "I'll be right back." Juliet turned back for a quick kiss.

Juliet returned carrying a large bag of food and climbed into the truck.

"Man, that smells good," Cedra commented.

"I know, so let's get home quick." Juliet grinned. "Remind me to give you your change later."

"No worries," Cedra replied and pulled into traffic. "We are going to eat good tonight."

"Yes, we are. Too bad the boys had to work. I bet they'll eat something good tonight too." Juliet chuckled. "Neither of them will skip a meal for sure."

When they pulled into the drive, Cedra looked at Juliet. "You take the food, and I'll bring my stuff." Cedra parked, and they climbed out of the truck.

When Juliet opened the door for them, she took a deep breath. "All right, Ma made brownies," she told Cedra. "I hope she had some pecans left."

"I surely did," Ma answered from the kitchen. "I've already got fine China out," she said, motioning to the paper plates and a roll of paper towels on the table. "What do you two want to drink?"

"I think I'll have more of your tea, Ma. It's the best around," Juliet praised.

"I'll second that and have some too," Cedra said with her eyes sparkling with excitement. "It has been pure misery driving home smelling this food. If it tastes even half as good as it smells, we're in for a treat."

"Then brownies for dessert." Juliet grinned as she unloaded the bag of food. "If we aren't comatose after dinner, Cedra and I wanted to know if you'd help us work on the CD cover."

"I don't know anything about making those," Ma replied.

"We just need your help to pick out the best photos to use," Cedra replied. "Juliet wants to have several for the boys to choose from."

"That I know I can do." Ma chuckled and carried the tea glasses to the table.

Ma opened her carryout container. "Someone must have been hungry when they ordered. I could never eat all this food."

"I know two young men who will raid the refrigerators for leftovers," Juliet said as she removed the foil from her corn. "Nothing ever goes to waste with those two around."

"They have healthy appetites, but you know they never gain weight, unlike me. I'll gain a pound just looking at all this," Ma grumbled.

"No way, Ma. We'll harvest more pecans tomorrow and burn this right off ya," Juliet promised.

"Those pies were delicious. Maybe I'll make more for dinner Thursday before your show," Ma suggested.

"Your pies are always welcome, Ma." Juliet passed Cedra the salt and pepper.

Cedra was still chewing a bite but quickly swallowed. "This is so tender. You hardly have to chew."

"I love how they add the burnt bits into the beans," Juliet said and then took a bite.

"That adds to the flavor," Ma replied. "Some folks would just toss those out as waste, but they really perk up baked beans."

Ma looked at her plate and then at Cedra's at the end of the meal. "I think we could have shared one. But, as you said, it won't go to waste."

"I guess I was a piglet," Juliet replied as she looked down at her plate. "It sure was good. Thank you, Cedra."

"My pleasure," Cedra replied. "I'll combine our two boxes Ma, while Juliet finishes."

"You can add my beans. I can't eat anymore," Juliet groaned. "Do you want to work a bit before brownies?"

"Good Lord, you're getting as bad as Keith," Cedra chuckled. "I couldn't eat a bite right now."

"That's just because you don't know how good Ma's brownies are." Juliet shot a wink to Ma. "We can wait, though. I'm going to get my laptop. Do you want me to take your stuff up as I go?"

"Thanks. That would be great." Cedra put away the remaining food. "Do you want some coffee, Ma?"

"I was thinking about it. Will you join me?"

"Sure will. Sit tight, and I'll start a pot." Cedra was filling the pot as Juliet came bounding down the stairs. "I'm making coffee. Do you want some?"

"Sure," Juliet replied. She placed her laptop on the table between Cedra and Ma and took a seat. "Ma, do you have a notepad and pen handy?"

"Sure do. There's one in the drawer under the phone."

Juliet retrieved the items and handed them to Cedra. "You are the writer of this bunch. We need to come up with some bios for the band," Juliet explained to them.

"Got it. I think," Cedra said. "Let's start with names. I know your full name, but I don't know Keith's or Wayne's."

Juliet frowned and looked to Ma for help.

Ma chuckled, "I got this. Keith's last name is Champion, from Lexington, Kentucky. Butler is Wayne's last name, and he's from Franklin, North Carolina."

"See, you're helping already. I wouldn't have had a clue," Cedra replied. "Stone Watson, and he's from Ocala, Florida. There, we're done, Ma," Cedra joked.

"Nope, we need to describe the roles they play in the band. For instance, you and Stone are songwriters, the instruments you play and vocals. Do that for each of us," Juliet said. "While you're thinking about that, take a look at these group shots."

"Oh, I like that one," Ma said, pointing out an image on the screen. "This one too," she added.

"They are all good. I agree with Ma's first pick, too. What about you?" she asked Juliet.

"I like those two and this one," Juliet replied, adding a third photo to the mix. "Let me add some text, and then we can see what all three look like," Juliet replied. "Keep working on the bios."

"Yes, boss," Cedra chuckled. "Let's see. I play guitar and piano. Should I just say keyboards?" she asked Juliet.

"Yeah, that sounds good," Juliet replied.

"Wayne plays guitar and drums. Keith, guitar and banjo. Stone, guitar, drums, and fiddle. What about you? Guitar and...?" she asked Juliet.

"I can play a mean harmonica," Juliet replied.

"Really? So, why haven't you played it?" Ma asked.

"There's not much call for a harmonica in today's country music," Juliet replied.

"That's true. I can't think of a song in the last few years that has harmonica music in it," Cedra replied. "It's a shame. That's a beautiful sound."

"Maybe if y'all get into a little Blue Grass, you could play some," Ma suggested. "Maybe some of the old cover tunes."

"That's a good idea, Ma," Juliet said. "What do y'all think about these?" Juliet turned the computer around so they could see the screen. She scrolled through three options for CD covers.

"I like what you've done so far," Ma said.

"I feel a 'but' coming on. What is it missing?" Juliet asked.

"A title," Ma replied. "How many tracks were you able to cut in the studio?"

"Four so far," Juliet answered.

"How many before you could put out a full CD?" Ma asked.

Juliet looked at Cedra. "At least ten, twelve would probably be better. What's your thought, Cedra?"

"I think a solid dozen. What are you thinking, Ma?" Cedra asked.

"What if you held off until you have a full CD to release, and you call it *Six Strings and a Dream?*"

Juliet's eyes lit up. "I love that idea, Ma. It may take us some time to record eight more tracks, though."

Ma shrugged her shoulders. "Why not wait to see what Carrie Brooks has to say before you release any recordings? Getting studio time wouldn't be an issue if she chooses to sign with you. I know that just in Cedra's songbook you have enough songs to record eight more, and you've barely gotten a taste of Stone's writing."

"That does make sense. Carrie could propel us forward much faster, and she'd eat the studio and production costs," Cedra replied.

Juliet's fingers flew across the keys as she typed the title of the CD at the bottom of the photograph. "Something like this?"

"Yes, use that for the front jacket and use this setup for the back jacket with a list of the songs," Cedra suggested.

Juliet added the four titles they had already cut to the list, put "Six Strings and a Dream" as number five, and then entered seven more blank lines. "All we need to do is select the next seven. I believe we can easily do that if each of us takes a favorite song to highlight individual talent."

"For certain, the one song from Stone's Open Mic. That was so good. Sorry, I don't remember the name," Ma said.

"I like the idea. Even if we don't get signed right away, we can do this on our own and hit the streets hard to market it to the local and national radio stations," Juliet said.

"We could get into the rotation at the Iron Horse to help pay for the production costs. I think with five of us working together, we could make that work," Cedra replied.

"That's a lot of pickle jars full of tips," Juliet joked. "I have a good feeling about us, though. We just need to showcase our talents well."

Cedra looked at Ma and then Juliet. "I didn't mention this around the others because I didn't want to get them nervous, but Carrie told me several other agents are planning to attend the Open Mic night. So at least we might generate some competition. I think that's why Carrie wanted to get an appointment set up early. She didn't want to get scooped."

"That's good to know," Juliet said. "If we can pack that place and the crowd likes what they hear, it will be a big plus."

"It seems like Carrie is very interested, and that can only work in your favor," Ma said.

"I'll check with Lisa Marie in the morning and see if we can do some word-of-mouth advertising. I'm sure she wouldn't mind the extra business," Cedra said.

"Speaking of tomorrow, it's getting late," Ma said. "Time for me to get up to my bed. You two enjoy the brownies and milk and then get some rest. The next week is going to be hectic."

"Dang, I had forgotten about the brownies," Cedra said.

"I haven't. I'll pour the milk if you cut a nice piece. Are you sure you won't have one with us, Ma? You know the pan will be empty in the morning."

"Lordy, I'm still stuffed from dinner. Eat what you can. Wayne and Keith will take care of the rest. Goodnight, ladies."

"Goodnight, Ma," Juliet answered.

"Thanks again for a great dinner, Cedra."

"My pleasure Ma. I'll see you bright and early." She turned to Juliet. "Corner or edge for you?" Cedra asked.

"Both," Juliet replied.

Cedra cut a corner for herself and a large slice with an edge and middle for Juliet.

"That looks perfect," Juliet said as she sat beside Cedra. She raised her milk glass. "Cheers."

Cedra laughed and picked up her glass. "Cheers."

"Oh, my goodness. These get better each time Ma makes them," Juliet said and moaned after taking another bite. "You know we could take the rest of the pan upstairs, and the boys would be none the wiser."

"Would you do that?" Cedra asked.

"I'll admit to being tempted, but no, I couldn't do that to them," Juliet admitted. "Do you have some ideas for the other songs for an album?"

"We can scan through the songbook and see if we can select a few more. Stone has several excellent songs too. What about you and the boys?"

"Nothing of the quality we need for an album," Juliet said. "We'll be leaning heavily on you and Stone for that."

"Maybe you and I can work on some together in the future. I want to write something for that harmonica of yours," Cedra teased.

Juliet nodded and took another bite of brownie. "I think we could come up with something with harmonica, banjo, and fiddle."

"I do, too," Cedra replied as she rinsed her glass and put it in the dishwasher. "Are you done or going for seconds?"

"It's tempting, but I think I'll stop here," Juliet said as she popped the last bite of brownie in her mouth and drained her glass. She handed her glass to Cedra and shut down her laptop. "You ready to head upstairs?"

"I'm right behind you," Cedra replied. "I love to watch you move," she teased.

Juliet wiggled her hips before taking the first step. "You want to change clothes and go take a look at some songs?"

"I'm good with that. Come over when you're ready," Cedra said.

"I will. I need to text one of the boys to bring some milk home. I'll be over in a minute."

Juliet changed into sleeping clothes and picked up her phone to text Keith. *Ma made brownies, and there are a few left on the table for y'all. Bring home milk. We're almost out.*

Juliet watched the bubble as Keith typed a response. *Will do. Thanks for saving us some.* He ended his text with a smiley face.

Good night. Don't work too hard.

Keith sent a thumbs up, and Juliet placed her phone on charge, then walked into Cedra's room.

They sat with their backs against the headboard on Cedra's bed and searched through her songbook until they had all but two slots filled. "We can leave these two for Stone, and maybe substitute another of his if you want," Cedra said.

"You've seen his work. Should we give him three?" Juliet asked.

Cedra turned to her and nodded. "I think we could easily pick three of his. Let's remove this one for now. He and I can go through his book tomorrow and plug in three songs while we're on break."

Juliet took Cedra's book and laid it on the bed. "I'd like to suggest something, and I hope it doesn't hurt your feelings."

"Go ahead," Cedra said with a smile.

"The song you sang tonight is beautiful, and I know it's our song. I could easily see it becoming a wedding song favorite if it's a duet sung by a male and female."

Cedra broke out laughing, then suddenly stopped when she saw the confused look on Juliet's face. "I'm sorry for laughing. I agree with you completely. It will always be our song and sung for you first."

Juliet turned to face her. "I think you and Stone should sing it. I think you both have the voices and the heart as songwriters to do it justice. What do you think?"

"I was thinking more of you and Stone, but we can try it both ways to see how it sounds. You have a stronger voice than me."

"Stronger, yes, but I can't mimic that tone of yours that can melt butter. Smooth and sexy all at once," Juliet told her.

"Oh, I like that." Cedra grinned.

Juliet looked at the clock. "Why does time always pass so quickly when I'm with you?" She picked up the book, placed it on the desk, and then turned off the lamp. "Come snuggle with me," she whispered to Cedra.

Cedra moved closer and laid her head on Juliet's shoulder, tossing a leg across her thighs. Her hand disappeared under Juliet's shirt to feel the warmth of her skin.

"I love snuggling into you," Cedra said as she settled into a comfortable position.

"Not as much as I love being with you." Juliet bent her head to kiss Cedra's forehead. "Are you coming straight home tomorrow?"

"Yes, as far as I know, and I've got Tuesday off. Is there something you need?"

Juliet chuckled. "A night when we don't have to rush and can take time to love each other properly."

"Tuesday night it is then," Cedra commented.

†

Cedra crept out of bed and turned off the alarm before it could wake Juliet. She smiled at her lover sleeping and had to restrain a laugh when Juliet rolled over and snuggled into

Cedra's pillow. She started the shower and stripped out of her clothes, showering quickly, and dressed before returning to her room for her keys and songbook. Cedra leaned over and planted a soft kiss on Juliet's cheek.

"I love you," she whispered.

"I love you, too," Juliet replied but did not stir awake. Cedra met Ma in the kitchen. "Good morning, Ma."

"Good morning. Did you sleep well?"

"Yea, I did after we sat up discussing songs for a bit. I think we are down to three, and I want to plug some of Stone's in to fill those slots."

"That shouldn't be hard to do," Ma replied. "Do you want anything besides coffee? I'd offer you a brownie, but they got wiped out last night," Ma said with a soft laugh.

"Imagine that," Cedra joked. "No, coffee is good. Thanks, Ma."

"You're welcome. When are you off this week?" Ma asked.

"Tuesday," Cedra answered. "Do you need something?"

"No, just curious. I know you and Juliet haven't had much time together. I would suggest a date night that doesn't include cafés or music. Maybe dinner and a movie?"

"I think we could handle that. What do you have planned for dinner Thursday?" Cedra asked.

"I was thinking of something simple like spaghetti or something easy. I know you will all be excited to perform that night. I'll get the clothes ready this week."

"I can help with that," Cedra offered.

"No need. It'll give me something to do other than a nap," Ma teased.

"Is there anything you need from town?" Cedra asked as she picked up her travel mug to leave.

"I think we're good for now. I may do some grocery shopping Wednesday," Ma replied.

"If you need help, drag Juliet along. I think she has this week free before she starts gigging again."

"Do you think that will change after this weekend?" Ma asked.

"That depends on what Carrie or another agent has to offer. If all goes well, hopefully, we'll be spending more time in a studio somewhere."

"Will you and Stone continue to work at the Redbird?"

"I don't see that dramatically changing for a while until we get other money coming in," Cedra replied. "Besides, Lisa Marie gave us jobs when we needed them, and I'd hate to leave her without an opportunity to replace us. I don't see it happening for several months at least, though, unless Carrie does work magic."

"I could easily see you guys taking off at the start of the year, so maybe she can arrange some studio time for y'all before she starts arranging out-of-town gigs."

"Yeah, that's only two months away. I think it's possible, though," Cedra replied. "Only time will tell. I'll see you tonight, Ma."

"Have a great day, Cedra."

"You too, Ma." Cedra collected her things and walked out to the truck. She was surprised to see frost on her windshield, and climbed in to start her engine and let it warm for a minute. *Won't be long before I have to dig out a jacket,* she thought as the window cleared and she could drive to work. Cedra had gone a mile toward town when the first deer darted across the road in front of her. "Yeah, it's that time of the year," she said to herself and drove a bit more cautiously. Stone was stepping out of his truck when she pulled into the lot.

†

"Good morning, sunshine," he called out.

"Good morning to you, kind sir. Did you see deer on your way in this morning?"

"Not yet, but I'm sure they are out there," Stone answered.

"I had one run out in front of me this morning. I guess it's that time of year."

"Yeah, we will need to drive carefully over the next few months. As my dad always said, where there's one."

Cedra broke into his line, "There's always more."

"That's right," Stone laughed. "Are you ready to get this week going?"

"I am. I have a project for us on our break," Cedra replied.

"What's that?"

"We need to pick out three of your songs to go on an album," Cedra replied. "So be thinking about it this morning."

"That should be fun. So, are we cutting an album?" Stone asked.

"One way or another, yes. Hopefully, we can get a signed contract with Carrie Brooks, and she can foot the bill for production. If not, we'll need to fill a bunch of pickle jars at Wild Bills," Cedra teased. "Either way, we want to be ahead of the game and have the other nine songs chosen."

198

"That sounds like a good plan to me," Stone said as he pulled the back door open. "It's nice to have some money coming in, and I can use part of my tips to pay my part."

"Hopefully, we won't need to, but with five of us pitching in, I don't think it will be too painful," Cedra replied. "We can always pull some extra shifts too."

"That's true. It seems like we can always use an extra set of hands around here," Stone said.

Cedra stored her keys and songbook under the counter, pulled on her apron, and picked up her order pad.

"You two want a quick cup before we get started?" Lisa Marie asked from the coffee station.

"Absolutely, boss," Cedra replied.

Lisa Marie poured two more cups and placed them on the counter. "Did y'all have a good night?"

"Yes, I think we both did. I treated Ma and Juliet to some fine brisket, and we had a relaxing evening at home. We started some work on a CD insert using the photos we took Saturday morning."

"That sounds very promising," Lisa Marie said. "You've gotten some studio time in also, haven't you?"

"Yes, we were able to cut four tracks, so just eight more to go for a full album." Cedra smiled at the look of surprise on Lisa Marie's face.

"Y'all are going full tilt on this, aren't you?"

"Yes, ma'am. Would you mind if we do some word of mouth promoting for the Open Mic night Saturday?"

Lisa Marie smiled and shook her head. "Heavens no. More customers mean more sales. Promote away. I think we'll have a good crowd, so I'm pulling in another server."

"I just pray everything turns out well," Stone said.

"We've practiced hard, got some new clothes, so we've done everything we can. It's in fate's hands now," Cedra smiled.

"I wish I could feel as optimistic as you," Stone replied. "So much is riding on this for all of us."

"Have faith in your skills," Lisa Marie said. "Are y'all ready to greet the masses?"

"Let's roll," Cedra said and took her cup to the sink.

"Good morning, gentlemen," Lisa Marie said as she swung the door open.

Cedra took a table of three while Stone attended to a man at the counter. "What can I get you, folks, to start?"

"Coffees all-around, little miss," one older man said.

She handed them a menu and said, "I'll be right back with coffee."

Cedra returned with a pot of coffee and started pouring. "Have you decided on breakfast, or do you need a few more minutes?"

"Do you have any recommendations?" one of the men asked.

"It depends on how hungry you are. I like the three eggs and double meat with hash browns. The pancakes or French toast are good as well. The country ham and biscuit are other options if you want something super light."

"I don't know about y'all, but I'm starving after last night's show," the first man replied. "I'll take the three eggs over easy with country ham, hash browns, and apple juice."

"Toast or biscuits?" Cedra asked.

"Bring both. Biscuits and some white toast, please."

"Not a problem. Who's next?"

"Can you toss some pecans in those pancakes and give me a side of city ham?"

"Yes, sir, I sure can." She turned to the final man and thought he looked familiar. "You, sir?"

"I'll take the eggs benedict and another pot of coffee." He smiled. "You can call me John," he added. "Calling me sir makes me feel old."

"Hell, you are old, bro," the first man answered. "I bet this young lady wasn't even born when you sang "Seminole Wind,"" he teased.

"You're John Anderson?" Cedra asked. "You wrote that song, too, didn't you?"

"Yes, ma'am. At least she knows my name, if not my face," he said with a smile to Cedra. "These two knuckleheads are my old school band mates, Leroy and Josh."

"Well, it's a pleasure to meet you. I'm Cedra, and I'll put your orders in and bring fresh coffee."

"Thank you, miss."

Cedra placed the orders and then grinned at Lisa Marie. "Did you know who that was?"

"John Anderson and his tribe. They were in town last night for a show at the Ryman," Lisa Marie said. "You may see some other familiar-looking faces today."

"That's cool with me." Cedra picked up a coffee pot and returned to the table. She topped off their cups and walked back to the counter. The cook pushed their plates of food through the window, and Cedra placed them on a serving tray with a large glass of apple juice. She carried the food to the table to serve them and waited for a second. "Is there anything else I can get you?"

"I think I'm going to need more butter for these pancakes."

"More butter. Anything else, jelly for your toast?" Cedra asked.

The big man nodded. "Apple, if you have it."

"We do. I'll be right back."

Cedra delivered the butter and jelly before greeting other customers who sat at a nearby table. "Coffee?" she asked.

"Yes, please, keep it coming," the woman answered.

Cedra turned over two cups and filled them. "I'll give you a few to look over the menu." She topped off the guys' coffee. "How is your breakfast?"

"Delicious as always," Josh said. "Thanks for the great service."

"My pleasure. Is there anything else I can get you?" Cedra asked.

"One more round of coffee and a check, please."

"Together or separate?" Cedra asked.

"Together. It's my turn to buy," John replied.

"I'll have it for you in just a minute." Cedra pulled out her order pad and ripped off the sheet with the orders. She pointed to the cash register. "Lisa Marie will cash you out, but if you need anything else, just catch me."

"Thanks, Cedra," John said and smiled.

"My pleasure. Enjoy your time in Nashville."

"Thanks. Good luck to you." He saw the confused look on Cedra's face. "Only a songwriter would know I wrote that song."

Cedra nodded and smiled back at him. "Thank you. I may not have been born yet, but it's a great song."

John left her a nice tip and the morning rolled into the lunch hour before she knew it.

"If you two want a quick break, I'd take it now, before the rush hits," Lisa Marie told Cedra and Stone.

They ordered breakfast and pulled out their songbooks while they waited. "The first one is easy. The one you ended Open Mic with," Cedra replied.

Stone nodded and turned to the page.

Cedra wrote the name of the song in the number five slot. "What else?"

"Read through this one while I grab our meals," Stone said and walked to the window.

Cedra's head bobbed to the imaginary music in her head as she read through the lyrics. "I like this. Do you have one that's more of a rockabilly tune as well?"

"Flip three pages back. Do you want juice?"

"Apple, please," Cedra answered. "Oh yeah, this is good," Cedra agreed when Stone sat beside her.

"Cool," he said and dug into a pile of hash browns. "Man, I was starving."

"You missed some great brisket last night," she teased.

"Did you cook?" he asked.

"No, but I bought. Juliet and I gave Ma a break from cooking."

Stone smiled. "Ma sure is a special lady."

"Yes, she is. She is so excited about The Bentleys."

"We all should be excited about this great opportunity. My wife was tickled pink when I told her."

"Too bad she can't come up this weekend," Cedra said.

"She is," Stone replied. "Dad bought her a ticket, and they are babysitting."

"That's excellent news, Stone. I look forward to meeting Sarah."

"She's excited to meet all of you, too. She says that's all I talk about anymore."

"That's not a bad thing, but make sure you give her some 'you' time this weekend."

"I plan to. Sarah gets in around four on Friday, and I'm taking her out to the Hermitage Steak House for dinner."

"Have you gotten a hotel room?" Cedra asked.

"I offered, but she said she wanted to experience how I lived, so she better understands why I do what I do," Stone explained.

"That's wonderful and cozy," Cedra grinned and elbowed him in the ribs.

The door opened, and Carrie entered the café. "Sit tight, and I'll get her seated while you finish eating," Lisa Marie said as she grabbed a menu.

"Thanks," Cedra said and finished her meal quickly.

"Leave your dishes, and I'll get them," Stone offered.

Cedra wiped her mouth and washed her hands as Lisa Marie poured a glass of tea. "You ready?"

"All set," Cedra answered and took the glass. "Here you go, one sweet tea."

"I didn't mean to interrupt your meal break," Carrie said.

"It was crazy busy for a Monday morning. You're early today, too."

"I had a break before an afternoon meeting," Carrie said.

"The usual?" Cedra asked, pointing at the menu.

"I'm feeling a bit rebellious today. Bring me a bacon cheeseburger, well done, and onion rings." Carrie laughed.

"Oh my, that is a change." Cedra smiled. "Everybody needs to splurge now and then."

"Yes, it's been way too long since I've had a cheeseburger, so I might as well go all the way."

"That's the spirit," Cedra grinned. "Should I check out the pie selection for you, too?"

"Why not?" Carrie chuckled.

"I'll put your order in and check out the pies."

Cedra placed the order and took a look at the pie selection for the day. Then she picked up the tea pitcher and made rounds filling customer glasses. When she got to Carrie's table, she filled the glass.

"The pies are wide open today. Everything from key lime to buttermilk and pecan."

"I can hardly say no to buttermilk pie after eating a cheeseburger," Carrie answered.

"I'll make sure to save a piece back for you. Coffee to go with it?" Cedra asked.

"Sure, that sounds good. Thanks, Cedra."

Cedra took orders from another table, and when she walked back to place the order, Carrie's food was coming up. "I have to admit, that does look good," Cedra said as she put the food in front of Carrie. "I may have to try one soon. Is there anything else I can get you?"

"How about a side of honey mustard? The ketchup gives me a headache," Carrie explained.

"Coming right up," Cedra said and walked into the kitchen for a container of honey mustard.

The café was packed with customers as Cedra wove between tables to deliver the honey mustard. "Let me know when you're ready for pie."

"Thanks," Carrie replied.

Cedra busied herself with taking orders, and even with Lisa Marie's help, she and Stone stayed swamped during the lunch hour. When Carrie motioned for her, Cedra walked over to the table.

"I'm going to have to take the pie to go," she said. "I received a call that the office needed me."

Cedra tore off her ticket and handed it to Carrie. "I'll get your pie boxed up to go and a fork. I hope everything is okay."

"Thanks, Cedra. I'm sure it will be," Carrie answered as Cedra turned away.

Cedra placed the pie box in a bag and handed it to Carrie to check out.

"Do try that cheeseburger soon. It was heavenly," Carrie smiled.

"I will. Have a good day. See you tomorrow," Cedra replied.

"Yes, you will, but back to a salad tomorrow." Carrie laughed and handed Cedra a ten-dollar tip.

"Wait, I'm off tomorrow, but will see you Wednesday. Thanks," Cedra said and tucked the bill in her pocket.

"This has been a crazy day," she told Lisa Marie.

"Very busy for sure. How about when this group moves out, the three of us sit down for a cheeseburger? That did look good."

"I'm sure Stone won't complain. We've already burned off breakfast." Cedra chuckled and picked up another tray for delivery.

It took another hour for the rush to die down, and Cedra could hear Lisa Marie asking Stone about a cheeseburger. "Oh, heck yeah," was his immediate answer.

Lisa Marie placed their orders and cashed the last patron out as Stone and Cedra helped bus and clean tables. When they finished, they sat at the counter and took a drink of tea.

"What a day," Stone said.

"I've never seen it this busy on a Monday," Cedra replied. "Is there something big going on in town?" she asked Lisa Marie.

"There was a bit of a reunion of artists from the 90s last night at the Ryman. You met John Anderson at breakfast, and a few lesser-known folks came through at lunch."

"We were so busy, I probably couldn't have recognized them anyway," Stone said. "It was a great day for tips."

"You need that for your big night Friday when Sarah hits town," Cedra teased.

"Your wife is coming to town? That's great news, Stone. For the show Saturday?"

"Yes, and to meet you and all the folks I'm constantly raving about," Stone answered.

"I look forward to meeting her," Lisa Marie said. "Come, help me with our plates."

Cedra took a bite of the cheeseburger. "Oh my gosh, Carrie was right. This burger tastes heavenly."

"The onion rings aren't bad either," Stone chimed in.

"What plans do you have for your day off tomorrow?" Lisa Marie asked.

"To sleep in, for starters. It may only be until seven, but I'll try. Then a relaxing day with Juliet and Ma and a night on the town with Juliet."

"That sounds like fun. Are you all set for Wild Bill's on Thursday and your performance here on Saturday?"

"As much as I can be," Cedra replied.

Lisa Marie turned to Stone. "Are you ready?"

"I'm going for a haircut and a close shave tomorrow night when I get off work. Ma has our clothes all pressed and ready. She plans on feeding us Thursday night, early."

"You play from seven until eight?" Lisa Marie asked.

"Yes, ma'am," Stone answered.

"I'll drop in and listen for a bit," she replied.

"A cold beer is on me," Stone told her.

"I think I can handle one and still drive," she winked at him. "This is so exciting for y'all. I'm very proud of you both for staying the course and writing what you want. Always remember that and don't get pressured into writing something that's not who you are."

"Sage advice," Cedra replied. "You're right, though. We need to stick to our roots."

"Y'all did well today. That was a heck of a crowd at breakfast and lunch. I don't know how I'll replace you when you get rich and famous."

"I don't think you have to worry about that for some time yet. We won't leave you high and dry," Cedra promised.

"You never know. Carrie may have big plans for you and get you on the road quickly."

"Well, she'll just have to allow us to give proper notice," Cedra said. "We won't leave you until you can replace us."

Lisa Marie scowled. "It may not work that way, but don't you pass on anything. I will just have to pull in some extra help."

Cedra's face lit up in a smile. "You know if we're all gone, Ma won't have anyone to cook for and look after. She's always up early to see me off. She could handle the counter for sure."

"That's not a bad idea," Lisa Marie said. "I'll keep her in mind."

"Let's just wait to see how everything goes before you start shipping us off." Cedra smiled.

†

Lisa Marie looked at Cedra and Stone when the evening crew came in. "You two head out. You put in a full day's work." She handed them their tips from the till. "I'll see you tomorrow," she told Stone. Then she turned to Cedra. "You enjoy a well-deserved day off."

"See ya," Cedra replied and grabbed her songbook.

Stone walked out with her. "It's going to be odd working with Jennifer tomorrow and not you."

"Trust me. You'll survive. Grab Carrie when she comes in for lunch. She's a great tipper. See you Wednesday," Cedra called out as she reached her truck.

†

When Cedra arrived home, Wayne, Keith, and Juliet were on the front porch. Ma was sitting in her rocker, listening to them play. They were practicing some of the songs they had chosen from her songbook to add to the album. Juliet's voice was pure as she sang a love song, and Cedra smiled at the sound of her lover's voice.

Cedra walked onto the porch just as the song ended. "Y'all are sounding great."

209

"We thought we'd practice a bit to kill some time before supper," Juliet said.

Cedra took a seat beside Ma. "Don't let me stop the music."

"You wanna grab your guitar and join us?" Keith asked.

"Nope, tonight, I'm a listener," Cedra replied. "Today's shift kicked my butt."

"Fair enough. Sit back and listen to the beautiful songs you've written," Wayne told her.

"I'm going to check on supper. Would you like something to drink?" Ma asked.

"Some tea would be great. Thanks, Ma."

"Were you and Stone able to pick out three more songs?" Juliet asked.

Cedra nodded. "Yeah, we did. I made copies for everyone and the two new songs as well."

"Pass them around, and let's take a run at them," Keith suggested.

Cedra opened her songbook and pulled out the photocopied pages. "I think these will do well to round out an album."

"We've got enough material in just your book alone to cut several albums," Wayne said.

"Hold your horses. We've got to get one cut and distributed first," Juliet reminded him.

"Y'all won't believe who came in for breakfast this morning," Cedra said.

"Who?" Juliet asked.

"John Anderson and some of his old band mates." She looked at Keith. "There was a reunion of some stars from the 90s last night at the Ryman."

"I guess I dropped the ball on mentioning that," Keith apologized.

Cedra laughed. "No biggie, but it was probably a great show. Did John sing 'Seminole Wind'? That was always my favorite of his songs."

Keith nodded. "He did, and there was some other great talent there, too. I'm sorry I didn't think to mention it to you."

"I'll forgive you this time," Cedra said with a wink.

†

After running through the new songs twice, Ma came to the door. "Are you all about ready to eat?"

"I'm always ready," Keith said.

"Let's eat then," Juliet said.

As they were eating, Juliet made an announcement. "I've got two nights at Iron Horse next week if anyone wants to join me."

"What days?" Wayne asked.

"Thursday and Friday from eight to nine," Juliet replied.

"I'm good. I've got both nights off," Keith replied.

"I've got to work Friday, but I'll see if I can take my lunch break then," Wayne said.

Juliet looked at Cedra, who nodded. "Of course. I'm sure Stone will join us as well. He'll be living out here by then."

Juliet took a drink of tea. "Sounds like a good deal. Hopefully, we'll get a signed contract soon, or we can pay for some time to get back into the studio."

†

211

After the guys went to work and Ma retired for the evening, Juliet and Cedra took a leisurely shower together and loved the night away. When Cedra fell asleep in Juliet's arms early in the morning hours, she smiled and curled up next to her lover, completely content.

They slept in until eight the following day and helped Ma with a few chores around the house. Ma had their clothes for Thursday night cleaned and pressed for their performance.

"We plan to go to dinner and a movie tonight, Ma. Is there anything you need from town?" Juliet asked.

"Nope. You two have a great time. I think me and the boys are having leftovers." Ma chuckled. "It's so rare that we have any."

Juliet looked at Cedra. "Are you ready to get dressed for a night on the town? Maybe I can show you some spots you haven't seen yet before dinner."

"That sounds like fun. I know there is so much more to Nashville than what I've seen so far."

Juliet chuckled. "You did hit the ground running, and you haven't slowed down since you got here."

"That's true. You've barely had any days off, always pulling extra shifts," Ma replied.

"Trying to build up a bankroll," Cedra teased.

"Let's get a move on then," Juliet said.

†

After showering, they separated to their rooms to dress. Cedra took a bit longer and found Juliet sitting on the porch with Ma. Juliet stood when Cedra walked out.

"Look at you," Cedra remarked. "New jeans, and they are even pressed."

"I needed to look presentable for our first official date night," Juliet replied.

Cedra loved the way Juliet's eyes sparkled when she was excited. Her eyes explored Juliet. "I am proud to go out on the town with you. You look very nice."

"Ma said I cleaned up pretty well," Juliet grinned.

"You do. Are you ready to hit the road?" Cedra asked.

"Let me grab my keys," Juliet stepped inside.

Ma smiled at Cedra. "You both look very nice. I hope you have a great time tonight."

"As long as we're together, we will, Ma," Cedra replied.

"I'll see you bright and early in the morning," Ma told Cedra when Juliet returned. "Y'all be safe and watch out for deer."

"Yes, Ma," they answered in unison as they walked to the car.

†

Juliet gave Cedra a tour of the other side of downtown, including the Titan's football stadium, Nissan Field, and other highlights.

"That's a big stadium," Cedra said. "I'd love to see us fill one like this in concert one day."

"We will," Juliet said. "All in good time." She reached for Cedra's hand and entwined their fingers. "There are so many great country music festivals all over the place these days. Hopefully, we can break into that circuit and take our music nationwide."

"If we can get some of the major stations to play us, I think we will catch on fire," Cedra said. "At least, I hope we will."

"If we can get just one song popular enough to record a music video for CMT and the Internet music channels, I think we will," Juliet replied.

"I didn't even think about a music video," Cedra admitted.

"It's in our stars," Juliet said as she pulled the car to a stop at the restaurant. "I'm glad we're here. I'm starving."

Cedra stepped out of the car and took a deep breath. "That smell is to die for."

†

They did not pay attention to anyone in the restaurant, or they may have seen Carrie Brooks sitting across the dining room. Cedra and Juliet were focused only on one another. Carrie, however, watched their interactions closely, clearly ignoring the attention of her date.

†

"There is so much to choose on this menu," Cedra said. "Do you want to get a couple of combos and split them so that we can try as much as possible?"

"I'm all for it as long as a ribeye and lobster tail are one of them." Juliet smiled.

"Okay, what if we get the spicy shrimp as an appetizer, you get the surf and turf, and I'll get steak and baby back ribs?" Cedra suggested.

Juliet reached over and caressed the top of Cedra's hand. "I do love the way you think."

214

Cedra was amazed at the size of the portions when the appetizer and salads came out. "If we eat all of this, we may not make it to the movies."

"I'm good with that. If we're too full after our meal, we can just head back home," Juliet replied.

"Or we can take doggie bags. I'm looking forward to buttered theater popcorn," she grinned. "I can't tell you how long it's been since I've been in a theater."

"There are some nice ones in Nashville, where you can eat your meal while you watch the movie from comfy reclining chairs," Juliet replied. "The one we are going to tonight is one of them."

"We could have just eaten there then."

Juliet shook her head. "No way. I would never trade this meal for theater food."

"Just the smells here are enough to make your mouth water."

They stopped nibbling on the shrimp when the main courses arrived. "Oh, my goodness, I could make three meals of this," Cedra replied.

"Pace yourself. There's no need to rush." Juliet chuckled as she smeared honey butter over her steak. The server had removed the lobster tail from the shell, and Juliet cut a bite and drenched it in melted butter. "Sweet Mother of Jesus, you have got to try this." Juliet dipped a section into the butter and offered it across the table to Cedra. A drop of butter landed on Cedra's chin, and Juliet gently reached over to wipe it away.

†

There is no doubt they are lovers' Carrie thought as she watched their interactions. She felt the tip of her tongue snake out to lick the imaginary butter from her lips. The soft touches and brilliant smiles quickly gave them away. *I've waited too long to make a move on Cedra. Or have I?* She tore her attention away from Cedra and Juliet.

"What did you say?" Carrie turned back to her date.

"I was asking if you wanted to go join them. You're ridiculously more interested in what is happening there instead of what's across from you," Carrie's date growled.

"I'm sorry. Those are two very talented artists I may be signing soon," Carrie replied with a fake smile. "I'm sorry, Linea, my attention is one hundred percent back on you." Carrie watched the blonde toss her hair back and give her a seductive smile. "I promise. All yours."

Linea was a model she had used on several videos, but she was nothing more to Carrie than a pretty face and a willing fuck buddy, if she could claim that. If it weren't for the great sex, Carrie probably wouldn't have given her a second glance.

†

Linea wriggled in her seat at the sexy purr in Carrie's voice. She knew what Carrie's statement inferred. After dinner, Carrie would take Linea home for several hours of mind-blowing sex, but Carrie would be gone the following day. That was all she ever got from Carrie, but for now, it was enough. At least she continued to answer her calls and texts, even if it was just for sex.

†

"I swear I can't eat another bite," Cedra said as she dropped a rib bone onto her plate. "Unless you were saving the last bite of lobster for me," she teased.

"It just so happened I was," Juliet said and twirled the tasty morsel in the butter. She reached the fork across the table and waited for Cedra to take the bite and moan.

"Oh yeah, that's what I was waiting for." Juliet grinned. "The sound of that moan was the best part of this meal."

The server placed the leftovers in containers and set the check on the table.

Cedra's quick reflexes grabbed the paper before Juliet could argue, but Cedra's face turned to a frown when she saw the balance of zero. She looked up the server. "I don't understand."

"Carrie Brooks paid your check," the server replied. "Including a generous tip."

"Well, I certainly won't complain. I didn't even see Carrie dining here," Cedra replied.

The server chuckled. "You couldn't keep your eyes off the hottie sitting across from you, but I can't blame ya there. Have a great night, ladies," she added with a wink and walked away.

"That was certainly a surprise," Juliet said. "It makes me wonder if Carrie is sweetening the pot. She may be worried about her competition."

Cedra shrugged. "That's fine with me. That's money I can add into the studio fund," Cedra replied.

Juliet stood from her seat and picked up the bag of leftovers. "Are you still up for a movie?"

"Honestly, I'd rather curl up in your arms," Cedra replied. "If Ma's still awake, maybe we can entice her into a movie on Netflix and some popcorn."

"That sounds like a perfect plan," Juliet replied and held out her elbow for Cedra. "Let's go home."

†

The house was dark when they arrived home. Juliet placed the bag of leftovers in the fridge. "Movie in my room?" Juliet asked.

"That works for me." Cedra followed her quietly up the stairs.

Juliet found a movie on a streaming service while Cedra changed clothes and set her alarm. When Cedra returned, Juliet looked at her. "Do you want popcorn?"

"I couldn't eat anything else tonight. That dinner was awesome."

"Yes, it was, especially since we didn't have to pay for it. It has me worried, though. There's no such thing as a 'free meal.' I wonder what Carrie's game plan is."

"As long as she keeps paying for steak and lobster, I don't care," Cedra replied as she stretched out next to Juliet.

Carrie's motives did worry Juliet, but she didn't say anything to dampen Cedra's spirits. "I reckon we'll find out soon enough."

Neither of them made it through the entire movie. When Juliet woke hours later, Cedra was fast asleep next to her. She set the alarm on her phone as a backup, turned off the television, and then snuggled in with Cedra.

CHAPTER ELEVEN

When the sound of alarms going off wakened Cedra, she tried to creep over Juliet to turn them off. Juliet grabbed her as she was about to step off the bed and rolled her onto her back.

"Not so quickly there, miss." Juliet chuckled and turned off both alarms. "I'm not ready to let you go just yet." Juliet kissed her softly. "Two more days of work for you, and then we'll be playing live," she told Cedra.

"What are your plans for the day?" Cedra asked.

"Some coffee with Ma and maybe breakfast. I'd like to take a trip into town later and look at some drum sets. Maybe see how much it would cost to rent a set."

"That's not a bad idea. I think a few of our songs could benefit from some drums. Check the studios, too, and see if they rent. There's no sense paying for a set until we start to get some gigs."

"That's true. I'll check on some studio costs, just in case. You know, I was thinking about something last night."

"Was that before or after I fell asleep on you?" Cedra asked.

"I'm not sure who went out first," Juliet replied. "I thought I would check on the cost of having two of your singles we've already recorded cut onto CD and maybe have a few for sale on your Open Mic night. I could easily make an album cover for you with what we have."

Cedra smiled. "That's not a bad idea. I could afford two dozen if the costs aren't too expensive."

"Hey, this is my idea. I'd love to have the CDs made for you. Besides, I have another thought too."

"You're one for one so far. What's the other idea?" Cedra asked.

"To print out some covers for *Six Strings* and print the song list on the back. We could pass them around after the show Thursday night. Maybe Ma would help with that. I know she's excited to be there."

Cedra smiled. "That would be some good marketing. Give them a taste, but leave them hungry for more."

Juliet nodded. "My thoughts, exactly."

"Have I told you lately how beautiful and brilliant you are?" Cedra said as she leaned in for a kiss.

"I do believe you whispered something like that before, but I never tire of hearing your praise."

"I would love to stay in bed and sing your praises all morning, but I need to hit the shower and get ready for work," Cedra said before climbing out of bed.

"Do you need someone to wash your back?" Juliet said, wiggling her eyebrows.

"Yes, but that will have to wait until tonight. I will surely be late if you join me in the shower. Go back to sleep for a bit if you can. There's no need for you to be up with the chickens, too."

Juliet propped on her elbow to watch Cedra leave the room. "Kiss me goodbye before you leave."

"I will," Cedra replied and left the room.

Juliet stretched out on her back, but her mind was whirling with excitement. There was no going back to sleep for her, but she would wait until Cedra left before going downstairs to share the plan with Ma.

†

Juliet heard Cedra's truck start, and she slipped into some sweats and slippers before brushing her teeth and hair. She grabbed her laptop and descended the stairs as Ma was pouring a cup. "Make it two, please, Ma."

"There must be a ghost haunting me. I could have sworn Juliet just asked for coffee at a quarter to five in the morning," Ma teased as Juliet entered the kitchen. "Are you feeling okay?"

"I'm just excited about some things I want to work on today," Juliet said as she placed her computer on the table.

"Cedra mentioned you came up with some good ideas this morning. Anything I can help with?" Ma asked as she sat a cup of coffee in front of Juliet.

"Yep, you can ride into town with me later and help me with some printing," Juliet replied. "I want to print out some covers for The Bentleys performance Thursday night and if I can make it happen, some for a two-single CD for Cedra's Open Mic performance."

"That sounds exciting. What can I do?" Ma asked.

"I will need you to use the cutter to trim the sheets of covers as I get them printed. If you can do that, it will speed things up tremendously."

"Show me what do, and I'll make it happen," Ma replied. "Do you want some breakfast? I'm hungry this morning. Must be the change in weather."

"I could eat," Juliet replied as she started tapping away at the keyboard.

"You keep working then, and I'll fix us some eggs and bacon. Do you want toast or biscuits?"

"Toast is fine with me. Thanks, Ma."

Juliet typed in the list of songs for the *Six Strings* cover and then added the lyrics to the two titles for Cedra's cover.

Ma was just finishing the bacon when they heard footsteps on the stairs. Wayne stopped in his tracks when he looked up to see Juliet sitting at the kitchen table. "Keith, I wasn't hallucinating?" he said, pointing at Juliet. "I did hear her down here."

"Yeah, bro, you did. Did we miss the memo about an early morning meeting?" Keith asked Juliet.

Juliet took a sip of coffee. "No, just woke up full of energy and ideas."

"One of you jokers can get busy making some toast," Ma said. "Fried or scrambled eggs?"

"Scrambled would be easier and faster," Keith replied. "I'll get the toast if you pour juice and coffee."

"I'm pretty sure I can handle that. I'll set the table, too, and Juliet can tell us what has her on fire this morning."

Ma cracked a dozen eggs and scrambled them while Juliet discussed her plans with the boys.

"I love the ideas," Wayne said. "I'd hold off on the drums, though. We can use a studio set for minimal cost. Especially if Carrie Brooks is behind the project."

Ma poured the eggs into a bowl. "Cedra said Carrie paid for your dinner last night. I wonder what she's up to," Ma said.

"I've been wondering the same thing," Juliet replied as she saved her files onto a jump drive and shut down her laptop.

"Yeah, no free lunches in this town," Wayne replied.

Juliet shrugged then reached for the bacon. "It felt kinda creepy. We didn't even know Carrie was in the restaurant. It was a hell of a meal, though."

"What's got you two up so early anyhow?" Ma asked.

"We don't work until late, and one of Keith's friends invited us to go deer hunting," Wayne replied.

"I didn't realize you two have rifles," Ma said.

Keith laughed. "Back home, yeah, but not here. My friend is going to loan us some."

"I don't even know if we'll see anything big enough to go after. It's more just the experience of boys being out in the woods," Wayne replied.

Juliet shook her head. "I don't see how y'all could shoot Bambi," she teased.

"Bambi makes for some good eating," Keith said. "I don't know about these skinny little Tennessee deer."

"It's not cold enough yet, to get the big ones moving," Ma said, and three sets of eyes turned to look at her. "Are you surprised that I know about hunting?"

"Well, yeah, Ma. You've never mentioned it before," Keith said.

"In all fairness, neither have you," Ma chuckled and bit into her toast.

"You've got me there, Ma," Keith replied. "What's the biggest you've brought down?"

"Go look above the door on the back porch," Ma replied.

Keith wiped his mouth and left the table. They heard the back door open, and seconds later, he came rushing back. "You got an eight-point buck?"

Ma laughed softly. "Probably before you were even born, but yes, I did. He fed us well for several months. My husband never bested that shot."

"Do you still have a rifle?" Wayne asked. "Do you want to join us today?"

"Yes. It's tucked away in my closet, but no, I'm helping Juliet out today. Maybe some other time."

"We will hold you to that, Ma," Keith said.

"You have a deal." Ma grinned. "I can't climb into a deer stand, though."

Keith smiled. "We will figure out a good spot for you, Ma. My buddy has shooting shacks, so you don't have to climb if you don't want."

"What about you, Juliet? Want to come along?" Wayne asked.

"Oh hell no. No way I'm getting out of a nice warm bed to go sit in the cold woods somewhere, looking for something I couldn't shoot even if I were starving."

Wayne burst out laughing. "I pretty much figured that would be your answer. If we do manage one, tell me you will at least try the meat."

"I can't promise you that, Wayne, but you have to get one first," Juliet shot back at him.

Juliet finished eating and picked up her laptop. "Let me shower and get dressed, and we can head into town," she told Ma. "You two have fun today, but I hope you don't shoot Bambi."

"I think Bambi is safe today," Keith replied. "Will y'all be back in time for supper?"

"I would surely hope so," Ma said with a chuckle. "Any special requests?"

"We were thinking we'd treat y'all to more of that brisket," Wayne replied.

"I could go for that," Juliet said. "We shouldn't be out past midday."

"If you just happen to go by the café, would you ask Stone if he wants to join us?" Keith said.

"I'm sure we could swing by there," Ma replied.

Keith nodded. "Cool, we'll come home and then clean up before we order the food. Dinner around five good?"

"That sounds perfect," Juliet replied. "See ya soon."

"See you later, Ma," Wayne said as he and Keith walked toward the front door. "Enjoy your trip out with Juliet."

"I will. You all stay safe," Ma said as she closed the door to the dishwasher.

CHAPTER TWELVE

Lisa Marie smiled at Cedra at the end of her shift Thursday. "Are you getting nervous about tonight?"

Cedra nodded. "A little. I haven't had that much experience in front of a live audience before."

"It will be great to have some practice before Saturday, although tonight's crowd will probably be bigger and rowdier." Lisa Marie placed a comforting hand on Cedra's shoulder. "Relax and have fun up there. Friends and family will surround you."

Cedra smiled. "I just want tonight to go well for all of us."

"I have a strange sense of belief it will, and The Bentleys will be a huge success."

"We will know for sure in a few hours." She looked over at Stone. "Come out as soon as you're ready. Ma will have dinner at 4:30 or so."

"I'll be there all bright and shiny," Stone replied. "You're still coming tonight, right?" he asked Lisa Marie.

"I wouldn't miss it for the world. I'll drop by on my way home and collect on that beer." She winked at Stone.

"I'm going to head out and make sure everything is ready at home. I'll see y'all soon." Cedra grabbed her keys and walked out to her truck.

†

When she pulled into the yard, Ma and Juliet were sitting on the porch. "Welcome home," Juliet said. "How was your day?"

"Busy, but good," Cedra answered. "Yours?"

"It was great. Ma and I have everything set for dinner. Would you like to stretch out with me for a while and relax before dinner?"

"Yeah, I'd like that. My stomach is full of butterflies. I'm not sure I'll be able to eat tonight, Ma."

"Just try a little. Maybe a salad and some bread," Ma suggested. "The butterflies will settle down, and y'all will be great."

"Let's go crash for half an hour, and then we can shower and get ready for dinner," Juliet suggested.

"I'm right behind ya. See you in a bit, Ma." Cedra followed Juliet into the house.

Cedra slipped out of her work clothes and pulled on a T-shirt to join Juliet on the bed. She snuggled in next to her lover and placed her hand on Juliet's stomach. "What's the secret to not being nervous? You seem as calm as a cucumber."

"Have faith in your skills and preparedness. We have worked hard to get ready for tonight. I believe the crowd will enjoy our performance, and if by some odd chance they don't, then we'll get back to work."

"I know you've done this so many times before. It's old hat to you."

Juliet laughed softly. "I've never performed with the woman I love, so this is a first for me, but I believe in us. We'll start out with "The Devil Went Down to Georgia." Wayne will take the first lead, and Stone will be sawing it hot," Juliet teased. "He does sound good on the fiddle." Her hand softly stroked Cedra's face. "That will give you time to settle in a bit and play for the second number."

"I hope you will always know the right thing to say to keep me grounded," Cedra replied.

"I will do my best. Your mother's song is beautiful, and the boys and I will be right beside you playing while you sing."

"That's a great comfort to have you on stage with me," Cedra replied.

Cedra's phone rang before Juliet could reply. "Hey, Daddy."

"Hey, Baby Girl. I just wanted to call and wish you luck tonight. I know you'll be great, and I wish I could be there."

"Thanks, Daddy. Maybe you can see us play somewhere when you come up for Thanksgiving. You're still planning on coming, right?"

"I wouldn't miss it for the world. Give my best to Juliet and the boys, and knock their socks off tonight. I love you."

"Love you, too. I'll call tomorrow and let you know how things go," Cedra promised. "Goodbye."

"That was sweet of him," Juliet said. "I can't wait to meet him."

"Dad's pretty excited to meet you, too," Cedra informed her.

"I think I'm more nervous about meeting him than I am our performance." Juliet chuckled.

"Relax. Dad's going to love you," Cedra replied.

Juliet's alarm sounded. "That's our cue to hit the shower." She stood and reached for Cedra's hand.

They dressed, and before they left their rooms, Juliet held out a small box to Cedra. "I want you to have this to remember our first performance together."

Cedra opened the box and gasped. Her fingers were shaking as they removed a gold and diamond bracelet. "It's beautiful," Cedra replied as she looked at Juliet with eyes full of tears. "I didn't think to get you anything."

"This isn't my first time on stage. It's our first together, and I want it to be a magical night. I love you, Cedra."

"I love you too. Will you put it on for me? I don't think I can work the clasp right now."

"I'd love to," Juliet said and gently placed the bracelet on Cedra's left wrist, then kissed her sweetly. "Are you ready to go knock their socks off?"

Cedra nodded, and they headed for the stairs.

†

Cedra chuckled when they arrived downstairs to find three young men sitting at the table with towels draped around them.

"Good move, Ma," Cedra said.

"I didn't work for hours to have them ruin their clothes with spaghetti sauce. In hindsight, I should have picked an easier meal."

"I promise we will be careful," Keith said as he picked up his fork.

"Did you two need bibs as well?" Ma asked.

"I think we're good. I'm going to have some salad and garlic bread," Cedra answered.

"Bring on the bib. I'm having a plate of your spaghetti, Ma. I'm not too proud to wear a bib." Juliet grinned up at Ma as she tied a towel around her neck.

†

Ma stored the leftovers while the rest checked their appearance before going downstairs. "Y'all are a fine-looking bunch. Would you mind if I ride in with you two?" Ma asked Cedra.

"You are more than welcome to ride with us. The boys are hauling most of the gear," Juliet said. "All we have is one small box."

"We loaded everything else this afternoon," Keith told Cedra.

"I guess we're all set then. Let's do this," Cedra replied.

"Before you rush out, I have something I want to give ya'll," Ma said and placed a box in front of Cedra. "It's not much, but I thought it would be nice and you could add it to your stash of swag or whatever it was Juliet calls the freebies."

Cedra opened the box and gasped. "These are fantastic, Ma." She reached into the box and pulled out a handful of black guitar picks with the band's name emblazoned in red. "When did you do this?"

"I have my resources too." Ma grinned.

"These are perfect, Ma," Wayne said and kissed her on the cheek after stuffing several picks into his pocket.

"Thank you, Ma. These are great and will be great to hand out to fans," Juliet said. "We need to keep a bunch here for us, though. These will go quickly."

"No worries, I'll buy another batch if I need to," Ma smiled. "I'm excited you like them."

†

When they arrived at Wild Bill's, Ma carried in the small boxes while the others took their instruments inside. They were still early, but there seemed to be a crowd already forming inside. Ma was lucky to find a small table close to the stage that would be big enough for her and Lisa Marie and offer them a great view.

Juliet showed them where they could store their instrument cases, and they had just finished removing them when Stone rushed backstage.

"Sorry, I'm late. I had to park a block away. There must be some big-name performing here tonight," Stone teased.

"There were a few spots left when we parked," Cedra replied.

"Not anymore. There's not an empty table in the place, either. I saw Ma and Lisa Marie at a table close to the stage."

Juliet hung her guitar strap around her neck and turned back to them. "This is it. I'll lead off by introducing everyone, and then we can get right down to making some

231

music. Does anyone have any questions about the playlist?
Know where your spots are on stage?" Juliet looked around
the small group. "Pretend we are jamming on Ma's front
porch," she told them. "We are going to knock their socks
off."

†

When the stage lights flickered, the group took their
spots. Cedra carried her songbook out with her and placed it
on a stool. She knew every lyric by heart, but it was a
comfort to have it nearby. Juliet watched her place it next to
her and smiled. The stagehand drew the curtain with a nod,
and the lights came up. Cedra was surprised by the intensity
of the lights and quickly determined the best angle to stand to
keep from being blinded. The bright lights also put out some
heat. Time seemed to stand still as Juliet took center stage,
and the crowd fell silent.

†

"Good evening, Nashville, and welcome to Wild
Bill's. My name is Juliet, and tonight I have the extreme
pleasure of offering you the first glimpse of Nashville's
newest band. Let me introduce you to The Bentleys. My
name is Juliet Tucker, from Blue Ridge, Georgia. To my
right is the beautiful and highly talented songwriter, Cedra
Tyler, from Monroeville, Alabama, who wrote several of the
songs you will hear tonight." The spotlight moved to Cedra,
and she bowed slightly. "Next, to my left, not quite as
beautiful, but also an accomplished songwriter and musician,
Stone Watson from Ocala, Florida." Stone also took a bow as
the spotlight moved from him to Keith. "These last two

jokers, you've probably seen and heard performing before. Keith Champion from Lexington, Kentucky, and Wayne Butler, from Franklin, North Carolina. I'd also like to make a quick shout out that Ms. Cedra Tyler has her first Open Mic event at the Redbird this Saturday night, so if you like what you hear tonight, come back for more." Juliet turned around to Wayne and Stone. "Let's hit it."

The band played a lively rendition of "The Devil Went Down to Georgia" and Wayne nailed the lyrics while Stone had the crowd on their feet at the sound of his fiddle. Cedra only played her guitar on this song, so she let he eyes adjust to the masses. The group was much larger than Cedra had anticipated, and everyone seemed primed for an evening of fun and good music. As the song wound down, Cedra felt her heart race as she stepped forward. Once the applause died down, Juliet gave her a smile and a nod. Her left hand grasped her guitar, and the glimmer of the bracelet on her arm made her smile. Cedra began to play, and as soon as the music reached her ears, the lyrics danced before her eyes.

†

Juliet looked at Cedra with pride and turned to find the audience mesmerized by the song Cedra was singing. They could feel the emotion of longing and heartbreak as Cedra sang her mother's song. Cedra's performance was flawless, and when she ended the music, the crowd appeared stunned for several long seconds. Juliet saw Cedra with a look of panic on her face, which quickly turned into a smile when patrons jumped out of their seats and gave her a standing ovation. Cedra humbly bowed and smiled at Juliet. Whistles and catcalls filled the honky-tonk, and when they quieted, Juliet began the next song.

Cedra breathed a sigh of relief when the audience finally reacted to her song, and she was overwhelmed that they had given her a standing ovation on her first attempt. Her confidence soared, and her voice was pure as she joined in the vocals on the following two songs. They had agreed they would end the set with "Backwoods Boogie," and when the boys began jamming to her music, her heart swelled with the love she shared with her new family. The music energized the crowd, and there was little doubt their first performance was a success.

When the final note sounded, Juliet again took the lead. "Thank you for allowing us to share our first performance with you. We are in the process of producing our first album. If you pay a visit to the lovely Ma Bentley," Juliet pointed out Ma's table, "she will give you a sample of our first album cover and the tracks we will be including. If you loved our music, please share our name with others, and we hope to be blasting through your stereo speakers soon. Thanks again, everyone."

They all stepped to the center of the stage and took a bow to a crowd roaring with applause. Cameras flashed as photos snapped, and The Bentleys left the scene. As soon as the curtain closed behind them, Juliet began sharing high-fives with the group. "We killed it," she told them.

"That was freaking awesome," Wayne said. He looked at Cedra. "I've never known anyone to earn a standing ovation on their first song. Ever."

"That was a great start," Juliet said. "It's just that, though, a start. We have a lot of work ahead of us."

Cedra heard the music begin and looked at Wayne. "They'll play from the DJ booth until the next band is ready, so we'd better clear out. I think we all deserve a cold one."

"Amen to that," Stone said.

Cedra placed her guitar in her case and then gasped when she realized she had left her songbook on stage. She turned back toward Juliet, who held it out toward her.

"This is gold. We can't leave it behind for someone else to steal," Juliet claimed as she handed Cedra her book.

"Thank you. In all the excitement, I nearly forgot it was with me," Cedra replied as she tucked her book safely into the guitar case.

"I've got your back," Juliet smiled and picked up her case.

As they emerged from backstage, the bar was packed and buzzing with excitement. They wove their way toward Ma's table and were stopped numerous times by well-wishers and calls of congratulations from the patrons.

When they finally arrived at Ma's table and propped their cases against the wall, they turned back to Ma. She was holding up three album covers. "Can I offer you a gift from the most exciting and talented new band in Nashville?" Ma asked.

"That's all you have left out of a hundred?" Juliet inquired.

"Yes, the crowd stormed the table after your performance," Ma replied. "You all were fantastic," Ma praised. "The guitar picks were very popular too."

"You did sound great, and the crowd was digging the music," Lisa Marie said. "You could have heard a pin drop after you finished your song, Cedra. That was amazing."

Cedra admitted. "I was almost in a panic when there was no reaction. I wasn't sure if I should run or just freeze like a deer in headlights."

"They were just stunned by the performance. It's not often you feel a song like they felt that one," Lisa Marie said. "I better get to hiring replacements soon if this crowd is any indication of how you're going to be received."

"Beers all around?" Keith asked.

"Absolutely," Ma replied.

Stone and Juliet rounded up chairs for Cedra and Juliet. "That was so much fun," Cedra told Ma. "I did like you said and took a deep breath and imagined we were jamming on the porch."

"Carrie was one of the first to stop by," Lisa Marie told them.

"I didn't even see her in here," Cedra replied. "How did she seem?"

"She was wearing a huge smile," Ma said. "She loved the way y'all sound together."

"That's a relief," Juliet said. "I was worried Carrie would be disappointed if Cedra wasn't solo."

Lisa Marie shook her head. "If she was, her actions sure didn't express that. She took several of the cover shots to send out to some radio stations."

"Some early hype over us won't hurt one bit," Keith said as he passed beers around.

When he moved to stand with Wayne and Stone, Cedra saw Carrie approaching. She was wearing a brilliant smile.

"I just wanted to stop by and tell you all congratulations on a great performance," Carrie told the group. "Will there be more of this, Saturday night?" she asked Cedra.

Cedra nodded. "Yes, the group will play one or two numbers with me."

Carrie raised the cover for all to see. "You all have twelve tracks cut already?"

"Four, actually," Juliet replied. "We are working on studio time for the other eight right now."

"Do you have it scheduled yet?" Carrie asked.

"Nope, not yet," Cedra replied. "Working on it, though."

Carrie looked at Cedra. "Would you have a problem if our meeting Monday is expanded to the whole band?"

"No problem at all," Cedra replied.

"Hold off on paying for any more studio time right now. I may have a solution for you Monday."

"Thanks," Juliet replied.

"Enjoy your celebration tonight. I look forward to hearing more from you all on Saturday," Carrie replied and turned away.

"Holy crap," Wayne replied. "I am taking off work Monday. We are going to celebrate in style that night."

"Ease up, cowboy," Juliet said. "Yes, we should be excited about a meeting with Carrie, but we also need to consider other potential offers and not jump on the first option out of the gate. I think she made it obvious she wants us tonight, but she needs to work for us. There may be other offers after Saturday."

Lisa Marie nodded. "I'd have to agree with Juliet. Carrie is chomping at the bit to sign you, which means she's worried about her competition. Hear what she has to offer, and let her know you have other options to explore before you make a decision. If you get a better offer, give her the option of sweetening the pot."

"I hate to leave such great company, but I have to get back to work," Wayne said. "Tonight was one of the greatest nights of my life. Thank you all."

"Take the truck. Stone is going to give me a ride home later," Keith said.

Wayne chuckled. "I guess we didn't plan that part out well."

"We got the important stuff. That's what counts," Cedra replied with a wink.

"I guess I'd better be moving along, too. There's no rest for the wicked. I'll see you two in the morning." Lisa Marie said. "Thanks for a great show and the cold beer."

"Our pleasure," Cedra answered. "Drive safe, and we'll see you in the morning."

"Can you guys handle hauling the instruments?" Juliet asked.

"No problem, they will fit easily in my back seat," Stone replied.

"Why don't we load everything into the bed of my truck, and we can drop you off at yours?" Cedra suggested. "I'm just outside the back door."

Juliet drained her beer. "That sounds great to me. Let's roll."

†

Ma had been mysteriously silent for several minutes, and when they climbed into Cedra's truck, Juliet asked. "Are you okay, Ma?"

"I feel a bit funny," Ma replied. "It's been a long time since I've had a beer, but I feel flushed."

"Your cheeks are a bit rosier than normal. Do you have a thermometer at home?" Cedra asked.

"Yes, I've got one of those fancy no-touch ones," Ma replied.

"Let's drop these boys off and get you home and checked out and tucked into bed," Cedra said. When Keith tapped on the side of the truck, she pulled out of the lot and drove to Stone's truck parked down the street.

"We'll see you at the house," Cedra said as they headed for home. Ma was still unusually quiet, which worried Cedra. She drove as quickly as she could."

When they arrived home, Cedra looked at Juliet. "Help Ma get upstairs and comfortable. I'll make her some ice water and be right up."

"I can make it up on my own accord," Ma fussed, but she didn't hesitate in taking Juliet's arm for support.

Cedra made a large glass of ice water, grabbed a sleeve of saltine crackers, and followed them up the stairs.

Juliet was helping Ma slip a nightgown over her head when she entered. "Where is your thermometer?" Cedra asked.

"In the bathroom medicine cabinet," Ma answered, sounding winded.

Juliet shot a worried look at Cedra. "Grab it, and let's see if she's running a fever."

Ma sat on the edge of the bed, waiting for Cedra to return. The flush on her cheeks was more evident under good lighting. Cedra turned the gadget on and aimed it at Ma's forehead. Juliet noted the frown on Cedra's face. "What is it?"

Cedra looked at the reading again. "She does have a bit of a fever. She's at 99.9 degrees. Do you have some Tylenol, Ma?"

"It should also be in the medicine cabinet," Ma answered.

Cedra placed the thermometer on the nightstand with a glass of water, then returned and handed them to Ma. "Do you have any other symptoms? Headache, body aches, chills, or nausea?"

Ma swallowed the medicine and sat the glass on the table. She shook her head. "No, just feel warm and a little wheezy," Ma replied.

"The Tylenol should help with the fever relatively soon. Do you mind if we come back in and check on you later?"

Ma looked up at Cedra. "I will be just fine. I've taken medicine and will lay down and get some sleep. There's no need for you to worry."

"I've no doubt you will, but I'll feel better if I see that for myself," Cedra replied.

"You have to be up in a few hours to work. You need your rest too," Ma reminded her.

Juliet chuckled. "I am a lady of leisure these days, so I don't have that excuse. I will come to check on you tonight. No argument."

Ma was too tired to fight and stretched out on the bed. Cedra pulled the covers over her. "I'm leaving my door open tonight, so just call out if you need anything," Cedra told Ma.

"Try to rest, and hopefully, you will feel better in the morning," Juliet said.

†

Juliet and Cedra were coming downstairs when Keith and Stone came in carrying instruments. "You look like someone just ate your last cookie," Keith said to Cedra. "Is everything okay?"

"Ma's not feeling well. She's running a bit of a fever," Cedra answered.

"Is there something I can do?" Keith asked.

"No, she's going to try and rest, but you've given me a great idea," Cedra smiled.

"Dare I ask what?" Keith said.

"It's time to make some cookies to celebrate. Can you stay for a few and join us, Stone?" Cedra asked.

"I'll preheat the oven," Juliet said.

"Chocolate chip?" Stone asked.

"Yes, indeed," Cedra replied.

"Do you think Ma would eat some?" Juliet asked.

"I'll bake extras for her. We can take them up in a bit when we recheck her temperature." Cedra said as she walked to the freezer and pulled out cookie dough.

"I sure hope it isn't that new virus everyone's been talking about," Stone said. "Some kind of new super flu sort of thing."

"I sure hope not too. If Ma's not better in the morning, Juliet will take her to the doctor."

†

Cedra filled two cookie sheets full of cookies and popped them in the oven. The others were sitting around the kitchen table. "I think I need someone to pinch me," she said as she sat next to Juliet. "Wait, it's just a figure of speech, but am I the only one that feels like I'm dreaming?"

"This whole night has been surreal," Stone said.

Juliet nodded. "It went off even better than I had hoped. I don't think I've seen that place so packed on a weeknight before."

"Thank you for allowing us to all be a part of your meeting with Carrie," Stone said.

Cedra smiled at him. "It's not all about me anymore. It's about The Bentleys, and we are all a part of that and should have a voice in the decision-making process."

"It's so exciting to think that we may have decisions and options to look forward to discussing," Keith said. "Other than you, Juliet, I don't think any of us have ever been this close to a potential contract."

"Definitely not me. I haven't even turned a head until tonight. The crowd genuinely liked us. I still feel the excitement rushing through me," Stone grinned.

"Me too," Cedra said as she walked over to check the cookies. "I'm not sure I'll sleep a wink tonight." She peered inside at the baking morsels. "Someone should start pouring milk. Juliet, will you bring me some fine china?"

"I'm all over it. You two sit tight, and I'll get the milk too," Juliet said. She walked to the refrigerator and opened the door. "We need to put milk on our shopping list," Juliet stated. She shook the jug. "There should be enough for cookies, but not much else."

"I'll run out in a bit and get a couple of gallons," Keith said. "I need a bit of unwinding, too."

Cedra looked at Juliet. "If we do get a contract, what do you think the first steps will be?"

"First off, it's "when not if," we get a contract. I'd bet my last dollar we will have something in the works by this time next week. I would think more studio time first to get a few more tracks and then interviews with radio stations to get our name out there. Maybe a small paying gig or two at first until the beginning of the new year."

"I don't think any of us should give up our jobs yet," Stone replied.

"No, we still have bills to pay," Cedra replied.

"I've got a bit of a bankroll saved, so I'm not stressing a job, but I thought I would take the lead on some marketing for us, unless Carrie or an agent takes that role away to a professional. Then I'll look for something."

"You could probably get some backup vocal work at one of the studios," Keith suggested. "I'll check if there's an opening at the Ryman that you could work."

Cedra removed the pans of cookies and painfully waited for them to cool a bit to harden enough she could use a spatula to serve them. She placed several on a plate for Ma. Juliet helped her carry the rest to the table.

"Man, those look good," Keith said as he took a bite and fanned his mouth. "Still plenty hot, though, so be careful."

After devouring the cookies, Stone excused himself to head back to town. "I'm going to run get more milk. Do we need cookies, too?" Keith asked.

Cedra nodded. "Those were good, so yes, get some more." She looked at Juliet. "Should we check on Ma and then try to rest?"

"Yeah, that sounds good." Juliet picked up the plate of cookies and followed Cedra upstairs.

The dim light in Ma's room made her look pale, but Cedra could see the pink on her cheeks. The way Ma was lying there made her think of her mom, and she hesitated just inside the room.

Juliet turned to look at her. "You okay?"

"Yeah, I'm good," Cedra said and proceeded to the table and picked up the thermometer. She looked at the reading and let out a deep breath. "She's back to normal," she told Juliet.

"Do you think she would eat a cookie, or should we just leave them for her?" Juliet asked.

"They smell too good not to eat," Ma said and popped an eye open.

Juliet sat beside her on the bed. "Doc Cedra says your fever is down. Sorry, we don't have milk to offer, but Keith is going out for more. How are you feeling?"

"Better, but still tired," Ma answered as she lifted a cookie to her mouth. "These are great, Cedra," Ma said.

Juliet huffed and put her hands on her hips. "How did you know Cedra baked them?"

"Juliet darling, as much as I love you, you are horrible in the kitchen," Ma said with a grin.

Juliet placed her hands over her heart. "That was brutal, but true. I know I'm not much help in the kitchen."

"But you make for excellent company," Ma said. "I want you both to know how very proud I am of you tonight. The boys, too, but I think the two of you have succeeded in pushing them out of their comfort zones."

"We were good, weren't we, Ma?" Juliet asked.

"The Bentleys performed like you have played together for years," Ma praised. "I can't wait to see what the future holds for you."

"Hopefully, we will know a bit more after Monday," Cedra replied.

"I'll keep everything I have crossed until then," Ma smiled. "It's getting late, so you better hit the sack. I'll see you in the morning for coffee."

"No, ma'am, Dr. Cedra is ordering for you to stay in bed. I can get my coffee."

"I'll get up and make it while she's in the shower," Juliet said.

Ma quirked an eyebrow.

"I'll go back to bed once she's gone," Juliet replied.

"I won't argue with you tonight, so thank you to both of you," Ma said.

"Goodnight, Ma," Juliet said. "Do you need more water or anything before we go?"

"I'm good. Thanks," Ma said. "Sweet sleep."

"You too, Ma," Cedra said and bent down to kiss Ma's forehead. "Call out if you need anything."

"I promise. Now go." Ma chuckled.

†

Cedra led Juliet into her room. "Ma's forehead still felt a bit warm. I need to get up and recheck her in a few hours."

"No, you don't. I will. I can sleep in tomorrow, remember." Juliet pulled Cedra in for a kiss.

"Check her temp and give her more Tylenol if her fever returns," Cedra instructed.

"I may not know much about the kitchen, but I can handle a thermometer and Tylenol." Juliet grinned as she began unbuttoning Cedra's shirt. "Let's change into sleep clothes and stretch out for a bit. I promise I'll check on Ma in a couple of hours."

†

Cedra climbed into the bed first and snuggled against Juliet when she joined her. It didn't take long for Juliet's warmth and the long day to catch up with her, and Cedra drifted off to sleep. Juliet smiled when she heard the soft purring Cedra emitted as she slept. She listened to the front door open an hour later as Keith returned from the store. She crept out of bed and met him in the hallway as he climbed the stairs.

"I hope I didn't wake you. I promise I was trying to be quiet," Keith whispered.

"You didn't. I was getting up to check Ma when I heard you come inside. That took longer than I expected."

"I had to drive around for a bit to wind down after tonight's show. I still don't know if I'll sleep much. How is Ma?"

"She ate cookies, and her fever was gone. I'm going to check on her a couple of times tonight, just to be sure it stays gone."

"If you need anything, just tap on my door," Keith said.

"I will. Try to get some sleep. You were great tonight."

"We all were," Keith reminded her. "See you in the morning."

†

Keith slipped inside his room, and Juliet walked into Ma's room. She stopped in the doorway and realized that seeing Ma lying there so still may have triggered a memory of her mom for Cedra. Juliet hadn't thought of that earlier, but Cedra had jumped right into caretaker mode and examined Ma. She must have had a lot of experience providing care for her ill mom until she passed. Juliet picked up the thermometer and pointed it at Ma's forehead. She looked at the reading and released a sigh of relief. Still normal. Thank goodness, she thought as she returned the instrument and left Ma's room. Juliet climbed back into bed and didn't stir until the alarm woke Cedra.

†

"Good morning, sweetheart," Juliet said as she kissed Cedra awake. "I'll go recheck Ma and start the coffee pot while you shower."

"How was she last night?" Cedra asked.

"I checked her around midnight, and her temperature was still normal," Juliet reported.

"Thanks," Cedra said and kissed her lover. "I'll see you downstairs soon."

Ma was still sleeping when Juliet entered her room. She quickly checked her temperature and found it elevated again.

"More Tylenol," she whispered and opened the bottle to pour out two capsules.

"Ma, I need you to wake up for a minute," Juliet whispered.

Ma startled awake and stared at Juliet for a minute. "Is everything okay?" she asked.

"Your temperature is up a little again, and Cedra gave strict orders to give you more Tylenol." Juliet smiled as she held out the medicine and the glass of water.

Ma swallowed the medicine and handed the glass back to Juliet. "I will be fine, so don't worry."

"You don't worry about anything. I'm making Cedra's coffee, and I will help the boys with breakfast when they get up. I'll continue to check on you, too, Ma. Do you think you can eat anything?"

"Not just yet. Maybe later you can fix me some toast."

"That I know I can handle," Juliet smiled. "Holler if you need anything."

"I will," Ma answered and laid her head back on the pillow.

Juliet heard the shower as she passed by their rooms and descended the stairs. She was surprised to find Keith sitting at the table eating a bowl of cereal. "What has you up so early?"

"The box of Cap'n Crunch I bought last night when I got milk. I've been thinking about it ever since I went to bed. I used to eat this stuff almost every morning as a kid." He pushed the box toward her. "Care to join me? I've already got the coffee brewed."

"Don't mind if I do," Juliet said. "Are you ready for some coffee?"

"Not until I finish eating," Keith replied.

Juliet pulled down a bowl and prepared Cedra's travel mug full of coffee. She placed it on the table and joined Keith in eating breakfast.

"Man, I haven't had this in years," Juliet announced.

"Loaded with sugar, but it never failed to get me going as a kid," Keith grinned and added more cereal to his milk. "How is Ma this morning?"

"Her temperature was up a bit, so I gave her another dose of Tylenol. I sure hope it isn't anything serious."

Keith wiped an errant drop of milk from his chin. "Me too. Ma is our rock."

Cedra started down the stairs, and Juliet stopped mid-chew to watch her. "How do you manage to make blue jeans and a pullover look so good?"

"You're just biased, silly," Cedra replied as she walked into the kitchen.

"Um, no, she's not. You do look nice." Keith agreed with Juliet.

"Cap'n Crunch time, huh? Did you check on Ma?" Cedra asked.

Juliet nodded. "I gave her more Tylenol. She was back to 100 degrees. I told her I'd be back to check on her and try to get some toast in her."

"Dry or lightly buttered with more water," Cedra replied.

"Got it, doc," Juliet said. "Do you have time for some cereal?"

"Not this morning. I'll call you during our mid-morning break to check on Ma, but please call if anything changes."

"Is there something I should be alert for?" Juliet asked.

"If her temp doesn't go down within the hour or it continues to elevate, or if she starts having other symptoms like difficulty breathing, headache, or body ache." Cedra picked up her mug. "Any of those, and I'd call her doctor's office and see if you can get her in. They can at least test her for the flu."

Keith frowned. "She had her flu shot a couple of weeks ago."

Cedra looked at him, surprised that Keith would know that. "Even though she's vaccinated, it may be a different strain than what's covered by the vaccine."

Keith smiled with a milk mustache. "I want to be smart like you when I grow up," he teased. "I don't go in until later, so I'll help Juliet keep an eye on Ma.

"Thanks. Pull something out of the freezer, and I'll cook some dinner when I get home," Cedra said.

"I'll grill some hamburgers if you cook some fries," Keith offered.

"You have got yourself a deal. Let me know if I need to bring anything home from the store."

"Don't worry about that. I may not cook, but I can surely shop." Juliet shot a wink to Cedra, who bent down to kiss her. "Have a great day, sexy."

"I will. Keep me posted on Ma."

"Drive safe and watch for critters," Keith warned.

"Will do," Cedra replied and pulled the door behind her.

"How did she get so smart?" Keith asked.

"She took care of her mom until she passed, so she learned a lot of things the hard way," Juliet said.

"I had forgotten about that," Keith replied.

"I did, too, until I saw the look of worry on her face last night as she watched Ma. She didn't say anything, but I know she had a flashback."

Keith reached for her empty bowl. "Why don't you try to get some sleep, and I'll get some hamburger thawing and make a list of anything we need from the store?"

"Don't worry about thawing some. I'll just buy fresh. I'll set my alarm for eight. Will you check in on Ma in an hour?"

"I'll take her some lightly buttered toast and fresh ice water," Keith answered.

Juliet smiled. "Thanks, Keith."

Juliet returned upstairs and buried her face in Cedra's pillow, and was asleep in no time.

†

Cedra stepped out of her truck just as Stone was arriving. She waited for him, and they walked in together.

"Good morning, sunshine. How is Ma this morning?" he asked.

"Still running a temp, but hopefully it's nothing serious," Cedra answered.

"I hope not, too." Stone swung the door open for them.

"Here's the dynamic duo," Lisa Marie called out from the counter. "Coffee?"

"Yes, please," Cedra answered.

"How's Ma this morning?" Lisa Marie asked.

"She's still running a bit of fever, but Keith and Juliet are watching her close today," Cedra answered.

"I hope she's just got one of those nasty fall bugs," Lisa Marie said. "You guys were awesome last night. I don't know if you realized it, but Carrie wasn't the only agent that saw the performance. I counted at least three that I recognized. There was a rep from Big Machine there as well."

"Wow, I had no idea," Cedra said.

"Big Machine has a great lineup of artists. Rascal Flatts, Lady A, Florida Georgia Line, Reba, and of course Tay Tay," Stone joked.

"Tay Tay?" Cedra asked.

"Taylor Swift's nickname. Or one of them," Lisa Marie explained.

"Those are some great artists and songwriters," Cedra replied.

Lisa Marie handed them a cup of coffee. "Yeah, and each one of them started just like you all. Nobody starts on top of the game. You gotta work your way there."

"We will get there," Cedra replied. "None of us are afraid of hard work. If we can get a bit of luck, that wouldn't hurt either."

Lisa Marie nodded toward the door. "The natives are hungry. Are we ready?"

"Yes, ma'am," Stone said, and he rushed over to open the door.

"Good morning, folks," Stone said as he held the door open.

"Good morning to you and great show last night," one of the men said as he entered.

"Yeah, you guys knocked it out of the park. We can't wait to hear more Saturday," his companion added.

Lisa Marie and Cedra heard the exchange. Lisa Marie looked at Cedra and winked. "Told ya so."

Cedra chuckled. She picked up a pot of coffee and followed the men to their table. "Coffee, gentlemen?"

"Served by the lady with the golden voice herself," one man replied. "Yes, please, and keep it coming," the other answered.

"I sure will. Do you know what you want to eat today or need a few minutes?"

"Three over easy with toast, hash browns, ham, and bacon, and a side of pancakes. I'm starving."

"Damn, Tom, that sounds good. Just double his order, Ms. Tyler."

"You can just call me Cedra," she smiled as she finished writing down the order. "Any juice?"

"One orange and one apple. You can call me Mick, and this here's Tom," he smiled.

"Thanks, guys. Let me get your order in, and it'll be out quick."

They were only the first of many patrons that morning who congratulated them on the performance the previous night, and Cedra thought her face would be sore from smiling. "I am amazed by the people who have complimented us today," she told Stone and Lisa Marie. "I knew the crowd was big, but with those lights, it was hard to see into the crowd."

"That's why some performers choose to wear sunglasses. The lights can be brutal," Lisa Marie said. "There were quite a few of our regular patrons there last night, and I bet we pick up more business with y'all working here."

"I hope so," Stone said. "You've been good to us."

Lisa Marie shook her head. "I should give y'all a raise. You're probably two of the better servers I've had in a long time."

"The tips are great, and your support is better than any raise," Cedra said.

"I appreciate you both. Ready for some breakfast?" Lisa Marie asked.

"Yeah, I've worked up an appetite," Stone said.

"Will you put an order in for us while I call to check on Ma?"

"Sure thing, Cedra. The usual?" Stone asked.

Cedra nodded. "I'm hungry, too."

Cedra pulled out her phone and dialed Juliet's number. It rang several times before Juliet finally answered. "Hey, is everything okay?" Cedra asked.

"I got the doctor's office to work Ma into the schedule. Her fever is still low grade, but I didn't want to take any chances. They just did a nasal swab for a flu test, and we are waiting for results."

"I won't keep you then, but please call and let me know the results."

"Sure will. Love you," Juliet replied.

"I love you, too. Hugs to Ma for me."

"Is she okay?" Lisa Marie asked.

"Juliet has taken her in to see her doctor and get a flu test. They are waiting on the results now. I hope everything is good for Ma." Cedra looked at Stone. "You got me worried about that super flu virus. I hope we don't see any of that here soon."

"I saw something about that on the news. It's not looking great to keep it out of the United States. It's spreading like wildfire across Europe, so it's just a matter of time," Lisa Marie said. "I may need to start stocking up on masks, gloves, and cleaning supplies. People always panic, and then there's a shortage. Maybe I can get ahead of the curve."

"We can handle things here if you want to go ahead and start making some orders. I'll holler at you if we get swamped," Cedra told her.

"Good deal. Hopefully, I won't be long," Lisa Marie said and walked into her office.

Stone looked at Cedra. "She's apprehensive, isn't she?"

Cedra smiled. "We all need to be careful until we know what's going on. Eat good, wash hands often, vitamins wouldn't hurt, and get plenty of rest." She grinned at him. "I doubt you'll be getting much rest this weekend. Are you excited about Sarah coming to visit?"

"Yeah, I can't wait. Only a few more hours, and my baby will be back in my arms." Stone let out a sigh. "It feels like forever."

Cedra nodded. "I'm sure she feels that way too. Enjoy the time you have together and pray it doesn't go by too quickly." The door opened, and it was their first lunch guest. "Finish up. I've got this."

†

The lunch crowd was busy, and Cedra was relieved when Lisa Marie emerged from the office and took over the counter. She had a worried look on her face, and the first chance Cedra got, she walked over to check on her. "Everything okay, boss?"

"It was a good thing I called to place orders. My suppliers are getting swamped with requests, so I placed an early order and set them up for weekly deliveries until I'm well stocked. I also got another call, I need to discuss with you and Stone, but that can wait."

"Okay, just let me know what I can help with," Cedra said as she picked up a fresh pitcher of tea and made the rounds. She heard the door open and smiled when she saw Carrie arriving with two men in tow. She walked to her usual table in Cedra's section and looked up with a smile as Cedra approached.

"Good afternoon," Carrie smiled.

"Welcome back. Tea for everyone to start or something else?" Cedra asked.

"Tea is fine," all three answered, so Cedra returned for three new glasses. "Do you need a few minutes to look over the menu?"

"I'll have my usual," Carrie said.

"No celebrating today?" Cedra teased.

"Not today, but maybe after Monday," Carrie teased back with a wink.

"I'll have the double cheeseburger and fries," one man answered, and the other looked up at Cedra. "Hey, you're one of the songwriters for The Bentleys, aren't you? Great show last night."

"Thank you, sir. My name is Cedra, and yes, I'm part of the group."

Carrie chuckled. "She's the modest one of the bunch. She's a terrific writer and performer. I was very impressed last night."

Cedra felt herself blushing. "Thanks. We all felt great after the show."

"I guess I'll have a Rueben and fries," the man finally ordered. "I hear you have an Open Mic performance here Saturday. Is that right?"

"Yes, sir, I do."

"Remind me to reserve a table with Lisa Marie before we leave then," he told Carrie.

"I've got you covered already, boss," Carrie answered.

"I'll go put these orders in," Cedra replied and walked back to the kitchen.

"That's Carrie's boss?" Cedra asked Lisa Marie.

"Yes, Mark, and he's also part owner of Big Machine, so don't spill anything on him," Lisa Marie teased.

"No pressure there," Cedra grinned and made the rounds to refill tea glasses. She glanced at the dessert counter to see what sweets were on the menu.

When she heard "order up" from the kitchen, Cedra returned to gather the tray filled with food.

"Remember, no spilling," Lisa Marie teased as she walked by.

Cedra loaded condiments on the tray before delivering the food. She served Carrie first and then the two men. "We have a huge selection of pie today, including buttermilk, if you have room left. Is there anything else I can get you?"

"This all looks and smells terrific, but please be sure to save me a piece of that buttermilk pie," Mark said.

"Me too," Carrie added.

"I'll be the oddball if you have coconut cream," the other guest replied.

"We certainly do. Just let me know when you're ready. I'll check back on you in a few minutes."

"Thanks, Cedra," Carrie replied.

When Cedra returned to the counter, Lisa Marie handed her the phone. "I answered it when I saw it was Juliet."

Cedra nodded and took the phone. "Hey. How's Ma?"

"She's going to be fine. It was an early case of the flu, but we've got medications and strict bed-rest orders for her to follow, so hopefully, it will remain a mild case. I'm going to drop her off at home for Keith to watch over her, and then I'll go shopping."

"That's great news. Do I need to pick up anything?" Cedra asked.

"No, I think I've got everything covered. We just pulled up at home, so I'll see you later. Love you."

"Love you, too."

"Everything okay?" Lisa Marie asked. She and Stone were patiently waiting.

"A case of the flu that will hopefully stay mild," Cedra said. "Meds and orders for bed rest and lots of fluids."

"I don't envy y'all having to keep Ma in bed," Lisa Marie said. "Be careful though, that you all don't get infected."

"Crap, I didn't even think of that," Cedra replied.

"Speaking of which, the artist that was to perform after you called and he can't make it because of illness. Do y'all want an extra hour?"

"Hell, yes," Cedra answered a bit too loudly. "I'm sorry he's ill, but we won't pass up an extra hour." She looked at Stone. "You okay with that? I know Sarah will be in town for a short time."

"She would kick me in the tail if I said no." He grinned.

"Awesome. Thanks, Lisa Marie," Cedra replied.

"Thank you. Now I don't have to scramble around for a replacement."

"We'll be more than happy to fill that slot." Cedra nearly floated back into the dining room. When she approached Carrie's table, they all looked up. "Are you ready for pie?"

"Sure, bring it on, Cedra," Mark replied.

Cedra cleared their lunch dishes and smiled. "I'll be right back," Cedra said and walked behind the counter to plate the pie.

When she delivered the pie, she looked at Carrie. "The artist that was scheduled to perform behind me Saturday is ill. Lisa Marie has offered us the extra slot, so maybe we'll be able to show you a bit more."

"That's great news for you. I'll be looking forward to hearing a bit more of the range from you all," Carrie replied.

"That won't be a problem. We can play a few of the other tracks we want to put on our album." Cedra replied.

"I am looking forward to that," Mark replied. "The title song intrigues me, and I hope it will be one you perform."

"You can bet it will be," Cedra replied. "Thanks. Do any of you want coffee to go with the pie?"

"That is a great idea. Thanks, Cedra."

She nodded and returned with three cups and a pot of coffee. "Just let me know if you need anything else."

"Just a check, please," Mark replied. "This pie is delicious."

"Here you go, and thanks for joining us today," Cedra said as she placed the check on the table.

"Thanks for the great service," Mark replied.

†

When the evening crew started coming in, Stone left for the airport. "I know it's late notice, but could you hang around for a couple more hours so I can pick up an order at a big box store?" Lisa Marie asked.

"Sure, that's no problem. Just let me call to let Juliet know. Are you that worried about supplies?"

Lisa Marie nodded. "Yeah, I am. Thanks, Cedra. I'll be quick."

Cedra picked up her phone, and luckily Juliet was still at the store. "Pick up a few gallons of bleach, some Lysol spray, and wipes if you can," she asked.

"Okay, that shouldn't be a problem. Whoa, there's only a few gallons of bleach left. Are we having a zombie apocalypse?"

"No, people are getting panicked over this new flu outbreak. Lisa Marie is heading out for supplies now, so I'll be a couple of hours late tonight."

"Is there anything else I need to stock up on?" Juliet asked.

"Hand sanitizer and antimicrobial soap. Surgical masks if you can find them."

"Wow, this does sound serious."

Cedra sighed. "I hope not, but at least we'll be prepared. We need to be cautious around Ma, too. She's probably contagious as long as she's running a fever. Grab some vitamin C and juice."

"Aw, crap, I didn't think about Ma being contagious."

"I know, I didn't think about it either, but I should have known better. I'll see you as soon as I get home. Grab some broth, too, in case Ma can't keep food down. Love you."

"I love you, too. See you soon."

†

Lisa Marie made it back in record time, and as soon as Cedra helped her unload and stock the supplies, she was ready to head for home.

"Thanks for staying late," Lisa Marie said.

"No problem. I was glad I could help out. I'll see you tomorrow night unless you need something else."

"Nope, I'm good. Thanks again, Cedra."

"Goodnight, boss."

†

Cedra made it home and could smell the grill burning. "Someone must be hungry," she said as she climbed the steps onto the porch. When she went inside, she had to stifle a laugh. Juliet was standing at the stove wearing one of Ma's aprons and was making French fries. Wayne was sitting at the table, slicing onions and tomatoes with tears running down his cheeks.

"If this isn't a picture of domestic bliss, I don't know what is," she said as she entered the kitchen and snapped a few pics. "How's Ma?"

"Go check on her. We've got her propped up on pillows in the living room. No fever, but recheck her, please." Juliet smiled at Cedra.

Cedra walked into the living room and took Ma's temp. "How are you feeling? No fever. That's good."

"Not too bad. I'm a bit tired and have a little headache," Ma answered.

"Do you want some Tylenol to see if we can knock it out?" Cedra asked.

"Yes, that would be good. How are you?" Ma inquired.

"I'm good. Lisa Marie asked me to stay over a bit so she could run to the store." Cedra doled out two Tylenol and handed Ma a glass of water. She sat the glass back down and pulled her phone from her back pocket. "You have got to see these." She pulled up the photos of Juliet and Wayne in the kitchen.

"Maybe I should be sick more often," Ma teased. "I need to get a smaller apron if Juliet is going to cook, though. She could wrap mine around her twice."

"I'm impressed she's learning to cook," Cedra replied. "Do you need anything? Have you tried to eat?"

"I just finished some chicken and stars soup not long before you came in."

"Good. A burger is probably too heavy for you, but do you want to try a few fries?"

"Juliet would probably be disappointed if I didn't," Ma smiled weakly.

"Okay, I'll have her bring you some in a few minutes. I'm glad you're feeling better."

"Me, too, Cedra," Ma replied.

"Holler if you need anything," Cedra said and left the room.

†

Juliet was pulling up a batch of fries when Cedra entered the kitchen. She washed her hands at the sink and smiled at her lover. "Those look good. Why don't you put a bit of salt on them and take some to Ma? I can take over here for a few minutes."

Juliet beamed at Cedra. "Mickey Dee's ain't got nothing on my fries," she said.

"That's right. You did great. Has Keith got the burgers on already?"

"Yeah, he just came in to report they would be ready in about five minutes," Wayne said.

"Seems like I timed my entry just right then," Cedra said with a chuckle.

"Perfectly," Juliet kissed her cheek and took a small portion of fries and some ketchup to Ma.

"Should I go ahead and set the table?" Wayne asked.

"Sure, set us up with some fine china and napkins," Cedra answered. "I think it's safe to pour some drinks too."

Juliet returned to the kitchen smiling. "Ma said they were the best fries she's ever tasted."

Cedra took one off the plate and bit into it. "I have to agree with Ma. These are great. Did Keith put the buns on the grill too?"

"Yeah, I think so," Juliet replied. "Should I check?"

"Yes, ask him if he needs a pan to put the burgers and buns in," Cedra said. She handed one to Juliet. "Just in case."

Juliet and Keith returned just as Cedra removed the last batch of fries and carried them to the table.

Keith sat the pan of burgers on the table, and everyone took their seats. "Good job, everybody," Cedra said. "This looks great."

"Let's dig in," Keith said. "Has anyone checked on Ma recently?" he asked before taking a bite.

"Juliet just took her some fries," Cedra answered. "Oh, guess what?"

"What?" Wayne asked.

"The artist scheduled after us on Saturday called out sick today to Lisa Marie, and she asked if we wanted a second hour."

"I sure hope you told her yes," Juliet replied.

"Of course, I did," Cedra replied. "I also met Carrie's boss, Mark, today, and he's part-owner of Big Machine records according to Lisa Marie. He will be in the audience

Saturday. Last night, he also caught our show, and he specifically asked to hear 'Six Strings.' He was impressed that we have tracks ready for an album."

"It's a good thing we saved that one and Juliet's song, too," Keith said. "I wish she and Stone could run through it one more time, though."

"Why don't you text him and ask him to come out after lunch, and we can run through it again," Juliet suggested. "He needs to come out to get his clothes Ma prepped for him anyhow."

"That's true, maybe we can spring for more brisket," Cedra replied.

"I'm on it," Keith replied and picked up his phone to shoot a quick text to Stone. His phone pinged almost immediately. *We'll be there. How's Ma?*

Feeling better, Keith texted. *Have fun tonight.*

†

After they finished picking up the kitchen, Keith grinned. "Anyone up for some picking?"

"Sure, it's still early. Do you want to ask Ma?" Juliet said.

"I'll be right back." Keith returned with Ma on his elbow a few minutes later.

"I'll gladly escape my sentence on the couch," Ma said.

"Let's get a throw for you. You don't need to get a chill," Cedra said and returned to the couch. She tucked it around Ma while the others grabbed their instruments.

"I'm sorry I'm going to miss the show tomorrow night," Ma said. "I've asked one of my old bingo pals to come to sit with me, so y'all don't have to worry about me."

"That was a great idea. I was worried about how we were going to leave you alone," Cedra said. "Especially now. We've got an additional time slot tomorrow night."

"That's excellent news. I just hate I'm going to miss it," Ma said.

"You might miss the live performance, but Sarah will be taking a video to show Stone's family. I'm sure she'll let you view it before she goes home," Cedra informed Ma.

"That would be great," Ma said. "Get to playing," she teased.

"I've got an idea," Cedra replied as she took her seat. "Since we now have a full hour, what about adding another cover song so we aren't giving away too much of the album?"

"You have something in mind," Juliet teased. "What is it?"

"We highlight Stone with "The Devil Went Down to Georgia" to show off his fiddle skills. Why don't we cover "Up on the Ridge" by Dierks Bentley to let Wayne share his banjo skills and Keith take the lyrics?"

"Hell yeah," Wayne said. "I love that song."

"Have you ever covered it?" Cedra asked.

"No, but I'd love to give it a shot," Wayne replied.

"You up to tackling the lyrics?" Cedra asked Keith.

Keith turned to look at Juliet. "Can you print them out for me?"

"Give me five minutes. Why don't y'all listen to the tune a few times while I'm printing?"

"That's no problem." Wayne pulled out his iPhone and brought up the song.

"The rest of us can add the guitar to allow you to focus on the lyrics," Cedra told Keith.

"That sounds like a deal to me," Keith said. "I don't remember it being a difficult song, but if I can concentrate on lyrics only, it will be easier to pick it up faster."

They listened to the song three times while Juliet printed out copies. She returned and handed each of them a copy. "We'll bring Stone up to speed tomorrow. We've bothered him enough tonight. Play it one more time if you would."

Cedra's head bobbed to the music. She looked at Wayne and Keith. "Are you ready to give it a run?"

"Let's do this," Wayne said.

After the third run, Ma nodded her head. "That one sounded good."

"I'll work on getting sharp on the lyrics tonight," Keith replied. "It feels good."

"Ma, are you ready to go to bed?" Cedra asked when she saw her dozing.

"I don't think I have much of a choice. I can't seem to keep my eyes open."

"I think we should call it a night then. Juliet and I will get her upstairs and tucked in for the night. I'm going to take a run at Ma's French toast in the morning, and we can make plans for brisket for a late lunch slash early dinner," Cedra replied.

"Wayne and I will take care of that, so don't worry. There will be plenty of good eats," Keith said. "We may even swing by the Farmers Market to get a nice dessert."

"Now we're talking. Maybe there will be a caramel cake tomorrow," Juliet said.

"Damn, that does sound good. Cedra, could we convince you to bake more cookies tonight?"

Cedra smiled. "Got milk?"

"Another full gallon if we finish this one off," Keith smiled.

"Go ahead and get the oven preheating and bring Ma some ice water. Could you eat more cookies, Ma?"

Ma nodded and smiled. "I do believe I could."

"Let's do this then. Wayne, can you bring our instruments inside? We can put them away later."

"You got it, Cedra," Wayne answered.

"Let's get you upstairs then, Ma," Juliet said.

†

Cedra and Juliet escorted Ma safely up the stairs. "You know it's going to take a little bit for cookies, Ma. Would you feel better if you took a bath or shower?"

"I probably would feel better," Ma answered.

"Would you mind staying with Ma to help if she needs it?" Cedra asked Juliet.

"Not at all. Shower or bath, Ma?" Juliet asked.

"A shower would be faster, but a hot bath sure might feel good to these old bones," Ma answered.

"I'll start drawing a bath then," Juliet said. "I've got some bath treatment that helps soothe everything. No bubbles, but very relaxing. Would you mind if I added some? It may help to relax you."

"Bring it on," Ma said.

"I'll be right back then." Juliet left the room.

"Do you want a nightgown or some pajamas to put on?" Cedra asked.

"I think a nightgown will be good. Would you mind bringing me a cup of coffee with the cookies?"

"You can have anything you want, Ma," Cedra said.

Juliet returned with a bottle of bath treatment and a glass of ice water. "Do you want to recheck her temp before we get her in a hot bath?" Juliet asked.

"That's a good idea," Cedra replied. She smiled when she found Ma's temperature back to normal. "Ma's good to go. I'll set up some nightclothes for her on the bed."

"I'll get you in the tub and wait out here. Just give me a holler when you're ready to come out, but take your time," Juliet said as she led Ma into the bathroom.

"Thank you, girls, for taking such good care of me," Ma said. "The boys, too."

"You take care of us all the time, Ma," Juliet said.

Cedra called after them. "That's the truth, Ma. You deserve all the good care we can give you, so tell us if you need anything."

Cedra placed a clean nightgown and underwear on the bed for Ma and then went downstairs to bake cookies.

"Everything okay?" Keith asked.

"Yeah, Juliet's staying with her while Ma takes a soothing bath," Cedra explained.

"Is Ma going to be okay?" Wayne asked.

Cedra nodded. "I think we caught it early, and the medicine seems to be working. We just need to make sure she rests, eats, and takes all of the medication even when she insists that she feels better."

"We all need to be careful in the future. The reports on this stuff they are calling corona virus sound deadly. Wash our hands often and stay away from folks who are coughing or sneezing," Wayne said.

Cedra nodded. "I agree. I asked Juliet to pick up some vitamin C at the store today. It wouldn't hurt us to take it to help keep our immune system strong. Lots of fluids, and if we start feeling ill, we need to let each other know immediately to keep from spreading it, especially now since Ma has already been sick."

"I'd hate to give that crap to any of us," Wayne said.

"Amen to that," Cedra said. The stove chimed that it was preheated. "I guess I'd better get busy making some cookies. Keith, will you make a half pot of coffee? Ma wants some with her cookies."

"I'm on it," Keith answered and walked to the pantry. "I'll grab some fine china, too." He laughed.

"I've been holding out on y'all, Cedra," Wayne confessed. "I can make French toast, so why don't you let me make breakfast in the morning? You don't have to carry the load of cooking."

"I won't argue with you on that," Cedra said. "Thanks, Wayne. We all need to work together until we can get Ma back on her feet and then maybe after, too, to give her a break now and then."

"That would be good, and we all need to be more independent," Keith said. "I'm open to any lessons."

Cedra placed the first two pans in the oven to bake. "Two batches tonight?"

"I sure won't argue with a second batch," Keith said.

"I didn't reckon you would after I saw the amount of cookie dough you bought," Cedra teased. "Hey, I need your help on something else. I want to write something with a harmonica, banjo, and fiddle. Do you think you can put your bluegrass hats on and help?"

Keith shot Wayne a look. "I think we can handle that. Give you the bones and let you pretty it up," Keith said.

"Good," Cedra said. "I feel like it should be a fun, cutting loose kinda song."

"I agree," Keith said.

"You know I just have a feeling tomorrow night is going to be great," Cedra told them. "Playing at Wild Bill's only confirmed to us how much fun we could have playing together and how well we sounded. Tomorrow night is going to be a continuation of that. As long as we enjoy playing together, there's no telling how far we could go." She smiled at the boys. "When Juliet showed me the Titan's stadium, I told her how I'd love to fill that place up one day. It sounded like a pipedream, but we could make it happen. If Carrie or whoever our agent turns into hooks us up with the right big-name band, we could take off."

"Like a rocket," Keith agreed. "Could you see us opening for someone like Eric Church or Little Big Town or Lady A?"

"Yes, I can," Cedra said. "With enough hard work and a little luck."

"That's it. Tomorrow, I'm going looking for a four-leaf clover," Wayne teased.

"Lucky penny, rabbit's foot, favorite pick. Whatever your mojo is, we keep using it," Cedra replied.

†

"Ma, you doing okay in there?" Juliet called out. She hadn't heard Ma stirring, but she didn't want to walk in on her.

"Yeah, this is so comfortable. I don't want to get out," Ma answered. "The water's getting cold, though."

"You know we can draw more hot water if you want to soak a little longer," Juliet said.

"Nope, the way I figure it, Cedra's just about ready to pull the first batch of cookies out, and by the time I get dressed for bed, she'll be heading upstairs with coffee and cookies."

"You are so clever, Ma," Juliet teased. She heard Ma pull the drain on the tub. "Do you need some help getting up?"

"It probably wouldn't hurt to have you on standby. My legs feel like jelly," Ma admitted.

Juliet entered the bathroom and tossed a towel over her shoulder. Ma was turned and used a handrail to pull herself up. She managed to stand and took Juliet's hand to step from the tub.

Juliet smiled. "There you go. Back on solid ground. Do you want me to bring your nightgown and slippers while you dry off?"

"That would be great. Thanks, Juliet."

†

Cedra gently removed the warm cookies from the pan and placed several on a plate for Ma before filling the pans and putting the fresh dough on to cook. She poured a cup of coffee and looked at the boys. "Don't eat them all before I get back," she warned.

"We'll try our best, but damn these are good, Cedra," Wayne replied.

"I'll be back in a few minutes." Cedra picked up the plate and cup of coffee. When she arrived at Ma's door, Ma looked at Juliet and broke out laughing.

"I'm glad I didn't bet with ya, Ma," Juliet said between snickers.

"Did I miss something?" Cedra asked as she entered the room.

271

"I predicted that your timing would be impeccable," Ma said. "You would arrive just as I finished dressing and sat on the bed."

"Ah, that explains the laughter. I'm glad I don't have something in my hair or stuck in my teeth," Cedra joked. "Hot from the oven," she said as she handed the plate of cookies to Ma. "I'll set your coffee next to you." She looked at Juliet. "Do you want me to bring you some up here?"

"Nonsense, you two go back and eat some with the boys. If you don't hurry, they may have already wiped them out," Ma said.

"I warned them not to, but there's a second batch cooking if they couldn't resist," Cedra smiled. "Do you think you will want more?"

"This will set me up just fine," Ma said. "Thank you both."

"We'll be back up in a bit with your last medicine for the night," Cedra replied. She looked at Juliet. "Let's go see if there are any left."

†

There were very few cookies left when they all had their fill. Cedra looked up at the clock and smiled. "This time tomorrow, we will have finished our second live performance."

"That's so exciting to think about," Keith said. "I was serious about us all going out to eat Monday night, though. Even if we don't have a signed contract in hand, we still need to celebrate. Meeting with an agency is the furthest any of us has ever made it."

"I don't think anyone will disagree with you," Cedra replied. "I'm taking off work early to come shower and change, and if she's feeling up to it, I think we should invite Ma to attend the meeting with us. She's been an advisor to us all along. Why stop now. She could be our lucky penny."

"I think she would be honored if we asked her to go," Juliet said. "Then we could hit a nice restaurant for a great meal."

Cedra smiled. "Do you think we should ask her when we go up to give her the next dose of medicine?"

Juliet nodded. "All four of us should go. So, you two get busy washing those baking pans while we get Ma's medicine. We'll wait for you to arrive, and then we can ask."

"All over it," Keith said as he headed to the sink. "I'll wash, and you can dry."

Cedra poured out Ma's medicine, and Juliet made a fresh glass of ice water before they started up the stairs. "That was a great idea," Juliet said to Cedra.

"Asking Ma? Or having them clean the kitchen?" Cedra asked.

"Both, actually." Juliet smiled.

†

Ma had finished her cookies and coffee when they entered.

"Did you get enough? There are a few left," Cedra replied.

"No, I'm good. The cookies were very delicious, though. Thank you."

Cedra handed her several pills and a glass of water. "Here you go. These should get you through the night."

Ma swallowed the pills and drank half of the water.

Keith and Wayne came charging up the stairs. "Can we come in, Ma?" Keith asked.

"Certainly," she replied. "Is there something wrong?"

"No, ma'am, we just have something we wanted to ask you together," Juliet replied. "If you're feeling up to it, we want you to go with us to our meeting with Carrie Brooks and dinner afterward. You've been our advisor from the start, and you're like our lucky charm."

Ma's eyes glistened with tears. "I'd be delighted, and I promise I will be well and ready to go."

"Excellent news. Thanks, Ma. I'm taking off early from work to come home to shower and change clothes. You can ride with Juliet and me."

"That sounds wonderful," Ma replied. "Are you all set for tomorrow night?"

"I think we're as ready as we can be," Juliet replied. "We need a good night's sleep and some good food tomorrow. We've got the meals all planned out, so don't you worry about a thing."

"I'm so very proud of you all," Ma said. "I hate I'm going to miss the show, but I do need to be ready for Monday."

"We're all going to have a restful day Sunday. We can tell you all about the performance, or if you want, we can give you a private show."

Ma chuckled. "I never get tired of hearing ya'll jam."

"I think we'll let you get some rest. Give us a holler if you need anything." Cedra picked up the plate and empty coffee cup.

"I'll take that back downstairs," Wayne said. "Goodnight, ladies," he said and left the room.

"I don't know who he thinks he's kidding. He's going after the last of the cookies," Keith said.

"Don't pout because he thought of them first," Cedra teased.

"Honestly, I don't think I could eat any more," Keith admitted.

"Well, I'll be damned," Ma said, and they all looked at her. "I never thought I'd ever hear him admit to being full of cookies," Ma said and began laughing.

"A red-letter day for sure, Ma," Juliet replied. "Let's go," she told Cedra.

"Goodnight, all," Cedra said and followed Juliet from the room.

CHAPTER THIRTEEN

Cedra stretched when the warm sun shining through her window woke her, and she realized she was alone in the bed. She listened for signs that Juliet was up and about, but the room was silent. A glance at the clock revealed nearly eight, and Cedra sat up with a start. After slipping on some sweats, brushing her hair and teeth, Cedra stepped out of her room and peeked into Ma's room to find it empty as well. As she walked toward the stairs, Cedra could hear laughter from the kitchen. When she entered, she found Wayne at the stove under the watchful eye of Ma as he cooked French toast. Juliet was the first to look up and see her approach.

Juliet smiled. "Hey, baby girl. I'm glad you decided to join us. I was about to come up to get you."

"I can't believe I slept so late," Cedra said as she headed toward the coffee pot. "It is smelling good in here," she said to Wayne.

Wayne pointed to a large plate of bacon. "There's nothing like the smell of bacon and fresh coffee to get you going in the morning."

"How is the French toast coming along?" Juliet asked.

"The first batch is almost done. You want to be my first victim?" Wayne asked Juliet.

"Bring it on and keep them coming. I'll let Ma have the first taste, though, so she can coach you if it's missing something," Juliet replied.

"I think he's got everything he needs, but I won't turn down the offer," Ma replied. She spread butter across the battered bread and covered it in syrup.

Wayne waited anxiously for Ma to take a bite and nearly burned the next batch.

"Very tasty, Wayne," Ma said. "However, you might want to flip those," she added with a laugh.

"Crap," Wayne cried out and turned back to the stove as the bread was beginning to smoke.

"No problem, I like mine crispy," Juliet replied.

Cedra carried the plate of bacon to Ma. "You need more coffee?"

"That would be great. Do we still have some apple juice?" Ma asked.

"We sure do," Keith answered. "Does anyone else want some while I'm pouring?"

"Yes, please," Cedra replied.

"Orange for me if we have some," Juliet said.

"Milk for you, bro?" Keith asked Wayne.

"Yes, please. We might consider getting a dairy cow," Wayne teased. "Especially if the price of milk keeps going up," he added.

"It has gotten a bit crazy. There is plenty of room for a small barn, but I'm not getting up early to milk a cow," Ma teased Wayne. "You two drink the most, so it would be one of y'all sitting out there in the cold."

"That's okay, Ma. I'll get a second job if I need to," Keith answered. "That dang rooster of yours is loud enough. The last thing we need joining Reggie's crowing is a cow mooing ready to be milked."

"Where is your sense of adventure, boys?" Cedra asked as she carried the next serving to Juliet.

"This is good, Wayne," Juliet praised after taking a bite.

"Thanks," Wayne answered and cooked until everyone had a portion. "Is anyone ready for seconds?"

"You sit and eat," Cedra told him, and I'll cook a few more slices."

"Are you done eating?" Juliet asked.

"Yes, I'm saving room for some delicious brisket," Cedra replied. "Has anyone called in the order yet?"

"I did that as soon as they opened," Keith said. "Martha Stewart," he grinned at Wayne, "and I will go pick it up at twelve while you, Juliet, and Stone do a final run-through of your songs."

Juliet wiped some syrup from her chin. "This is our big day, guys. I can't believe it's finally here."

"You all will be wonderful tonight," Ma assured them. "Just make sure Sarah videos the performance so I can see it tomorrow. Do you all plan on eating in town after the performance?"

Keith shook his head. "No, ma'am, we've ordered enough brisket to have plenty left over for sandwiches when we come home."

278

"We plan on buying a bottle of bubbly to celebrate, if you'd like to join us," Wayne said.

"I'd be just as proud to share another cold beer with y'all unless you just really want champagne," Ma told them.

"A case of beer it is then," Wayne said. "Would you mind if Stone and Sarah, park his truck out here so they can join us?"

Ma shook her head. "Not at all. Stone's a Bentley, so he's more than welcome. He only has another day or two at the campground, so he can just get an early start."

"That way, nobody is on the road, and everyone will be safe," Juliet said.

Cedra held up the frying pan. "Who's ready for more?"

"Ma, can you split a pair with me?" Juliet asked.

"I do believe I can." Ma smiled.

"You boys want two more each?" Cedra replied as she served Ma and Juliet.

"Yes, please." Keith and Wayne chimed in together.

†

After cleaning up, the group brought their instruments downstairs and played until Stone and Sarah arrived. Stone introduced Sarah to the group and pulled out his guitar.

"I feel like I know you all already," Sarah said. "Stone talks about you so often. Especially the guardian angel that taught him how to be a server at the café. He can be all thumbs, but it sounds like he's doing well."

"We make a good team," Cedra replied. "I've found him quite teachable," she added with a wink to Sarah. "He talks about you and Destiny all the time, and he hates being away from y'all."

"We miss him, but we want him to have every advantage in chasing his dream. We know he can be successful, and it sounds like you all have created a great partnership."

"Hopefully, we'll know if the hard work is paying off next week," Juliet said.

Stone looked at Cedra. "Are you ready to take a run at your song?"

"Yes, I feel pretty confident, but I think it could be a perfect wedding song if we nail it," Cedra replied.

"Let's do it then." Stone grinned and pulled out his pick.

Cedra began playing, and it still felt odd to sing the song with Stone instead of Juliet. She agreed the marketing would be more successful with a male and female duet, but it would always be Juliet's song in her heart. As they played, she could see the passion in Stone's eyes and imagined that he was thinking of Sarah, just as she was thinking of Juliet.

When they finished the first round, Sarah smiled. "Damn, that's good. I can easily see that becoming a popular wedding song. You two sound great together."

"Thanks. I wrote it for Juliet, and Stone helped me with the music," Cedra explained.

Sarah placed her hand on Stone's shoulder. "He told me all about the song and how jealous he was that you could create something so beautiful with such ease." She leaned down to kiss his cheek. "I have to admit, watching the interaction between you, I understand how easy it was for you." She smiled at Juliet, then Cedra. "It's obvious how much you love each other."

"I'm the luckiest girl in the world," Juliet said.

"No way. I'm the luckiest for having met you," Cedra said, and leaned over to kiss Juliet.

"I think we are all lucky that fate has brought us together. There is a reason, and we need to ride this wave of good fortune," Keith said.

"Well said, lil bro," Wayne said. "Are you ready to go grab our food, so we can get this afternoon rolling?"

"Sure, but I'm driving. You're too dang slow," Keith teased. He looked at Stone. "Do you want to ride with us?"

Sarah smiled and nodded to him. "Go, I'm going to enjoy this rocking chair and the company of the womenfolk."

"We'll be back soon," Keith said.

"I'll go set the table," Ma said.

"No, ma'am, you won't. I'll get it," Juliet replied. "You just sit back and relax."

Ma looked at Cedra. "You heard the boss," Cedra teased.

"It won't take but a few minutes. I'll be right back," Juliet said.

"Is there anything I can help with?" Sarah asked.

Juliet smiled. "Naw, I'm good, but thanks."

Sarah looked at Cedra. "I do appreciate all you and the others have done for Stone. He's so excited to live out here with all of you and to be a Bentley."

"He's been a welcome addition to the family," Ma replied.

"It's been a lot of fun working with him and writing together. He's very talented," Cedra added.

"Stone says the same thing about you. Stone says you're his idol, but don't ever tell him I said that, please."

"It'll stay our secret then." Cedra grinned.

"He's so worried he'll let y'all down," Sarah said. "Seeing all of you together, I know that fear isn't valid. You all will lift each other and continue to grow together as one."

"Yes, they will," Ma said. "I can see so much progress in all of them over the last month. I know they are going to perform beautifully tonight."

"I told Stone I would video the performance for our family to see, and I'll bring it out tomorrow if that's fine with you?" Sarah said to Ma.

"I would love to see it," Ma replied. "I'll pay for a copy if you will send me one. I think it might be good to remind them where they came from." Ma chuckled.

"I can do that. No problem. I'll get a copy made and send it to you," Sarah promised.

"Thank you."

Juliet returned and sat beside Ma. "All set in the kitchen."

"I think after we finish eating, we need to get the instruments packed into Keith's truck and then start showers so everyone can be fresh and shiny for tonight," Ma said. "You and Stone are more than welcome to use my bathroom."

"Thanks, we can even double up to conserve some hot water," Sarah shot a wink to Juliet.

"I do like the way you think." Juliet smiled.

"Thanks for pressing and laundering his outfit. Ironing has never been Stone's strong suit," Sarah said to Ma.

"He's not the only work in progress," Cedra teased and bumped shoulders with Juliet.

"But I love my slept-in look."

"That's perfectly fine around here, but not on the stage," Ma advised. "You have a band to represent now."

"Yes, Ma. I know, but I can't resist teasing Cedra."

†

After feasting, Keith and Wayne loaded the equipment while Cedra and Juliet helped Ma store the leftovers. Stone and Sarah showered and dressed in Ma's room and waited on the porch swing while the others prepared for the show.

Ma waved to them from the porch as they pulled away, eager to arrive and get set for the performance. "Good luck," she hollered out to them. Juliet smiled and waved back to her.

†

When they arrived at the café, the band set up their instruments, and Cedra arranged her stool. Because it was her Open Mic night, she would lead off the show, and then after she sang her numbers, she would call the others onto the stage for the rest of the show.

Cedra joined them at the table and took a long drink of sweet tea.

"Nervous?" Stone asked Cedra.

"A bit, yes. I've never performed solo, so it's a new experience," Cedra replied.

Stone covered her hand with his. "I survived my Open Mic, and you will be fine, too. Besides, we will be right here cheering you on."

"Hell yes, we will," Lisa Marie said. She had walked up to speak to the group. "This place has never been so packed this early before a show. We're already hopping with orders."

283

"You need us to help out for a bit?" Cedra asked.

Lisa Marie scowled. "Absolutely not. Tonight, is your night to shine. Knock them silly. I've counted no less than five agents here already."

"That's fabulous," Cedra said and took another sip.

"Relax for another five minutes, and then I'll get the show started. I'm grabbing one of these, too, before they disappear," Lisa Marie said as she picked up a copy of Cedra's songs on the CD. "I'll add it to my collection," she winked.

Carrie, Mark, and several other people entered and took their seats. Carrie saw Cedra and walked toward the group. "Give us the best of you tonight," Carrie told them. "This night is huge, and I know you won't let the audience down. Give us more of what you did at Wild Bill's."

"We will," Cedra replied. "Thanks for being here."

"My pleasure," Carrie said and turned away.

Juliet saw Cedra running her fingers across the bracelet she had given her. "I'll be right there," Juliet said and touched Cedra's wrist.

"No, ma'am. You are right here," Cedra said and pointed to her heart.

"Awww, that's so sweet," Keith teased. "I hope I find a Cedra one day soon. I love you, Li'l sis."

"I love you guys, too," Cedra replied.

Lisa Marie walked over to the table. "Ready?" she asked Cedra.

Cedra nodded. "Let's do this."

"Take your seat, and I'll introduce you," Lisa Marie told her.

Juliet took her hand. "You got this," she smiled.

Cedra stood and walked to her stool. She strapped her guitar around her neck and glanced over at her songbook. *You got me here, so it's time to work our magic.*

Lisa Marie picked up a microphone, and the crowd fell silent. "Ladies and gentlemen. I've had the pleasure of getting to know our next performer over the past few months, and I've never seen a harder worker or someone so dedicated to the craft of writing her songs." She turned to Cedra. "Join me in welcoming Ms. Cedra Tyler to the Redbird stage."

Lisa Marie left the stage, and when the crowd died down, Cedra positioned her microphone. "I'd first like to thank Lisa Marie, not only for giving me a job but also for allowing me a chance to showcase my music for you tonight. Thank you all for coming tonight and the support you've given me," she said as she looked at her band sitting at the table. "I have several songs that I have written and would like to share with you, and then the rest of the performers from our new band, The Bentleys, will join me on the stage to play a few other songs I have written or co-written with them, and maybe a tune or two you may have already heard." She took a deep breath. "I wrote this first song about my mother, who tragically died way too soon."

Cedra looked out to find Juliet smiling and began to play. Once the sound of her guitar filled the air, the lyrics danced off her tongue, and Cedra rocked like she did when she played on Ma's front porch. Cedra made eye contact with the crowd and found them smiling back at her, more than one wiping a tear from their eyes. When she finished the song, the crowd filled the air with applause. Juliet nodded and smiled back at her.

I've got this. Cedra felt her confidence soar as she began the next song and then the one after that. At the end of the third song, Cedra waited until the crowd quieted. "For the next song, Stone Watson, fellow writer, and band mate will join me for a brand-new duet."

Stone pulled up a seat near Cedra and smiled at her. Cedra began playing and leading with the first chorus. Stone's eyes shone back at her with excitement as they played and sang the beautiful love song together. When she dared a glance at the audience, several were swaying in their seats, wearing huge smiles. Juliet gave her a thumbs-up, and Cedra and Stone finished the song. Cedra caught Carrie's eye, and she gave her nod of approval as the crowd filled the room with applause and a standing ovation.

Cedra turned to Stone. "Thanks for joining me, Stone. Are we ready to have some fun?" Cedra asked the room.

"Hell, yeah," the crowd yelled back.

"While the rest of The Bentleys join me on the stage, I want to tell you about this next song. I wanted to write a song that I hope every artist who has ever hit Nashville, Detroit, or Atlanta could relate to their struggles to chase their dreams of making it big. This next song, called 'Six Strings and a Dream' is also the title of the first album The Bentleys will be producing soon." She looked around the stage to find everyone ready. "Let's hit it."

The Bentleys performed the song, and the audience caught on to the chorus quickly and joined in with the band. Cedra's heart swelled with pride at how well the audience reacted to the song. After the song ended, Cedra introduced the rest of the band to the audience, and they continued their performance of original songs and the two cover songs. Keith and Wayne nailed "Up on the Ridge", and then Cedra announced the last song, "Backwoods Boogie," and the group played their hearts out, giving the audience their best performance ever of the tune.

Cedra looked around at her band as they finished the last song. They were breathless from the music, so she took her mic and walked to the center of the stage.

"Thank you for coming tonight and letting us share our music with you. Once more, The Bentleys," Cedra said and turned to her partners. The crowd erupted with applause, and several patrons shouted "Encore." Cedra looked at Lisa Marie and nodded to her. Then she turned back to Stone and the others. ""Devil Went Down to Georgia"?"

"Why the heck not?" Stone said and grabbed his fiddle.

Cedra turned back to the crowd. "You might know this tune from Charlie Daniels," she announced and then nodded to the boys.

The room was buzzing with energy after the final notes ended. Cedra took the lead once more. "Thanks again. We hope you enjoyed our music tonight as much as we did."

†

As they packed up their instruments, the next performer walked on stage and grinned at Cedra. "How the hell am I supposed to follow you?" he asked.

"Sing your heart out," Cedra said and hugged him.

Lisa Marie returned to the stage. "Give us ten minutes to get the next performer set up, and we'll get back to tonight's show.

Lisa Marie pulled Cedra into a hug. "I'm so damned proud of you. You were fantastic, and when the band joined you, magic filled the air."

"We did good, huh, boss?" Cedra asked.

"Beyond good. That was one of the top performances ever, and business was booming. Thank you for that."

"Lisa Marie, none of this would have happened if it weren't for you," Cedra replied.

Lisa Marie shook her head. "The hell it wouldn't. You guys are great. I'm proud to have been a part of it, but you guys did all the work. I pity the next performer for having to follow that performance."

"I do too, but I'm glad we performed well," Cedra replied.

"I'm glad I grabbed a CD when I did. They are already gone," Lisa Marie chuckled. "I may have to buy some of them to sell here for autographs while I still have you working here."

"We're not going anywhere soon."

Carrie and Mark were already at the table to congratulate the band on the performance. "I can't wait to meet with you all Monday. Thank you for playing "Six Strings". You nailed that one," Mark said.

"We'll see you Monday," Cedra promised.

Several patrons dropped by to give their thanks, and they left the café that night with the business cards of eight agents that wanted to speak with them. The boys packed the instruments, and after a quick thanks to Lisa Marie, the group headed for home as the next artist was finishing his set. "I think you should give him a rain check to come back," Cedra whispered to Lisa Marie. "Tonight, was a bit unfair to him."

Lisa Marie nodded. "I was thinking the same thing. Be safe, and I'll see you Monday."

†

Ma was sitting in the kitchen, talking with her friend, Patsy, when they arrived home. Juliet walked in and held up her hand, as she fanned out the business cards like playing cards.

"What's that?" Ma asked.

"Not one, not two, but eight business cards from interested agents," Juliet crowed.

"Y'all must have kicked butt tonight," Ma said. She introduced Patsy to the group.

"I have to admit, Ma, we sounded pretty damned good," Cedra replied. She sniffed the air. "Have you already got the meat in warming?"

"Patsy helped me. I knew you all would be starving, so we got a jump on the leftovers. They should be nice and warm by now. We've got buns in warming, too."

"Thanks, Ma. How are you feeling?" Cedra asked.

"Good enough to beat me in six hands of gin rummy," Patsy growled.

"Much better," Ma replied. "It's been nice catching up with Patsy, but I hated missing the show."

Sarah looked at Juliet. "Do you have a laptop?"

"Yes, ma'am, I do. I'll be right back." Juliet left the table and rushed upstairs.

Sarah smiled at Ma. "I can download the video on Juliet's laptop, and you can see it tonight. I'll still get a copy burned for you, too."

"Thank you so much, Sarah," Ma said. "That means a lot to me."

Cedra jumped into action while Juliet and Sarah loaded the video.

"Stone, will you bring the fine china and napkins from the pantry? Keith, can you start pouring drinks? Stone, there are a couple of bags of chips in the pantry, too."

"What can I do?" Wayne asked.

Cedra pulled the oven open. "You can pull these out and help me set them on the counter, and then we'll begin making plates. Stone, will you grab the macaroni and potato salads from the fridge?"

"You got it, boss," Stone teased.

Sarah helped him set the table and put large serving spoons in the cold salads. Cedra and Wayne built sandwiches and filled a tray, which Cedra carried to the table while Wayne brought the steaming baked beans.

"Sauce," Keith said. He walked to the counter and pulled out several small bottles of sauce.

Cedra looked at Ma. "Will you bless this meal?"

Ma nodded and said a quick prayer of thanks for the excellent food and good friends, and for blessing The Bentleys with a house-rocking performance.

"When you're ready, I'll hit play," Juliet said.

Ma nodded and smiled.

Juliet started the video. "Can you see it and hear it okay, Ma?"

"You could turn it up just a bit," Ma grinned.

The group watched the video while they ate and when everyone got their fill of brisket, Cedra turned on the coffee pot.

When the video came to an end, Cedra asked, "Other than Keith and Wayne, who is ready for some caramel cake?"

"Oh, heck yeah," Juliet said. "I had almost forgotten. Get to pouring milk, Keith, while Wayne and I clear the plates. Cedra can cut and serve. Who wants coffee?"

"I'd love some," Ma answered. "What about you, Patsy?"

"I should have left an hour ago," she said. "What the heck, why not?"

"Keith and I can drive you home when you're ready, to make sure you arrive safely. It may be a bit foggy tonight," Wayne said.

"That would be lovely of you, young man. Bring on the cake and coffee." Patsy chuckled.

"So, what did you think of the performance, Ma?" Keith asked.

"That was your best by far." Ma turned to Cedra. "You did a lovely job presenting not only your talent but the rest of the group as well."

Patsy chuckled. "I bet the women in the audience were swooning over that love song you and Stone performed," she said.

"Oh, they were," Sarah replied. "It was a great performance."

"I can easily see that being a popular wedding song one day," Ma said. "It's so romantic and heartfelt."

Cedra felt her heart swell with pride. "That's what I intended listeners to hear."

"You did, quite well, dear," Patsy said. "It was so beautiful."

"Thank you." Cedra smiled. "Anyone for seconds?"

"Maybe just a small slice, and then we'll take Miss Patsy home if she's ready," Keith said.

"I'm way past my bedtime, but it sure has been fun meeting you all and listening to your performance," Patsy said. "I hope to hear you on the radio soon."

"I hope we do, too, Miss Patsy," Juliet said.

"Ma, would you mind if I run through the shower? Those stage lights were brutal," Stone said.

"You can use ours Stone while we take Miss Patsy home. It's now yours, too," Wayne winked.

"That's right. You're officially a Bentley. Oh, goodness, do you know what we forgot this week?" Ma asked Cedra.

"Halloween candy," Cedra replied and smacked her head. "No worries. I'll go to the store in the morning, pick up some and hide it until it gets dark. Do you get a lot of trick or treaters?"

"Not as a general rule, but you never know. What doesn't get passed out won't go to waste, with these three around."

"Ahem, you better make it four, Ma. Stone loves Butterfingers and Reece's Cups," Sarah reported.

"That's good to know. Any other special requests?" Cedra asked.

"Chocolate and lots of it," Wayne said.

"If you can find those mini gummy bears, I love those," Keith said.

Cedra turned to Ma. She laughed, "Any of the above. I love the banana or strawberry Laffy Taffy too."

"Oh, heck yeah," Keith said. "He stood and pulled a ten out of his wallet, and Wayne did the same.

Stone reached for his wallet when Cedra said, "Stop right there. I'm not buying out the whole candy aisle."

"I'll go along to make sure she gets all the right stuff," Juliet said with a wink.

Miss Patsy stood. "It was a pleasure meeting all of you tonight, but it's time for this old woman to get in the bed."

"I hope you'll join us again soon," Cedra replied.

"Don't be a stranger, Patsy," Ma said.

"I won't." Patsy looked at Keith and Wayne. "Are you boys ready?"

Wayne stuck his arm out. "Waiting on you, young lady."

"I see why you love these kids," Patsy told Ma.

"Be careful, boys. I think I'll head up to bed too," Ma said as they walked to the door. "I'll see you in the morning. Biscuits and gravy sound good to you?"

"Heck yeah, Ma, but only if you're up to cooking. I know I sure haven't mastered gravy, much less biscuits," Wayne told her.

Ma smiled. "I'll be fine to cook breakfast in the morning. You all have kept me down long enough."

When the door closed, Juliet looked at Sarah. "Are you going to conserve water, or would you like to use our shower?"

"I'm all about conservation," Sarah answered. "Let's go get some fresh clothes."

"Ma, do you need us for anything?" Cedra asked.

"No, you have done more than enough. I'm going to hit the sheets and get a good night's rest. I'll see y'all in the morning."

"Goodnight, Ma," Juliet said and took Cedra's hand as they walked upstairs.

†

Cedra stretched out on her back as she waited for Juliet. She watched the shadows from the flickering candle dance on the ceiling. She was smiling when Juliet entered the room.

"What's that beautiful smile for?" Juliet asked.

"Several things. The way the shadows dance on the ceiling, the great night we have had with friends, and the beautiful woman who is about to join me in the bed," Cedra answered. She tossed back the covers for Juliet to climb into bed.

"It was a great night, wasn't it?" Juliet said as she snuggled next to Cedra.

"Everything went amazingly well. I am thankful that it will be my only time on stage without you beside me. It was a great comfort to see you watching, but even better when you were at arm's length away."

"I was pleasantly surprised by how everyone performed tonight. We turned some heads. I still can't believe we have eight agents interested in us."

"Believe it. I think tonight was the easy part. Next week meeting with all the agents and weighing our decisions will probably be the hard part."

Juliet propped up on an elbow. "How will you feel if Carrie's isn't the best offer?"

Cedra smiled. "Disappointed, but we have to take the best deal for us."

"I don't believe that will happen," Juliet replied. "I think Carrie is going to bring out the biggest guns to sign us. There were several other big-name agents, but I don't think they can hold a candle to what Carrie and Big Machine have to sell."

"That may be true, but bigger may not always mean better. We need to keep an open mind when we meet with the others," Cedra answered.

"Do you want me to try to get our meetings scheduled next week?" Juliet asked. "I have the luxury of time that you and the boys don't."

"I'm off Wednesday and Thursday next week. I think Stone is off Wednesday, too. We can get the boys to give us their schedules tomorrow, and you can see what you can get set up."

Juliet stroked her fingertips across Cedra's cheek. "I don't want us to rush into a decision, but I think we need to meet with agents as quickly as we can, before they hear someone else they may be interested in signing."

"Strike while the iron's hot," Cedra replied.

"Yes, that's it exactly. Circumstances change quickly in this town. We can't play hard to get for long."

"I won't play hard to get with you," Cedra said and pulled Juliet's face down for a kiss.

Juliet rolled on top of Cedra and deepened the kiss. One kiss led to others, and they loved the rest of the night away. Cedra cuddled into Juliet, tenderly running her fingertips across Juliet's stomach. "I can't believe this, but I'm hungry, and that caramel cake is calling to me."

"Sit tight, and I'll sneak down and bring us both a piece. Will you split a soda with me? Now that you mention it, some cake does sound good. I just pray the boys didn't come home and wipe it out."

"Hurry back," Cedra said.

"Second option if the cake is gone?" Juliet asked.

"Nope, my heart is set on the cake," Cedra teased.

"Cake you shall have then, my love, even if I have to make a midnight store run," Juliet said as she slipped a long T-shirt over her head.

"There's no need to leave the house. It won't be the end of the world if I don't have cake," Cedra replied.

Juliet opened the door and tried to be quiet as she descended the stairs. The glow from the kitchen lit her path, and she was surprised to find Keith and Wayne sitting at the kitchen table. They looked up at her with guilty faces when Juliet entered.

"There better be some cake left," she warned.

"There should be just enough for you and Cedra," Wayne said. "We were about to do the rock, paper, scissors thing to see who would get the last chunk."

"Then you better thank your lucky stars I showed up when I did then," Juliet teased. She looked inside the box, and there was a large slice left. "I don't need to make a store run." She pulled out a soda and a fork while Wayne placed the cake on a plate.

"Maybe you and Cedra could pick up another when you go for candy," Keith suggested.

"I'm sure we could arrange that. Goodnight, boys," Juliet said and headed for the stairs.

Juliet was laughing when she entered the room. "Five more minutes, and we would have been out of luck. Wayne and Keith were preparing to do rock, paper, scissors for the final piece."

Cedra shook her head. "Those boys."

"They asked if we would get another one tomorrow when we go for candy," Juliet said as she handed Cedra the soda and sat down on the bed.

"I think we can manage that." Cedra watched as Juliet cut a bite with the fork and offered it to her. Cedra smiled and opened her mouth to allow Juliet to feed her the cake. "That tastes even better when you treat me."

Juliet's smile grew. "There's nothing I won't do for you if I can. If cake makes you happy, then I'll do everything I can to ensure you have as much as you want."

"While I love the sentiment of your gesture, we better go easy on the cake, or I'll blow up like a house," Cedra teased.

"Nope, that'll never happen. I'll love it off you," Juliet said and popped a bite in her mouth. "I do hope you never learn to bake this. It really could be dangerous."

"Lucky for you baking isn't my strong suit," Cedra said and opened her mouth for the next bite.

Juliet placed the empty plate on the desk and offered Cedra the last sip of soda before blowing out the candle.

CHAPTER FOURTEEN

The group spent a leisurely Sunday morning together. Cedra and Juliet had returned from shopping for the Halloween candy and caramel cake and returned to find the boys hovering around the grill. Stone was grilling chicken for a late lunch. He planned to leave to take Sarah to the airport for the flight home at three.

Cedra was sad to see her leave. Stone had smiled the entire time she visited, and she knew the separation was difficult for both of them.

They heard Sarah and Ma laughing in the kitchen when they entered the house.

"Welcome home," Ma said as they placed the cake and bags of candy on the table.

"Thanks, Ma. Where should we hide the candy for now?" Cedra asked.

"I will put some of it in the bowl on the foyer table and the rest in the pantry. Hopefully, after we eat, the boys will be full for a few hours," Ma replied.

"They sure have the air smelling good," Juliet said.

"Stone is sharing his secret for moist chicken with Keith and Wayne," Sarah replied. "They might swap stories for an hour after that."

"We've already made a salad, have beans in the oven, and corn on to boil. Is there anything else we want to add?" Ma asked.

"That with the cake should be plenty. Is there anything we can help with?" Juliet replied.

"No, I think we've got it from here." Ma smiled. "Go check on the boys and see if they need anything."

Juliet reached for Cedra's hand. "Let's go see what kind of trouble they are getting into out there."

Cedra took Juliet's hand, and they walked out the back porch to where the boys were hovering around the grill. "You know what they say about a watched pot," Cedra teased.

"Hey, we didn't know y'all made it back already," Keith replied.

"We had to sneak in with the candy so we could hide it from y'all," Juliet told him.

"That is just downright cruel," Keith groaned.

"There is plenty for you to devour after we dole some out to any trick or treaters tonight," Cedra promised. "We hit a good sale for last-minute shoppers."

Stone lifted the lid on the grill, and the air filled with fragrant smoke. He used a squirt bottle to mist the cooking meat. "What's the secret recipe?" Cedra asked.

"Water, a dash of lemon juice, and a splash of Tabasco sauce," Stone answered. "Misting with this mixture keeps the meat from drying out when it's cooking. Doesn't make it spicy, though," he added.

"That's a brilliant idea," Cedra said. "Can we run an idea past y'all quick?"

"Sure," Wayne said.

"We have a lot of meetings we need to arrange this week. Juliet has planned to make all of the appointments for us. I know we have all agreed to meet with Carrie tomorrow, but how would you feel if Juliet, Ma, and I attended all the others, so we don't have to take off work? If you're off already, that's no problem."

"I wouldn't have any problem with that," Stone said. "I know y'all will look out for our best interests."

"Same here," Keith and Wayne both answered.

"Great. We need to get the meetings done quickly, then decide as a group what the best offer is before someone else catches their eye," Juliet said.

"Yeah. I agree. Things move quickly in this town. We need to strike while our iron is hot," Stone replied.

"Speaking of hot, I believe you need to dowse those flames, bro," Keith told Stone and pointed to the grill.

Stone had forgotten to close the lid, and the flames were licking up around the meat. Stone rushed over to close the lid and cracked it open to ensure the fire went out. "That was a close call." He grinned.

Cedra looked at them. "Thanks, guys. I think that will help us speed up the process next week. I believe Carrie will be aggressive, but I want us to hear what the others are offering as well."

"I think the two of y'all and Ma can advocate for the group, and it will save us from having to sit through meetings," Stone replied.

"That's settled then. Do you need anything?" Juliet asked.

"No, we're good. The chicken will be ready in about fifteen minutes," Stone replied.

"You need sauce or anything?" Cedra asked.

"Nope, we whipped up several different sauces earlier, so everyone can choose their favorite," Wayne said.

"That was a great idea," Juliet replied.

"We've got everything covered. I hope. We've got Alabama white sauce, North Carolina mustard sauce, and Kentucky bourbon sauce. Or you can just have it plain," Keith added.

Cedra shook her head. "I'm going to try them all."

"We'll let Ma know the ETA on the chicken and get the table set," Juliet told them and reached for Cedra's hand.

"That is so damned cute," Wayne said with a wink to Cedra and Juliet.

"Eat your heart out boys, she's all mine," Juliet teased back. "We'll see you in a few."

†

After a fantastic meal, Stone and Sarah left for the airport. Stone returned just after dark and joined everyone on the porch to wait for potential visitors. Ma smacked Keith's hand every time he reached toward the bowl of candy sitting on the table. It was creating an overwhelming temptation for the king of sweet tooths.

"No, you don't," Ma reminded him. "If we don't have any kids by eight, you can dive into the bowl, but not until."

Wayne looked at his watch. "Only two hours to go," he teased.

"Why don't y'all get your instruments and jam a while. That will at least keep your hands busy," Ma joined in the teasing.

"That's a good idea," Juliet said. "Let's go, boys."

†

They only had one truckload of kids drop in for trick or treating, so promptly at eight Ma looked at Keith. "Now, you can have some candy." When the bowl was empty, Ma smiled. "Will that hold you for a while?"

"At least until midnight, when I get up for a second or third slice of cake, Ma," Keith replied.

"I think we need to get you to a doctor," Ma teased. "I've never seen anyone crave sugar the way you do."

"I've checked before, and the doctor couldn't explain it either. He just told me I have a super-high metabolism. There is no blood sugar or thyroid issues."

Ma shook her head. "I wish you could share some of that with me. I swear I look at a mini candy bar and gain a pound."

"You look good, Ma, and don't let anyone tell you differently," Stone said.

Ma smiled at him. "You are so sweet to me."

"I hate to leave this sugar parade, but I need to hit the sack to be ready for work tomorrow. Are you riding with me in the morning?" Cedra asked Stone?

"I think I'll drive tomorrow since you're coming home to change and pick up Ma and Juliet. I can wash off and change in the truck and meet you at Carrie's office."

"Or we can swing by the café and pick you up. The parking downtown is ridiculous." Juliet reminded him.

"You're right. I'll wait on y'all." Stone answered.

"Goodnight then. Thanks for a great day," Cedra replied and left the porch.

"I'll see y'all in the morning," Juliet replied and followed Cedra inside.

†

"I think I'll run through the shower tonight, so I don't wake anyone in the morning," Stone said.

"We sleep like rocks, so wait until the morning if you want. You won't wake us," Wayne replied.

"I'll already be up drinking coffee. You can use my shower as well," Ma told Stone. "I usually make a travel mug for Cedra in the morning. Should I make you one as well?"

"That would be great, Ma. Thank you. I'll see you bright and early then. Goodnight." Stone left the porch heading to his truck.

"And then there were three," Wayne said.

"Nope, two. I'm going to call it a night, too." Ma smiled. "It was a good day and a great weekend, but I'm tired. Goodnight, boys."

"Goodnight, Ma."

†

Cedra and Juliet changed into sleep clothes and stretched out on the bed. "This was a fun but busy weekend," Cedra said. "Are you excited about tomorrow's meeting?"

"Yes, I am. I'm eager to hear what Carrie has to offer. I'm sure she witnessed the high level of interest from other

303

agents, so hopefully, she will bring her best offer to the table."

"I think she will," Cedra replied. "I guess we will find out tomorrow."

"I'll call and see if I can schedule an appointment with another agent for Tuesday afternoon after you get off work and then try to fill Wednesday and Thursday since you'll be off. Maybe by Friday, we can be finished and ready to make our decision."

"This is all so exciting. Nerve-wracking too," Cedra replied.

"Yes, it is. Not near as exciting as being with you," Juliet replied and rolled on top of Cedra. She kissed her breathless and smiled at Cedra. "I am so thankful that fate brought us together."

"That makes two of us. I do have one question for you, though," Cedra informed her.

"What is that?"

"Are you going to kiss me or what?" Cedra asked. She chuckled at the look on Juliet's face.

"Until you beg me to stop," Juliet replied, and Cedra's laughter stopped. Juliet removed her sleep shirt and reached for Cedra's. "Ah, that's much better." Their bodies moved together as Juliet's kiss deepened, and she broke the kiss with them both gasping for air. "I want you so bad right now."

Cedra smiled and pushed a stray lock from Juliet's face. "I am all yours."

"Forever and a day," Juliet whispered against Cedra's cheek.

"That would make a great song title," Cedra replied.

Juliet placed her hand on Cedra's temple and mimicked turning a key. "I need to turn that off for just a little bit while we make a different kind of music."

Tender caresses elicited moans of pleasure and soft purring sounds as Juliet made love to Cedra. Cedra's hand slipped between their bodies, and her fingers slid deep inside Juliet, bringing them to climax together.

"I promise one day we will never have to worry about time, but we both have to be well-rested for tomorrow. I feel our future will unfold for us after the meeting with Carrie."

Cedra stretched and snuggled into Juliet. "I'm both excited and petrified. I don't want any of us to be disappointed by her offer."

"Call me cocky, arrogant, or whatever is appropriate, but I don't think Carrie intends to let us pass her by."

Cedra blew out the candle. "I sure hope you're right."

Juliet chuckled. "Of course, I am, sweet dreams, my love."

"Goodnight, my sweet," Cedra said and pulled the covers over them.

CHAPTER FIFTEEN

"Today is the big day," Ma said as she placed Cedra's mug on the table. "I haven't seen Stone yet."

"He may not come in for coffee this morning since he's driving separately today," Cedra replied. "I'll be back shortly after the noon rush to get cleaned up and ready for our meeting."

Ma smiled. "I'll be ready to go, and I'll make sure Juliet looks presentable. I've already got a pair of jeans pressed for her. I just need to know what shirt she plans to wear."

"She'll look good in anything she wears," Cedra answered.

"Thank you for allowing me to attend this one with you," Ma replied.

"Not just this one. All of the meetings, if you can and want," Cedra clarified. "We appreciate your business sense and want you to help us make the right decision."

Ma's face filled with a smile. "I'll do my best."

"I know you will. You are a good judge of character and see through the BS quickly."

Ma nodded. "I think Carrie is going to cut to the chase pretty quickly. She wants you all badly, and I'm almost certain Mark has given her free rein to do whatever it takes to sign the group."

"I believe her offer will be our benchmark for decision making," Cedra said.

"I do, too. I don't know of anyone in Music City that has the clout her agency has right now," Ma added.

"I guess we will find out soon," Cedra said. "I better get moving. I have a feeling this day is going to go by in a blur."

"Have a great morning, and we'll see you when you return. Should I have a sandwich ready for you?"

Cedra shook her head. "I'll try to eat a hearty breakfast. I don't want to spoil our dinner celebration tonight, and I'm sure I'll have a nervous stomach until after the meeting."

"Just relax and have faith in your talent. Carrie sees a great opportunity, so she should be the nervous one, not you."

Cedra chuckled. "Now you're beginning to sound like Juliet."

"If I don't know anything else, I know good music when I hear it," Ma assured her.

Cedra picked up her mug. "I'll see you soon."

†

Stone's truck was already gone when Cedra walked outside to warm hers for the drive to town. She smiled when she pulled into the parking lot to find he had already arrived, and when she entered, Stone and Lisa Marie were drinking coffee at the counter.

"Good morning. Will you join us for a cup?" Lisa Marie asked.

"Yes, but I need to get rid of some first," Cedra answered.

"Go clock in, and I'll pour you a cup," Stone told her.

"You left early. Did you sleep at all last night?"

Stone smiled. "I slept like a rock and couldn't wait to get this day started."

"I know how you feel. I'll be right back." Cedra walked into the back office.

"Jennifer is coming in at noon, so I want you to head out as soon as she gets here. I can't wait to hear how the meeting goes this afternoon."

"We will give you all the details in the morning," Cedra promised.

Lisa Marie grinned. "I think good fortune will be on your side today. I heard Mark tell Carrie to offer whatever she needs to get you all signed."

"She will be our benchmark offer, I'm sure," Cedra replied.

Stone nodded. "She's got the biggest guns in town right now, and she won't want to miss a good opportunity."

"Did Stone tell you that Juliet, Ma, and I will be meeting with the other agents this week?"

Lisa Marie swallowed a sip of coffee. "Yes, he did. I think it's wise to make a decision as quickly as possible. If you need more time off, just let me know."

"I think we're good as long as Juliet can get things scheduled this week, but I'll let you know. We hope to decide by Friday," Cedra replied.

"Good. Things move quickly in this town," Lisa Marie warned. "Strike while your iron is hot."

"We plan to do just that," Cedra replied.

†

The morning passed by so quickly, Cedra didn't have time to watch the clock. Stone had ordered them breakfast while she waited on her last customer, and when they left, her breakfast was on the counter waiting for her.

"That was perfect timing," Cedra said as she sat next to Stone and picked up her fork.

"Who said that was for you?" Stone teased.

"I'll order my own then," Cedra replied, thinking he was serious.

"Sit down. I'm only teasing you."

"That was pretty mean, Stone," Lisa Marie called from the cash register.

"I am so sorry. Please accept my most heartfelt apology," Stone replied.

Cedra punched him hard in the arm.

"Ouch, you beast," Stone joked.

"That serves you right. Better be glad I didn't miss and hit that pretty face of yours," Cedra told him. "I'd hate for you to attend our meeting sporting a shiner."

Stone playfully rubbed his arm. "You've been around Juliet and the boys too much. Where did the sweet Cedra go?"

"She's still around, but you started it by being mean," Cedra replied and took a bite.

309

"I swear you two are sounding more like siblings every day," Lisa Marie said with a chuckle. She looked up at the clock. "Another hour, and you are out of here. Are you getting nervous?"

"Maybe just a little," Cedra replied.

"I'm terrified," Stone answered.

Lisa Marie nodded. "I'd be worried if you weren't a little nervous, but just relax and be yourselves. Carrie already knows who you are and how badly she wants you."

"I'll just be glad to get this first meeting under our belts, so I know what to expect," Cedra said.

Stone took a sip of juice. "I think this will be the one that counts."

"Just don't decide before you hear all the offers. You may be surprised," Lisa Marie warned. "Just the fact of how much Carrie wants you will up the game for the others."

"I hope you're right, Lisa Marie. I feel like Carrie's will be the benchmark for all the other offers."

"More than likely, Cedra. As much as she will pressure you for an answer, don't let her bully you into a rash decision."

Cedra listened to Lisa Marie's warning. "Carrie seems tame when she comes in to eat, but I haven't seen her with her game face on yet."

"No, she will be much more professional and aggressive at the bargaining table," Lisa Marie agreed. The door opened, and an early lunch customer arrived. "Sit tight. I've got this one."

†

"I'll meet you outside Carrie's office at a quarter to three," Stone said as he finished eating. "Will that be early enough?"

"That should be perfect. We should be prompt, but not too early," Cedra replied.

"Sarah already texted to wish us luck." Stone smiled.

"It's too bad she couldn't stay in town a little longer," Cedra replied.

"Maybe next time. Sarah said Dad had the flu when she got home, so it was good timing for her return."

"I hope it's not a serious case," Cedra replied.

"Dad is a pretty tough customer, so I don't think he'll be down for long. My mom will run him out of the house if he starts whining," Stone chuckled.

"That sounds familiar. My mom always said men were big babies when it comes to pain tolerance, and they would never have survived childbirth."

Stone nodded in agreement. "That certainly would have curtailed the population explosion. I was in labor and delivery with Sarah when Destiny was born, and I thought I was going to pass out several times."

Cedra drank the last of her juice. "I reckon we'd better get prepared for the lunch crowd. I'll start rolling some silverware if you'll set up the tea pitchers."

"I'm on it," Stone said and carried their dishes to the kitchen.

Cedra washed her hands and prepared the silverware until customers started rolling in.

Jennifer arrived just as Cedra had rung up the last of her customers. "That's good timing. It's been a busy lunch hour already."

"I'm glad to hear that. I'm a bit short on my rent this week," Jennifer replied. "I'll take all the extra work I can get."

"I'm sure Lisa Marie would let you come in early a few days this week, if you asked," Cedra replied.

"I'll keep that in mind. Lisa Marie lectured me on budgeting last time I was short," Jennifer replied with a roll of her eyes.

"It is important," Cedra said with a wink.

"Hit the clock, hotshot," Lisa Marie called to Cedra. "Good luck. I can't wait to hear how it goes."

"You will be the first to hear in the morning," Cedra replied and walked to the back office. "I'll see you soon," she said to Stone as she passed by him.

†

Cedra blinked as she stepped into the bright sunlight and walked to her truck. When she arrived home, Ma and Juliet were finishing up a sandwich.

"Are you sure you don't want a sandwich?" Ma asked.

"I'm good, Ma. Thank you. I'm going to stretch out for a few minutes, and then I'll shower and get dressed. Stone said he would meet us at a quarter to three."

"Wayne and Keith are on their way home to get ready as well," Ma replied.

"Are you feeling okay?" Juliet asked.

"Yeah. I just need to wind down a bit. This morning was hectic," Cedra answered.

"Okay, I'll hang with Ma for half an hour and then come up. Is that enough time?"

"Yes, that should be fine. You can come up earlier if you want. I will stretch out but won't nap."

Juliet smiled at Cedra. "I'll see you in a few minutes then."

Cedra nodded and started up the stairs. Her phone began ringing as she entered her room. She smiled when she saw her dad was calling. "Hey, Dad."

"Hey, Baby Girl. I just wanted to call and wish you luck this afternoon. Let me know how things go."

"I will, Dad. We are going out to eat afterward, but if it's not late, I'll call when we get home."

"Call me regardless of the time. I'll be sitting on pins and needles. Besides, I can sleep in a bit in the morning if these danged kittens will allow it."

"Okay, Dad, I will. I love you."

"Love you, too, Baby Girl."

Cedra plugged her phone in to charge and kicked off her shoes before stretching out on the bed. "Man, this does feel good." She closed her eyes and relaxed until she heard Juliet enter the room.

Juliet walked over and kissed her. "I've been missing you all day," she said.

"Here I am," Cedra replied.

"Looking fine, too, I might add," Juliet said. "Would you mind some company for a few minutes?"

"Sure, but please set a timer for twenty minutes. We don't need to get behind schedule." Cedra moved over on the bed to make room for Juliet. "Time passes so quickly when I'm with you."

"I've noticed that, too," Juliet replied as she pulled Cedra close. "How are you feeling about our meeting?"

"A little nervous, but I know we'll be fine," Cedra admitted.

"Yes, we will," Juliet replied and kissed her softly.

†

Cedra, Juliet, and Ma arrived promptly at Carrie's office building at a quarter to three. Wayne, Keith, and Stone were chatting when they parked and joined them.

"Are we all set, boys?" Juliet asked.

"Lead the way, fearless leader," Keith teased.

The group was ushered into a large conference room and offered drinks. Cedra accepted a bottle of water, and Ma requested coffee. Cedra placed her songbook on the table to take notes. She tapped the pen nervously until Juliet reached over to cover her hand and smiled.

"Relax, it's going to be fine," Juliet promised, just as the door opened and Carrie and Mark stepped inside.

†

Cedra took comfort in the feel of Juliet's thigh pressed against hers, but she felt a trickle of nervous sweat roll down her spine. As Carrie made the introductions, Cedra picked up her pen, prepared to take notes to hide her nerves. Her eyes scanned the photographs in the room of some of the biggest names in country music, and her mouth went dry.

Carrie cleared her throat. "I want you to know right off the bat, Mark and I want to sign you for Big Machine. We see a great deal of talent sitting around this table, and we'd be fools to allow you to go with a smaller agency."

"That being our opening statement," Mark said, "we have developed a list of benefits in signing with us that we'd

314

like to cover with you all today." He passed each of them a sheet of paper to review.

"I think you realize by now that Big Machine represents some of the hottest bands in the market today, and we see that potential in The Bentleys," Carrie stated.

"After we reach an agreement, we'd like to get you in the studio as quickly as possible to finish the album you have begun. I love the music you've created so far," Mark continued. He smiled at Cedra. "If the size of that book of yours is full of lyrics, I'd say you have a considerable advantage over most of the new bands in town."

Cedra smiled. "This is just one of a few that are full. Stone has several songbooks as well."

"A band rarely has one good writer, so you have a distinct advantage with two creative minds," Mark replied. He smiled at Juliet. "You have a charismatic lead singer and good musicians with a variety of instruments." He paused for a moment. "The fact that you have put egos aside to create a band tells us that you are all dedicated to the serious work it will take to make it in this business. Each of you has the talent to succeed independently, in time, but together the arc to success will occur much faster."

"We want to be the agency that helps you achieve that success," Carrie told them. "We can provide opportunities that many of our competitors can't, and we hope to use that to our advantage."

"If you look at the list of artists on the top of the page, they all started right where you are today. Good talent with a desire to reach the top." Mark paused to take a sip of water. "We can open the doors to help you realize that dream. We've outlined the steps of your progression from finishing an album and getting it out to major radio stations for some playtime. We'd get you lined up for interviews and promote you as up and comers."

"That's a significant advantage we have over some others. We have the experience and ownership in some of the largest radio markets across the country. We can book you into venues that it would otherwise take months or years to reach on your own." Carrie smiled. "I know you've had some experience opening for a few small names," Carrie said to Juliet. "You are much better than that. We aren't promising an opening set for Taylor or Rascal Flatts just yet, but you have the talent for that."

"We'd love to have the opportunity to promote The Bentleys and provide you the resources and a chance for a fast break that is rare in this business. That's how much potential we see in you." Mark relaxed in his chair. "Tell me what some of your goals are?"

Juliet smiled. "We want to play in a stadium full of fans one day."

"I would say that is highly achievable with hard work," Mark replied. "What else?"

"I'd like for us to have a number one song on the country charts," Cedra said.

Mark smiled at Cedra. "I've heard several of the songs you've written that artists would jump at every chance to record. I think "Six Strings" will do well once we add a professional sound to it, and you have the perfect wedding song. Your writing appeals to most country fans, and no matter if The Bentleys record your songs or someone else, you will have that number one song."

"What potential do we have of selling the songs we write to others if the band doesn't want to record them?" Stone asked.

"We require our writers to give us first option at anything they want to market," Mark replied. "We provide the technology and equipment to make songwriting a more straightforward process to our top writers. We don't expect you to record everything you write or to sell every song, but we can put the perfect artist together with the pieces that fit their style."

"Cedra's already got a jump on that," Keith blurted out.

"How so?" Carrie asked.

Keith looked at Cedra. "May I share with them?"

Cedra felt the heat rise her cheeks. "Sure, go ahead."

Keith nodded. "When we first met and got a glimpse of her songbook, we noted that Cedra had names of bands or artists penciled in at the top of each new song. We wondered if she could hear their voices singing the lyrics as she wrote them."

"Could you?" Mark asked.

"For some, yes," Cedra answered. "Lately, the writing has focused on the voices in the group. I can imagine how Juliet's voice would sound singing a song, or Keith or Wayne, and write it to match their strengths."

"Amazing," Mark said.

Juliet studied the page for several seconds. "Other than getting us into the studio, what are we looking at for potential live performances?"

"We'd start with some of the more prominent country music festivals and work you into opening slots for some of the tours we promote. If things go well, you could be the headliners one day and have others opening for you," Carrie answered.

Mark cleared his throat. "I'd like to focus your attention on the financial breakdown for a few minutes to explain these. The top line is the personal advance we will pay each of you for the production of *Six Strings*. We will cover all the production costs and get the album in the hands of the media markets. Next is the royalty section. Twenty-five percent of sales, video, CDs, and other marketable materials at fifty percent will get divided between the five of you. We will cover the royalty fees to the production manager out of our share of royalties."

"What are the term limits to the length of the contract and copyrights?" Juliet asked.

"Our standard contract is two years to ensure enough time for a debut album to receive maximum exposure," Carrie explained. "The copyright ownership spans five years in today's market. The terms have swung much further back in the artist's favor from the days that lifetime copyrights were standard."

Mark leaned forward in his chair. "We hope to sign you for the long term, and you will have ample opportunity to negotiate contract changes after two years."

"What happens if we sign with you and two months down the road Carrie leaves to start her own business or work with a competitor?" Ma asked.

"All of our contracts have a 'Key man' clause that would allow you the opportunity to leave the label," Carrie explained. "Don't worry. I'm not going anywhere."

"What are the marketable materials?" Wayne asked.

"T-shirts, autographed photos, key chains, cups and mugs, calendars, all the items typically sold at concerts. Once the cost of production is covered, it's pure profit," Mark explained. "For example, if we sell a T-shirt for forty dollars and it costs us six dollars to mass produce the item, the profit of thirty-four dollars gets divided fifty-fifty."

"Is that typically a large source of income?" Stone asked.

"Fans love band swag," Carrie replied. "They generally don't balk at paying for items at concerts."

"What rate are we accountable for completing albums?" Cedra asked.

"Most typically, one per year," Mark said. "That may change depending on tour schedules. We don't want to burn anyone out by requiring too much. We sign artists for the long haul."

Stone shifted in his seat. "As the only one here with family obligations, I have to ask what happens if I need to leave the group for unforeseen reasons?"

Carrie nodded. "That's an excellent question. Your role as a songwriter wouldn't necessarily change, and the band has ample talent to perform live without your presence. Your continued participation in future royalties would be the decision of the rest of the band. We contract with the group for royalties and other revenue. How it's divided is up to the group to decide."

"I hope it never comes to that, but it would be prudent for us to decide," Juliet responded.

"I hope so, too," Stone replied.

"Do you have any other questions?" Mark asked.

"I think we are good for now," Juliet replied. "I'm sure once we've had time to digest some of the information, we may have questions."

"I realize that we aren't the only ones interested in the group," Carrie said. "We only ask that if someone else's offer interests you, that you will allow us to counter-offer before you sign with anyone."

"We appreciate that you chose to meet with us today, and we feel like we put the best offer on the table, but if we need to renegotiate a stipulation, we are open to it, as Carrie stated." Mark took a deep breath. "We want you to sign with us, of course, but we will accept your decision if another offer better meets your needs."

Cedra smiled at Mark. "Thank you both for your interest in us. We hope to decide by the end of the week once we've talked to everyone."

Carrie returned her smile. "I'll go ahead and draft a contract and contact you when it's ready for you all to review before deciding."

"That sounds great," Juliet said. She stood and offered a handshake to Mark and Carrie. "We'll be in touch."

The group left the office and assembled at Cedra's truck. "That is a lot of information to digest," Cedra replied. "Let's head to the restaurant, and we can discuss over a great meal."

"Do you want to ride with us, Stone?" Wayne asked.

"That would be great," Stone answered.

"We'll meet you there," Wayne told Cedra.

†

Juliet, Ma, and Cedra climbed into her truck. Juliet turned to Ma. "What do you think of the offer?"

Ma laughed softly. "Honestly, I don't think anyone will be able to come close to the offer but wait to decide until you've spoken to everyone and we review the contract."

"Granted, I know nothing about business contracts, but it sounded almost too good to be true," Cedra replied.

Juliet nodded. "The royalty rates surprised me, and the advance payments were much more than I'd anticipated. I think Mark has put most of his cards on the table to get us."

"Were you able to schedule the rest of the appointments?" Cedra asked.

"Our last one is Thursday afternoon. I expect we will hear from Carrie before then," Juliet answered.

"Are you interested in being our manager?" Cedra asked Ma.

"Heavens no," Ma said with a soft laugh. "You know I'll help you in any way I can, but I'm too old for that responsibility. I doubt there's anything that you and Juliet can't handle on your own."

"As long as we can bounce ideas off you, I would agree if you're not interested," Juliet told Ma.

"Advice is free," Ma replied.

Cedra suggested. "Why don't we enjoy a good meal and then head home to discuss what we heard today? It will be a better atmosphere for us to have a serious discussion."

"I think that's smart," Ma said.

"I do, too," Juliet replied.

†

Cedra pushed her plate away. "That was a fantastic meal."

"Who's up for dessert?" Keith asked.

"Man, you are just not right," Wayne teased.

"I can't eat another bite, but you go right ahead," Juliet said.

Keith ordered and devoured a slice of chocolate pie while the others watched in disbelief. "I don't see how you can eat like that," Stone teased.

When the waitress brought the check, Ma reached for it.

"No way, Ma," Juliet said. "We've got this."

"Please, let me do this tonight to celebrate," Ma told them.

Juliet nodded her head. "Thanks for a great meal."

"It was fantastic," Cedra replied.

"Thanks, Ma," the boys said one after the other.

"You are all so welcome. I'm very proud of you," Ma stated. "You've all come so far."

"With your guidance and advice," Wayne said. "Will you become our manager?"

Ma laughed softly. "Juliet and Cedra have already tried that. I'll give you all the free advice I can, but you all need to make the key decisions."

†

When they returned home, Ma put on a pot of coffee, and everyone took a seat around the table.

"Is anyone else blown away by their offer like me?" Stone said.

"I think we are all in a bit of shock," Juliet said.

"Just the fact that they are willing to lay out that kind of an advance should tell us how serious they are about signing us," Cedra said.

"I think both Mark and Carrie were honest on how much they wanted the group," Ma said.

"What did you think of the offer, Ma?" Keith asked.

Ma tapped on the fact sheet in front of her. "I don't think any other agency will come close to what they proposed. When you get a copy of the contract, you need to read all of the fine print to make sure there are no hidden clauses, but I doubt there will be."

"Don't shoot me for admitting this, but I never realized we were this good," Wayne said.

"I'll be honest and admit I had some doubts too," Stone replied.

"Not me," Juliet said. "We are worth every penny of this."

"Just a word of caution," Ma said. "Don't go crazy spending the advance. Put a good chunk of it back for a rainy day. Carrie guaranteed to provide the technology and equipment you need, so let them pay for it."

"Does that mean I can't buy that VW camper bus for our tour bus?" Cedra asked Juliet.

Juliet shook her head vigorously. "Definitely not. We can get the studio to spring for transportation until we need something bigger. I don't think we are a large tour bus material yet."

"Is that something we need to ask about?" Cedra asked.

"Yeah, probably. I hope you wrote down everyone's questions from today. Great job, by the way, guys," Juliet said.

"I did. I'll add any additional ones we want to ask, too," Cedra replied.

"Thursday, we will have completed all of the meetings, so we need to meet Thursday to make a decision," Juliet commented.

Cedra nodded. "I expect we will get a call from Carrie either tomorrow or Wednesday about a draft contract."

"Can anyone think of anything else we didn't ask about today?" Juliet asked as Cedra scribbled notes on transportation.

"I hadn't even considered songwriting software," Cedra replied.

"I nearly choked when I saw they would provide us with Mac books and Master Writer software," Stone replied.

"They have software to add music to lyrics too," Keith said.

Cedra smiled. "I don't think I'll ever entirely move away from pen and paper."

"We can still scribble notes everywhere and then upload them into a laptop," Stone replied.

"I'd love to add a bass guitar in the future to give us a bit more depth to our sound," Keith stated.

"I think the studio will have a variety of instruments, mixers, and keyboards we can experiment with," Juliet said. "I did a backup gig at Big Machine. I am still in awe of the studios there. Top of the line everything."

"If we can arrange for the same days off, there isn't a need to quit the café yet, is there?" Stone asked Cedra.

Cedra shook her head. "I would think two to three days a week in the studio would be ample for starters."

Juliet smiled at Cedra. "If you can teach me the software, I can add the songs in your notebooks to the laptop."

"I'm sure I can teach you. You already know more about computers than I do," Cedra replied and reached over to touch Juliet's arm. The clock in the hallway chimed ten. "Why does time always fly by when we're having fun?"

"I was wondering the same," Stone said. "Some of us have to get up early in the morning, so we can't hang out with you night birds."

Ma yawned. "It has been an exciting day, but I'm going to turn in also."

Keith looked at Wayne. "Will you hang long enough to drink a cold one with me?"

"Sure, bro. I don't have to go into work until six tomorrow," Wayne answered.

"Enjoy, boys," Juliet said as she stood and reached for Cedra's hand.

"Goodnight, everyone. I'll see you in a few hours," Stone told Cedra.

"Goodnight. Sleep well," Cedra said. "Don't stay up too late," she told Wayne and Keith.

"Yes, boss," Keith teased. "One beer, and we'll be ready to hit the hay, too. Thanks for a great day, everyone."

"One of many to come, I hope," Juliet said. She and Cedra headed for the stairs.

†

After they undressed and slipped under the covers, Juliet turned to Cedra. "It was an incredible day. I don't think it's sunk in just how close we are to making a significant change in our lives."

"It was pretty amazing, wasn't it? I still feel like I'm dreaming sometimes. First, meeting you, and now we are about to sign our first contract."

"You make me feel like the luckiest woman alive," Juliet said and kissed Cedra.

"I think we're both lucky to have met. I've never felt this way for anyone before, and it has challenged me to put my feelings into words," Cedra replied.

Juliet held her close. "I think you're doing a great job of that so far, and I only see it improving as we grow together as a couple and a band."

"Did Stone's question surprise you?" Cedra asked.

"Initially, yes, but I understood he has more than himself to think about, unlike the rest of us," Juliet responded.

"I hope nothing happens that would necessitate that kind of change, but it does make us think. I believe Stone should continue to receive his share of royalties at least for the remainder of the contract, or at least for the tracks of his songs," Cedra replied.

"I think either of those would be reasonable. I'd lean more into paying royalties on Stone's songs since we will be the ones producing and performing them. He won't be on the road with us."

"We can cross that bridge if it ever comes to it," Cedra said as she snuggled into Juliet.

"Right now, it's one step at a time. Would you mind if I read through more of your songbooks tomorrow? I know the current one is just the tip of the iceberg."

Cedra pointed to a small stack of books on her bookcase. "Knock yourself out," she chuckled.

"I will," Juliet said and turned out the lamp. "Goodnight, baby girl."

"Oh, crap. I forgot to call Dad." Cedra sat up in the bed. "Will you turn on the lamp and hand me my phone?"

Juliet chuckled. She turned on the lamp and searched for Cedra's phone. "It's not too late?"

"He made me promise to call no matter what time it is. I won't stay on long," Cedra replied.

"Talk as long as you want," Juliet said.

Cedra hit the speed dial. When her dad answered, she said, "I'm sorry it's so late, but it's been an exciting day. Yeah, the meeting went better than I think any of us could hope. We have several more meetings this week, but Carrie's offer is going to be hard to beat."

Cedra listened to him for several minutes. "I will call again earlier tomorrow, Dad, and fill you in on the details. I love you too. Goodnight." She handed the phone back to Juliet. "Dad said to tell you hello and congratulations. He sounds as excited as us."

"Just wait until the first time he hears us on the radio. I bet he calls before the song ends," Juliet teased.

"Probably so," Cedra agreed and snuggled into Juliet's warmth. "Goodnight, my love."

"Sweet dreams," Juliet said. "Love you, too."

†

Cedra and Stone updated Lisa Marie on the meeting the following day, and it was difficult to determine which of them smiled harder during the shift. When Carrie came in for lunch, she also wore a broad smile.

"Will you drop by the office when you finish work? I'll have the draft contract done by then," Carrie asked.

"Sure, Stone and I get off at three, and we're carpooling," Cedra replied.

"Perfect. What does the group think of the offer so far?" Carrie asked.

"We all feel that it's a generous offer to start, but we want to examine all offers thoroughly," Cedra answered.

"I would expect nothing less," Carrie said with a smile. "I better get busy," she said and paid her bill. "See you in a couple of hours."

"Thanks," Cedra replied.

"What was that about?" Stone asked after Carrie left.

"She asked we stop by the office to pick up a draft contract," Cedra told him.

"That's cool. It will give us a few days to review all the fine print," Stone replied.

"My cousin is an attorney, and I'm sure she wouldn't mind looking it over for you. If you'll stop by and make a copy, I'll get with her tonight," Lisa Marie offered.

"That would be awesome," Cedra replied. "We'd be willing to pay her for a review."

"Nonsense, you are family, too, so she'll do it for free," Lisa Marie said.

†

After work, they stopped for the contract and then dropped by to copy the document for Lisa Marie. When Cedra pulled into the yard, Juliet sat on the porch with her feet up on the railing. reading. Cedra could see a stack of her songbooks on the chair beside her lover.

Juliet looked up to see Cedra and Stone returning from work. "Welcome home."

"Thanks. Have you had a busy day?" Cedra asked.

"Very productive. I've almost made it through your songbooks." Juliet smiled. "You've got a great collection of songs."

"Thanks. There's quite a few I'd like to offer to others that I don't think fit us as perfectly as I like." Cedra stepped onto the porch and handed Juliet a copy of the contract. "Lisa

Marie has a cousin who is an attorney, and she offered to have her review this, too."

"It can't hurt to have someone with legal experience to look it over," Juliet replied. "Have you read through it yet?"

"Nope, I was waiting until we got home," Cedra replied. "Where's Ma?"

"In the kitchen baking a couple of pecan pies to go with the pot roast she's cooked for dinner," Juliet said.

"I was wondering what was smelling so good," Stone commented.

"Dinner is early tonight before Keith and Wayne have to go to work," Juliet informed them.

"Does Ma need some help?" Cedra asked.

Ma pushed through the screened door. "No, ma'am, I just took the pies out to cool. How was your day?"

"It was busy, but Carrie had the contract draft ready, so Stone and I stopped by after work. Lisa Marie has an attorney to review it for us, too," Cedra answered.

"That's not a bad idea," Ma said as she took a seat and looked at the document Cedra handed her. "Anything that has surprised you yet?"

Juliet chuckled. "Just one thing."

Cedra wrinkled her face in a frown. "What?"

"Carrie must not appreciate our wardrobe. She's added five thousand for apparel."

"That's a thousand each," Stone stated. "Can we say shopping spree?"

"That's if we sign with them and we find out what apparel they expect us to purchase," Cedra said.

"I'll do anything but skirts and a cowboy hat," Juliet growled.

Cedra looked at her. "I think you'd be adorable in a nice leather skirt."

Juliet smiled at Cedra. "For you, I might wear one, but never on stage. I couldn't concentrate on singing for fear of what I was flashing fans in the front row."

"I love you in your jeans," Cedra assured Juliet.

Juliet nodded. "We do need to ask about expectations. Many of the tours have major sponsors, and I'd hate to show up at a Wrangler tour wearing a pair of Cinch or Levi's."

"That's a good point," Ma said. "The rest of the information looks like the conversation notes from yesterday."

"I agree with Ma. I think we've covered everything else, and I don't see any small print," Juliet grinned.

Cedra looked at her watch. "Do I have time for a shower before we eat?"

"Absolutely," Ma answered. "I told the boys we'd eat at five."

"Perfect," Cedra answered. She kissed Juliet. "I'll be back in a little bit."

"Hey, don't forget to call your dad before it gets late," Juliet reminded her.

"Thanks for reminding me," Cedra said and walked inside.

"Are you about to finish up out here?" Ma asked, nodding toward the stack of songbooks.

"I've got two more to go through, but they can wait. It's amazing to see the growth in Cedra's writing," Juliet said with pride.

"I'd love for you to go through mine and give me your opinion on what to keep and what to market," Stone said.

Juliet nodded. "Anytime you're ready. Just bring them over."

"I will," Stone answered. "I think I'm going to stretch out for a bit if you don't need any help."

"No, we're all set. See you at five," Ma answered.

CHAPTER SIXTEEN

Business meetings took two days for Ma, Cedra, and Juliet. Each night, they updated the group, and it became apparent that Carrie's offer was still the best on the table.

"Should I call Carrie to arrange a meeting if we have agreed to sign with Big Machine?" Cedra asked.

"I think we agree Carrie has the best offer," Keith replied.

"I can call and schedule that since you have to go back to work tomorrow," Juliet offered.

"That works for me. I don't know about y'all, but I'm anxious to hit the ground running and get into the studio to finish *Six Strings*," Cedra replied.

"There's not much else we can do until we get that wrapped up other than playing some local gigs. I think they have made that a priority for us, so maybe we can get studio time quickly," Wayne said.

"Don't be surprised if we have to start from scratch, too. The studio will probably want to engineer the four tracks we've cut with their staff," Keith said.

"I'm good with that if it produces a better sound," Stone said.

"Their studio is state of the art," Juliet replied. "I was blown away by their process."

"Let's do this then," Cedra said. "Any objections?"

"None whatsoever," Juliet replied.

"Make the call in the morning then and see what we can get set up," Cedra suggested.

"Everyone good for three tomorrow?" Juliet asked.

"We'll have to come straight from work, but that's not a problem," Stone said.

After Wayne and Keith left for work, Ma, Cedra, Juliet, and Stone sat on the porch drinking coffee. "We won't have too many more nights that we can sit out here like this," Cedra said. "It's already getting chilly."

"Do you want to go inside?" Ma asked.

"I think I'm good, but you don't need to get a chill," Cedra replied.

"I'm good for one cup, and then I'll head upstairs to watch some television," Ma replied. Ma looked over at Stone. "How's your dad feeling?"

"Sarah says that he seems better, but not his regular self yet," Stone replied.

"We don't bounce back as quickly as we used to," Ma replied and smiled at him.

"I know, but I still worry about him," Stone said. "He's the rock in our family."

"Have faith that he will be as good as new soon," Ma encouraged.

Stone nodded and took a sip of his coffee.

Juliet held up her cup. "This time tomorrow night, we will be signed artists." She touched her cup to Cedra's, then Ma's, and Stone.

"A dream come true," Cedra replied.

"A dream just beginning," Juliet added.

"Now the hard work begins," Stone told them. "It was fun getting to this point, but we will have to work even harder in getting the album cut."

"I think we've got a good head start in at least knowing which tracks we want to record," Cedra said.

"That's if Carrie and Mark approve all of them. That's the downside to signing a contract. We give up much of the control to what we record," Juliet informed them.

"I hadn't thought of it that way," Cedra said. "That's a bit of a downside."

"I think as motivated as they are and the money they have invested in us; they will give us some control, but not entirely. We have to remember this is a business to the studio." Juliet smiled. "Maybe that should be something we discuss with Carrie tomorrow before signing."

"It wouldn't hurt to clear the air a bit," Ma agreed.

"Well, that's a few more questions we need answers to," Cedra said. "If anyone thinks of anything else, we need to write it down."

Juliet grinned at Cedra. "You're our designated scribe. That's all up to you."

"I don't mind that at all. Just let me know what to add," Cedra replied.

Ma shivered. "I think it's time for me to head inside."

"Great idea, Ma. It's starting to get cold," Stone replied as he stood and offered his arm to Ma. "I'll see you in the morning," he said to Cedra as he walked Ma inside.

"Have a great night and say hello to Sarah for me," Cedra answered with a smile.

"I will. Goodnight, ladies," Stone said as he walked off the side of the porch heading to his truck.

Juliet looked at Cedra. "It's just you and me. What do you want to do for the rest of our evening?"

"Like you have to ask," Cedra said as she stood and pulled Juliet to her feet. "I want to be wrapped in your arms."

"Lead the way, my love."

CHAPTER SEVENTEEN

"All set?" Juliet asked the group assembled outside of Carrie's office building.

"Yeah, let's do this," Keith said. He swung the door open.

The receptionist escorted them to the conference room when they entered the lobby. "Mark and Carrie are waiting for you all."

Mark stood when they walked into the room. "I am so glad to meet with you all again today. I hope this is the beginning of a long-lasting relationship."

"We hope so, too, but we have a few more questions to ask first," Juliet replied.

"Take a seat and let's get started then," Carrie said. "I hope you found the contract acceptable."

"We did," Cedra replied and opened her notebook. "We noticed that you added money for apparel and wanted to know what the studio's expectations are?"

Mark nodded. "Wrangler sponsors many of our tours, so we hope you will invest in some of their products. Not exclusively, but we hope you will respect their investment in you if the band gets chosen for one of their events."

"That's easy enough," Juliet replied.

Cedra looked at Carrie. "We understand how important it is for us to complete *Six Strings*. How much control do we have to select the tracks for this album and future albums?"

Carrie didn't hesitate to answer. "We are committed to allowing you control over the tracks as long as we approve of the final product. If the sound doesn't meet our standards, we can re-engineer it to improve the sound, or you can choose another track to produce. This album and future albums."

Cedra nodded. "Final question, unless anyone else has a question. When can we get into the studio to get to work?"

Mark smiled. "Can you start tomorrow?"

Juliet smiled. "We can."

"I have one final question," Keith said.

All heads turned toward him. He raised his hands. "Where do we sign?"

The group broke out laughing. Carrie looked at Keith with a serious face. "Do you have a knife?"

"Yes, ma'am, but what do we need that for?" Keith stammered nervously.

"I figured you wanted to sign in blood," Carrie teased, bringing another round of laughter around the table.

Mark opened a file folder and pulled out a document. "Let's get this official. Then we have a surprise for you."

Cedra quickly compared the document to the draft and found it identical to the one Lisa Marie's cousin said was good as gold. She was the first to sign and then passed it to Juliet. Once everyone had signed, including Carrie and Mark, Carrie called her secretary into the room. "Please make five copies for us."

"Yes, ma'am. Congratulations," she told them.

"We hope you don't have dinner plans," Mark said. "Carrie and I would like to treat you to the Hermitage tonight."

"That sounds perfect," Juliet replied. "What time?"

"We made reservations for seven to allow Cedra and Stone a chance to clean up after work since we met so early, but we can change them if needed," Mark replied.

"Thank you. I think we both need to shower off the café," Cedra replied as the secretary returned with the copies.

Mark placed their copies in a folder and handed them to Cedra with the Mont Blanc pen used to sign the contract. "I hope you use this to write more beautiful songs."

Cedra smiled at him. "I'll give it my best."

Carrie looked at Stone. "If you will follow me back to the office, I have two more things for you and Cedra. We have your Mac Books loaded with all the software you will need."

"Now we're talking," Stone said as he rubbed his hands together.

"We'll be right back," Carrie said and left with Stone on her heels.

When Stone returned carrying two laptop bags, he wore a huge smile. "I may not sleep for days." He grinned.

"You better rest up. We've got work to do," Cedra teased back.

"I'll book you for tomorrow morning at nine at the studio," Carrie told them as the group moved toward the door.

"That will be perfect," Juliet replied. "We'll see you at seven tonight. Thank you both, for everything."

Mark smiled. "Thank you for choosing us. I think together we can take you all far in this business."

"We'll hold you to that," Cedra smiled. "We will work hard to make that happen."

"I know you will," Mark replied. "We'll see you tonight."

†

"Congratulations," Ma said when they walked outside. "I hope you all are pleased."

"I don't think we could ask for any better opportunity," Juliet said. "We need to go easy on the celebration tonight, so we will be fresh to start to work tomorrow."

"I can't wait to get started," Keith said.

"What time do y'all have to work tomorrow?" Juliet asked.

"I go in at seven," Keith said.

"Eight for me," Wayne said. "Both days."

"I lucked up and got Sunday night off," Keith said.

"Maybe we can get some studio time Sunday, too," Cedra said. "Stone and I are off until Monday."

"I'm sure we will have to go through some orientation at the studio in the morning, but I hope we can make some good headway on the tracks," Juliet stated. "We neglected to

339

ask who our producer would be. I'm crossing everything I can that we get Bud Roberts. He's top-shelf."

"Maybe we should ask tonight at dinner," Wayne suggested.

"Good idea. Let's head home so Stone and I can get cleaned up. I'm starting to get hungry," Cedra replied.

"I'm going to order that porterhouse I've been dreaming about for months," Keith said.

"Now you're making me hungry," Ma said. "Let's go."

†

Cedra rushed upstairs to shower, and when she stepped into her room, she found a box sitting on her desk. She placed the items she carried on the table and picked up the package. Cedra unwrapped the box and found a pair of Ray-Ban glasses. She put them on and looked in her mirror. "You look good," she said to herself.

"I'd have to agree with your assessment," Juliet said from the doorway. "I noticed how the stage lights affected you, and I wanted to get you a pair."

"I've never owned Ray-Bans before, but I love them. Thank you," Cedra replied.

Juliet smiled. "You're welcome. I got a matching pair." She held up her sunglasses.

"The boys are going to be jealous," Cedra teased as she began undressing.

"They can buy their own," Juliet replied. She reached for Cedra's dirty clothes. "Hit the shower, so we can go eat," she said as she tossed the clothes in the hamper.

"Remind me to call Dad on the ride to town, please. I need to tell him we are officially signed artists. Man, that sounds good."

"I know. It still seems too good to be true," Juliet replied as she sat down on the bed.

"I think it will feel real tomorrow when we get into the studio," Cedra called from the bathroom.

"It will be interesting to see how much better the sound will be at Big Machine. They have state-of-the-art everything." Juliet stretched out on the bed.

†

"That's cruel," Juliet said when Cedra entered the room with a towel wrapped around her waist as she dried her hair.

"What?"

"Looking so delicious when we committed to going out for the evening," Juliet pouted.

Cedra dropped the towel from her body and smiled. "Save room for dessert," she teased.

Juliet stood and pulled Cedra into her arms. "Seconds and possibly thirds, ma'am," she promised.

†

The meal was spectacular, and the group was excited when they learned Bud Roberts would be their producer. "We want you to start with the best," Mark explained. "He works well with new artists and is a crowd favorite."

"That's what we were hoping for," Juliet replied. "We want the best."

"Bud will work you hard to produce your best," Carrie replied. "Don't expect to leave tomorrow with a full album cut. You'll be lucky to get four tracks done, and that will take most of the day. He may ask you to record each track five or six times before he hears what he wants."

Mark nodded. "Bud has an ear for selecting the right sound for award-winning music. If anyone can help you rise on the charts quickly, it will be Bud."

"We are looking forward to working with him," Cedra stated. "Thank you for a fantastic meal, but if you will excuse us, we have a busy day planned tomorrow."

Carrie grinned. "That's the work ethic we expect from you all. Work hard, and your dreams will come true."

"Will you be there tomorrow?" Cedra asked Carrie.

"Don't be surprised if I show up in the booth to listen. Bud doesn't like distractions, so I won't be able to stay long."

Juliet stood. "We'll see you at some point tomorrow then. Thanks again for a great meal."

"Do great things tomorrow and have fun," Mark said.

"We always have fun when we play together," Keith said.

"Goodnight, then," Mark said.

†

"Is breakfast at seven going to give y'all enough time in the morning?" Ma asked when they arrived home. "I was thinking bacon and French toast."

"That sounds perfect, Ma," Cedra replied. "I'll help with the bacon."

"Too late," Ma teased. "Stone has already offered."

"Alrighty then." Cedra smiled at her writing partner. "We'll see you in the morning. Get some rest, boys. It's going to be a long day."

"I've heard he makes ya play until your fingertips bleed to get it right," Wayne said.

Juliet shrugged. "We just have to get it right after the first run or two. We'll give it our best and see what Bud wants to change."

Keith bumped into Wayne. "That's the price we pay for getting the best producer. Bring your 'A game,' and we'll be good."

"I'll see y'all in the morning. I have a laptop to play with," Stone said.

"You need rest too, so don't stay up too late," Cedra warned.

"Yes, boss," Stone replied. "Goodnight, everyone."

Keith was in the kitchen scouting ingredients in the refrigerator. "You can't possibly be hungry," Juliet teased.

"Sure, I can," Keith answered. "Dessert was just a tease."

Ma shook her head. "Make me a cup of coffee, and I'll bake some cookies."

"I'm in for that," Wayne jumped on board. "I've got the coffee."

"Do you two want cookies?" Ma asked.

"Not tonight, Ma, but thanks," Juliet said.

Ma smiled and nodded. "I'll see you in the morning. Get some rest."

"Goodnight," Cedra replied and followed Juliet upstairs.

†

Cedra closed the bedroom door behind them. "I love cookies, but I remember promising you a different dessert."

"One that I plan to collect on, too," Juliet said as she spun Cedra in her arms.

Cedra laughed as she danced in Juliet's arms. When she stopped, she could see the passion burning in Juliet's eyes, and her breath caught in her chest. She felt her hand fly to her neck.

Juliet saw the immediate change in Cedra's facial expression. "Are you okay?"

Cedra nodded with tears in her eyes. "Yes, I've never had anyone look at me the way you are right now, and it caught me by surprise."

Juliet cocked her head to the side. "Like you're the one that makes my heart race with joy?"

"That could be one way to describe it," Cedra said. "I always thought coming to Nashville to make my way in the music business was my dream, but meeting you has been better than any dream I could imagine."

"Our dreams are just beginning, and I'm glad we will travel down that path together. You make me feel things I've never felt before, and my love for you grows every day," Juliet answered.

Cedra stepped forward and began unbuttoning Juliet's shirt. "Let's grow some more," she teased.

Midnight in Nashville

Songwriters Series Book 2

Chapter one

"That was much better, Cedra, but let's run through it one more time," Bud Roberts called out from the production booth. Cedra Tyler and the rest of The Bentleys band had been in the studio for their first day of recording for four grueling hours. They had managed to nail down one track and were almost to the point of finishing another.

Cedra nodded to Bud. "What do I need to improve?"

"Take the range up just a bit when you hit the harmony this time. After this track, we will take a lunch break," Bud promised. "You all have done very well today."

"Thanks, Bud," Juliet said as she took her seat beside Cedra. "I think we're all ready for a break," she said to Cedra with a wink.

"Bud told us this morning in orientation this wouldn't be easy, but I like the sound of the first track. I will nail this one so that we can have a break," Cedra replied. "Ready, boys?"

Stone, Keith, and Wayne all nodded. "One, two, three, four," Cedra called out and began playing. Bud's voice rang through the studio when she sang the last chord. "That's it. That's the one I was waiting on. Good job, guys."

"Hallelujah," Keith said. "My kidneys are about to explode."

"Lunch is set up in the break room. I'll see you there," Bud replied.

Cedra placed her guitar in the stand and stretched her arms above her head. "This has been a great first day, don't you think?"

Juliet smiled. "My fingertips aren't bleeding yet, so I consider this a win. Seriously, it's not as difficult as I thought it would be. We've managed to cut two of our original four tracks already."

Stone smiled. "I can't wait to hear what they sound like; they sounded great from in here."

"Maybe Bud will play them for us after lunch," Wayne said. "Let's go. I'm starving."

Juliet looked at Wayne. "You're beginning to sound a lot like Keith."

Wayne smiled at Juliet. "Ma's bacon and French toast are long gone. It seems like days ago since we had breakfast."

†

Bud and Carrie were already seated around the table when they entered the break room. Cedra hadn't seen their agent in the studio. "I didn't know you were here. Good afternoon, by the way."

"Carrie has been here for the last two hours," Bud replied. "I wouldn't let her into the production booth, so she's been watching from here." Bud picked up a remote and turned on a large monitor.

"You all sounded great," Carrie said.

"They have done well so far today. Are you all up for a few more hours? I want to shoot for one more track," Bud told them.

"We are good until seven tonight," Keith said as he returned from the restroom.

"I don't think it will take that long, but that's good to know. How about we take a run at "Backwoods Boogie" after everyone gets refueled?" Bud asked.

"Oh, heck yeah. That song always gets us re-energized," Wayne said.

Cedra placed a turkey sandwich on her plate and picked up a bag of chips. She walked to the table and sat beside Carrie. "Are you eating?"

"I've been nibbling for the last half hour," Carrie smiled.

"Do you want water or something else?" Juliet asked Cedra from the drink area.

"Some water would be great. Thanks, Juliet," Cedra answered.

When everyone settled around the table, Bud spoke. "I am very impressed by your work ethic today. I've worked you pretty hard, and there hasn't been one complaint from any of you."

"We are all excited to be here, and we appreciate everything you are doing for us," Juliet said.

Bud smiled at her. "Eat up then, and I want to share the first two tracks with you. We have them nailed down, but I want you all to agree that the sound is what we are looking for."

Carrie stood and walked over to a cabinet and took out seven pairs of headphones, placing one in front of each of them. "These will block out any external noise and give you the pure sound of what we recorded," Bud explained.

"Eat up guys, I can't wait to hear this," Cedra said.

All heads turned to Keith. "I'm eating as fast as I can without choking," Keith said between bites.

"Be thankful there are no cookies or sweets, or we could be here for a while," Cedra informed Bud.

"Those will be available after the next track," Bud said. "We will break again around four and see how everyone feels. I don't want to wear you out on day one, but damn, you all are doing great."

"We all agreed to work as long as the sound was good, or you tell us it's time to quit," Juliet told him.

Bud looked at Carrie. "I already love working with this group."

"I told you so," Carrie smiled at Bud. "They are hard workers and dedicated to being successful."

Bud nodded his head and looked around at the smiling faces. "I have an excellent feeling about you all. I believe you're going to do well in Nashville."

"Thanks for all your hard work, Bud," Cedra replied.

"You all are making it easy for me. All I have to do is sit back and listen. Are you ready to hear what we've created so far?"

"Heck yeah," Keith said.

Bud pushed a button on the remote, and their first track started playing. He paused after the song ended and smiled at Juliet and Cedra. "What do you think?"

Cedra was the first to answer. "I am shocked by how great it sounds."

Juliet nodded. "I knew it was good, but this is amazing. Every note sounds so pure."

Bud chuckled. "Big Machine has spared no expense in purchasing the best equipment possible. Are you ready for track two?"

"Bring it on," Stone replied with excitement.

The duet with Cedra and Stone was the best version of the song. Their voices blended perfectly, and Cedra smiled as she saw tears pooling in Juliet's eyes. "I believe that was just the sound it needed," Cedra told Bud.

Bud nodded to Cedra. "I'll admit to a dilemma. Carrie asked me to recommend a song for your first release, and it will be hard to decide between that one and "Six Strings," and we haven't even recorded it yet."

"All he's heard so far is the recording I made on my iPhone Saturday night," Carrie replied. "Even when he heard that version, Bud told me we have to record that song."

"Yes, I did. We could work on that next if you want or wait until you are fresh tomorrow," Bud suggested.

"Let's stick with 'Backwoods' for now, and if that goes smoothly, maybe we can take a run at 'Six Strings' today while still energized," Juliet suggested.

"That works for me. I have no problem cutting four tracks today as long as you all are feeling good," Bud said.

"We have waited all our lives for this opportunity," Juliet replied. "We're all good."

"I love it," Bud said with a chuckle. He looked at Carrie. "Thank you for bringing them to me."

Carrie stood and began picking up the headphones. "I knew you wouldn't be disappointed."

Mark came rushing into the break room. "Hello," he said to everyone. "I just finished listening to the first two tracks. Damn, they sound good."

"We have worked hard this morning, and we hope to have one to two more done today," Bud told him.

"Would you mind if I stayed to watch for a bit?" Mark asked.

"You can join Carrie in here," Bud replied. "You're too much of a distraction in my sound booth," Bud added with a soft laugh. "I will turn the video on so you can watch."

"That works for me. You all do sound great," Mark told them.

"We have been pleased so far," Juliet remarked.

"I'm going to head back to the booth but take your time and come back to the studio when you're ready," Bud told them and left the room.

"So, what do you think about Bud?" Mark asked.

"He's a genius and so much fun to work with," Cedra replied.

Keith held up his hands. "No bloody fingertips yet."

"He will work you hard as long as he sees effort in you," Mark said. "I believe he's enjoying working with you all. I haven't seen him smile like that in ages."

"We hope to keep him smiling then," Cedra told him. "I need to hit the ladies' room, and I'll be ready if y'all are."

"That's a good idea," Juliet said and stood to leave the room with Cedra.

†

Cedra locked the door behind them and took Juliet in her arms for a kiss. "I've been wanting to do that for hours."

"I have, too," Juliet admitted. "How do you think things are going so far?"

"Better than I thought possible. I like the way we sounded on those two cuts. Bud, Mark, and Carrie seem pleased as well."

"Yeah, they do. I hope we can do two more today. I think we've performed 'Backwoods' enough we've got it down pat," Juliet said.

"I think so, too. Let's hurry and get back out there," Cedra suggested. "One last kiss, though, to hold me until later."

Juliet kissed Cedra, and then, after they used the facilities, they returned to the studio.

†

It took two tries to get the sound Bud wanted for "Backwoods." It was hard to tell who was more excited to take a run at "Six Strings."

"Do you need a break?" he asked from the sound booth.

"No, we're good to go," Juliet answered.

"I'm ready when you are," Mark said.

"Let's do this," Cedra said, and they began playing. Cedra looked into the booth halfway through the song to find Bud smiling and his head bobbing along with the music.

When the song ended, Bud's voice came over the speaker. "That was a good first run, but let's do another. A bit heavier on the banjo and bass this time, boys."

Wayne and Keith nodded. "Heck yeah," Keith replied.

"Just don't go crazy with it," Juliet teased.

"I'm ready when you are," Bud said.

Juliet looked at Cedra and nodded. "One, two, three, four," Cedra called out and began playing.

"Meet me in the break room in five," Bud said. "Something's missing, and I want to let you hear it for yourself."

"Let's hit the ladies' room," Juliet told Cedra.

Juliet turned to Cedra. "What do you think it is that's missing?"

Cedra's face scrunched up in thought. "The only thing we've done differently is the bass guitar. Why don't we ditch it for this one and go back to Stone's fiddle?"

"That's what I thought too. The bass isn't suitable for this song," Juliet answered. "Let's see what the boys come up with."

Keith couldn't resist a cookie as he entered the room. He grabbed two and took a seat at the table.

"You are such a sweet hound," Cedra teased.

Bud joined them and played "Backwoods" first. "I think we're good on this one. That's a fun song, by the way. Something is not clicking on "Six Strings", but I can't put my finger on it," Bud said.

"We have an idea but want to hear the recording and see what the boys come up with," Cedra told them.

They listened to the track, and Keith was the first to answer. "As much as I loved playing it, the bass just doesn't fit that song."

Juliet nodded with a smile. "That was our conclusion too. The bass was the only thing we did differently. Let's drop it and go back to Stone's fiddle."

"Yes, that's precisely what it needs," Bud answered. "I was hoping you would come up with the same solution."

"We passed our test then?" Cedra teased Bud.

Bud nodded. "Yes, ma'am, you did. I need to make sure that I stay on the same page with the artists when suggesting changes. No one knows your sound better than you."

"Can we take another run or two at it today?" Juliet asked.

"I'm certainly up for it if y'all are," Bud answered.

"Let's do this," Juliet said.

They huddled up in the studio before they began playing. "I know we've all worked hard today, but let's finish the day with our best," Cedra replied. "I want there to be no doubt in Bud's mind that 'Six Strings' is our debut single."

The band picked up their instruments, and when Bud nodded, they began to play.

Cedra closed her eyes for a second and envisioned being on Ma's porch. Her lead-off stanza was terrific, and she opened her eyes to watch each of her band mates perform their parts. The harmony in the chorus was perfect, and when they stopped playing, they all looked at the sound booth for Bud's reaction.

"That is it!!" Bud said with excitement. "Come listen."

Carrie and Mark were back in the break room when they entered. "That was the best yet," Mark said.

Bud walked into the room and picked up the remote. He looked at Mark and Carrie. "We have our debut single." He pushed the button, and they all listened carefully.

Juliet smiled broadly. "That's the best we've ever done on that song."

"I agree," Cedra replied.

"How long will it take to burn fifty copies?" Mark asked.

"I'll have one of the assistants do them tomorrow," Bud replied.

"We will start shooting them out to radio stations on Monday then," Mark said. "That's too good to wait for the entire album."

"Hell yes," Cedra high-fived Juliet.

"You all have had a heck of a great day," Bud said. "Why don't we call it done? Are we on for tomorrow?"

"Same time, same place," Cedra answered.

"We should be able to finish two or three more tracks tomorrow. My goal is to get halfway through," Bud replied. "I think you're going to take off like a rocket, and I don't want fans to have to wait long for the album."

"What studio time is available to us next week?" Juliet asked.

"Any time you are ready," Mark said.

"We'll compare work schedules tonight and let you know tomorrow," Cedra replied. "Two or three more sessions to complete the album?" she asked Bud.

"Definitely by three," Bud replied.

Carrie looked at Juliet. "I know you've had photo-shoots and have begun working on the cover art. Will you bring in your files tomorrow, and we can have our artist review and take over from there?"

"Consider it done," Juliet said. "Will you need full lyrics for each of the tracks?"

"Yes, as well as the writer's name," Carrie replied.

"That should be easy enough," Juliet replied.

"Oh, before I forget," Mark said and pulled an envelope out of his briefcase. "Your advances and apparel allowance. We split everything five ways on the apparel. Have fun shopping. Go easy on the Wrangler goods. I think you will receive plenty of their products when you go on your first tour."

"Thank you so much. Let's load up and head home," Juliet said.

"Great first day, guys. I'll see you tomorrow," Bud said.

"Goodnight," Cedra said and followed the rest back to the studio.

†

"I am so excited about today," Cedra said as she entwined her fingers with Juliet's on the ride home. "We had an incredibly productive day."

"Yeah, we did. I was amazed we got four tracks cut. Bud was easier to work for than I expected. He's a really nice guy."

"I was expecting someone much more aggressive, but he treated us with respect and allowed us input. I've heard horror stories about some producers having *carte blanche* and taking all the controls away from the artists," Cedra replied. "I was happy to find he was the complete opposite."

"That was a huge relief, and I think he genuinely enjoyed working with us today," Juliet said.

"What's not to love about working with us? We gave it everything we could, and I think he appreciated our effort."

Juliet lifted Cedra's hand to her lips. "That sounded just like something I would say." She kissed her hand.

"I think you're a good influence on me," Cedra replied.

Juliet chuckled. "I hate to sound like Keith, but I hope Ma has something cooked for dinner. I'm hungry."

"You know she'll have a spread ready for us," Cedra replied. "My sandwich is long gone, too."

"After dinner, do you want to help me collect the lyrics for the album cover?" Juliet asked. "I've got a few of them typed up already. I don't have Stone's, though."

"We can ask him to type up his three tracks and email them to you while we work on the rest," Cedra suggested.

"That sounds like a plan," Juliet said as she turned into the drive.

The boys had already arrived and were piling out of Keith's truck. They waited for Juliet and Cedra on the porch before entering the house.

"I guess this would be a good time to pass out checks," Juliet said.

"I agree. I think everyone is anxious to have the first advance in their hands. It's so exciting," Cedra said.

Juliet parked and pulled the envelope out and handed it to Cedra. "Would you do the honors?"

"I'd love to," Cedra replied. "How about a payday?" she asked as they stepped onto the porch.

"Hell yeah," Wayne said.

Cedra began sorting through the checks and handed each of them an advance payment and apparel allowance.

"Thanks," Keith said and kissed her cheek when she offered him the pair.

"The first of many, I hope," Cedra said. She left hers in the envelope.

"Amen," Juliet replied. "You want me to take yours upstairs as I go?"

"Yes, please. I need to take a picture to send to Dad," Cedra said.

"That's a great idea," Stone said. "I'll be right back."

"Don't be too long," Ma said from the front door. "Dinner will be on the table in ten minutes."

"Yes, Ma," Stone said and jogged over to his truck.

"I hope y'all had a great first day in the studio," Ma said as they filed into the house.

"We did, Ma. We got four tracks cut," Wayne said. "We got our first advances, too," he said and showed her the checks.

"That's a fine day all around," Ma said with a proud smile.

"The best part is that we've recorded and decided on 'Six Strings' to be our debut single. Bud is burning the copies tomorrow. Mark and Carrie will begin sending them out Monday. We could be on the radio soon, Ma," Juliet reported.

"I can't wait to hear it," Ma said.

"We were blown away with the sound," Cedra replied. "The quality of the studio equipment made a huge difference."

"Is that your fried chicken I smell?" Wayne asked.

"Yes, it is," Ma responded.

"That was my first meal in my new home," Cedra replied. "It's still one of my favorites."

357

"We also have a big bowl of fried okra, rice, and chicken gravy, green beans, corn, and biscuits," Ma informed them.

"That sounds perfect, Ma. Thank you for another great meal and for cooking some of our favorites." Cedra leaned down and kissed Ma's cheek. "You are so good to us."

"You all make it easy on me. I cook it, and you eat it with never a complaint," Ma answered.

"There's never anything to complain about," Juliet said as she returned to the kitchen. "What can we do to help?"

"You can pour drinks and help me get dishes set on the table," Ma replied.

"No problem." Juliet walked to the counter and began filling glasses with tea. "Oh, dear Lord, pecan pie for dessert? I have died and gone to heaven."

Ma's chuckles filled the kitchen. "You are also incredibly good for my ego."

Stone rushed in just as everyone was taking their seats. "Oh, my goodness. This meal looks and smells terrific."

"Have a seat and let's get to eating," Ma said. "I think we need to bless the good lord for this meal and the success of The Bentleys," Ma said. She reached for Keith's and Cedra's hands and then blessed the meal for them.

"Thank you, for everything, Ma. We wouldn't be here without you," Juliet said as she speared a piece of chicken as Wayne passed it around the table.

Ma shook her head. "I wouldn't be here, and as proud as I am, if it weren't for the five of you. I could never have selected a better family."

"This is so delicious, Ma," Cedra praised.

"I'm glad you are enjoying it," Ma replied. "What's the next step for y'all?"

Juliet passed the bowl of okra back to Cedra with a smile. "To finish the other eight tracks for the album and finalize the cover art. Cedra, Stone, and I need to copy the song lyrics tonight. Once Carrie and Mark begin distributing the debut track, we hope to get some airtime and maybe an interview or two."

"I wonder how they would feel if we continued to play live at Wild Bill's or the Iron Horse," Keith asked.

"That would be a question for Carrie tomorrow," Juliet said. "I think it could go either way, but they may want us to limit free performances until they can start gigging us."

"This is the first time since I moved out of my parents' home that I didn't have to worry about money," Wayne said.

"Just don't go crazy with it. It can go away just as fast as we make it," Juliet said. "I'll feel more confident once we have regular checks rolling in or consistent gigs."

"I'm sending the majority of mine home," Stone said. "Sarah will spend it more wisely than me." He grinned.

"I finally have enough to open a checking account," Keith said.

"I think we will all enjoy going to the bank next week," Cedra said. "Okra, anyone?" Cedra held up the bowl.

"Go for it, sweetie," Ma said.

"I don't mind if I do," Cedra replied and scraped the last of the fried delicacy onto her plate. "So damned good."

"Is there anything you need around here, Ma?" Wayne asked. "A bigger freezer or anything?"

"If I did, I wouldn't use your hard-earned money, but thank you for the offering. You deserve to spend that on you or your family," Ma replied.

"I've got you now, Ma," Wayne teased. "You have told us many times you are claiming us as family, so you are considered family. A chest freezer or upright?"

"An upright we could fill with cookies and milk, so we'd never run out," Keith said.

"They do have a point. We could fill it with vegetables from the Farmers Market for the winter," Juliet replied.

"I don't have room for it," Ma said.

"Nonsense, it will fit right by the backdoor," Wayne said. "You just need to tell us if you want white or white," he said with a grin. "I don't think they come in any other color."

"You don't have to do anything," Ma said.

"Please just let us have this one little win?" Keith said. "Wayne and I will split it."

"Cedra and I will take you to the Farmers Market to buy the vegetables you want to freeze," Juliet replied.

"I guess that leaves me gallons of milk and a couple of cases of cookie dough." Stone joined in on the fun.

"I guess it's white then, boys," Ma replied.

"Yes!" Keith answered. "We can get it Monday and get it cooling down."

"That reminds me. What is everyone's work schedule next week? We need to reserve more time in the studio," Juliet reminded them.

"I'm off Tuesday and Wednesday," Cedra replied.

"Wednesday and Thursday for me," Stone answered.

"When do you guys work Wednesday?" Juliet asked.

"I'm off," Keith said.

"I go in at eight," Wayne answered.

"Do we want to try for as many hours on Wednesday as we can? If we have another good day tomorrow, maybe one more full day will be enough," Juliet said.

"If not, we can do some late afternoons when Cedra and Stone get off work," Keith suggested.

"That works for me," Cedra replied.

Juliet turned to Stone. "Can you type up the lyrics for the three songs of yours we are using and email them to me tonight? Cedra and I will do the rest."

"Sure, that won't take long at all," Stone agreed.

Keith smiled at Ma. "I'll clear the table and load the dishes if you start serving pie."

"We can all pitch in, Ma. We won't let Keith destroy the dishes," Cedra teased. "You can supervise him putting away the leftovers."

Wayne chuckled. "That won't take long at all. There's not much left to store."

"You can start a pot of coffee," Ma said to Wayne.

"What can I do, Ma?" Stone asked.

"You can empty the garbage can and put in a new liner," Ma said.

"Easy enough," Stone said. "I'll wait on the dishes to be emptied first."

"What do you all want for breakfast?" Ma asked. "I assume you're going in at nine again?"

"How about biscuits and gravy? Your gravy was off the chain tonight, Ma," Wayne said.

"I'll make a fresh batch of biscuits in the morning if that's good for everyone," Ma stated.

"I'd never turn your cooking down, Ma," Stone said.

"That's easy enough then," Ma said. "Keith, will you bring me a pie, a knife, forks, and some fine china?"

"You bet I will, Ma," Keith answered and went to work.

Wayne worked on the coffee pot while Stone carried plates to the kitchen counter for Cedra and Juliet. "I knew my serving skills would come in handy," Stone teased as he balanced a large stack of dishes.

†

Juliet sat on the bed with her laptop as Cedra sat at her desk. "I'll start from the bottom and work up if you want to start with the first tracks," Juliet offered.

"This shouldn't take us long at all," Cedra replied. "Especially with three of us working together."

"Did you take a picture of your checks to send to your dad?" Juliet asked.

"Thank you for reminding me," Cedra said. She quickly snapped a photo and sent it to her dad. "I bet my phone will ring within five minutes."

"Probably less," Juliet replied. "I wish my family was as supportive as your dad."

Cedra's head turned to look at Juliet. She was about to comment when her phone rang. "Hey, Dad," she answered and put the phone on speaker.

"Hey, Baby Girl. That's impressive money for day one," he chuckled. "Is Juliet with you?"

"Yes, she is."

"Hey, Dad," Juliet called out from the bed.

"Hey, Juliet. So, which one of you can I borrow from?" Hank teased.

"Either one or both," Juliet replied. "What do you need?"

Hank chuckled. "Nothing, sweetie, I am just teasing. You all should be very proud. I know I am. What's next?"

"Another day in the studio tomorrow and then one to two more next week to hopefully finish the tracks for the album. Bud, our producer, has already selected 'Six Strings' as our debut single. Mark and Carrie will begin distributing them to the media Monday."

"Wow. Things are moving quickly," Hank said.

"Yeah, Daddy, they are."

"I'd better start keeping the radio on twenty-four seven then," he said.

"If we get a heads up, I'll let you know," Cedra promised.

"I'm so proud of y'all. I know your mother has to be smiling," he said.

Cedra could hear the heartache in his voice. "I know she is. I feel her with me all the time," Cedra told him. "Thank you for encouraging me to follow my dreams."

"This is only the beginning, Baby Girl. There is so much coming your way. I can feel it in my bones."

"I sure hope so, Daddy. I can't wait for you to come up in a few weeks. We will have a jam session for you when you're here."

"I'm looking forward to that. I bet I will hear you on the radio before that."

"I pray you're right."

"I won't keep you tonight. I know you've got stuff to prepare for tomorrow. I wanted y'all to know how proud I am for you."

"Thanks, Daddy. I'll call you soon. Hopefully, with more good news. Goodnight."

"Goodnight, ladies. Love you both."

"Love you too, Dad," Cedra and Juliet answered.

Cedra turned to look at Juliet and saw tears in her eyes. "What's wrong, baby?"

"I wish my dad would talk to me like that," Juliet answered.

"You never talk much about them. Do you talk to your family often?" Cedra asked.

"No, but it's my fault. The last time I talked to Dad, he was so negative, I went off on him. That was months ago."

"Maybe it's time to reach out to him again?" Cedra suggested.

"Not until we have a song on the radio. I don't want to jinx anything." She wiped a tear from her eyes.

"I don't think you can jinx us, but I will support your decision. Does your dad know anything about the band?"

"Nope, nothing at all."

"Would you mind if I make a suggestion?" Cedra asked.

"Not at all, sweetie."

"Why don't you get a copy of the single tomorrow and send it to him? I was thinking of asking for a copy for Dad and Ma."

Juliet smiled. "That's a good idea. Thank you."

"I know Daddy has enough love for two, but I believe family is important, and you should try to keep a relationship with them," Cedra replied.

"I'll send them a CD, and we'll see where it goes from there," Juliet promised.

Cedra leaned over and kissed her. "I love you."

Juliet smiled. "I know you do, and if your love is all I have, it's enough to carry me through."

"More people than me love you," Cedra replied. "Just keep me at the top of your list."

"Always," Juliet said. Her phone pinged with an email from Stone. "Stone's done with his project. I guess we'd better get busy."

"Yes, boss," Cedra smiled and turned back to her laptop. She emailed the first four tracks to Juliet, who saved them on her jump drive an hour later.

"I'm almost done too. Do you want to go back down for another slice of pie?" Juliet asked.

"That does sound good. Coffee? I can go get a pot started while you finish," Cedra suggested.

Juliet nodded. "That works for me. I'll see you in a few."

Cedra leaned down to kiss her. "Don't be too long."

"I won't. Hopefully, the boys left some pie," Juliet smiled.

"Good point. If not, I'll bake us some cookies."

"That works too," Juliet replied.

†

Cedra walked downstairs, and the lights were on in the kitchen. Ma and the boys were sitting around the table. "Is there any pie left?" she asked Keith.

"Why are you asking me?" Keith smiled.

"Because you are the biggest sweet tooth in the house," Cedra said as she looked at the coffee pot. "Will you drink some coffee, Ma?"

"I could do another cup," Ma replied. "The pie is in the fridge. Do you want me to heat some for you?"

"I'll get it, Ma. Juliet is coming down as soon as she finishes the last of the lyrics."

"I got the coffee," Wayne offered.

"What have y'all been up to?" Cedra asked.

"Just dreaming," Keith answered. "We've been planning our first tour."

"Where are we going?" Cedra asked.

"We thought it would be cool to play the college towns in the south. Most of the larger schools have country venues in town that would help grow our younger fan base," Keith explained.

"That's not a bad idea. Is this something that is done regularly with new artists?" Cedra asked.

"I think it's a possibility until the music festivals start in the spring," Wayne answered as he filled the coffee pot.

"Maybe we should pick Carrie's brain about it tomorrow to see what her plans are for us," Cedra replied. She cut two pieces of pie and placed them in the microwave.

Juliet arrived just as Cedra removed the pie. "That was good timing," she said as she entered the kitchen.

"Coffee will be up in a minute," Wayne said.

"The boys have been planning our first tour of college towns," Cedra told her as she brought the pie to the table.

"Not a bad idea," Juliet said as she picked up her fork. "Towns like Athens, Gainesville, Knoxville, Baton Rouge, and Lexington have some awesome country venues." She cut a bite of pie. "We could travel on Fridays, do a show Friday night, Saturday, and be home on Sunday. You may have to drop down to working four days a week."

"I don't think that would be a problem for any of us," Keith said. "The winter months can be slow at the theater."

"I could bartend part-time too," Wayne said.

"Lisa Marie asked if I would consider some part-time work at the Redbird," Ma said. "Maybe I could fill in on the days when y'all are on the road."

"That would be good. You're an early riser, and you wouldn't have us to look after," Juliet teased.

"Working at the café would be cake compared to tending to us," Keith said.

"You all aren't bad," Ma said. "It's quite a comfort having you around."

Cedra finished her pie and sipped on her coffee. "I know Lisa Marie would benefit from your help. You wouldn't have to worry about cooking but one meal. She'll feed you well for breakfast and lunch."

"This is sounding better by the minute." Ma smiled at Cedra. "I think I could handle two or three days a week."

"I'm sure you could, Ma," Cedra replied. "It would get you out more, too."

"That's an added benefit I hadn't considered."

"Thanks for the pie. I reckon we all need to get some rest. Tomorrow will be another long day," Cedra stated.

"I hope it's as productive as this one was," Wayne said. "Goodnight, ladies."

"Goodnight, boys," Ma said.

"Do you two have any recommendations for dinner tomorrow night?" Ma asked Cedra and Juliet.

"How about a taco night? We haven't done one of those in ages," Juliet said.

"With an ice cream sundae selection for dessert?" Ma asked.

367

"That works for me," Cedra said. "Do we need to pick up anything from the store?"

"Naw, I'll go shopping after y'all head to the studio tomorrow," Ma replied. "It'll give me something to do."

"Why don't you invite Patsy over too for some company and dinner? I'll drive her home," Juliet replied.

"That's not a bad idea. Maybe we can sip on a Margarita while we cook," Ma chuckled.

"There ya go. I can't do the liquor, but I'll have a beer with you when we get home," Juliet promised.

"Have a great night and get some sleep. I'll see you for breakfast."

"You too, Ma. Goodnight." Juliet reached for Cedra's hand, and they climbed the stairs.

†

Cedra and Juliet stretched out on the bed as the flame from a candle danced on the ceiling.

"Today was a great day," Cedra commented.

"Yes, it was. I wasn't expecting it to be so productive," Juliet admitted.

Cedra turned toward Juliet. "Will you do something with me Monday when we get home from work?"

"Sure. What do you want to do?"

"I want to go shopping for some boots. I've never had a nice pair before. I know you have a collection, so you could guide me on what to buy."

"I love going boot shopping. If I didn't have six pairs already, I'd buy more," Juliet answered. "I know just the spot to take you."

"Thanks," Cedra said and snuggled into Juliet.

"We sounded good today, didn't we?" Juliet asked.

Cedra frowned. "I think everyone was surprised. It won't be disappointing to fans if we don't sound so perfect when we perform live, will it?"

"No, not at all. We sound good when live. Fans realize the acoustics and studio environment enhance the quality."

"When we start performing gigs, will we still do some cover songs?"

Juliet's smile grew. "We will mix some in, but I think we will need to play mostly songs from *Six Strings*. Maybe some others as we develop them to prepare fans for our next album."

Cedra laughed softly. "We haven't finished cutting our first album yet, and you are already planning a second."

"Of course, I am. You have so many songs already written we could be busy for months in the studio, even after you offer some to other artists."

"I love that you have that much confidence in me," Cedra said.

"You have such a beautiful talent for writing tremendous lyrics," Juliet replied. "I fully believe once Carrie and Mark get their hands on the lyrics in your songbooks, they will go wild promoting them."

"I hope the words never leave me," Cedra said.

"Just write from your heart and the music you want to hear created and not try to conform to a template. Too many artists fail to write new tunes, and their music has the same sound with different words. That's so bland and lacks imagination."

"I have to agree with you there. Even if the first song was successful, it could be ruined by diluting it with different lyrics."

ABOUT THE AUTHOR

Ali Spooner lives in beautiful northwest Florida with several fur babies. Ali's writing began as a hobby, and with the assistance of the Affinity Rainbow Publishing team has advanced her love of storytelling to a new level.

Ali's characters are primarily everyday people, from cowgirls to psychics. Ali also has created a few supernatural characters in her paranormal series. Several of her twenty-plus books have been Amazon-rated number one choices and always include a happily ever after. Ali's hobbies include photography, reading, travel, college sports, and spending time with family and friends.

OTHER AFFINITY BOOKS

<u>Trouble in Paradise-Trophy Wives Club book 4</u> – Ali Spooner & Annette Mori

The gang from the Trophy Wives Club is back, but this time they're taking their fun to a new and exciting location. Lindy and Remy prepare to make a huge announcement that has the gang nervous about their future with the club. As it turns out, the Club's future is bright and Lindy simply wants to reward the crew with an all-expenses paid trip to paradise over the holidays. With everyone coupled up, Lindy feels a little out of her element.

Soon after arriving on the Island, an attractive stranger catches the eye of more than one person in their tight-knit group, but Lindy is especially intrigued. Could Angel Dubois, the owner of an all-woman financial planning company be the answer to Lindy's crushing feelings of loneliness. Along with fun in the sun, the gang navigates treacherous waters to ring in the new year, while finding new ways to love one another.

Georgetown Glen by Annette Mori

Lucy Manetti is positively euphoric over her recent purchase of an old ghost town. Unfortunately, she failed to consult with her wife, Bea, before buying the abandoned village. Predictably, Bea is not as enamored with transforming the ghost town into a sapphic retirement community, but Bea's love for her wife trumps her displeasure over Lucy's impulsiveness. The mature couple hires Fiona, an expert at restoring old houses, and Saville, a certified electrician, to bring the ghost town back to its glory days.

According to the adorable real estate agent who recommended the pair, Fiona and Saville have *history*. Lucy detects a spark between the two young women and decides, against the advice of her wife, to play matchmaker, bringing her beautiful niece into the mix. As the ragtag team begins their work on the old saloon, they discover a lot more than they bargained for, including ghosts, long-buried secrets, an abused golden retriever, and maybe even love.

Serenity by KB Belmar

After Kirby MacLennan had lost her partner and her only sibling in a horrific accident, all she wanted to do was move from the city and live the rest of her life alone in a small mountain village. When she meets Samantha Parker, the village sheriff, they soon become friends. Samantha's cousin Jackie, and her wife Beth, along with their children, moved into the old farmhouse next door to Kirby. Something makes

Kirby uneasy about the couple's relationship and she finds herself drawn to Beth, and her silent plea for help.

Can Kirby overcome her own trauma of the past to help a neighbor in need? Will she finally accept love back into her life, enough to move out of the shadows and into the light?

Along Came Sally by JM Dragon

Angela Barossa is content with her life as the local realtor in the small town of Whistler. Until a request to see a property that can only be sold to a local or ex-local disturbs her.

The name of the potential client…Sally Maguire. Why on earth would her childhood nemesis want to return to Whistler? Angela needs to be dispassionate in her dealings with Sally, but can she?

Simply a timeless romance.

Artist Free Zone by Annette Mori

Melissa just moved to a conservative part of Washington State. A move designed to set her and her longtime partner up for early retirement. But best laid plans go awry when her partner, Colette decides, out of the blue, their relationship isn't working for her. The only thing left to do is sob all over her beloved kitties. Vowing never to get involved, ever again, with another artist.

Colette is torn up about hurting Melissa. She hasn't been entirely honest about her reasons for leaving and that tears her up even further. She keeps calling to make sure Melissa is okay. Life is exciting and wonderful for her because she's met her soulmate and plans on moving to Alaska. But will Karma exact its revenge?

This is a raw and honest portrayal of love lost and love found again.

Not to mention the soothing influence of a beloved feline.

Finding her Heart by Samantha Hicks
Ellis Davis's self-imposed isolation is blown apart when a new neighbour moves in next door. Having spent the last five years working from home, shutting herself away from the world she once knew. The last thing Ellis wants, or needs, is the woman next door challenging her beliefs about herself and bringing out feelings Ellis has never experienced before. Melissa Cole moves into her new home as a recently divorced woman, raising her young son as a single parent with the help of her parents. Melissa is instantly intrigued by her mysterious neighbour next door.

Forever Home by Ali Spooner
Nat, Marissa and Maggie survived their first winter by the ocean. Spring brings new growth, friends, and unwelcome visitors to the homestead. Find out how Nat and Marissa's tiny community deal with the hazards and rewards before them, as their homestead continues to grow and prosper. Expect romance, adventure, danger, good fortune, and the odd meal or two, in this sequel to The Bee Charmer.

Disconnected by Annette Mori
Vanna has always felt like something was off with her parents, leaving her feeling oddly disconnected. She decides to move across the country and establish a new and independent life after college. On the way to her new position in Flagstaff, Arizona, Vanna meets out and proud Trey, who loves to flirt.

Trey has never forgotten the beautiful young woman she met briefly and is determined to ensure their paths cross again. Thousands of miles from home, Vanna finds out more about herself, but not her feeling of being disconnected from her parents. Will Vanna ever form the connection she desperately seeks? Does Trey's determination work out?

Darcy Comes Home by Jen Silver
After twenty-five years Darcy and Angie meet again and from the faintly flickering embers of their forbidden teenage love, a flame erupts. Family complications arise including a reluctant engagement, secret surrogacy, and a persistent ex-wife.
Villagers in Professor Darcy Belsfield's childhood home of Sycamore Haven remember her being sent away to a Christian conversion camp in Canada when her father discovered her making love to her school friend, Angie. Angie has never married but she does have a past and some unenthusiastic plans for the future. Will the differences in their lives doom the chance of Darcy and Angie discovering if they can build a future together?

Hat Trick by Ali Spooner and K.L. Gallagher
Alexandra "Alex" Hawthorne is on the fast track to the top of one of the most formidable, white-collar, criminal defense law firms in New York. She can ill afford any distractions, especially those with dark-brown eyes, who can rock a power suit while coaching professional hockey players. Not now. Not when Alex is so close to making senior partner. Not after

all she has sacrificed.

After a devastating end to her playing career, Janelle Leblanc channeled her passion into coaching and reached the pinnacle of success as the first female head coach in NHL history. Despite her accomplishments, she hears whispers that she was hired as nothing more than a publicity stunt. Janelle's focus needs to remain on the ice if she is to prove them wrong, not on a certain curly haired attorney with the most arresting emerald-green eyes she has ever seen.

Once the spark is lit, their chemistry is impossible to ignore. Can Janelle break down Alex's walls to give them a real chance? Or will Alex's past heartache be too much for them to overcome?

The Lone Star Collection *II* by Various Authors

Saddle up for a wild ride! *The Lone Star Collection II* has something for everyone! If you enjoy romance, Kris Bryant and Dena Blake have penned hot contemporary stories in *Heat* and *Horseplay*, while *Pins and Needles*, by Julie Cannon, is a historical adventure. Annette Mori also contributes to the romance fare with a beautiful, enduring love story in *Rainstorm*. If you want sizzling erotica check out *50 by 50*, from Renee Mackenzie. What would a collection be without fantasy, paranormal and swashbuckling adventures? *Lured to the Rocks*, a unique work of fantasy by Barbara Ann Wright. In *The Devil's Backbone*, Lacey L. Schmidt spins a thriller about overcoming evil and personal loss. MJ Williamz explores dark passion in *Take Me All the*

Way. Del Robertson offers *Return to Me* a classic pirate story, and Yvette Murray tosses in the *Ghostly Galleons*.

Footprints by Ali Spooner
Sandy, the youngest sibling of Gator Girlz, Inc., has worshipped her older sister Cam all her life and wanted nothing more than to be just like her hero. *Footprints* provides readers with Sandy's story of growing up in the Bayous of Louisiana. When the devastating floods of 2016 impact the Baton Rouge area, Cam and Sandy join the Cajun Navy to help rescue families trapped in the rampant floodwaters. The story also revisits Sandy's victory over Bubba Gump and how Sandy's injuries started her down the path to find the love of her life. Food, adventures, and great family relationships fill the pages of *Footprints*.

eBooks, Print, Free eBooks

Visit our website for more publications available online.

https://affinityebooks.com/

Published by Affinity Rainbow Publications
A Division of Affinity eBook Press NZ LTD
Canterbury, New Zealand

Registered Company 2517228

"Exactly my point. You take a winning song and don't create beyond that. I don't want us to ever do that. With the skills you and Stone have, I don't think we are in fear of running out of good material anytime soon."

Cedra rolled over and blew out the candle. "We won't. If anything, my writing has dramatically increased since we met. Lyrics just seem to pour from my head onto paper."

"It must be love," Juliet replied and kissed Cedra.

"It's definitely love. Goodnight, sweetie."

"Goodnight, my songwriting wonder."

Cedra laughed and snuggled into Juliet's warmth.

Publication date September 2022